WHEN IT
FEELS RIGHT

Visit us at www.boldstrokesbooks.com

By the Author

Visiting Hours

Bird on a Wire

Across the Dark Horizon

And Then There Was Her

Queen of Humboldt

Swipe Right

Two Knights Tango

Almost Perfect

When It Feels Right

WHEN IT FEELS RIGHT

by

Tagan Shepard

2023

WHEN IT FEELS RIGHT

ISBN 13: 978-1-63679-367-2

This Trade Paperback Original Is Published By
Bold Strokes Books, Inc.
P.O. Box 249
Valley Falls, NY 12185

First Edition: April 2023

CREDITS
EDITORS: ASHLEY TILLMAN AND CINDY CRESAP
PRODUCTION DESIGN: SUSAN RAMUNDO
COVER DESIGN BY TAMMY SEIDICK

Acknowledgments

I wrote this book in a time of wild upheaval in my life, but I drew inspiration from a time when I thought I had the whole world figured out. It was an interesting experience to say the least! I'm still not entirely sure how I managed to get the words onto paper. It never would have happened without a few wonderful people.

The early stages of this manuscript went to my incredible mentor during the GCLS Writing Academy. Rey Spangler gave me some wonderful advice and I am forever indebted to them for their help.

As always, my thoughtful and patient editor Ashley Bartlett kicked my ass and cheered me on in equal measure.

Rad, Sandy, Cindy, and Ruth at BSB are sent directly from heaven. Thank you all for being you.

And, of course, nothing in this life would be possible or worthwhile without the love and support of my wife, Cris. You're my favorite person and the best roommate ever!

Dedication

For all the folks who figured themselves out later in life
and for all the folks who are still figuring themselves out

PROLOGUE

*Y*ou should stay here. I'm pretty good company."
"I'm flattered, but I'm not gay."
"Are you sure? Because you walk pretty gay."

Marlene played the words over and over in her mind as she spun her Manhattan on the tabletop. Each time she repeated the conversation, anger flared. She couldn't think of anything else. She couldn't dance with her best friend or her coworkers. She couldn't steal glances at the gorgeous bartender. She couldn't do anything except seethe at the stranger's comment.

Walk gay? What did that even mean? How could someone walk gay? And if there was a way to walk gay, she didn't do that. She walked like a lady. A successful woman. Marlene forced herself to stop spinning her now room temperature drink and forget what the stranger had said. She stood, preparing to go out onto the dance floor.

She was standing in front of the stranger before she realized she'd started walking. She put down her drink slowly, turning her eyes to Marlene with a languid grace that sent a zing of interest up Marlene's spine.

"You're back."

The sound of her voice grated along Marlene's nerves. Or it was supposed to. Marlene straightened her shoulders, trying to focus, but she wasn't fast enough.

"I knew you would be." The stranger waved two fingers in the air to signal the bartender. "Let's get you a beer, shall we? I think you'd rather have a beer than that fussy drink you had before, right?"

"I like Manhattans," Marlene said. "And they aren't fussy."

"Any drink that includes a cherry and bitters counts as fussy. Let's go for something simpler, shall we?" She turned to the bartender and said, "Abby, get my new friend a beer, would you? Let's see. She's not the IPA type, that's for sure. Something simple. An American lager."

Marlene tried to stop Abby, but one look into her smiling, playful eyes and Marlene lost all ability to speak. She was stunning. Enough to turn anyone's head no matter how straight they were.

That thought shook Marlene out of her daze and reminded her why she'd marched across the bar to tell this woman off. When the bartender walked away, Marlene turned her glare back on the stranger. "Look, I don't know who you think you are."

"Penelope."

"What?"

"It's my name. Call me Pen." She leaned in close and said in a husky whisper, "It'll be easier for you to shout the short version of my name when I make you come."

A thrill snaked through Marlene at the words spoken with a hint of promise, but it shriveled quickly. She'd been here before and it never went anywhere.

"I told you before, I'm not gay."

Pen winked, bringing a flush to Marlene that she told herself was anger. "Sure."

"I'm not." Marlene slapped her palm on the bar in frustration. She took a deep breath, reminding herself that ladies didn't get angry. After another deep breath, she was able to calmly ask, "What did you mean when you said I walk gay? I don't walk gay. That's not a thing."

Pen slid the bottle of beer across the counter into Marlene's hand. She hadn't even noticed it being delivered. Where had the bartender gone?

"It's not just the way you walk. It's everything about you," Pen said.

"No. It isn't." Marlene took a sip of the beer without thinking. It was delicious. Smooth and cold and not as bitter as she remembered. She hadn't had a beer in years. Not since her sophomore year in college. Ladies drank wine or, if they couldn't stand the stuff like Marlene, cocktails.

"Yeah. It is." Pen reached out and flicked at the loose collar of Marlene's silk blouse. "Like this costume you're wearing. You know you look ridiculous in this, right? Like a kid whose big sister dressed him up in drag."

Marlene's mouth fell open and she couldn't catch it. A throbbing started in her temple and humiliation washed through her like a tidal wave. She suddenly felt the weight of her clothes. How her blouse stuck to her skin and how her slacks pinched at her waist. The way her lace bra chafed her armpit and the awkward way her bikini briefs left part of her butt bare. Everything felt wrong and awkward and she wanted to peel out of her skin.

"Fuck you," she spat and turned, marching to the exit without seeing it.

The night air slapped her when she hit the sidewalk and she looked around. She had no idea where she was. She had a vague recollection of handing her keys over to a valet, but she couldn't quite remember. Was that here, or was it at dinner earlier? A throat clearing feet away made her jump. The moment she saw the attendant's politely confused smile, she remembered the whole exchange. She handed the valet a ticket she found in her pocket, pointedly avoiding eye contact until he jogged off with her keys in hand.

Marlene gripped her phone hard as she watched the street, waiting for the headlights that would be her escape. She plotted the trip in her head. The valet would return in a few moments with her car. The drive to her condo would be quick at this time of night. In an hour, she'd be home, preparing for bed and forgetting this night ever happened.

"You shouldn't wait out here alone."

Marlene closed her eyes at the sound of Pen's voice. Why wouldn't she just go away? Hadn't she done enough damage?

Pen appeared at her side, standing shoulder to shoulder and looking at the busy street. "Not that Adams Morgan is a dangerous place, but there's a lot of us around here." She leaned in to whisper close to Marlene's ear, "Lots of queers on the streets out here. How many women have nodded at you as they walked past? We can spot our own, you know."

"Goddamn it, what is your problem?" Marlene spun, her clenched teeth inches from Pen's smug smile. "You can't bully me into sleeping with you. I'm not interested."

"I'm not bullying you. I'm trying to help you."

The words bit into Marlene deeper than the cool night air, chilling her anger. Without the rage clouding her vision, she noted the softness in Pen's eyes. The sincerity.

"You're shivering." Pen took off her suit jacket. "Here, put this on."

"I'm not shivering because I'm cold." Marlene distractedly slipped an arm into the jacket as the anger bled back into her. "I'm shaking because I'm pissed off. You're rude and mean and I don't want to spend another second in your company."

"Uh-huh." Pen's eyes scanned her torso, making a slow trip down past her hips and back up.

"Will you look at me when I'm shouting at you!"

Even the roar of her rebuke wasn't enough to take Pen's eyes off her body. She was staring unabashedly at Marlene's breasts and the hunger in her eyes was chipping away at Marlene's anger and making her feel something else entirely. She pulled the sides of her suit jacket together, hoping that covering more of herself would take away the weight of those eyes on her. To her surprise, however, the spark of interest in Pen's stare only flared as she adjusted the jacket.

Pen's eyes flicked up to meet hers and a smile grew on her lips. She jerked her chin over Marlene's shoulder. "Look."

"What?"

"Look at yourself."

Marlene turned to the window behind her. Blackout curtains hung behind the glass, protecting the club's ambiance from stray light. With the streetlight just behind her, the window acted like a mirror and Marlene could see her reflection clear as day. Could see herself wearing Pen's suit jacket.

It wasn't like the blazers Marlene bought from the women's section. It was cut for a man, with full shoulders and strong, straight lines. Every blazer she owned was darted to highlight breasts and hips. She hadn't really understood that until now. She'd known that they were the things professional women wore and so she wore them.

Marlene turned, examining the way the jacket fell around her slim hips. It didn't really fit her well—Pen was wider across the shoulders than she was—but that didn't matter.

"It looks." Marlene swallowed hard, fighting against the need to cry or maybe throw up. "It looks…"

The warmth of Pen's body pressed against her and Marlene could see the reflection of her smile. That smile and the warmth of her breath against her ear sent a spike of desire through Marlene like nothing she'd ever felt before.

"The word you're looking for is hot," Pen said. "You're so fucking hot when you dress like yourself."

Marlene didn't think or feel or consider. She just moved, grabbing Pen by the collar and crushing her against the window. She'd never kissed anyone like that in her life. She'd never allowed herself to devour someone. To take what she wanted from their mouth. And no one had ever kissed her back the way Pen did. She didn't hear her valet honking behind her or the whistles from women passing by them on the sidewalk. For once in her life, Marlene blocked out the world around her and acted on what she wanted.

Marlene didn't stop to process what had happened when she left Pen's house in the morning. She didn't chat or even say good-bye. She just scrambled to collect her hastily discarded clothes from Pen's bedroom floor and ran out of the house with her shoes in her hand with all the dignity of a stray cat in heat.

There wasn't time to go home and shower or even change. She just put her brain on autopilot and drove to the bank in a daze. One minute she was pulling away from Penelope's townhouse, the next minute she was sitting in the bank parking lot, staring at the back door with both hands on the wheel. Fortunately, the all-clear sign was up, so she didn't have to rush inside and check for intruders.

Then she was sitting at her desk, her office door and all the blinds closed. She stared at her hands, clenched together on the desktop, every knuckle white as bone. The only thought that banged around her mind was what those hands had done last night. The places she'd touched on another woman's body. Each touch had felt better than the next. Each body part she encountered more perfectly shaped to fit into her hands. There was a strange, strangled noise in the room. It took her way too long to figure out it was her own, ragged breathing echoing in her ears. She made a concerted effort to breathe normally and all she managed was a gasping, scratchy sound like a fish yanked out of their pond.

Knuckles tapped against the glass door. She tried to answer, but the door swung open before she managed a word and Ellie barged in.

"Do you like strawberries?" Ellie asked, pushing the door shut with her hip.

"Yes. Wait. No? Maybe? I did yesterday."

Yesterday was kind of a long time ago.

"Cool." Ellie dropped a white bag on her desk. There was a peppy logo for the new bakery down the street stamped on the front. It was thin on the bottom right, like the stamp had landed awkwardly and no one had bothered to push down on that corner. "I got you this."

Maybe Marlene hadn't said all that out loud. Maybe she'd just said "yes" and debated her like or dislike of strawberries internally. It was possible. It was equally possible that Ellie hadn't listened to a word she'd said.

"Did you hear? Lucy officially announced her retirement." Ellie dropped into the chair across the desk and put her feet up on the blotter. "You should apply for the job. You're the best branch manager Fairfax Trust and Loan has. It's only natural for you to move up."

Marlene's clothes were hanging oddly and she couldn't quite make them fit right, no matter how much she shifted. "I don't want Lucy's job. I've got enough on my plate. Look, Ellie, it's not really a good time."

Too late. Ellie had noticed her fussing with the blouse and now she was scanning her from head to toe. "Is that the same outfit you wore yesterday?" Her eyes narrowed as they focused back on her face. "And where did you go last night? I looked for you, but you disappeared."

"I, um, left."

"Yeah, no shit." Her eyes followed Marlene's hands as she finger-combed her hair. It was a tangled mess. Especially in the back. "But if you went home why are you wearing the same shirt?"

It was time to get Ellie out of the office. "I don't want to talk about last night, okay? Just let it go."

She knew the moment the words were out of her mouth they were a mistake. Ellie sat there, staring at her over her gleaming loafers, for so long Marlene thought she might scream. She couldn't work up the nerve to tell her to get out. Her palms had started to sweat by the time Ellie finally spoke.

"Oh my God."

"Ellie, don't."

"You went home with someone!" She dropped her feet to the ground and leaned her elbows on the desk, her eyes glimmered and Marlene's stomach took up permanent residence in her shoes.

"I'm not going to discuss this."

"But we went to a dyke bar," Ellie said, completely ignoring her. It was like she wasn't even there. Ellie scrunched her eyebrows together the same way she did when asked to perform even the simplest math. "Who could you have gone home with at a dyke bar?"

"Ellie." Marlene was on her feet before she knew she'd moved. Her voice was too loud and if she didn't calm down someone would come to check on them. "Drop it, okay?"

Ellie flushed scarlet at her neckline and her mouth pulled into a tight, unsmiling line. The muscles in her jaw flexed rhythmically. "Fine."

"Ellie."

"No." She stood and marched to the door. "It's fine."

It wasn't fine, though. Marlene's best friend was pissed at her and she'd just slept with a woman and Ellie was the only one she could talk to about this.

Marlene said in a rush, "I walk gay."

Okay, not the words she'd meant to say. They worked, though.

Ellie stopped and turned back. "What?"

All the fight leaked out of Marlene. She wasn't the kind of woman who was constantly wracked with emotion, but she'd been on the verge of tears for twelve hours now. She slumped back into her chair. The leather squeaked as she leaned back and stared at the ceiling.

"I walk gay." Marlene glanced at her and whispered, "Why didn't you ever tell me I walk gay?"

"Walk gay? What does that even mean?" Her words trailed off and her eyes slipped out of focus. "Huh. You do walk gay."

Every muscle in Marlene's body lost its battle with gravity simultaneously. Her head dropped. "Fuck."

"Holy shit! Did you—"

"Yeah." Marlene cut her off because she didn't want to hear Ellie say the words.

Ellie's hand rested lightly on her forearm and her voice was soft. "Did you get drunk and do something stupid?"

"No." Marlene's words slurred against her palms. There was still a whisper of lavender on them from Pen's sheets. "I did something stupid stone cold sober."

"Oh." The surprise in Ellie's voice was both sweet and insulting. "Did you like it?"

Understatement of the century. "Oh yeah."

"Wow. Okay. Hey! This is a big moment for you then. This is exciting, right?"

Marlene's answer sounded more like a question. "It's confusing?"

"You never thought that maybe you liked women?"

"Not really?" Marlene finally looked up. Ellie's face was a mask of happiness and Marlene had never felt so safe. "I mean I kissed a few women at parties in college, but then who doesn't?"

"Straight people."

"Ellie, I'm serious."

"So am I, Marlene. Why didn't you ever tell me about this?"

Marlene shrugged and looked away, hoping the heat on her cheeks didn't translate to color.

"What are you embarrassed about? It's okay to not be exactly straight," Ellie said.

"I know, it's just." Marlene swallowed hard and closed her eyes so she didn't have to see the hurt on Ellie's face. "I thought maybe I was a little bit bi or something, but nothing ever came of it and then I met you and I, um, wasn't attracted to you."

"Ouch."

To Marlene's surprise, the word came with a burst of laughter. She opened one eye to see Ellie smiling at her. The relief of that laughter gave her the strength to continue. "I figured if I got to know this really cool lesbian and didn't want her, it meant I was straight, right?"

"Or maybe I'm just not your type?"

"Apparently."

"So wait, back up to the kissing girls in college. It didn't go further than kissing?"

"Never." Marlene could remember those nights like they were yesterday. Each one had been seared in her brain. The best parties she'd ever been to. She thought the joyful atmosphere had led to the kissing, but maybe it was the other way around? She'd collected more than a few phone numbers that she'd never called. In the light of day, those kisses had confused her and even scared her a little. Those kisses were not part of the plan her father had laid out for her.

"Why not?"

Marlene shrugged and again the silk felt like sandpaper against her skin. "What would that even look like? How does one navigate a relationship with a woman? Sex with a woman?"

"Pretty sure you figured that out last night."

A coil of pleasure snaked through her at the memories of last night, but she shook it off. "But that's one night. It's totally different."

Ellie laughed again and dropped back into the chair. "How did it even happen? I mean, what was different last night from all those times in college?"

Marlene knew the answer instinctually, as though it had always been there at the edge of her vision, just waiting for her to turn her head enough to catch sight of it. But how could she explain to Ellie what it felt like to finally see herself?

"I wore her jacket."

"Huh?"

"She was wearing a men's suit jacket and I was cold. I put it on and saw my reflection and—Jesus, Ellie, I don't know how to explain what that did to me."

Ellie pulled on the lapel of her suit jacket. It was a lot like the one Pen had worn last night. The one she'd worn last night. "You don't have to."

Ellie's smile was soft and kind, like Pen's had been last night. Even with the similarities, Marlene still didn't feel that pull of attraction to Ellie. In fact, this morning she couldn't even say Pen would catch her eye if she saw her again. Maybe it hadn't been Pen that had turned her on last night and given her the most incredible sex she'd ever experienced. Maybe it had less to do with Pen and more to do with Marlene and the way she looked in that jacket.

"Hey," Ellie said gently. "You had an experience that can be really exciting and really scary at the same time. How are you processing that?"

"By flipping out." Marlene's voice squeaked. "Haven't you been paying attention?"

Ellie laughed and wrapped her in a hug that was warm and comforting and smelled like baked goods. "Why don't we go out for a drink after work to talk about this?"

"No." She was too loud again, but the idea of going out again tonight was too much. If they went back there she might see Penelope. Or the sexy bartender. She was way too confused for that. "Come over to my place and we'll get takeout?"

Ellie stood and squeezed Marlene's shoulder. "Sounds good."

Ellie made her way to the door. When she turned the handle, Marlene blurted, "What am I supposed to do now?"

Ellie smirked and said, "Whatever feels right."

CHAPTER ONE

Six Months Later

Abby grabbed a pinch of flour and held it at chin level, like her mother taught her. She whipped her wrist and it floated down to the pasta sheet like a dusting of snow. Two more trips through the pasta roller and it would be ready to stretch. She pressed the tips of her fingers into the dough while she spread the flour. Maybe three trips.

She had almost finished the ravioli, her pastry bag of ricotta filling, delicately flavored with tarragon and lemon, hovering over the perfectly stretched sheet of pasta when she heard a key in the lock.

Abby smiled and a little moan of anticipation hummed in her throat. Josie was early. Even better.

Just thinking of Josie made her heart rate pick up. Abby dotted the final ravioli's filling more sloppily than she intended, eager to get the bag out of her hand and her girlfriend into them. Wiping her hands clean on the towel tucked into her apron string, she walked around the counter and struck a sexy pose.

Josie said it was Abby's smile that first drew her notice. Her first message through the dating app a year ago had mentioned Abby's smile and the confidence in her eyes. When they met in person, Josie's jaw had hit the floor the minute Abby had walked in. She'd stammered her way through the date and Abby had loved every second.

Maybe it was silly to celebrate the first anniversary of chatting on a dating site. Most folks would celebrate the first date, but Abby had known from that first message that things would work with Josie. It was worth celebrating. Besides, they could celebrate their anniversary twice. It just meant two opportunities to spoil her baby.

"Hey, Abs." Josie froze in her greeting, looking around the kitchen. "What's up?"

Not the thrilled reaction Abby had hoped for, but it was close enough to their anniversary that Josie might be worried she'd forgotten something.

"Just a special dinner for my special honey." Abby pushed aside the cold greeting with her widest smile. "You're early."

"Yeah." Josie dropped her briefcase on the chair but didn't resume eye contact. "I thought you had to work tonight."

"It's Monday." Abby smoothed down her apron. "Date night."

"Oh." Josie was definitely avoiding her eyes. "Right."

"It's okay if you forgot." Abby untied her apron and dropped it on the barstool. "You can make up for it."

Abby pouted her lips in anticipation of one of Josie's aggressive kisses. She balanced her fingertips on her twisted hip and stuck her cheek out with a flirty grin.

Abby's hair flowed down to her shoulders in waves of dark chestnut, except for a large chunk of her bangs, which was vivid pink. Josie had mentioned a few months back that she preferred Abby's natural hair, so now she saved her brightly colored wigs for work. The upside of that change was that she could wear her Pin-up girl inspired wardrobe more often, as it went better with the swoop of pink bangs.

Tonight, she wore a vintage wiggle dress in blue velvet. The skirt fell just above her knees and the halter top pressed her ample cleavage into a provocative but not indecent display. Later, Josie would get to discover that she wasn't wearing anything else. It was the sort of dress that made Abby feel sexy as hell. It also showed off her sewing skills, as she'd had to alter the vintage dress to match her size-twenty frame.

"I don't have time, babe." Josie marched past her toward the bedroom. "Maybe later."

Abby watched her go, her heart sinking into her stomach. Not once in their year together had Josie refused to kiss her. "What?"

"I have to go." Josie turned, a challenge in her eye. To Abby's surprise, there was also something like anger flashing there.

Abby squared her shoulders and dropped her fists onto her hips. She'd never been the type to deny a challenge. "Where are you going on date night?"

"I didn't know it was date night, okay?" Josie said.

"It's literally every Monday. My one guaranteed night off. How could you not know?"

As Abby had known she would, Josie flinched first. She turned away and continued to their bedroom. "I forgot. But I've got work plans, so we'll have to skip it this week."

"Skip it? Did you see all the trouble I'm going to?" Josie retreated into the walk-in closet and Abby waited for her in the bedroom. "And what do you mean, work plans?"

"It's a client dinner." A hanger zinged against the metal rod as Josie grabbed clothing. "I have to go."

"Oh, baby." Abby marched to the bathroom to wash flour off her hands. "Why didn't you say something? I could've spent this time getting ready rather than cooking food that'll go to waste."

Silence greeted her. She checked her makeup and found it perfect, so she hustled back into the bedroom. She froze just inside the door. There was no mistaking the anger in Josie's look now. She stood across the bed, her shoulders up around her ears and a new jacket half on her arms.

All of a sudden, Abby realized what was happening. Why Josie was home so early and why she looked mad. Josie had been trying to dodge her. To get in and out before Abby was back from her studio so she could go to the dinner alone.

"You're not coming," Josie said.

Abby's mouth went dry.

"You aren't invited, Abby."

"I don't understand. Is this not a couples client dinner?" She knew the answer. Firms like Josie's always had partners come to client dinners. It created a sense of family and people were less likely to fire family. Abby had a standing invitation to every client dinner, issued by Josie's boss himself, since last summer.

"It is, but I'm going solo tonight," Josie said.

Abby didn't say a word. She stared at Josie, waiting for further explanation. She knew she'd get it. If there was one thing she knew about her girlfriend, it was that she was honest.

"Look." Josie crossed her arms over her chest and stuck her chin out. Abby had always loved her fighting stance. Tonight, she wanted to sock Josie in that stupid chin. "I can't have another fiasco like the Harreford dinner."

"How was that a fiasco? It was a lovely dinner."

"It was a fantastic dinner. I just didn't know I'd be bringing the show to go with it."

Abby sat down hard on the mattress.

"Can we talk about this later?" Josie said. "I'm going to be late."

"Frankly, Josephine, I don't give a rat's behind if you're late. You are going to stand there and explain just what you meant by that."

"See, that's why I tried to avoid this whole scene." Josie threw her hands in the air and started pacing.

"Mrs. Harreford specifically asked to sit next to me. We talked all night long. We laughed, we gossiped, we had an amazing time."

"You did. Did you see Mr. Harreford?"

"He was your job."

"He was smiling, too," Josie said. "Like a fucking cat. And so were Bill and Mark and Jonathan. All they could talk about after that dinner was you."

"And that's a bad thing?"

"It's not like they were talking about how classy you were, Abigail."

A light dimmed inside Abby, and she felt its passing like a candle being blown out. Tears built behind her eyes, but she loved herself too much to let them fall. It wasn't the first time this had happened. Sooner or later, Josie would get around to using the exact words and then Abby could at least have closure.

Realization of her unkindness seemed to strike Josie, and her shoulders slumped. A few years ago, Abby would have tried to make things easier on her partner. She would have said something like "it's okay" or "I understand" to give Josie the out she was looking for. But it wasn't okay and Abby didn't understand, so she let the silence stretch.

"It's just." Josie ran a hand through her hair, ruining that perfect spit-curl that made her look like Superman. "At first this whole look was fun and quirky."

There they were. The words that always came with the breakup.

"Add in the flirting and you're the life of the party. But I need someone more serious in my life," Josie said. "Someone I can take to work events who won't pull focus. I love you, babe, but I hate the costume."

Abby's smile tasted bitter on her lips as she said, "It's not a costume. It's who I am."

She smoothed down the satin brocade of her dress. She didn't feel as sexy now as she had when she'd put it on, but she knew she looked amazing. If Josie was going to break up with her, she was going to break up with her while she looked like a bombshell.

"It's not who I am," Josie whispered.

"Yeah, I know." Abby went to the bedroom door and stopped, looking out onto the hall because she didn't want to see Josie again. "I'll get my stuff out by this weekend."

Josie offered a weak, "I'm sorry."

Abby waved it off with a hand dripping in silver rings. She went back to the kitchen and finished her ravioli. She started the cream sauce after she'd sealed the last one. Josie came out of the bedroom in the blue pinstripe suit that tapered to her ankles. Abby turned away as soon as she heard the bedroom door close, but she heard the click of high heels on the hardwood.

Abby was busy cutting golden beets into wedges for her salad when the front door opened. She battled with herself, trying to decide if she wanted to turn around. Clearly, Josie was battling, too, because the door stayed open for far too long. Abby's conviction won out, and the front door clicked closed.

Seventeen minutes later, she lit the mismatched tapered candles on the dining table. She took the time to carefully portion and pack away the rest before sitting down to eat alone.

Marlene sat at the stoplight, her knuckles white on the steering wheel, the click of her blinker echoing in the silent car. If she craned her neck she could see across Legato Road, past the fire station, and barely catch a glimpse of her condo's balcony. She let out a long, shallow breath and glanced back at the red light.

"You can do this," she said. "Just pull up nose to nose with Mr. Phan's van. Then throw it into reverse and back in. Turn the wheel sharply to the left to line it up, then ease off once you see the air handler in the rearview. It's okay to pull forward and realign. No one's watching."

Just the thought of someone watching her try to park her SUV in her own driveway made her palms damp. She shook her head and chided herself. This was ridiculous. Getting worked up over parking. Everyone in the neighborhood struggled with it. Whoever designed the community was the real jerk here. Who put air handlers on one side of a driveway and columns on the other? It was like trying to park between two pickets in a fence.

Marlene recognized the symptoms of another spiral and shook her head, clearing out complaints. She focused again on the movements, running her hands loosely over the steering wheel in practice. She saw the angle in her mind's eye. She pictured herself being successful, just like her therapist taught her.

She really should set up another appointment with her. It was probably a bad sign that she couldn't remember her therapist's name.

A horn blared behind her and Marlene lurched into the intersection. Half a block down Legato and there was the turn onto her street. She could do this. She'd been living here five years. She'd successfully parked in her own driveway dozens of times.

Rolling past the visitor parking with an overwhelming sense of yearning, Marlene had to screech to a halt to avoid running over Mr. Phan walking his arthritic Maltese, Mrs. Fluffy. She held up an apologetic hand and met his scowl with a half-smile. Following his path across the parking lot, Marlene was surprised to see her driveway occupied.

Dawn's brother, Dustin, emerged from the garage, his arms stretched to wrap around a cardboard box. He looked up, saw Marlene, and paled visibly. His half-smile was far more apologetic than Marlene's offering to Mr. Phan.

"What the hell?" Marlene asked the steering wheel as Dustin dropped the box into the bed of his truck and hurried back inside.

She'd been dating Dawn for almost five months now and she hadn't spent much time with her family. They hadn't really moved out of the honeymoon phase, so they didn't leave the condo much. Dustin had been at a couple of family dinners Marlene had attended, but he'd never come to the house. He was a nice guy, but Marlene wasn't interested in entertaining at the moment. It was fine, Marlene supposed, for him to stop by, but it had been another long day at work and she just wanted to relax. Not to mention his reaction to seeing her and the cardboard box in his truck. She really didn't have the energy for strange family stuff tonight.

Marlene pulled perfectly into a visitor's spot and hopped out of her SUV. She just had to trust that either Dustin would move his truck or Dawn would hand over the visitor's pass they shared before a tow truck happened by.

She headed for her front door instead of cutting through the garage. The condo faced the playground of a grade school, so, as usual there were a gaggle of children laughing and running around playing on the sidewalk. She scooted around them and slipped inside, carefully locking the door behind her.

Dustin disappeared out the back door before she could greet him. At least he'd closed the garage door behind him. Marlene had the hardest time getting Dawn to remember, even with the bitter January chill. Marlene peeled out of her peacoat as she trudged up the three flights to her place. She kept meaning to hang a coat rack in the entryway, but the weekend never seemed long enough. She always spent most of it emotionally recovering from the past week at work and emotionally preparing for the week to come. It wasn't until she scooted around a stack of boxes on the landing that she realized there'd been one in the entryway, too. She looked up the long final staircase. There was a suitcase waiting at the top, next to the open powder room door. One day she'd figure out how to explain to Dawn how important it was to her to keep that damn door closed.

"Dawn?" Marlene called. She heard a rustling upstairs and sighed before mounting yet another staircase. "Babe? You home?"

She heard Dawn's annoyed sigh and followed it into their bedroom. Dawn's clothes were piled high on the unmade bed. A pile of shoes spilled out from a cloth shopping bag by the footboard. Dawn marched out of the walk-in closet, her arms full of a tangle of dresses, a hanger still dangling from one. Her eyes lit on Marlene and then slid off her as she continued over to the bed, shoving the clothes unfolded into an open suitcase.

Dawn's gaze had done that a lot recently. Flitted over her as though she was a glass ornament. Semi-transparent and unremarkable. When they'd met, at a queer art exhibit celebrating Pride last summer, Dawn couldn't keep her eyes or her lips off Marlene. Her lips still seemed interested, at least, even if her eyes weren't. They certainly had been last night, anyway.

"Babe?" Marlene asked again.

"Yeah?" Dawn's voice was usually seductively gravelly. Today it was stony.

When Dawn didn't seem likely to offer an explanation, Marlene said, "I called for you. Didn't you hear?"

"Yeah." She continued to shove three suitcases' worth of clothes into one. "Obviously, you knew I was home, so I didn't answer."

Marlene cringed, felt her cheeks blaze with embarrassment, and cringed even harder. Her long bangs came loose and she tucked them back behind her ear. "What's going on?"

"What does it look like?" Dawn caught herself and sighed heavily. She stopped packing and pinched the bridge of her nose. "Look, Marlene, I just can't do this anymore, okay?"

The words slapped Marlene and she took a step back. Her chest tightened and she couldn't draw a deep breath. She fumbled behind her for the dresser and leaned heavily against it. "You're leaving me?"

"You know as well as I do that this isn't working," Dawn said.

"I do?"

"Come on." Dawn's eyes narrowed and some of the warmth leaked out of her features. "Don't act like this is a surprise."

Marlene forced her brain to move, to think back over the last days and weeks. Try as she might, she couldn't see a single clue that this was coming. Things had been hot and heavy from their very first night. Dawn had moved in less than a month later. They went out together and stayed in together and this very morning Dawn had kissed her good-bye when she'd left for work.

"It is a surprise," Marlene said. Her gaze strayed to the rumpled sheets, and she pointed at them as evidence. "We made love last night."

Dawn shrugged.

Shrugged.

What kind of girlfriend shrugs about making love?

One who knew she was breaking up with you before taking you to bed, Marlene thought.

When her suit jacket caught on the drawer, Marlene realized she was sliding to the floor. She tried to stop. To straighten her knees and push herself back to her feet, but her body didn't respond. Her jacket slipped off the knob and her butt landed on the carpet with a thud.

"Look." Dawn walked around the bed and stood over her, crossing her arms. "You're really sweet and all."

She trailed off and Marlene's heart thudded in her ears, waiting for an explanation. "But?"

Dawn threw her arms into the air. "But I'm not interested in teaching a baby gay the ropes, okay?"

Each word slammed into Marlene's oxygen-deprived lungs like a punch. Her vision actually blurred for a moment and she didn't know if it was from tears or lack of air.

"You're breaking up with me because I just came out?"

"No," Dawn said, but the whine in her voice and the way she avoided eye contact told a different story. "We just don't have anything in common. Like, you don't have the cultural reference for this relationship."

"Cultural reference?" That sounded an awful lot like Dawn's BFF talking rather than her. She had practiced this with her friends, for Christ's sake. "I could. I mean, I listened to the music you suggested. And I have a list of movies to watch."

"That's the problem. It's like you're studying how to be gay and I really just need a partner who's already passed the exam."

Dawn circled the bed and went back to jamming her clothes into the suitcase. Marlene stared at the spot where her sneakers had left imprints in the carpet. Her brain replayed the words Dawn had said, but she was having a hard time processing them.

"Studying how to be gay," she said, her voice thick with tears.

"That's the other thing I just can't take anymore."

Marlene looked up, the image of her girlfriend swirling in the tears pooling in her eyes. "What?"

"Butches don't cry." Marlene flinched and tried to stop the tears, but it was a losing battle. Dawn counted off her faults on her fingers. "Butches aren't needy. Butches don't bottom. I need a real butch, okay?"

Silence wrapped around Marlene as the words echoed in the still air. Dawn moved in and out of Marlene's peripheral vision, but never said another word. At some point, Dustin came in and spoke to Dawn, but Marlene didn't look up or try to listen. She let Dawn's words tumble over and over in her brain while she listened to them stomp down the stairs. Sometime later she realized they hadn't come back up. They must've left while she stared at the crushed carpet fibers.

Sometime after that, she stood up and grabbed the vacuum from the laundry closet. She'd only intended to clean up the shoe prints, but it made sense to continue with the rest of the bedroom. When the bedroom was done, she vacuumed the hallway and the other two bedrooms. One had been set up as an office for Dawn, but it was empty now except for a table lamp sitting unplugged in a corner. Marlene had bought Dawn the lamp for her birthday. She'd bought her the leather desk chair, too, but Dawn had apparently kept that.

Going back into the bedroom to put away the vacuum, Marlene caught sight of the disheveled bed. She started to make it, but then smelled the hint of Dawn's expensive perfume on the pillowcase and pulled away. She didn't want to sleep on those sheets again. Not after last night.

Marlene untucked one corner of the fitted sheet before the last molecule of energy leaked out of her. She stood completely still, her hip pressed against the bedframe and the sheet still clutched in her fist. She blinked twice.

"Fuck it," she said, her voice echoing off the window panes.

She stripped out of her suit, flinging it to the ground on her way back to the closet. When she emerged a few minutes later, she wore a pair of men's jeans that hugged her upper thighs and a thick, warm flannel shirt. It was her second favorite one. Black and red with a few threads of blue stitched into the pattern. The sleeves were too long, but then sleeves were always too long for her short, petite frame. She rolled them up as she clambered down the stairs in her chunkiest, heaviest boots.

Dawn had left the visitor's parking pass on the kitchen counter next to her key. Marlene ignored them both and grabbed her wallet. She pulled up directions to Riveter's Cocktail Lounge on her phone and grabbed her coat on the way out.

CHAPTER TWO

A sliver of satisfaction ran through Abby's body as she smacked paint against stretched canvas. With a flick of her wrist, her brush danced, dragging the reluctant pigment along with it. Abby coaxed the brush into a graceful arc and the gloopy paint trailed along, bringing the dull canvas to life.

Abby lost herself in the act of creation. Unlike many of her classmates in art school, who stopped every few strokes to examine their work, Abby hovered close to the easel, only pausing to collect more paint. It wasn't until every pore in the canvas was bathed in color that she took a single step back and looked for ways to improve the painting.

She snatched a tube of primary blue acrylic paint from the floor, then squirted a dollop on her palette. She'd barely twisted the top back onto the tube before she slapped her brush, laden with a scoop of red and a touch of white, into the pool of blue paint. The purple she mixed had shades of lavender, but no pastel paint colors made their way to Abby's canvases. She dropped the faintest touch of black into the mix and the purple swirled into a shade closer to royal.

When she dragged the royal purple around to the wrapped side of her canvas, her elbow smashed into a cardboard box.

"Fork." She squealed as the brush dropped from her tingling hand. "Double fork."

Examining the canvas first, she noted the interesting doubling back brushstroke the impact had caused. She liked it, so she moved to examine the brush, snatching it off the floor. She bypassed her rinse cup in favor of the deep-basined sink in the corner. It wouldn't do to leave dust in her rinse cup. A paper towel to clean the floor was next, followed by an examination of the box. The only damage was to the precarious balance of mismatched cartons, which she adjusted to a sturdier arrangement.

Lastly, she checked on her own arm. The numbness from hitting her funny bone had passed, but her elbow felt raw. She couldn't quite move her arm to an angle to see the skin, so she waded through columns of boxes to her standing mirror, tucked between the wall and a wardrobe box.

The mirror revealed a minor scratch and a smear of purple paint. Abby ignored the scratch but wiped the paint clean as best she could. The last thing she needed was a paint smear on her couch. She was just clearing off the last of it when her phone spasmed with a cheerfully electronic tone.

Abby sighed and silenced the timer. She grabbed her palette and scraped the remnants of royal purple paint into the trash. It had been a lovely shade, but she could make it again. Or better yet, she could make a version slightly lighter to highlight that interrupted stroke. She laid her palette across the trash can to dry and moved back to her canvas.

She traced the path of her brushstroke, her finger an inch off the still wet canvas. A highlight here and here. Or maybe a lowlight. She could add more black and a little less red.

Her phone buzzed again, dragging her away from her canvas. She scribbled a note to herself before dropping onto her studio sofa. It sagged and groaned under her and she wondered for the hundredth time if she'd leave it here when she found a new place. It had found its way here when she moved in with Josie, whose sofa was much bigger and much nicer than Abby's. Now she was used to having a place to relax in her studio, even if it was too big for the space.

Everything was too big for this space, especially now that she was living here.

She reached for the nearest box, which had originally carried bottles of Jack Daniels to Abby's day job at Riveter's, but was currently overflowing with shoes. She wrestled around inside and extracted a pair of gray and neon pink striped Vans. As she exchanged her studio shoes for the paint-speckle-free Vans, she couldn't keep her eyes off the towers of looming boxes.

Never would she have guessed that she would still be lugging around her life's possessions in old liquor boxes at this age. Most people were settled by forty-one. Her friends all had their own places and their own furniture. Heck, even notoriously single-and-chasing-skirts Pen had settled down into a stable relationship. What did Abby have? A studio full of boxes and her a couch for a bed. She needed to get her life together.

The problem was, she thought she had her life together. She'd thought Josie was the one. But the further removed she was from her time with Josie, the more she realized how wrong she'd been. She had loved Josie, sure. She had been content and could have spent the rest of her life with her. But content had never really been Abby's thing.

She looked at the stripe of royal purple paint drying on her latest piece. That's how her life felt. A stripe of bold, brazen color that jerked to an unexpected halt. Maybe it hadn't been the breakup that had caused the stilted brushstroke in her life, though. Maybe it had been the relationship itself.

Josie had enjoyed the quirkiness Abby had brought to her life. The intensity of her color. But bright colors tired the eye of some viewers. That's what she had been to Josie. The shiny, distracting object she'd liked for a while, but had exhausted her in the end.

But what had Josie been for Abby? Warmth without depth? A safe place to land? Obviously not. No matter how much Abby had wanted Josie to understand her and love her, it had never felt quite right.

Next time, she assured herself as she flipped the box lid shut. Next time she'd get it right. She wouldn't settle.

She squeezed past the closest cardboard stack to perch her shoe box on top of the stack against the wall. She tried not to stare too longingly at the label on the top. She knew her jewelry box was inside, full of all her favorite bracelets and bangles. She definitely didn't glance over at the next stack, which contained two boxes of lovingly packed wigs in different shades and designs. Brushing them out when she landed somewhere new would be a nightmare, but she craved that day.

Touching the short spikes of her undercut and the messy ball of her bun, she sighed. She loved her hair. Loved the rich brown of her natural shade and the vibrant pink in her bangs, but her natural hair felt more like a costume than her wigs did. Without her twenty-sided dice earrings and lime-green wigs, everything felt slightly off in her life.

She had to turn sideways to maneuver her wide hips through the forest of belongings. When she was finally free, she smashed her knee into the corner of her canvas storage box.

"Biscuits!" She bent to rub the sore spot and smacked her elbow into her easel. She caught the wobbling painting just in time but smeared wet paint across her knuckles. "Crackers!"

Squeezing through to the safety of the doorway, she groaned in frustration. She needed a new studio. One spacious enough to allow her to display her work as well as create it. Selling her artwork online was hit or miss even at the best of times. Most artists sold through websites like Etsy or Society6, but those worked best for prints rather than the large format canvases she produced. Each of her pieces were original, and originality didn't sell well online.

What she needed was a place to show her work to art loving— and art purchasing—crowds. That meant one of the high-class studios in the area, like Workhouse or the Torpedo Factory. But she had bigger fish to fry at the moment. Like finding somewhere other than this tiny studio to live.

She'd already looked at rentals online, but she hadn't put much effort into it. There didn't seem to be a lot of good options. She could probably afford a tiny apartment if she stuck to the fringe suburbs, but she didn't relish the idea of driving into the city all the way from Manassas. More than the commute, she hated the idea of living alone. She got plenty of human interaction on the three nights a week she worked at Riveter's, but her studio was in a converted motel too far off the map where each studio had a separate entrance. Her art days would be far too solitary if she lived alone.

The shared living options didn't look great, either. The getting-to-know-you phase with a new roommate was always tense, and Abby didn't need any more tension in her life right now. The hetero crowd in DC was pretty open-minded, but acceptance often stopped at a fat lesbian with wild wigs, loud, nerdy jewelry, and a double-sized personality. After Josie, she had no interest in sharing space with someone who didn't completely accept her. But she couldn't keep living in her studio.

By the time she made it around the Beltway to Austin's apartment in Chantilly, Abby was feeling pretty low about life. It helped to see Austin's beat-up sedan parked crookedly in her usual spot.

❖

Austin answered the door so quickly Abby wondered if she'd been waiting on the other side for her arrival. She wouldn't put it past her friend. She was one of the friendliest people Abby had ever met. Despite the age difference between them—Austin was fifteen years younger than Abby—they'd been best friends since they met on Austin's first day at Riveter's.

Austin did her best to fade into the background most days. From her unremarkable brown hair to the green eyes that were pretty in a forgettable kind of way, it was easy to write Austin off. But Abby found that looks were often deceiving, and Austin had proven her right. The moment Abby spoke to her that first day, Austin's kindness and openness shined through, and neither the frustrations nor the monotony of bar life had dimmed her spirit. Now they did pretty much everything together.

"Going all out for D&D tonight?" Austin asked as she sprawled on the couch.

"I wish," Abby said, dropping onto the other cushion. "My usual stuff is still packed."

Every other week, Abby and Austin carpooled to the Palisades to meet their queer Dungeons & Dragons group. Abby usually used the event as an excuse to show off her most outlandish wigs and whip up a fancy new snack, but neither was in reach for her these days.

"I told you to bring some stuff here," Austin said through a mouthful of pretzels. "You could've changed here."

"You're sweet, but I don't want to clutter up your living room with my stuff. Besides, I'm gonna find my own place soon."

Austin was still upset that she couldn't invite Abby to stay with her. Her living room was so small that her couch was more of a love seat since this room was also her dining room and office. She'd offered to ditch the desk in favor of a dresser, but Abby wouldn't hear of it. Abby was a bartender through and through, but Riveter's was just a stepping stone for Austin post-college and she needed an office once she scored her dream job in politics. Nothing of Austin's could go, so there wasn't room for Abby here. No amount of shifting furniture could make it a more comfortable spot for Abby to crash than her studio.

"Seriously," Austin said, her guilt shining through her eyes. "I know the couch isn't much, but it's safer than staying in your studio overnight. Is there any security there at all?"

"No, which is why I can stay there overnight. Zoning doesn't allow for live-ins, so I'm sneaking in and out."

"See what I mean? You should stay here with me. It'll be fun."

Even as she offered the solution, her eyes darted around the crowded room. Her bedroom was worse. Austin wasn't a slob, per se, but there was more than one pile of discarded clothing on the floor in front of her bed.

Abby said, "It would be fun, but we both know it wouldn't work."

Austin pouted, and Abby used it as an excuse to pull her close. She smelled like fresh cotton and ginger ale and Abby didn't want to let go. She did, though, 'cause she'd spent enough time over the last two weeks crying on Austin's shoulder. More big hugs like this and the water works would start again. She didn't want to cry about Josie anymore. She didn't have her own place or any money, but she had good friends now and good times ahead. That was all she cared about.

"Thanks, pal. Let's go have fun, shall we?"

CHAPTER THREE

"How did we end up stuck with this job?"

Ellie snatched an old magazine from the table and tossed it in the direction of the trash can. It missed by at least a foot. Marlene paused in the middle of gathering up condiment packets to pick up the magazine.

"I mean, this bank is full of straight women with kids and shit," Ellie said. She dropped into one of the plastic chairs and half-heartedly wiped at a pile of spilled salt with a dishcloth. "But here we are, the two dykes, assigned to cleaning duty."

"We're assigned to clean up duty because I said so." Marlene snatched the cloth from Ellie and neatly swiped the salt into her hand. "And I don't like the term dyke."

"Lesbo? Is that better? How about carpet muncher?"

"Seriously." It took all her willpower not to crush the salt into dust. "Just try not to talk when Lucy and Brad get here, okay?"

Ellie shrugged and hopped up, retrieving the battered serving tray from the cabinet over the sink. She had the sense to wipe it off with a paper towel before setting it out, but not the sense to dry it before she reached for Felice's famous double chocolate chunk cookies. Marlene sprinted over and dried the tray just in time.

"Relax," Ellie said. "You're making me nervous."

"You're not capable of the emotion," Marlene said.

Ellie snorted and said something in response, but Marlene ignored her in favor of checking the bathroom for the tenth time. The bathroom wasn't dirty, but there was a dinginess to it she wished she could dispel. This building had passed through many different owners before settling with Fairfax Trust and Loan. When she took over as branch manager three years ago, she'd done her best to spruce it up, but the bottom line was it had been built in the seventies and looked it.

The break room was dark and dreary, the carpet in the lobby was threadbare, and the teller line still didn't have protective glass walls to prevent line-jumping robberies. The only positive part of the layout was the second-floor business offices. Her office and the desks for account representatives were elevated so they could keep an eye on the teller line traffic but remain separated from the bustle. Marlene needed that separation. It was the only reason she could survive in this soul-sucking job day after day.

After adjusting the air freshener so it perfectly lined up with the toilet tank, Marlene looked at herself in the mirror. As always since coming out, the sight of herself, dressed in the clothes that matched the way she felt inside, sent a thrill through her. She'd chosen her best new suit for today's meeting. She'd had to get the men's suit altered, not because of her curves—she didn't have many of those—but because she had short arms. And short legs. And a short torso. None of that really mattered because the suit fit like a second skin and her excellent tailor said the pinstripes helped elongate her body.

She'd gone without a tie, leaving her throat exposed. She didn't want to hit her new boss with the full butch lesbian image quite yet. Marlene knew next to nothing about him, so she decided to play it safe. She had hope, though. The first time Lucy had seen her in a tie, she had squealed with delight. Lucy had been her mentor for years and Marlene trusted her judgment. She'd hand-picked her successor. She would've picked a good replacement.

Tucking a piece of hair behind her ear, Marlene let out a long breath and headed back into the breakroom. Ellie was in her chair again, Felice's cookies scattered across the tray and crumbs littering the table. There were also crumbs littering Ellie's bottom lip. She lounged back, her feet up on the nearest chair, her gaze fixed on her phone.

"You're supposed to be helping, not eating all the cookies."

"Helped," Ellie mumbled through a mouthful. She waved the hand holding half a cookie toward the tray. A cascade of new crumbs danced across the table.

Marlene shoved her feet off the chair as she passed, snatching some paper towels from the dispenser. "Thank you so much for your help. Go back to work."

"Wow, someone hasn't gotten laid in a while." Ellie shoved the rest of the cookie in her mouth and brushed her hands across her pants. "You should've gotten Dawn to take care of that. Don't want to be a grouch when you meet the new boss."

Marlene nearly lost her grip on the tray. Her whole body swayed as a wave of nausea rippled through her. Dawn's words rattled through her mind.

I'm not interested in teaching a baby gay the ropes, okay?

Marlene gripped the edge of the table to steady herself and willed the tears not to come.

Butches don't cry.

"Whoa." Ellie dropped a warm hand on her shoulder. "You okay?"

"Yeah. I'm fine." Marlene cringed at the petty lie. This was Ellie. Her best friend. "Dawn, um, left. She broke up with me."

"Fuck, Marlene." Ellie wrapped her in a tight side hug. "I'm sorry. When did this happen? She didn't fucking leave last night? Not when you have such an important day today."

Marlene tapped Ellie's arm in an attempt to get air. When she could breathe, she said, "No. It was three days ago. I just didn't want to talk about it."

"Fuck."

Ellie pulled her close again and this time Marlene let herself be hugged. Lucy and Brad would be there in a minute, but she needed this. A hug for one minute would make everything feel so much better.

"Knock, knock," Lucy said as she walked into the breakroom.

Marlene leapt out of Ellie's arms so fast she banged her thigh against the table. One of the cookies slipped off the tray, but she didn't have time to adjust it before Lucy marched in. Marlene didn't think she'd seen the hug, but Brad's scowl made her wonder if he'd seen the embrace over Lucy's shoulder.

"There's my favorite manager." Lucy opened her arms to Marlene.

The day Lucy had introduced herself to Marlene, she'd started with the warning that she was a hugger. Having grown up with a stern single dad, Marlene wasn't great at physical affection, especially when it came from an authority figure. Soon enough, however, she'd found the warmth comforting. She'd been fresh out of college then and taken the first job she could find. After a month of training, she'd arrived at the branch and found the area manager, several levels of management above her, sitting at her desk, waiting to welcome her. Through all the promotions that led her to this point, Lucy had been there. The first to congratulate her. Lucy had been the constant in her life for years, but now she was retiring right when things in Marlene's life were the most chaotic.

"We're going to meet the tellers." Lucy slapped Brad playfully on the shoulder. Her many bracelets rattled on her slim wrist and Brad's smile looked a little too fixed. "Then we'll be back. Oh! Did Felice make cookies? Bless that woman, I'm going to miss those cookies. My waistline won't though."

She giggled as she slipped through the door, dragging her successor with her. Marlene hadn't taken a breath since she'd stormed into the room, and she collapsed into a chair the moment they left.

"Damn I'm going to miss her." Ellie grabbed another cookie. "She's hot as hell."

"She's old enough to be your mother."

"That's half the appeal," Ellie said, waggling her eyebrows. "You okay?"

Marlene tried to catch her breath, but she couldn't get the image of Brad's disapproving glare out of her mind. She leaned forward, hands gripping her knees and forced herself to take slow, even breaths.

"I don't think he likes me," Marlene said.

"Bullshit."

Marlene couldn't explain even to herself why she was so certain, so she didn't bother trying to convince Ellie. Maybe it was Brad's professional track record that made her so nervous. His MBA was from Cornell, and he'd spent the entirety of his twenty-year career bouncing from one mid-sized bank to another up and down the East Coast. Every entry on his LinkedIn profile proved him to be the quintessential old school banker. He'd never worked in a branch, but his numbers in upper-level management spoke for themselves. He came into a position, bolstered sales and satisfaction surveys, then moved on to the next big step. He'd be CEO somewhere in the next five years.

Marlene hadn't spoken to him yet, but he'd given a speech at the big manager's meeting the week before. He charmed everyone with his smile and wavy hair, then he'd lit into them for underperforming. He'd said FTL should be the biggest bank in Northern Virginia, and Marlene agreed. She hadn't agreed that managers being lax with their staff and ambivalent about their sales goals was the cause for the bank's underperformance. In fact, she hadn't thought they were underperforming at all, but he was the new boss and he had a great track record. Not to mention he was intimidating as hell.

"Seriously," Ellie said. She squatted down in front of her so Marlene had no choice but to look into her earnest eyes. "He's going to love you for the same reason Lucy did."

"Because she likes to collect strays?"

"You're not a stray and that's not why she liked you. This branch has been the company's top earner for how many years?"

"Five," Marlene said.

"Exactly. Our sales cover his entire quarterly bonus." Ellie stood and held out her hand. When Marlene took it, Ellie pulled her to her feet and straightened her lapels. "He's the one who'll be sucking up to you."

Marlene didn't think Brad had ever sucked up to anyone in his life, but Ellie wasn't wrong about their sales. She hated this job and the never-ending pressure to outperform herself as well as everyone else each quarter, but she always managed to do it. There was nothing about her job performance he could criticize, and all she had to do was keep working hard. Her results would bear out and he would respect her the same way Lucy had.

The break room door swung open and Lucy entered, her elbow entwined with Felice's. Ellie immediately joined their conversation, which appeared to revolve around cookies and Lucy's retirement travel plans. She turned on the charm so hard she had Felice shaking her head, but then Felice was always shaking her head at Ellie's antics.

Marlene was left to pull on a hasty grin and hold out her hand to Brad. "Nice to meet you again." He stared her down and she stammered as she said, "We met at the managers' meeting last week." When he still didn't say anything, she said, "Marlene Diggs?"

Brad finally wrapped his meaty paw around hers, but he didn't shake it. His palm was clammy and Marlene released it as soon as she could, resisting the urge to wipe the moisture off on her pants.

"Of course," he said. His voice was low and the cadence of his speech so slow Marlene had trouble taking in the words. "How could I forget?"

Lucy pulled him into their conversation, which gave Marlene a chance to step away and regroup. She didn't like the way he said he couldn't forget their meeting. Maybe she was reading too much into it, but the sentiment hadn't sounded pleasant. She took a moment to look him over, and the sight didn't exactly inspire warmth.

He wore a suit not unlike her own, though he probably hadn't bought his in the young men's section. He was at least a foot taller than her and equally wider at the shoulders. His shirt had the highest collar she'd ever seen and the knot in his tie was bigger than her fist. He looked like a bishop who'd walked into the wrong party but was too professional to retreat. His smile today was even less warm than it had been at the meeting and his eyes kept flicking between her and Ellie, eyeballing them as though he were trying to classify a new species.

"If there's one crew you won't have to worry about, it's this one," Lucy said. Slinging an arm around Ellie, she beckoned Marlene over. "Marlene's had this branch booming for years. She's the best you've got."

"Thanks, Lucy," Marlene said. "It means so much to hear you say that."

"I'm sure you're right," Brad said in a monotone.

"I'll miss you, kid." Lucy patted Marlene's cheek, and Marlene had to fight to hold in her emotion.

"I'll miss you, too, Lucy. It's been an honor."

"The honor's all mine," Lucy said.

She gave Marlene a squeeze and Brad flexed onto his toes a few times. In Lucy's reflected glow, Brad looked distinctly smaller than he had a moment before. It occurred to Marlene that he must know how big the shoes were that he was trying to fill. It must have been daunting, to take over for someone who was both beloved and respected. He was used to making his own mark, but that didn't make the job any easier. It would take him time to find his comfort level here. Marlene decided not to judge him too harshly early on. She could give him time to find his place at FTL.

"Okay, okay." Lucy grabbed a couple more cookies, wrapped them in a napkin, and slipped them into her pocket. She said, "No more mushy stuff. We'll let you get back to work. Take care, everyone."

Felice offered Brad a cookie, but he declined. He was the last one out of the room, following Lucy and Felice as they chatted their way out into the lobby. He threw one last, unreadable look over his shoulder before slumping off behind them.

The minute the door closed, Ellie was on her. "That was great! What a success."

"Was it?"

"Sure it was. Lucy had your back the whole time."

Marlene doubted Ellie would have felt that way had she heard her stilted conversation with Brad, but she was right about Lucy. Hopefully, she had been as effusive in the months she'd spent training him to take over.

"Want to grab a drink to celebrate?" Ellie asked. "Riveter's?"

Marlene's face went cold at the thought. She'd gone there every night since the breakup, and every night she'd left crying. Maybe it would be better with Ellie there. More relaxed. Ellie had never let her sulk.

"Sure," Marlene said, forcing cheer into the words. "Sounds great."

CHAPTER FOUR

Even though Ellie lived closer to the city, Marlene made it home to change and already had her first beer in hand before she showed up. It probably had a lot to do with how much effort Ellie put into her appearance. She swaggered through the door in dark washed jeans and a baby blue chambray shirt. Women nearby followed her with their eyes as she passed.

Marlene averted her eyes, focusing instead on the half-peeled label of her beer. She hadn't even bothered to look in a mirror before she'd left the house. She'd just shucked out of her suit and dragged some jeans on. The first button-up she'd grabbed had a stale, unwashed smell to it, so she'd tossed it on the floor near the hamper and grabbed another one. Sitting here now, her head slumped into her shoulders, she noticed that this one didn't smell fantastic either.

Ellie slapped Marlene on the back, sending her chest into the edge of the bar. "Hey, boss. How ya doing?"

"Please don't call me boss."

Before Ellie could respond, the tall bartender appeared in front of them. Marlene didn't know her name. She wore a rotating collection of graphic tees that highlighted wide shoulders and stretched across her ample chest. She was also shockingly young and made Marlene feel old and plain, so Marlene avoided conversation. That wasn't much different from usual since Dawn had left, though. Marlene avoided most people, especially clients, which was starting to show in her sales numbers even after just a few days.

Instead, she looked around the bar that had become her second home. Riveter's looked exactly the same tonight as it had six months ago, when Marlene had first crossed the threshold and changed her life forever. The lighting was still dim, coming from vampire chic wrought iron sconces that barely illuminated the royal purple walls and velvet trimmed furniture. The bar's vibe was vintage meets industrial meets techno and, while it didn't entirely mesh with Marlene's personal style, the crowd was gay, the drinks were dynamite, and Abby, the sexy bartender she'd drooled over even while she went home with Pen, was still there to light up the room with her megawatt smile.

"Okay," Ellie said after the bartender had filled her order. "Time to tell me what happened with The Blonde."

Ellie had only used Dawn's name for the first month or so they'd dated, then she'd started calling her The Blonde. Marlene suspected it was because her friend had never liked Dawn, and that meant she wouldn't like this story too much.

"I'm not really sure what happened," Marlene said.

"Tell me everything. We've got a full bar and all night."

The story didn't take all night, but the two of them did make their way through a lot of the bar. Once she started the tale, Marlene found it pretty easy to relate. Maybe too easy. She filled Ellie in on parts of their relationship that she hadn't been as open about before. Including how they'd spent the night before the breakup.

As the story continued, Marlene collected a pile of shredded beer bottle labels next to her discarded coasters. She rarely made eye contact with Ellie and even less often looked around. When she got to the part where Dawn had referred to her as a baby gay, Marlene's stomach clenched. She barely managed to list Dawn's descriptions of how she wasn't butch enough. Her lungs were nearly too tight to take in enough air to say everything.

Ellie, who occasionally demonstrated tact, put an arm around her shoulders. "That's really harsh. God, Marlene, I'm so sorry."

"Thanks," Marlene mumbled to the bar top.

She looked up to see Abby come out of the stockroom, her arms loaded with bottles. The tall bartender took two of them, saying something Marlene couldn't hear over the throbbing music and hum of conversation. Whatever it was, it made Abby toss her head back and laugh.

Marlene's guts did a momentary nosedive. While she hadn't paid much attention to the other bartenders at Riveter's, she had definitely noticed Abby. Her wild jewelry and wilder hairstyles were hard to miss, but that wasn't what constantly drew Marlene's eye. Abby was stunning. Her eyes shone with joy even on the busiest nights, and her smile was the most genuine, devastating thing Marlene had ever seen. The first night Marlene had come here, celebrating Ellie's birthday with the rest of her staff, she'd spotted Abby and been mesmerized. Repeated exposure hadn't made Abby any less tantalizing. Quite the opposite, in fact.

Ruining her former tact, Ellie said, "And y'all screwed the night before, too? Jesus, that's cold. How could she do that?"

Marlene cringed, keeping an eye on Abby for a reaction. She didn't flinch or look over, so maybe Ellie hadn't been loud enough for her to hear. Why had she told Ellie that part? She hadn't meant to. She'd meant to take it to her grave, but her best friend always managed to get the full story out of her.

"Hey, look. Abby's here. She makes the best Manhattans. You like those right? Want to get a couple?" Ellie asked.

"No thanks. I'll stick to beer." Marlene took the opportunity to look at Abby again. She wasn't wearing a wig tonight. Marlene hadn't seen her wear one in weeks. As much as she liked the way those vivid pink bangs played off Abby's pale skin, she missed the flamboyant hairdos.

"I'm starting to get jealous," Ellie said, shaking Marlene out of her reverie.

"What?"

Ellie jerked her chin in Abby's direction. "Every time we come here, you ignore me and watch Abby all night."

"That's not true."

"No? You're looking at her again."

Damn. She was. While Ellie was talking, Abby had picked up a pair of bottles and seamlessly poured two streams of liquor into a cocktail shaker. Marlene let her eyes slip from the bottles to Abby's hands, her mind wandering to places it really shouldn't go.

"I can't blame you," Ellie said. "She's super hot."

"How's she not your type?"

"I don't go for high femmes. Or the pinup look. I prefer women a little more androgynous."

Marlene shrugged and turned her attention back to her drink. Yet another thing she didn't understand because she was a baby gay. She wasn't even clear on what Ellie meant by high femme. Shame enveloped her as she realized this was just more proof Dawn had been right about her. She mumbled acceptance and took a pull off her lukewarm beer.

Ellie grinned at her. "She's totally your type, though, isn't she?"

"Why would you say that?"

"Well, The Blonde was the same flirty femme type, wasn't she?"

"That's one person."

"Well, you've only ever dated one woman."

The comment smacked Marlene in the gut like a blow. Dawn's sneer flashed in front of her eyes and any protest she would have given died on her tongue. Ellie wasn't wrong. She had only dated one woman. Here she was, thirty-eight years old and just coming out of a closet she hadn't known she was in. A woman as vibrant and confident as Abby would never want anything to do with her.

"Hey, you two." Abby's hands appeared on the bar in front of Marlene's downturned gaze. "Nice to see you back again."

"Hey, Abby," Ellie said. Marlene couldn't help notice how extra friendly she pitched her voice. Like she did with clients she'd just been gossiping about. "How's it going?"

"Well, it's Wednesday. You know what that means."

Ellie chuckled. "What's so great about Wednesday?"

Marlene finally peeled her eyes off the bar, looking up to see Abby's radiant smile directed at her.

"Not sure yet," Abby said. "I'll let you know when I find out."

Ellie laughed, but again it sounded like how she interacted with clients. Nothing genuine or even warm to the sound. Abby's returned laughter had all the life Ellie's didn't, and Marlene leaned into it, letting it settle into her bones and cheer her.

"Want another round?" Abby swept Marlene's shredded labels into her hand with a damp towel.

"I'm good," Ellie said.

"Me too. Sorry about the labels. Nervous habit."

Abby dumped the pile into a trash can and grabbed a fresh coaster. She stood it on its end, then flicked one side and it spun like an upright coin on the bar top. As it started to slow, Abby slapped it down, holding it in place for a second before picking it up and setting it on its edge again.

"That's my nervous habit," Abby said. Setting a stack of coasters between the two of them, she winked at Marlene. "Give it a try. It's fun and you don't get glue under your fingernails."

"Wouldn't want that," Ellie said, picking up a coaster. She tried to stand it on edge but couldn't get it to stay.

Marlene's hand shook slightly, so she plucked the top coaster quickly to hide the tremor. Hers stood on end just fine, but it took her two attempts to make it spin. Her slap was more tentative than Abby's, and the corner bent at an odd angle under her palm.

"Not bad." Abby leaned forward, grinning at Marlene. "You're a natural."

With difficulty, Marlene held Abby's gaze and offered a weak smile.

"Beginner's luck." Ellie still couldn't make her coaster stand up.

Abby pushed off the bar and turned back to her customers. "Have fun."

"You too." Marlene stuttered the words.

Ellie's chin landed on Marlene's shoulder. "You're getting drool all over the bar."

Marlene shoved her off, tucking a strand of hair behind her ear. "Stop. It's not like that."

Her eyes betrayed her, though, following Abby's form as she squeezed past the tall bartender to the far corner of the bar.

"Sure," Ellie said. "Whatever you say, boss."

They played with their coasters and sipped their beers for a long time in silence. Just as Marlene was forgetting the reason they were there in the first place, Ellie said, "I cry sometimes."

"Yeah, I know. I've seen you watch sports movies."

The teasing was as natural as breathing between them, so it took a minute for Marlene to figure out why Ellie had brought up crying. When she did, a new wave of embarrassment washed through her.

She felt her shoulders come up again and her hands shook so much she knocked over her coaster.

"I'm serious," Ellie said. "She doesn't get to tell you how to be butch."

A lump formed in Marlene's throat, making it too hard to speak. If her femme and out forever girlfriend couldn't, who exactly could tell her how to be butch? Especially the part about how to have sex as a butch. Maybe she was getting one or two things right, but it wasn't enough. For the first time in her life, Marlene liked what she saw when she looked in the mirror. She thought that certainty would translate to the rest of it. To the day-to-day of being queer and being someone's girlfriend. But she hadn't gotten it right.

This was the spiral she went into every night perched on this barstool. It was the same spiral that had made her turn down the few women who had asked to sit next to her or buy her a drink. It was the same spiral that was making her wonder if the clothes really mattered.

Ellie growled at a coaster that wouldn't stand up for her and crunched it in her hand. After draining her beer bottle, she turned to Marlene and said, "Let's dance it out."

"That's more your thing than mine."

"Then do it for me."

The request came with a pouty lip that made Marlene laugh despite herself. She shrugged and followed Ellie to the dance floor, deciding that it couldn't hurt to let Ellie try to cheer her up.

CHAPTER FIVE

"L eave it to those two to make a bad Saturday night even worse," Austin said, looking over Abby's shoulder.

Abby had been dabbing cranberry juice and vodka off Austin's T-shirt, but took a break to follow her line of sight. Penelope had finally arrived to join her girlfriend, Kieran, at their usual spot at the bar. She was leaning over, whispering in Kieran's ear. Abby had to admit, the way that smile grew on Kieran's lips was exactly forty percent heartwarming, sixty percent heartbreaking.

"I don't know." Abby handed the towel back to Austin. "I wouldn't mind finding someone who made me smile like that."

Penelope leaned down and swiped her lips across her girlfriend's. The mix shifted to seventy percent heartbreaking.

"Think I can save it?" Austin held out the tail of her shirt.

Abby turned back and examined the stain. Austin had been right in front of a drunk patron who'd tossed her drink in her girlfriend's face. Or rather had tried to toss it in her face. Considering how many of the cosmos she'd swallowed before she threw that one, she was lucky to even get the liquid out of the glass. Most of it had ended up on Austin, who'd come over to break up the argument. It looked like Austin had dumped red paint on her tits.

"Sorry, friend. I think it's a goner."

Austin tossed the towel down. "Damn. My favorite *Star Wars* shirt, too."

By the time Abby made it across the bar to Kieran and Penelope, they were full-on making out. Since they were regulars, Abby didn't begrudge them the PDA. It was nice to know Penelope had found happiness. She'd spent too many years picking up every woman who'd walked into Riveter's. Kieran was definitely good for her.

"Shoot, y'all," Abby said when they came up for air. Her neck was feeling distinctly warm. "You could charge admission."

"You couldn't afford us," Pen said, her eyes never moving from her girlfriend's lips.

They were a fun pair and Abby chatted with them for a little while. She thought her spirits might be lifting, until Pen told her she was the best. Everything that had bubbled inside her since Josie came home early from work spilled out.

"Tell that to my girlfriend." She tried to swallow, but her throat wouldn't loosen up enough for that. "Or make that ex-girlfriend."

They were really kind about the breakup, saying all the right things. Except all the right things didn't make anything feel right. If Abby was honest, things hadn't felt right for a long time. That's the realization she'd come to while she'd eaten ravioli alone at a candlelit table. Things had never felt right with Josie. It didn't make the breakup sting less. It maybe hurt worse because of that. Because she wasn't surprised.

"Wasn't meant to be," Abby said with a flippant shrug that wouldn't have convinced a stranger, much less someone as intuitive as Penelope.

Abby turned away, pretending to check on Austin but really just needing a break from their kind eyes. Looking toward the door, she saw her newest regular slump in. Abby had liked Marlene from her first trip into Riveter's. She hadn't known she was gay then, just joined a queer colleague for a drink and happened to cross paths with Penelope. The next time Marlene had come in for a drink, she looked like she did tonight. Like the poster child for newly out butch lesbians everywhere.

Pen and Kieran were talking to her, but Abby couldn't focus on their words. Marlene looked like she was three minutes from crying as she peeled off her jacket and dropped it onto the stool. She'd looked like that for a couple of weeks now. Abby thought things were going to be better after she talked to her friend last week, but she went right back to drinking alone after. As sweet as she was, it was a shame to see Marlene look that defeated. Abby said her good-byes to Pen and Kieran and made her way across the bar.

Propped up on the barstool, Marlene looked even smaller than she had walking through the door. Abby wasn't as tall as Austin, but she towered over Marlene, who couldn't have been much more than a few inches over five feet. It wasn't just her height, though. She was thin, with wiry arms and legs that never quite filled out her clothes. Her face was long, too, even when she didn't wear the hangdog look she was currently sporting. There'd been days when she'd come in to the bar with her girlfriend and a smile had lit up her face, making her look like a preteen heartthrob. She had elf-like features, with a small, upturned nose, dimples, and slightly prominent ears. Not long after coming out, she'd cut her long brown hair into a distinctly gay, asymmetrical pixie. It suited her, making her brown eyes sparkle with confidence. All that confidence was gone now.

Abby snagged a bottle of Fat Tire from the beer cooler on her way across the room. She dropped a coaster on the bar and cracked the top off the beer. "How's it going, Marlene?"

Those brown eyes dragged themselves up to meet Abby's. "Hey, Abby."

If it hadn't been for Josie bailing, Abby would think she had a crush. But it wasn't a crush, it was loneliness, and Marlene didn't need to be hurt even more. Still, the way her stomach danced when Marlene looked at her was hard to ignore.

"Thanks for the beer." Marlene handed over her credit card.

Abby shifted gratefully to the register to start her tab. A million questions bounced through her brain, all of them inappropriate and overly personal. Their answers were destined to make her stomach continue its cha-cha, so she went with something more neutral.

Returning her card, Abby asked, "Need anything else?"

"No." Marlene picked at the label on her beer. "I'm good."

"Sure? We're doing truffle fries tonight. Nothing goes better with a crappy day at work like potatoes and white truffle oil."

"No." Marlene met her eyes for a heartbeat, then looked back at her beer. "Thanks, though."

She pushed a stack of coasters across the bar. "Call me if you change your mind."

She moved on to take an order from the couple at the corner of the bar, telling herself to leave Marlene alone. She'd open up in her own time. If she had any intention of opening up to Abby at all.

❖

Marlene watched Abby go with a mix of regret and relief. Marlene had always liked Riveter's quirkiest bartender. Abby was actually the reason Marlene first came to Riveter's. Ellie had convinced the whole team that Abby was the best bartender in DC, and she had an amazing collection of wigs and jewelry that made her even more awesome. Maybe if Marlene had spent more time paying attention to Abby that first night and less time getting horizontal under Penelope, she wouldn't be crying into her beer right now.

Speak of the devil, Marlene thought as she glanced across the room. Penelope was sitting across the bar, her nose inches from her girlfriend's face, smiling and laughing and being the picture of relationship happiness. Not that Marlene actually knew what that looked like. She'd thought she did. Two weeks ago tonight she had fallen asleep, her sweaty, naked body entwined with Dawn's, thinking her whole life was figured out. If there was a prize for being the most wrong person in the world, Marlene was surely in the running.

Marlene turned her attention back to her beer. She brought it to her lips and took a long, cold pull. Setting it back down, she watched with the inevitability of a car crash as suds erupted from the lip of the bottle and cascaded down to soak the paper coaster beneath. Her right ear heated up to the point of pain and she cut her eyes around the room, checking to see how many people were laughing at her. Miraculously, the only person watching her was Abby, who gave her a wide smile that was all warmth and no mockery, before turning back to chat with the other bartender.

As usual, when she locked eyes with Abby, Marlene's fingers and toes tingled. Abby was, by far, the most carelessly erotic human Marlene had ever met. Her personality was larger than life and it filled her body to bursting. There was nothing about her that was average. She was on the taller side for a woman, and she was heavier than average. She wore both well. Marlene had never met a woman who didn't slouch to hide their height. Abby probably wasn't even capable of slouching. Her shoulders were always thrown back, her round face perpetually cut into a smile that made her gray eyes sparkle.

Movement out of the corner of Marlene's eye distracted her, and she looked over to see Penelope's girlfriend pull her into a kiss with more than a little heat.

Great, Marlene thought. They both kiss perfectly. Of course they do.

Those two got together after she and Dawn did, but where Marlene's love life had crashed and burned, theirs was still going strong. Stronger than ever if that shared sparkle in their eyes and the hasty way they paid their tab was any indication. They practically sprinted to the exit.

Dawn had never been so eager to take Marlene to bed. Okay, that wasn't true. She had been a little too eager early on. Then she'd moved in and it seemed like every day she was less and less interested in being in Marlene's company. In the two weeks since she'd left, Marlene had been over every minute of their relationship. There had been good times, for sure, but Dawn had been right. The signs had been there for a long time before she left. How she'd offered her cheek rather than her lips for Marlene's kiss. The missed dinners and long nights on the couch after Marlene had gone to bed. The mechanical way she'd touched Marlene that last night.

Marlene forced herself to stop thinking about it. That night of sex was the rabbit hole memory that would leave her crying on the floor and she didn't want that here.

"Annoying, aren't they?"

Marlene looked up into Abby's smile, her forehead crinkling. Abby jerked her chin toward Penelope's retreating form.

"Pen and Kieran," Abby said. "They're so in love. It's obnoxious."

Marlene watched as the door swung shut behind them. "I didn't know her name."

"Penelope?" Abby asked, leaning against the bar. "But I thought you two—"

"We did." Marlene hurried to cut her off before she said the words out loud. "I meant the other one."

Abby laughed and it made Marlene's heart skip a beat. Well, that and the fact that she just now noticed how low-cut Abby's shirt was. The way she was leaning on the bar left little to Marlene's imagination and Marlene had quite the imagination. Especially when it came to Riveter's gorgeous bartender.

"Want another?"

"Huh?" Marlene tore her eyes away from Abby's cleavage. Her ear flamed hot again, but Abby was reaching into the beer cooler and may not have noticed the ogling. "No. Thanks." Marlene snatched a coaster off the bar and tried to stand it on edge.

"Hey, I hate to pry," Abby said, her voice an octave lower than usual. "But are you okay? I've seen you in here for a few days now looking pretty bummed. Need to talk about it?"

Her ear was heating up again, so Marlene settled deeper into her shoulders. "It's okay."

"Seriously." Abby reached out and laid her hand over Marlene's, stopping it from picking at the coaster. "You can talk to me."

Marlene couldn't quite meet Abby's eye. Her gaze stuck on Abby's lips. They were painted the same rich, fleshy pink of her hair, and they glistened in the bar's low light. They were a perfect bow, arched up a fraction at the corners. Marlene's tongue touched her own bottom lip, a thin, pale imitation of what a mouth should be. Abby's lips were the roundest, fullest she'd ever seen.

Marlene swallowed hard and decided to take the plunge. "My girlfriend broke up with me. She moved out. Couple weeks ago."

"Oh, sweetie." Abby gave her hand a gentle squeeze as she spoke and Marlene had to bite her cheek to keep from flipping her hand over and gripping her palm. "I'm sorry. That sucks."

"Yeah."

"Had you been together long?"

Marlene cleared her throat. "Five months."

Abby's other hand joined her first, cradling Marlene's. "You were living together, huh? Will you be able to keep the place?"

"Yeah, it's mine." Marlene forced herself to look away from Abby's lips. "I own a condo in Fairfax. Dawn moved in with me."

"Least you've got a place to stay. That's good. Need anything?"

"No, I'm—"

"Don't say okay. I know you're not okay."

"It's just strange." It was easier to look at the bar than Abby's eyes, so Marlene didn't look up. "How empty the place feels now. It didn't feel that way before she moved in. Now I just hate being there alone."

"That's to be expected," Abby said. "You're going through a tough time and you're lonely."

Abby released her hand and stood up straight to check the drink levels around the bar. When she twisted to look around, her shirt sleeve pulled up far enough to reveal a massive red-purple bruise just above her elbow.

"That looks like it hurts."

Abby twisted her arm awkwardly to look at the bruise. "The hazards of living in a tiny art studio. You're not the only one who's been dumped, but I didn't have the luxury of my own place."

"You? Really? Someone would break up with you?"

It wasn't until Abby laughed that Marlene recognized how pathetic bordering on creepy that had sounded. It hadn't helped that her voice got squeaky, either.

"It happens to the best of us, I guess."

"I'm really sorry to hear that," Marlene said. That put a genuine smile back on Abby's luscious lips and Marlene continued before she could stop herself, "How long were you together?"

"A year," Abby said. "Just long enough to get invested in the relationship. If only it had happened sooner so I could U-Haul with the next hottie to come along, then I wouldn't have to search for a new place to live."

When Abby laughed, Marlene's stomach dropped. She was pretty sure she should be laughing along, but she didn't get the joke.

"Sorry," Abby said. "I shouldn't be making jokes. Not when you're so upset."

"No, it's fine." Marlene could feel Abby pulling away and she didn't want that. She wanted Abby to stay more than anything. Quickly, she said, "I'm sure it was funny. I'm just not good at this."

"Not good at what?"

Marlene waved her hand around, indicating the room full of happy queer people. "This. Being—you know."

Abby leaned back in, her genuine concern and kind eyes drawing Marlene in. "Being what?"

"Being gay," she said. "That's why Dawn broke up with me." Marlene wanted to stop talking. To stop announcing her shame to the world, but Abby's whole demeanor invited confidence. "She called me a baby gay. She didn't want to teach me how to be a lesbian."

"That was a horrible thing for her to say." Abby squeezed her hand again, rubbing her knuckles gently. "And it's also bull poop. There isn't a way to be gay. You just are."

"But I didn't get your joke," Marlene said. "About moving on to the next hottie. That's what she meant."

"It's okay to not know all about queer culture," Abby said.

Marlene wanted to argue. Wanted to explain how wrong Abby was. How Marlene didn't feel comfortable in her own skin again. She'd felt that way most of her life, then she came out and everything started to make sense. How could Abby, who surely had always accepted herself unconditionally, understand what Dawn's words had done to her?

"Sounds to me like you two can help each other out."

The new, unexpected voice made Marlene jump. Clearly, Abby was surprised by the interruption, too, because Marlene looked up in time to see her cut her eyes over her shoulder.

The young bartender shrugged and almost looked apologetic. She reached into the beer cooler next to Abby and said, "Abby needs a place to stay, you want a roommate and someone to teach you how to be a lesbian. Win-win."

"She doesn't need to be taught anything, Austin," Abby said with a bite in her voice.

Austin held up both hands in surrender, then took the new beer to her customer, leaving them alone again.

"Sorry about that," Abby said. "I didn't know she was listening."

Marlene didn't register the words; her mind was reeling from Austin's suggestion. Was it really that easy? Austin's idea scared and excited her in equal measure.

"She's right."

"I told you not to believe what Dawn said."

"Not Dawn. Austin." When Abby just looked at her blankly, Marlene continued, "You could teach me how to be a lesbian."

"Honey, you don't need anyone to teach you anything. The cultural stuff will come. Even if it doesn't, that doesn't matter."

Abby didn't understand. She'd been a lesbian much longer than Marlene. She couldn't understand how Marlene felt. So out of place in a community that defined itself by these cues. And she was too old to be so new to this. How could she ever fit in? How could she ever find someone to love her when she was so incomplete?

"Please?" Marlene heard the desperation in her voice, but didn't care. "Just teach me some of the jokes and references? I'll give you a break on rent for gay lessons."

Abby laughed and patted her hand. "That's funny." When Marlene didn't laugh, Abby squinted at her. "Are you serious?"

The way Abby's lips curved up just slightly, not to mention the still prominent cleavage so close to her, made another shiver pass through Marlene's stomach. This crush certainly wouldn't go away if they lived together. She should say no. Take back the offer and slink off into the night.

"Of course I'm serious," Marlene said.

Abby squealed adorably, and Marlene finally managed to tear her eyes away from her lips. It was an excellent decision. As captivating as her lips were, they were nothing compared to the smile in her eyes. Abby's eyes were a stormy gray and, at the moment, they shone brighter than the purple sconce behind her.

Austin came over and leaned in close. "Everything okay over here? I'm sorry for sticking my foot in it."

Abby threw an arm around her neck. "You're nosy, but I'll forgive you this one time."

While the two of them discussed Abby moving out of her art studio, Marlene attacked her long-neglected beer. She tipped it back and chugged while trying to figure out what she'd just done. One minute, she'd been contemplating Abby's lips, the next minute she'd invited a near stranger to move in with her.

Marlene had only ever lived with three people in her life. Her father, her freshman roommate, and Dawn. The first two had been assigned to her against her wishes. The last had been a disaster of epic proportions. She didn't like sharing her space. She wanted to come home from work, change into pajamas, and watch TV with her feet on the coffee table. What she didn't want was a sexy, confident bombshell sleeping right down the hall.

But she needed to figure out how to exist inside her new skin and Abby could teach her. All she had to do was ignore the crush until it went away.

Austin clambered away toward someone waving their credit card in the air and Abby leaned back in. Marlene caught a brief glimpse of soft eyes before Abby's hand enveloped hers again and those bewitching lips started to move.

"Are you sure about this? I still don't think you need to take a crash course in lesbian. If you want to take it back, you can."

"No way." Marlene swallowed hard and said, "I'd love you to be my roommate."

CHAPTER SIX

Christ's sake, Marlene. Why didn't you get the condo on the first floor?"

Marlene leaned her side of the mattress against the wall on the landing and Ellie followed suit, dropping her hands to her knees and sucking in long breaths. Looking over her friend's shoulder, Marlene wondered the same thing, not for the first time.

"The first-floor condos are a thousand square feet smaller."

"Perfect." Ellie wheezed. "Then you couldn't have a roommate."

"I also couldn't have a guest room for when you get hammered and stay too late."

"You haven't had a guest room in ages."

Marlene said, "Then you have nothing to complain about."

Ellie waved her arm up the stairs. "Wanna bet?"

There wasn't much arguing with her. Marlene looked up the stairs again and winced. The length of it stretched ahead of them, as daunting as a dark hallway in a horror film. Each of the units in her complex were either the first and second floor or the third and fourth, but they all had ground entrances. That meant Marlene had to carry everything up from the front door, around a couple of short flights and landings, and then up this final stretch of stairs that were narrow, low ceilinged, and the length of a floor and a half. It was hard enough when she was carrying groceries, but moving a queen-sized bedframe and mattress was torture. She probably should have left the guest bed set up when Dawn moved in, but she'd foolishly moved it to storage to make way for a second office. If she'd known how quickly Dawn would dump her, she wouldn't have bothered.

Shaking out her arms and lamenting again her inability to put on muscle, she bent to grab her side of the mattress. "Come on. This is the last of it. Once we get this upstairs, we can take a break."

Ellie heaved the mattress up and shuffled up the stairs. Her words came in strained gasps. "There better be a beer waiting for me on the other side of this."

Marlene tried to respond with snarkiness, but the mattress slammed into the ceiling and she put all her focus on not tumbling back down the stairs. They took another break when they got their load up to the main floor. Marlene dropped to her butt on the hardwood and gritted her teeth through the pain in her arms. Ellie leaned heavily on the powder room door and groaned at the ceiling. Once she'd caught her breath, her head rolled to look around the open living room. The usual admiration for the huge space and comfy furnishings lit her features.

"One of these days I'll land a really big client so I can put a down payment on a place like this," Ellie said.

Marlene struggled to her feet and looked up the much less intimidating staircase to the top floor. "It took me a ton of really big clients to earn a down payment on this place. And that was five years ago. FTL's commission structure was much more generous then."

"I can do it."

"Of course you can." Marlene gave her friend's shoulder an encouraging squeeze. "And I promise to help you move all of your furniture in when you do."

"Fuck that. I'm hiring movers."

The rest of the trip upstairs and down the hall was uneventful if exhausting. They'd built the frame on a previous trip, so all they had to do was drop the mattress in place. Five minutes later, Ellie was sprawled on Marlene's couch, beer in hand.

"Lucy's officially gone, huh?" Ellie asked, burrowing into the chaise built into the end of Marlene's couch. "How was the fancy dinner?"

"Fancy." Marlene swallowed back the knot of embarrassment that had formed in her throat. "She cried during her speech."

All of Lucy's branch managers, the core of FTL's sales and service team, had been invited to an intimidating restaurant the night before to celebrate Lucy's retirement. Lucy had been as sweet and supportive as always, wishing everyone well and pouring the wine with a heavy hand. Brad had lingered in the corner, his glass untouched, and watched. He was probably watching everyone, but Marlene's skin crawled with nerves and she sweated into her three-piece suit. He hadn't said a word to her all night, but he seemed chummy enough with everyone else.

"Did you schmooze with the new boss?"

"Um."

"Come on, Marlene." Ellie swatted lazily at her shoulder. "You've got to be your own biggest fan, remember?"

"Yeah. I know."

"Were you your own biggest fan last night?"

Marlene shrugged. "Sure."

"That means no."

"That means I didn't have a chance to talk to Brad." It was mostly true. She didn't have a chance because she steered as far from his judging glare as possible. "It can wait for work hours."

"True," Ellie said. "You'll be working together for a long time. Until you take his job."

"I have no interest in his job."

"You're not being your own biggest fan."

"Yes, I am. I hate management."

That wasn't the whole truth, of course. It wasn't just management she hated. It was the pressure and the sales and the regulations and the constant, quiet fear that some idiot with a gun would walk through the front doors any day. Marlene was teetering on the edge of admitting she hated banking in general and her job specifically. In fact, she'd been teetering on the edge of that truth for a few years now.

"You're good at managing me," Ellie said.

"No one can manage you. I've just kept you from getting yourself fired for a few years."

Ellie spread her arms wide and her smile wider. "Like I said, you're good at managing me."

Marlene chuckled deep in her throat and shook her head. "You're an idiot."

Ellie drained her beer bottle and settled back into the couch, closing her eyes to the glare through the windows. Marlene let herself relax now that talk of work had ended. If she was lucky, she could keep the conversation light for the rest of the day. She had no interest in letting her work anxiety bleed into this weekend. There was enough domestic anxiety to deal with.

"So who is this new roommate I'll be carrying boxes for anyway?" Ellie asked. "And how'd you find them?"

Marlene picked at a loose thread on the throw pillow. "It's, um, Abby. From Riveter's."

Even while avoiding the sight of her, Marlene knew Ellie's jaw dropped. She shoved herself up to a sitting position so fast Marlene jumped back. She finally met Ellie's gaze and the annoyance she'd expected was there in spades.

"Abby? You mean Hot Abby? The one you've been crushing on for months. The one you practically topple over the bar drooling at every time we go for a drink? That Abby?"

"I don't topple." It had only been once. "It's fine."

"It's one hundred percent not fine. You cannot, under any circumstances, move in with the girl you're crushing on," Ellie said.

"I'm not." Marlene continued in a small voice, "She's moving in with me."

"Did you learn nothing from shacking up with that blonde?"

"That's not fair." The sting of Ellie's words brought Marlene to her feet. "This is way different than Dawn."

"Is it?"

"Totally."

"What if Abby sleeps naked?"

A shiver traveled through Marlene's body, settling low in her belly. She tried to shake it off, but her voice squeaked as she said, "It doesn't—I mean—I wouldn't know."

"Oh yes you would. How's that going to feel, knowing she's naked, right down the hall every night?"

"It doesn't matter. We're not together or anything. She can do whatever she wants."

"Exactly." Ellie crossed her arms over her chest, towering over Marlene. She tossed out her next words like a stage villain. "How about when she brings someone home? When that person spends the night? Will everything be fine when you listen to her banging someone else in your house?"

"Stop it." Marlene's fists shook at her sides. "Just stop. It was stupid. I know it was stupid. You think I haven't thought about this? About all of it? I'm not an idiot."

Ellie's shoulders dropped and she put a hand on Marlene's arm. "I know you aren't, but this is a really bad idea. I just thought you'd have learned something after what happened with The Blonde."

"The Blonde has a name, okay?" Marlene threw Ellie's hand off and stalked across the living room. "And I did learn something from Dawn. I learned that I suck at relationships."

"That's not true."

"Yes, it is. I'm not good at relationships, so it doesn't matter that Abby is cute as hell or that she might be sleeping naked right down the hall. Nothing will happen."

Ellie made a sound somewhere between a laugh and a choke. "Shut up."

"Seriously. I'm done with dating."

"Grow up, Marlene." Ellie rolled her eyes.

"That's exactly what I'm doing." Marlene's phone chirped and she crossed to the dining room table to retrieve it. "This is growth."

"Bullshit. This is fear."

"She's here." Marlene leveled a challenging look at Ellie. "Are you still going to help?"

Ellie's face slumped, but she shook her head and walked to the stairs. "Of course, you big doofus. Let's get your hot new roommate moved in so you can start undressing her with your eyes."

"Are you sure about this move?" Austin asked as she maneuvered the rented truck through traffic on Route 66. "You can still move in with me instead."

"Sweetie, I love you, but I can't sleep on a couch forever," Abby said, laying her head on Austin's shoulder. "Besides, I would just lady block you."

"Lady block?"

"Well, the usual term doesn't apply to us. That seemed more appropriate."

"Maybe so, but you won't let anything block me. I never bring anyone home from work." She shot a quick look over at Abby's raised eyebrow and shrugged. "Okay, maybe once."

"Once? Is that once the redhead from last Thursday or the long locs from last night?"

Austin grinned. "Those were epic locs, weren't they?"

"Oh yeah, that's why you were flirting that hard with her. Cause you liked her hair." They laughed together, but Abby sobered as they exited the highway onto Fair Lakes Parkway. "Look, I need to start over. This is the perfect chance."

"I'm all for you starting over, but how much do you know about Mary?"

"Marlene," Abby said. "Not much, but she seems nice."

"Like how locs seemed nice?"

"No, not like that at all." Abby tried to hold back her smile, but she couldn't keep the corner of her ruby painted lips from creeping up. "Well, maybe like that, but let's take it slow."

"As long as she's not some uptight asshole like the last one, I'm all for it."

They pulled into the turn lane and waited for a line of cars coming the opposite direction. The delay gave Abby a chance to scope out her new neighborhood. The Fairchase community was a collection of different homes. A block of rental apartments loomed behind them, several stories higher than Marlene's place. A long, open field and patch of trees separated them, however, and Marlene's block of condos looked out over the field and followed the tree line away from the road. With any luck, Abby would wake up to just enough nature to make it feel suburban, but retaining the urban buzz of traffic from the busy road.

A break in traffic allowed Austin to lumber across the street, the truck groaning with renewed movement. Abby shifted her focus to her little patch of neighborhood. This block was separated from the rest of the condos and townhouses with a small but charming retention pond dotting the end of the cul-de-sac.

"Here we are." Austin pointed to the number over the garage. "This is you. Shame it's not an end unit. Pretty tight quarters here. Should I pull into the driveway?"

Abby shot off a quick text to Marlene, announcing their arrival, then turned her attention to the parking situation. "No way. You suck at parking. You'll definitely smash the air handler. Then you'll try again and smash the column on the other side. Why don't we just throw on the hazards and you can flirt with anyone who gets pissy about it."

Austin grumbled as she complied, adding that she wasn't that bad at parking. She went quiet after that, probably remembering some of her more disastrous driving incidents. Abby threw open the door and climbed out, looking happily around.

The neighborhood was everything she could want. The buildings were all luscious red brick on the face, creamy siding on the back. Each had a nice sized balcony, the lower ones shaded by the ones above, the upper ones fully open to the watery winter sunlight. Abby loved nothing more than sitting on a balcony in the morning, sipping her coffee and reading a trashy romance novel. She hadn't had outdoor space in so long, the prospect of reclaiming that vitamin D thrilled her.

"Hey." Marlene came around the corner with her hands in her pockets. "You found it."

"Sure did," Abby said, charging over to meet her. "I can't tell you how much I appreciate you taking me on as a roommate."

The closer Abby got, the rounder Marlene's eyes grew, until she looked like a gangly baby deer staring into the sun. A smile fought to form on her lips, but a blush made it to her cheeks and ears first. "Yeah. Of course. No problem. Anytime."

Another woman stepped out from behind Marlene. "What this idiot means to say is you're welcome."

"Uh, yeah." Marlene tucked her bangs behind her ear, pulling them tight across her wide forehead. "You're welcome."

"I'm Ellie. Marlene's employee."

Abby shook Ellie's hand and raised her own eyebrow. "Employee?"

"She's just joking." Marlene's blush deepened as she spoke, and she was avoiding Abby's gaze like an expert. "She's my friend. But I mean, technically I'm her boss."

Abby looked between them, trying to work out the dynamic. Marlene was petite, at least six inches shorter than Ellie and probably half her weight. She had a firm handshake, so there was obviously some muscle, but it was on a distinctly small frame. Ellie, on the other hand, looked like she played for the WNBA. She was tall and muscular and looked about the same age as Austin.

"It's okay." Ellie punched Marlene's shoulder like an older sibling. "I don't listen to what she says."

"Hey there." Austin held her hand out to Ellie. "I've seen you at Riveter's."

"Yeah. For sure."

Ellie pumped Austin's hand like a pair of bros and Abby wanted to share an eye roll with Marlene, but couldn't catch her eye. She sighed and told herself to be patient. She could draw Marlene out of her shell. Judging by the way her faded blue jeans hung low off her flat hips, Abby was going to enjoy the process far more than she should.

"Ready to get to work?" Austin asked, rubbing her hands together.

CHAPTER SEVEN

Marlene did everything in her power to convince Ellie and Austin to stay, but they insisted on returning the rental truck and retrieving Austin's car. If Marlene didn't know better, she'd think Ellie was interested in a hookup, but their energy was more like brothers than lovers. That made Marlene even more irritated about being abandoned. If Ellie was angling for a girlfriend, that would be one thing. Since she was just looking to bond over March Madness, Marlene felt justified in her resentment.

"Get a grip." Marlene deposited a box on the counter in the guest bathroom. Eyeing herself in the mirror, she said quietly, "You'll be alone with her all the time now."

That was the problem though, wasn't it? Marlene had known it was stupid to invite her crush to live with her, but she needed Abby's help and this was the price. Besides, Abby wasn't a major crush. She was just a cute woman Marlene had noticed. Ever since her sexual awakening, she had noticed lots of cute women. In fact, ever since she'd emerged from Penelope's bedroom, the world seemed to be overcrowded with gorgeous ladies.

So no, it wasn't a big deal that Marlene had thought the quirky, dressed up, and coiffed Abby was cute. The big deal was that she had noticed today that disheveled, sweaty Abby was way more than cute. She was scrape-your-jaw-on-the-ground, crawl-on-all-fours-to-beg-the-honor-of-kissing-her-toes, mouth-wateringly sexy. She'd kept that twinkle in her eye long after the rest of them were dragging themselves up the many stairs. When the three butches couldn't take another step and collapsed on the hardwood floor, Abby had bounced off to the kitchen and made them all big glasses of water with slices of cucumber and leaves of basil from the plant over the sink. Who knew water could be so tasty? Especially when their fingers brushed handing the glass back and forth.

Even now, after they'd been moving for hours and Marlene was at the limit of her strength, Abby still walked with purpose. More than that. She was brimming with excitement and energy. That acknowledgement of seemingly endless stamina didn't help her fluttering heart and awakening libido.

"Need some help with that?" Abby's voice crooned from behind her.

Marlene jumped, knowing that Abby hadn't read her mind, but blushing all the same. She tucked her bangs behind her ear and glanced at Abby in the mirror. Big mistake. Strands of bright pink hair stuck to her brow and beads of sweat stood out on her neck. Her pale, slightly flushed neck. Which led up to the broad curve of her jaw and cute little ears.

Marlene swallowed hard and swiped at her hair again, but found it already firmly stuck behind her ear. "I don't really know where you want all this."

"It depends." Abby marched into the bathroom, brushing against Marlene's arm. Goose bumps zinged up her bicep. "Is it okay if I take this bathroom?"

Even as Marlene focused on the press of Abby's slightly chilled arm against hers, she noticed the hesitation. Abby must've gone down to the garage for the last box. Marlene had been counting on that trip to cool her own face, and swapping it for Abby standing so close to her wasn't helping her overheated skin.

When Marlene didn't answer, Abby said, "If you want to keep it for guests, that's totally fine. I can keep my toiletries in my room."

"Guests?" Marlene's mind was sluggish, and she could tell from the amused smile creeping across Abby's face that it showed.

"Yeah. Like friends or family who might want to come and stay. You have guests sometimes right?"

"Uh, no, actually."

The smile bloomed and a laugh escaped her lips. "Then why do you have a three-bedroom condo?"

"It was nicer than the ones downstairs."

"What?"

Marlene said, "The upstairs units are bigger and have more natural light."

"Even though you were living alone?"

"Yeah."

"Why?"

Marlene swallowed hard and her brain finally kicked into gear. "It was the better unit. So that's the one I bought."

There was a twinkle in Abby's eye that she couldn't read, but it was gone in a flash. Abby shrugged and took the box, opening it to reveal enough makeup and beauty products to fill Sephora. "So it's okay if I take over the bathroom?"

"Sure. Of course. Make yourself at home."

"Thanks."

After checking the contents, Abby pushed the box aside and leaned on the counter, her full attention on Marlene. Her stance pressed her ample cleavage into a distracting sight and Marlene forced her gaze away.

Abby said, "Speaking of home. Care to show me around? We can set ground rules at the same time if you want."

"Yeah. Tour. Right." Marlene looked around, completely clueless. Dawn hadn't asked for either a tour or ground rules. In retrospect, the ground rules would've helped them a lot. "This is your bathroom."

Abby chuckled low in her throat, making Marlene's head spin again. "I gathered that. Cute shower curtain."

Marlene looked over her shoulder and groaned. She'd never used this bathroom, so hadn't thought about it, but the shower curtain was a gag gift from a former boyfriend who had no sense of humor. It was covered in cartoonish clowns, all with grotesquely sharp teeth inside their exaggerated smiles.

Marlene said, "You can change it if you want."

"No way. There has to be a good story behind it."

"Not really." Marlene glanced at Abby's playful grin and away again before her stomach could do another tango. "An ex of mine thought I was afraid of clowns."

"You aren't?"

Marlene said, "Nope. Just don't like them. They're just annoying, not scary."

"And she didn't get the nuance?"

"He didn't, no."

"Oh, sorry. Didn't mean to assume."

"It's okay." Marlene shrugged, trying to keep her tone light. "I was a late bloomer."

"Yeah. I remember your first time at Riveter's," Abby said.

"You do?" She hadn't thought Abby would've noticed her.

"Sure. I thought you'd punch Penelope. What did she say to you to piss you off so bad?"

Judging by the heat coming off her skin, Marlene was sure her face had gone fire-engine red. So she'd seen Marlene yelling at Penelope that night. Had she seen them making out? Or leaving together? Was Penelope the type to brag to the bartender about her conquests? Marlene was sure she was the butt of many jokes between Penelope and her friends.

"I'm sorry," Abby said, her voice soft. "I shouldn't have asked. That was rude of me."

"No, it's okay."

"How about that tour?" Abby bounced on her toes like a kid on Christmas morning.

"Yeah. The tour. We should do that."

The bigger of the two extra rooms had been set up as Abby's bedroom, but Marlene showed her the other, completely empty room as well. "You can have this room, too. I don't use it for anything. My ex had an office in here."

"That's not really fair for me to take both. Don't you need an office?"

"Mine's downstairs next to the living room, but I don't really use it." Marlene fiddled with the light switch, which somehow had acquired a swipe of blue paint. She picked at the paint with her thumbnail. "I spend pretty long hours at work. I can't bring much home. Privacy laws."

"Ooh, privacy laws. Sounds important." Abby walked over to the double windows and peered through the blinds. "Are you a spy?"

Marlene laughed, finally managing to get the paint off the switch. "Definitely not."

Abby turned and tapped her chin with one long, bright pink fingernail. "That's exactly what a spy would say."

Marlene was blushing again, and her tongue felt too big for her mouth. "I'm definitely not cool enough to be a spy."

Abby's hips swayed as she crossed the room and leaned against the closet door. She was so close to Marlene, but she couldn't make herself back up. "I think you're cool enough."

It took every ounce of Marlene's will power to keep her knees locked so she didn't crumble onto the floor. She tried to chuckle in that seductive way men did in movies when they flirted. It sounded like a cat choking on a hairball. "I'm a branch manager for Fairfax Trust and Loan Bank."

"Oh," Abby said. Was Marlene imagining the chill that had crept into her voice? "That's cool, too."

Nope, Marlene wasn't imagining it. The simmering flirtatious undertone was completely absent. What had she expected? That a fun, sexy woman like Abby would go wet over a banker? If her job could make her rich like a stockbroker or a lawyer, maybe. If it could make her famous like a musician or a reporter, definitely. But there was nothing glamorous or sexy about opening savings accounts for grandparents.

"You can have both closets, too," Marlene said to cover the awkward moment. "Mine is huge and I only use like half of it."

"Really? Can I see? I love a walk-in closet."

"You want to see my closet?"

"Is that weird?" Abby's forehead crinkled and her smile twisted. "I'm so weird. I know. I'm sorry."

"No." Marlene hated to see embarrassment on Abby's face. Not someone who was so open and accepting. She never wanted to make Abby feel bad. "It's not weird at all. It's actually like the best closet ever."

Marlene swallowed a joke about how long she'd spent living in one. She was terrible at telling jokes and didn't want Abby to find that out quite yet. Instead, she spun on her heel, missing a collision between her shoulder and the doorframe by inches, and strode off down the hall toward her bedroom.

"Double door entrance," Abby said. "Fancy."

Marlene shrugged. "I never open the other door."

"You should." Abby reached up and unlatched the second door's surface bolt. She pulled the doors closed and then flung them open and marched across the threshold, her grin as wide as her out-flung arms. "Make a grand entrance."

Marlene chuckled and followed a few steps behind, her hands deep in her pockets. "I'll have to try that sometime."

"And a king-sized bed." Abby ran her fingertips along the built-in shelves on the footboard. "Very nice."

"Best one I could afford," Marlene said with a shrug.

In truth, it had been better than she could afford, but she'd been single at the time and settled for microwave dinners for a few months so she could make the payments. The mattress had hurt even more, but her long work days required a good night's sleep.

"I love your style." Abby examined the matching dresser. "Lots of clean lines and warm tones. I love Mission-style furniture. Feels homey. I've always gone with mid-century modern myself. Don't know if you could tell, but I like things a little funky."

Abby flicked a chunk of pink bangs out of her face and gave a flippant shrug. It wasn't self-deprecating exactly, but gave Marlene the sense Abby didn't take herself too seriously. It was a refreshing change after Dawn, who had shrugged in a far more dismissive manner when she'd seen Marlene's bed.

"Is that the famous closet?" Abby pointed over Marlene's shoulder.

"Sure is."

Abby hung back, so Marlene led the way. She leaned her shoulder into the door, which always stuck in the winter from heat rising to the fourth floor. Flipping on the lights and stepping aside, Marlene welcomed Abby in with a sweep of her arm. She was happy she'd been the one to enter first, because watching Abby's eyes light up at the sight of so much closet space was a treat she didn't want to miss. Her mouth hung open as she looked around, but she actually squealed when she turned the corner and saw the built-in shoe cubby.

"This is awesome," Abby said, breathless for the first time on this busy day.

"Thanks." It felt like a compliment, though Marlene supposed the builder was really the one who deserved praise. "I like it."

"This place is only like half-full." Abby caught herself and turned apologetic eyes on Marlene. "Sorry. I'm such a jerk."

Marlene scrunched her eyebrows together. "No, you aren't. Why would you be a jerk?"

"Well, I mean, your ex just moved out. She must have taken up some of the space." Abby waved a hand laden with chunky rings toward the empty clothing racks.

"Oh. Um. No, actually. She didn't use this closet. She used the others."

Abby jerked her chin to the side, eyeballing the empty space. "Then why is it so empty?"

"I don't have a ton of clothes, I guess." Marlene gestured to the one full rack to her right. "I just have my work suits." She gestured to the half-empty shorter wall to her left. "And the stuff I wear out. I—um—recently changed my style."

Abby fingered one of the flannel shirts on the after-work side. It was Marlene's favorite, a two-toned brown check that was soft and ridiculously warm. "Yeah. I've seen you wear this one a couple times. I like it. It matches your eyes."

Marlene's ears heated up and she transferred her gaze to the beige carpet. "Thanks. I like it, too."

"You've got three times as many work suits as you have fun outfits. You should spend more on yourself, you know?"

Marlene shrugged and wandered back into the bedroom. "It just seems like a waste. I work so much. I don't really have time to go out."

"I guess I'll have to drag you out of the house sometimes. I can arrange some field trips for our course on lesbianism."

Abby's voice came from just over her shoulder, close enough that her breath tickled Marlene's neck. She sucked in a breath and hurried over to the bathroom. "So this is the bathroom. Um. Obviously."

"Oh. My. God."

Marlene whirled around, worried something was wrong, only to see that wide-eyed joy on Abby's face as she stared at the tub. "What?"

"What do you mean, 'what'?" Abby pointed an accusatory finger at the tub. "That is, by far, the most amazing soaking tub I have ever seen."

Marlene forced herself not to shrug again, but she couldn't help preening a little bit. Abby's approval of the condo felt way too much like approval of Marlene herself. Her chest puffed out and her shoulders felt wider. She tried to shrink back into her normal posture, but she couldn't manage it while Abby was skipping across the tile floor and leaning over the tub.

The tub was spectacular, even Marlene had to admit that. It took up a quarter of the bathroom, which was a feat since it was a massive bathroom. Tucked into the corner, the tub had two seats and a wide shelf all the way around. The sleek line of the faucet jutted out over the basin, but was tucked away enough to avoid blocking the entrance step. Of course, the only time Marlene had climbed in was once a month to wipe the accumulated dust off.

"You're welcome to use it any time," Marlene said. Abby turned to her, one eyebrow arching seductively. Marlene choked on her explanation. "I mean, I leave early for work and I guess you probably get up late. Being a bartender and all."

"Aw, darn." Abby leaned back against the counter. "That wasn't an invitation, then?"

Abby's ample cleavage, still barely glistening with sweat, drew Marlene's gaze and every drop of moisture left her mouth. She opened it to deny the proposition, but she'd forgotten how to form words.

After a moment of her mouthing soundlessly, Abby put Marlene out of her misery. "I'm sorry. I shouldn't joke like that. But thank you for letting me use your tub. I'll totally take you up on it."

"Sure. Yeah. Great. No problem. Yes."

Abby chuckled as she passed Marlene on the way out of the bathroom. "Come on and show me the living room."

CHAPTER EIGHT

Marlene hadn't seen Abby at all in the three days since she'd moved in. Most of Abby's shifts at Riveter's were closing these days, meaning she didn't make it home most mornings until four. By the time Marlene got up for work, she was already asleep. Abby had assured her it wouldn't always be like this, as her schedule changed constantly, but it was a strange feeling to have a phantom roommate.

The only evidence Marlene had of Abby's presence was the slow but methodical unpacking on Abby's side of the condo. Through the open door of her room, Marlene could see the stack of boxes disappear in conjunction with a subtle shift in the condo's energy.

Abby's style couldn't be any more different from Marlene's. Her walls were decorated with bold, abstract canvases easily recognizable from the few times Marlene had seen her artwork. Wigs in dazzling colors and gravity defying styles appeared on foam heads on her vanity and dresser. The most obvious change, however, was the ever-present and enticing scents of floral perfume and citrus soap. Marlene preferred more subdued, almost masculine scents, and the two complemented each other better than Marlene thought possible.

Marlene was pondering whether her crush would dissipate thanks to this unintended separation when she went downstairs to find Abby in the kitchen. One look at her wide smile and soft gray eyes made any thought of a diminished crush evaporate.

"Good morning, roomie," Abby said.

"Um, hi." Marlene could have slapped herself for the lukewarm greeting. "Good morning. Or is it still night for you? I didn't expect you to be awake."

"Awake is a strong word. I felt bad we haven't seen each other, so I thought I'd stay up to have breakfast with you. Is that okay?"

"Of course, but you didn't have to do that. You must be exhausted."

"I'm looking forward to forty winks, for sure, but I thought we should talk logistics." Abby stepped to one side, revealing a mismatched pair of boxes on the counter. "I even bought donuts for the occasion."

"Thanks." Marlene stepped into the room, forcing herself to ignore her sweaty palms and butterfly-filled belly. She was going to have to get used to seeing Abby every day, now was a good time to start. "Logistics?"

"For your lesbian lessons. If I'm going to teach you about all things gay, I need a plan."

"A plan sounds good." Marlene liked plans. Plans were structured and not at all sexy. She needed to focus on not sexy things at the moment. "Can the plan include coffee?"

"I thought you'd never ask," Abby said. "I don't know how to use your coffee maker and I'm dying for a pick-me-up."

Focusing on coffee preparation turned out to be just the distraction Marlene needed. She lost herself in a tour of the kitchen cabinets and debating on the optimal strength of their morning beverages. The mundane task made her feel in control. She needed that before embarking on either sitting down to a meal with Abby or discussing her ignorance of her own identity.

Once the machine was happily gurgling away, Marlene grabbed a pair of mugs. "How do you take yours?"

Abby collected a pair of plates. "You don't have to make mine. I can do it."

"I insist." Marlene pulled a carton of half-and-half from the fridge, making sure to show Abby where she kept it on the shelf. "It's the least I can do."

"The least you could do is put a roof over my head."

"You're paying me for that. Let me do something for free."

When Abby didn't answer right away, Marlene turned to look at her. There was a curiously soft expression on her face, which made the butterflies take flight again. It didn't feel like a big thing—making Abby a cup of coffee—but if she got that sort of response every time, she'd make it a habit.

"Light on the creamer, no sugar," Abby said.

Marlene tried not to put too much weight on the fact they took their coffee the same way. After all, it's not like that meant they would be compatible in other ways. The thought of other ways they could be compatible made Marlene's hand shake so much she spilled half-and-half on one of the plates.

"Shit. I'm sorry."

"It's okay." Abby swapped out the soaked plate for a fresh one. "I didn't know what type of donuts you liked, so I got an assortment."

That was an understatement. Not only did the boxes contain what appeared to be one of everything on the menu, they were from two different stores.

"You didn't have to go to all this trouble," Marlene said. "I'm not picky."

"Well, I am."

Abby's tongue peaked out between her bright red lips as she scanned the treats. She plucked up one that was so heavily covered in powdered sugar it fell like snow onto her plate and another with a thick layer of pink icing and sprinkles.

Marlene chose a plain glazed from one box, then panicked about her second choice. Normally she'd take the plain cake donut, but she didn't want Abby to think she was that boring. But what did adventurous donut eaters go for? There was another sprinkled option, but Marlene didn't like sprinkles. They got stuck in her teeth, oozing sugar for far too long. She wasn't a huge fan of chocolate, so that was out. Maybe one of the powdered options? But what was inside? There were so many filling options that looked the same. What if she thought she was getting Bavarian cream only to bite into lemon? Or worse, one with white icing like an inside out birthday cake. She didn't know if her nerves could handle that much sugar right now.

"Too many options to contemplate, huh?" Abby asked. "It's a big decision for this early in the morning."

Great. Now Abby thought she was indecisive as well as unadventurous. Before she could further embarrass herself, she grabbed one at random and dropped it onto her plate.

"Maple glazed. Excellent choice." Abby grinned and snatched up her coffee. "I wasn't sure if you had a favorite in the great donut debate. I'm a Dunkin' gal myself."

Since Marlene rarely ate donuts, she didn't have a preference, but she didn't want to shrug off another comment. Better to have an opinion. "My ex preferred Krispy Kreme, so I'm fully in the Dunkin' camp, too."

Abby laughed and Marlene congratulated herself for the answer. She would do just about anything to keep Abby from writing her off as dull and a whole lot more to keep Abby laughing.

"My ex wouldn't be caught dead eating donuts," Abby said.

"Was she a health nut or something?"

"Not especially. Donuts are too pedestrian for her. She's more of a French patisserie type."

Marlene swallowed a bite with difficulty. Of course, Abby dated women who were effortlessly classy. Her ex probably got the taste for fancy pastries while visiting Paris or something else equally enticing. Marlene had been to plenty of fancy restaurants, but only because her wealthy clients recommended them. She made a mental note to research bakeries in the city later.

Abby wiped her fingertips on a napkin and washed down a bite with coffee. "What do you have in mind for these lessons?"

Marlene's shoulders immediately tensed. She'd known they'd have to talk about this, but it felt so awkward. What if Abby hated doing this? What if it ended up souring their relationship? She tried to shake off her doubts, because she knew she needed this.

"I'm not sure exactly. I was hoping you'd tell me."

Abby said, "Let's start with timing. I was thinking weekly classes? There might be some homework, but I think you'll like it."

"Homework?"

"We can't watch all the movies or listen to all the music in one hour a week. You'll have to do some research on your own."

Marlene could do that. She liked research. Research was easy. There was a clear goal and easily defined steps in research. "Okay," she said, her confidence boosted. "I noticed you don't work at Riveter's on Mondays. Maybe we could do Monday evenings?"

"That works just fine." Abby finished her donut and pushed her plate away. "I'm surprised you noticed I don't work Mondays."

Marlene's face burned. Now Abby thought she was some sort of creep. "I wasn't keeping track or anything. I just started going there more often recently and noticed you weren't there."

She'd expected Abby to distance herself, but she didn't seem bothered at all. Instead, her eyebrows knitted together and she reached out to cover Marlene's hand with hers. "Can I ask, are you coming in more because of your breakup? It seems like this one hit you hard."

As usual when she thought of Dawn and the demise of their relationship, a flood of shame poured into Marlene. She could feel tears coming and she internally berated herself until they dried up. The last thing she needed was for Abby to know she wasn't butch enough. Just the thought had the lingering donut glaze turn to acid on her tongue. She had to swallow hard against the awful taste in her mouth and she couldn't look at Abby anymore. Her eyes fixed instead on Abby's hand on top of hers. The weight was comforting and the touch was gentle, almost soothing, but her fingers were still sticky from the donut, making the heat from Abby's hand uncomfortable.

"Yeah," Marlene said. "It did."

"Was she the first woman you've dated?"

Marlene nodded and looked away from their hands to her loafers perched on the barstool supports. She wanted to say something. Anything to change the subject or defend herself to Abby. But how could she pretend she was experienced when Abby already knew otherwise?

"Okay, then. Monday nights," Abby said as though the subject of Marlene's loneliness hadn't come up. "What do you want to know?"

"Everything." When Abby laughed at her answer, Marlene worried she was asking too much. "I mean, whatever you can teach me."

"Being gay is one of my favorite things about me, so I can teach you lots." Abby leaned her elbow on the counter and stared into the distance. "I'll have to think about a curriculum. History, terminology. I'll keep it light, though. Not too many documentaries."

"I like documentaries," Marlene said without thinking.

Abby gave her another of those warm smiles and all the fears and shame that had filled her moments ago vanished. "Of course, you do. You're the smart one in the house, for sure."

"Oh no, you're really smart. The other day you were talking to Austin about the school lunch bill the state senate is debating. You know way more about that stuff than me."

Abby looked surprised again and maybe even a little proud. "Thanks, but Austin is the one who's into politics. Her degree's in public policy. I'm just a flighty artist."

"Flighty artists are usually smarter than the rest of us."

"You're sweet," Abby said.

When Abby smiled at her like that, Marlene melted into an awkward puddle. If she kept this conversation up, she was likely to say or do something really embarrassing, so she decided to cut her losses.

Marlene gathered her dishes. "I better get to work."

"Yeah, I should get to bed."

"Will you be able sleep after drinking coffee?"

"There is very little that could keep me from sleeping right now," Abby said.

"Do you work tonight?"

Abby slipped their plates into the dishwasher. "Nope, so I can focus entirely on making your curriculum. I think I'll start with toaster ovens."

The non-sequitur threw Marlene off. "I prefer a regular toaster. I melted a bag of bread on top of a toaster oven once in college and I've been wary of them ever since."

The way Abby laughed, Marlene was pretty sure she'd missed a joke.

"This is a very different type of toaster oven," Abby said. "I'll tell you all about it on Monday."

CHAPTER NINE

How are things going with your tiny new roommate?" Austin shoved a raspberry kombucha into Abby's hand.

"She's not tiny," Abby said. She had to look up to glower into Austin's eyes, despite the tall heels on her vinyl boots. "Just cause you're a giant."

"Six foot doesn't make a giant. Not that Marlene would know. Also she probably weighs a hundred pounds soaking wet. I thought you liked ladies with a little meat on their bones."

"I like girlfriends with a little meat on their bones. Marlene's not my girlfriend. She's my roommate. She can have as little meat as she wants."

Their conversation was interrupted by the arrival of a pair of matching elves and a cowboy with a pink axe. They all assembled in the kitchen, laughing and munching on dainty snacks while showing off the newest pieces of their cosplay. While their Dungeons and Dragons group usually had a strict rule that each player had to dress as their character for biweekly quest night, they'd given Abby a pass while she was between houses and had to pack away all her favorite things. Now she was back with a vengeance, her outfit and her mood shiny and loud.

Abby's bard, Elanderose, had a penchant for miniskirts and midcalf go-go boots. She'd shaped a new beehive wig for her triumphant return tonight. It was a swirl of cotton candy pink and lime green, and she had to be cautious around the ceiling fans in their dungeon master's Palisades bungalow. She was also debuting a new article of equipment tonight—a lute she'd been refinishing and painting in her spare time for the better part of a year. Not only did it shimmer in Elanderose's signature flashy sixties color scheme, but it actually played well. She'd watched countless hours of YouTube videos on how to get just the right sound back into the old instrument. Of course, she hadn't yet learned to actually play it, but that was fine since Elanderose preferred a well-told tale to a song.

With the whole party assembled, they descended more intently upon the snack table. Abby had made her signature brie puffs, but added a homemade cranberry chutney this time to the delight of several players. Abby grabbed a plate and settled into her favorite old leather armchair. Austin was sitting on an ottoman nearby, looking very much like an enemy lying in wait with her long elf ear prosthetics and artfully soiled jerkin.

"So, tell me about the roomie," she said around a mouthful of seitan skewer.

"She's great," Abby said. "Quiet and neat and she insisted on me taking both the spare bedrooms. I have acres of closet space. I think it'll work out."

"Quiet and neat." Austin drawled with a suggestive smile. "Just your type."

Abby dropped back against the chair. "Exactly my type. That's the problem."

"Fuck. She's a lawyer, isn't she?"

"Worse. A banker."

"Seriously? How do you attract the most boring, uptight people?"

"I don't think she's uptight. She seems awkward. Not uptight."

"She seemed terrified while I was there. Is that because she's got the hots for you or because she thinks you're too much?"

Abby scowled at the phrasing. "Not sure. Probably too much. I tried flirting with her a little, but she looked like she might cry."

Austin giggled, a high-pitched, joyous sound. "That sounds like she's smitten."

"So maybe both then?" Abby put down her empty plate and snagged her kombucha. "That would be my type for sure."

"Hey." Austin's mirth evaporated. She put her hand on Abby's arm and said, "Josie was a dick. Don't take what she said to heart. Not everyone's like that."

Abby patted the hand and pushed to her feet. "I'd believe you if it was just Josie, but it's happened too often for that. I think I'll find a completely new type for my next dating adventure."

"Too bad for tiny Marlene."

"Too bad for you." Abby walked toward the massive dining room table where their DM was setting up the board. "I brought a Decanter of Endless Water tonight. My turn to be the group hero."

"Hey. No fair."

Austin chased her to the table, earning a laugh from the rest of the group for her antics. They stopped laughing pretty quickly. Their DM had a penchant for deceptively difficult campaigns, but she was such an excellent storyteller that the experience was always a blast. Besides, there were always just enough easy adventures to make the overall experience fun.

Tonight was not one of the easy adventures.

The group barely made it out of the haunted forest intact, and they were all exhausted by the experience. Austin actually groaned when they ended the night's adventure with a teaser of a ruined castle in the distance, a faint sinister glow lighting the night sky. Abby couldn't blame her for the fear, even though her mind raced with possibilities.

Abby only stayed to chat for a few minutes after the game was done, before making her way back across the river to her new apartment. She still had to use her phone's directions to find her way, but she was starting to recognize landmarks already.

Pulling into the neighborhood, her headlights flashed on the shiny silver of Marlene's SUV, snuggly parked in one of the guest spots. Abby continued to the driveway, popping her Mini Cooper into the narrow lane with ease. She discarded her boots at the front door, preferring to tackle the long staircases in her stockings rather than platform heels. It was past eleven when she arrived in the living room, and she was surprised to find Marlene awake, sprawled on the sofa with a paperback.

"Here I thought you were a morning person." Abby leaned her lute against the wall.

"Couldn't sleep," Marlene mumbled.

Abby held out the Tupperware container. "Hungry? I've got brie puffs and there's some chutney left, too."

Marlene slid a business card into the book to mark her page and looked up. Her eyes, which had been drooping until her eyelashes brushed her cheeks, flew open wide the moment they landed on Abby.

"You like it?" Abby struck a saucy pose, one hand on her vinyl-clad hip, the other flicking her latex ear tips. "I've been adventuring."

Marlene scrambled to sit up straighter on the fluffy sofa cushion. The movement pulled her baggy sweatpants low on one hip, exposing a flash of brightly colored waistband. Abby forced herself not to peek and see what brand underwear her new roomie preferred.

She told herself not to be a creep.

"But not a hair out of place," Marlene said, her lips lifting into a crooked smile.

"Well, we try to keep the excitement on the character sheets." Abby smoothed the side of her wig. "But Elanderose is pretty high maintenance."

"Uh, yeah. Totally." Marlene smoothed down her own hair. It was a little mussed in the back where she'd been resting it against a cushion.

Abby laughed, tossing down her boots. "Gimme a sec and I'll explain. Want something to drink?"

"Sure. I'll take a beer. Help yourself if you want."

Abby brought Marlene a beer and settled on the far side of the sofa with a glass of sparkling water. The sofa was massive, with deep cushions and a chaise on Marlene's side. Marlene had tried giving Abby the chaise side, but it was obviously her favorite spot. Abby was more than comfortable with her feet tucked beneath her. Owing to the extra cushions between them, they could've been on separate pieces of furniture.

"Have you ever played Dungeons and Dragons?"

"No." Marlene looked a little sheepish. "I've heard of it, but I don't really know what it's about."

"It's not that complicated, really. It's a fantasy role-playing game. Basically, a group of friends get together and make up stories about killing dragons and looting treasure."

"Sounds like a lot of pressure."

Abby sighed, thinking of the wickedly strong goblin her team had faced tonight. "You aren't wrong there."

Marlene squirmed, her body coiling tighter into the corner of the sofa. "I'm not sure I'd like that. I did an escape room once with a bunch of managers from the bank. It was supposed to be a team building thing, but I just spent the whole time worrying I wouldn't be able to figure it out and let the group down."

"That's the great thing about D&D. Abby can't ever let anyone down. I don't go adventuring, Elanderose does."

"Elanderose?"

"Elanderose is the name of my Dungeons and Dragons character. She's a bard. Half-elf, half-human. She likes a good story or song, but she's also very resourceful and brave."

"She'd have to be to wear boots like those into battle."

Abby couldn't hold back a laugh, not least because the more Marlene spoke, the more she smiled. Marlene had an absolutely adorable smile. Abby had noticed it when she'd come into Riveter's, especially after she'd cut her hair and started dressing more comfortably. Like the woman herself, the smile was shy and understated, but the gentle curve and slight pucker spoke to unexpected depths and a compelling kindness.

One of the main reasons Abby loved dating butch women was the way they treated her like a lady. Holding doors and escorting her with a hand on her lower back. Putting their coat over her shoulders when it was cold and ensuring she was served first. All the little things that felt condescending or controlling from men made Abby's heart gallop when they came from a woman. The idea of that attentiveness and strength coming inside a quiet, unassuming package like Marlene's was intoxicating.

Abby said, "Oh the boots are nothing. Try wrestling a forest troll in a skirt this short."

Marlene's eyes whipped off her and her cheeks flamed red. Damn. She went too far with that one. All Abby had wanted was those eyes to settle on her thigh, but she'd gone and made Marlene uncomfortable. She'd been right. There was no interest there. Which was a good thing, she reminded herself. Banker. Stuffy. Not interested in a flashy woman who likes bright wigs and a little attention from everyone.

"Actually, Elanderose doesn't do the wrestling," Abby said. "She leaves that to the fighters on the team. She mainly charms monsters and villagers."

Marlene flashed another of those shy smiles. "That doesn't surprise me. Abby's pretty charming. I'm sure Elanderose is, too."

"You're sweet."

Marlene shrugged and turned away from the compliment and Abby decided it was time to change the subject. "Tomorrow's Monday. Ready to start Lesbian 101? Week one will be jokes and stereotypes."

To her surprise, Marlene shifted on the sofa, looking even more uncomfortable than when Abby flirted. Considering how insistent she was that Abby teach her, she assumed Marlene would be itching to get started.

Marlene said, "No rush. You're barely settled. We can start next week if you want."

Abby still didn't think Marlene needed any of this instruction, and she figured the sooner Marlene realized that the better. Coming out was a confusing time and Marlene would eventually feel comfortable in her own skin. If this is what it took to make that happen, Abby was happy to help.

"Whatever you want, I'm ready to go."

Marlene mumbled her thanks and went back to staring into her beer bottle. It was sweet and sad and Abby wanted to pull her into a hug, but it was probably a bit early for that sort of thing.

"Okay, let's do it. Let's start tomorrow," Marlene said.

"Of course." Abby pushed herself off the sofa. "I'm dead on my feet. Think I'll head up to bed."

Just as her toes landed on the first step, Marlene said in a rush, "Good night, Abby."

Chapter Ten

"What's your deal today?"

"What? Nothing."

"Sure." Ellie grabbed a soda from the fridge and tossed it to herself, catching it midair with the other hand as though it were the easiest thing in the world. "You're acting totally normal."

"I am?" Marlene could tell it came out more like a question than a statement, so she straightened her back and tried again. "I am totally normal. Just tired. Didn't sleep well last night."

"You've used that excuse three times in the last week," Ellie said.

"It's not an excuse. I'm really not sleeping well."

"Of course you aren't." Ellie turned the plastic chair around and straddled it, dropping her sandwich onto the break room table in front of her. "Too busy having wet dreams about your roommate."

Marlene choked on a carrot stick. "Are you trying to kill me?" She lowered her voice, looking around the empty room. "I'm not having wet dreams about anyone. Certainly not Abby."

"Sure." Ellie took a bite of sandwich and barely chewed. "Keep telling yourself that."

In truth, Marlene hadn't had an inappropriate dream about Abby the night before. But two nights earlier, when she came home in her revealing D&D outfit—well, that was a different story. Her eyes had nearly popped out of her head when she'd seen it and she hadn't been able to focus on her book after Abby had gone to bed. All she'd been able to focus on was the memory of her creamy white thigh and the briefest flash of bright blue panties she'd revealed when she'd gone up the stairs. Marlene hadn't been right since.

Before Marlene could make more of a fool of herself and thus confirm all Ellie's teasing, the break room door swung open. This was a usual occurrence, since the staff bathrooms and lockers were stuffed into the tiny room along with the fridge and lunch table. The person who walked in, however, was not a teller in need of a bathroom break. Brad's shoulders took up most of the doorframe, just as his scowl took up most of his face.

Marlene had just shoved another baby carrot into her mouth, intending to use her lunch as an excuse to avoid conversation with Ellie. Sadly, now her cheeks, puffed out with carrot, mixed with her eyes, bulging in surprise, to create what she was sure was a less than impressive view for her new boss.

Hopping to her feet, Marlene swallowed her mouthful with difficulty and held out her hand. "Brad, what brings you out here to Main Street Branch?"

Brad glanced at her outstretched hand and pointedly folded his at his waist. "I make it a habit of dropping in unannounced to all my branches. It ensures I see my staff's true habits, not the show they put on when the boss is stopping by."

"Of course." Marlene dropped her hand and tried to imitate his relaxed, professional demeanor. "We were just finishing up lunch."

"Don't let me interrupt you." His sneer made it clear she would be in serious trouble if she continued her break.

"I'm all set. Shall we go to my office?"

"Wash your hands," Brad said.

He turned on his heels, presumably heading to Marlene's office. She didn't waste time saying anything to Ellie. Instead, she washed her hands as quickly and thoroughly as she could and sprinted out of the room. She was able to catch up with Brad before he made it upstairs to her office, and she didn't miss the way he looked down at her hands.

"I've been looking at your team's numbers." He settled into the guest chair as she shut the door. "They're adequate."

They were a damn sight more than adequate, Marlene knew. All branch managers were copied on the weekly sales reports and she checked them obsessively. She had the best sales of any branch apart from Clark Richards, and he had the prime spot inside the exclusive Reston Town Center.

"We work hard," Marlene said, treading the line between professional and defensive. "I have a very talented team."

Brad's lip twitched like he smelled something off-putting and crossed his ankle over his knee. "Talent is all well and good, but image is what sells a bank. We have to project stability. Tradition."

"Sure. Of course."

Marlene didn't have the slightest idea what he was talking about, but she had always been quick to match the management style of a new boss. Not to mention, she was a great listener. It's what made her a good banker, if not a happy one. Earning trust from a client often boiled down to listening and selling them only the accounts they needed, not the ones you wanted them to open. She could do the same listening with Brad.

"Banks don't need branches anymore," Brad said, obviously warming to his theme. "Everyone does their banking online these days. Customers who bank in person have particular needs. They have a level of sophistication our small fish, single account holders lack."

"I don't know if that's the case," Marlene said. She hated when anyone, particularly a bank employee, looked down on their smaller account holders. "I try to treat every account holder with the same level of respect and professionalism. Just because they don't have huge accounts with us doesn't mean they—"

"That explains it."

"Beg pardon?" Marlene felt like she was missing at least half of the conversation. "What explains what?"

"Your more buttoned-down approach." He waved a hand in her direction. "You're trying to make the smaller account holders feel comfortable by dressing down. It's a choice, but I don't think we should be playing quite so heavily to our weakest clients."

Marlene looked down, examining her outfit. It was a new suit, one that she'd purchased in the men's department of a very expensive store and had tailored to fit. Her periwinkle tie was designer and complemented the suit color. Sure, she didn't carry the outfit with the same gravity that Brad did, but then he'd probably worn suits like that his whole life. This was a new look for her.

She touched the knot of her tie, making sure it was centered at her throat, and chose to ignore the clothing comment in favor of defending her sales style. "I'm not playing to any of our clients more than the others. Part of our success is treating everyone who walks through those doors with the same level of respect."

"It's a safer bet to appeal to our older, wealthier clientele." Brad touched his own tie knot. It was wider than Marlene's, the full Windsor style she thought was too aggressive. "They prefer their bankers to look like bankers. You understand?"

Maybe Marlene was imagining the scorn in his look, but she certainly understood the implication. He meant they prefer their women to look like women.

"Yes," she said with an empty smile. "I understand."

"Good." Brad slapped his knee and pushed to his feet. "Let's take a look at your sales leads. You'll need to work hard to get back on top."

Marlene spent the rest of the day locked in her office with Brad. He insisted on talking through every potential sale in the area, no matter how flimsy. Like his tie knot, Brad's sales style was far more aggressive than Marlene's and he didn't like to be contradicted when she indicated she'd take a different approach. He was relentless and, though they were like oil and water, she could see how he'd been so successful in life. Brad was the type of businessman who radiated confidence and that was enough to get most men ahead.

The branch lobby closed at five o'clock, but the drive-thru stayed open until six. It was Ellie's night to stay late to assist the tellers with closing, but Marlene sent her home when the doors were locked. Brad left with her, though they didn't speak, and Marlene had a whole hour of peace and quiet in her office to recover from the long day.

Since she'd never had a chance to finish her lunch, she was ravenous by the time she pulled into her neighborhood. She had no idea what was in the refrigerator, but there were dozens of options for delivery. Her only hope was that traffic was light so her dinner wouldn't be cold by the time it arrived. It was most likely a forlorn hope, but she didn't have much choice.

Climbing the stairs to her condo, Marlene was enveloped in the rich aroma of onions caramelizing and potatoes roasting. She followed her nose into the kitchen, not bothering to drop off her briefcase.

"Hey there, roomie," Abby said, her grin wreathed in steam from a pot of boiling water. "Hungry?"

"Starving. You cook?"

"I love cooking." Abby dragged the words out as she dropped fresh tortellini into the water. "Hope you don't mind me taking over your kitchen?"

"It's our kitchen and I don't mind at all. I don't have the energy to cook anyway."

"Tough day?"

Abby fished the tortellini from the water and dropped them into the frying pan with the onions. She followed the pasta with a handful of chopped herbs and then flipped the pan continuously with her wrist, sending the contents briefly into the air as she mixed everything together. Marlene had seen that on cooking shows but had never mastered the move. Each time the food fell back onto the ceramic surface of the pan, it sizzled enticingly.

"My boss dropped by for a surprise visit." Marlene set her briefcase next to the fireplace and loosened her tie. "He came by in the middle of lunch and didn't leave until close."

Abby gave a sympathetic groan as she pulled a sheet pan of crispy brussels sprouts from the oven and sprinkled them with another pinch of chopped herb. Marlene gave the air an inquisitive sniff but couldn't tell if Abby was using oregano or thyme.

"That sounds dreadful." Abby switched off burners and turned to Marlene. "Sounds like you could use a beer. Or maybe a glass of wine will go better with the pasta?"

"Oh, is this for me?"

"Of course." Abby's smile widened and little lights flashed in front of Marlene's eyes. "I don't mean to be presumptuous, but I thought we could have dinner together. If you'd rather cook for yourself, I can clean this up."

"No. Thank you. This is great. I just don't want you to think you have to cook for me."

"I know I don't have to, but I like to." Abby scooped pasta into a wide, flat bowl and then nudged a line of potatoes beside it and handed it to Marlene. "What do you say about a drink? Beer? Wine? Water?"

"Beer would be great."

Marlene took the bowl and held it awkwardly in front of her while Abby snagged a bottle from the fridge. She didn't want to go into the dining room and feel even more like Abby was serving her, but the bowl was getting hot in her hands and she didn't know what to do with it. She opted to shuffle it around between her hands so as not to burn her palms while Abby served herself. When Abby floated off into the dining room, Marlene followed and sat down. Then she hopped right back up.

"Do you want a beer?" Marlene asked.

"No, thanks, I don't drink."

"Wait, what?"

Abby settled into her chair and spread a cloth napkin across her lap. She waved Marlene back into her chair and said, "I don't drink."

"But you're a bartender. Isn't that hard for you?"

"It's not because I can't drink. I just never really liked alcohol."

Marlene felt awkward with a beer in front of her now, so she ignored it in favor of setting her own napkin on her lap and pushing her food around. "Still seems an odd job for someone who doesn't drink."

"I guess." Abby speared a steaming tortellini on her fork. "But bartending pays really well and I like talking to people. I don't know if you've noticed, I'm a bit of an extrovert."

"I did notice," Marlene said. Then she realized that might've sounded rude from someone so obviously not extroverted. She forced herself to swallow a potato that was way too hot so she could say, "Which is good. You're a great bartender."

"Thanks. I bet you're a great banker, too."

Marlene's mood turned and her scorched throat seemed to tighten. "I thought so, but my new boss isn't a big fan. He thinks I'm catering too much to small account holders."

"Isn't that a good thing? There's more folks with small accounts than big ones, right?"

"True." Marlene went back to her food, half to give herself something to do and half because the pasta was phenomenal. "Besides, I don't focus on one or the other. I think my team has a lot to offer everyone."

"That doesn't surprise me in the slightest," Abby said. "I can tell you're thoughtful and fair. I bet your clients love you."

There was a twinkle in Abby's eye when she said "love" that made Marlene's neck feel hot, but she changed the subject, asking Abby about her day. Without intending to, Marlene fell into easy conversation, forgetting about Brad and even managing to forget about how Abby made her feel weak in the knees most of the time. The more she got to know her new roommate, the more Marlene was convinced they'd get along well. At the very least, the quality of food in the house was going to be better.

After dinner, they settled onto the couch with bowls of fruit and cream. Marlene was about to ask Abby if it was time to start their lesson when Abby asked, "When did you start wearing suits? After you came out, I assume?"

Abby was wearing a wide smile, so Marlene didn't feel as self-conscious as she normally would have. The tension that had left her when talk of Brad ended came back with force though. "Yeah. After I came out. Ellie took me shopping."

"It's a really good look. Being a butch lesbian suits you."

Marlene's mouth went dry, but she wasn't sure if it was because she was proud or self-conscious. She'd felt the same until Dawn's complaints, but it had been harder to believe recently. "Thanks. It feels better."

"Did you burn all the dresses or whatever you used to wear?"

Marlene shook her head, thinking of her closet. She couldn't quite bring herself to fully reject her old life. Part of her worried she couldn't make this work and she'd need those clothes again one day.

Abby said, "It's okay to hold on to part of that old life, especially while you figure out the new one."

Marlene nodded along, but it felt too much like faking her way through the conversation with Brad earlier. The whole point of having Abby live with her was to ask the hard questions. Before she could second guess herself, she asked in a rush, "What's it like to be a lesbian?"

Abby's eyebrow shot up, as did the corner of her mouth. She said, "I'm pretty sure you already know about the physical part. Pen is the expert on that, after all."

Marlene's insides shriveled. Mostly it was the thought that Abby knew she'd gone to bed with Pen, but there was also a part of her that wanted desperately to know if Abby knew about her expertise from personal experience. She wasn't sure she could handle the knowledge that Abby had slept with Penelope.

"Not that," Marlene said. "The rest of it."

Abby smiled sweetly and patted her knee. "That question is really hard to answer. It's too broad. Let's start with something specific."

Marlene didn't have to think about it too hard. She'd been squirming internally over this question since she'd asked Abby to move in. "When we were at Riveter's, you made a joke. About how us moving in was quick even for lesbians. What did you mean?"

"It's called U-Hauling," Abby said. Everything about her from her voice to her eyes was soft when she explained, so it wasn't nearly as humiliating as it could have been. "There's this old joke. What does a lesbian bring on a second date?"

"What?"

"A U-Haul. Because we commit really quickly and have a tendency to fall in love fast and hard. We move in with partners much more quickly than male-female couples."

"Really? Why?"

"Probably because women have less trouble with commitment and accepting our feelings than men. If you multiply that times two, you get U-Hauling."

"So you and I U-Hauled?"

Abby smiled. "It only counts if you're dating first, so not with us."

"My ex moved in after two months. It wasn't the second date, but is that U-Hauling?"

"Sounds like it. See. I told you that you already know how to be a lesbian. You're a natural."

Marlene laughed and it felt good to let go of a sliver of her fear. If she had lived out a lesbian stereotype without even knowing it existed, maybe Abby was right. She had never been a natural at anything.

They went over a few more basic stereotypes and inside jokes after U-Hauling. Some of them—like a penchant for flannel—Marlene was aware of, but most were new. Marlene had expected to feel inadequate during these lessons. That learning how much she didn't know would only deepen her shame. Abby was a gentle teacher, though, and taught with a sense of wonder and an obvious desire to nurture that Marlene felt comfortable from the start.

Abby yawned, covering her mouth with her fingertips. "Well, that's the first lesson completed. Next week we'll have lesson two. I'm exhausted."

To her surprise, Marlene was just as tired. She hadn't been to bed this early in ages, but she decided to give her body what it wanted. She trudged upstairs in Abby's wake, promising to wash up in the morning since she was too tired to tackle the dishes before bed.

CHAPTER ELEVEN

A bby was fully alert and out of bed the moment her eyes opened. Within minutes, she was in her bathroom with toothbrush in hand and the shower warming up. She was always like this on studio days, but today she was particularly peppy.

After three weeks in Marlene's condo, she was finally starting to feel settled. Curtains were up in her many windows, pictures were hanging on the walls, and the bathroom carried the lingering scent of her plumeria-based perfume all the time. Even better, she'd spent the previous morning with her hair stylist and her hair was now a slightly artificial, cherry-heavy auburn. As much as she'd loved the pink, it was time to reinvent her look.

Today she felt like Abby.

She decided to do a simple pompadour bang hairstyle since she'd be slinging paint all morning and loved how the height accentuated the richness of her new hair color. On a whim, she pinned back the sides as well and threw in a leopard print bandana, tied in a big bow on the side. Matched with a lavender tank top and her paint-speckled overalls, she perfectly embodied the pinup girl vibe that made her feel so good in her own skin. A bright red lip topped the whole thing off, even though she knew she'd leave half of it on her coffee cup.

Marlene must have read her mind, because she stepped out of the bathroom to the alluring aroma of freshly ground beans. As she skipped down the stairs, Abby could hear the tell-tale signs of Marlene moving around the kitchen. One of the first things Abby had noticed about Marlene, well before they'd moved in together, was the way she marched into a room. There was a confidence in her stride, completely at odds with her personality, which was far more reserved and even timid. Abby still hadn't decided if the walk was affected or if the timidity was new, a product of her coming out late in life. What she could say with certainty was that the aggressive set of Marlene's shoulders when she walked was wildly distracting.

"Good morning." Abby allowed the giddiness of her morning to make the words sing-songy. "You're up early."

Marlene's shoulders twitched inside her beige blazer, and she dropped the butter knife she'd been using to spread cream cheese on a bagel.

"Sorry." Abby bent to pick up the knife. "Didn't mean to startle you."

Abby looked up to find Marlene blushing bright red. "I'm such a klutz. Sorry."

"It's okay. It's hard to get used to someone new in your space."

"This is your space, too. I was just lost in thought."

The sincerity of her words touched Abby. Marlene was making such an effort to ensure Abby felt at home here. With all the turbulence in Marlene's life, her thoughtfulness was extra sweet.

"You're up early, too." Marlene stacked containers of food into her lunch bag. "Didn't you bartend last night? You can't have gotten much sleep."

"I'm a morning person, so I sleep a few hours at night then take a nap during the day."

"I guess I've never noticed because I'm at work. Coffee?"

"Please, thank you." Abby accepted the mug and settled onto a barstool. "Plus, my studio is quieter in the morning and I get more done. Artists aren't known for being early risers."

"That explains the overalls." Marlene nodded toward Abby's outfit as she filled her travel coffee mug.

Abby hooked her thumb under the strap of her overalls. "You like?"

"Very much."

Marlene seemed to realize what she'd said and clammed up, so Abby took pity on her. "I'm working at Riveter's tonight, too. You should stop by. Wednesday nights are always slow, and Austin isn't working. Come keep me company?"

Abby didn't know Marlene well enough to be sure, but she thought there was a hint of surprise and joy in her expression. "Sure. That would be fun. But you don't have to spend your whole shift talking to me. I'll invite Ellie along in case you get busy."

"Sounds great."

After a long moment of silence, Marlene snatched up the bag and headed for the door. "I should be getting to work."

"Already? The branch doesn't open until nine, right?"

"Yeah, but I have some paperwork."

"Don't forget your coffee." Abby waved her own beverage at the travel mug across the counter.

"Oh. Right. Yeah."

Marlene snatched it up and practically ran down the stairs. Abby didn't realize until she heard the front door slam that Marlene had also forgotten her bagel, waiting smeared with cream cheese on a plate by the toaster. She shrugged and got up, wrapping up the bagel to take with her on the drive to her studio.

Marlene sat in her car in the gravel lot a block from Riveter's and tried to get her nerves under control. When she noticed that her hands were literally shaking in her lap, she squeezed her fingers together, trying to calm them. The lot attendant had stopped looking quizzically over at her ten minutes ago. Apparently, he had accepted that she might never get out of her car.

"You're being ridiculous," she said to her reflection in the rearview mirror. "It's just Abby. She doesn't bite."

That didn't do much to calm her down. Mostly because she'd heard Abby's response to that joke more than once in her evenings at the bar. Abby always said the same thing in a sultry, flirty tone.

I only bite if you ask nicely.

God, why did her roommate have to be so overwhelmingly sexy? If only Ellie had agreed to come out for a beer. She could handle tonight if Ellie was with her. Her best friend would tease her about her crush and then the crush wouldn't feel so unconquerable.

"Stupid client meeting," Marlene said as her phone dinged with a notification.

Abby had texted her to ask if she was still coming out. She'd added a string of sleeping emojis that made Marlene smile. There wasn't a single other person in Marlene's life who used emojis. Or GIFs. Abby always sent the funniest GIFs. Texts from Abby were like a little performance. Full of energy and humor. Nothing else in Marlene's life made her feel so alive as being around Abby.

That thought gave her the confidence to finally open the car door. The lot attendant jumped at the sudden noise, but Marlene ignored him. Instead, she marched across the street, shooting back a text message to say she was walking in the door.

"Thank God," Abby said the moment she saw Marlene. "I was worried I might die of boredom tonight."

"You might still." Marlene slid onto a barstool. "I'm not that much fun."

Abby wrenched the cap off a bottle of Marlene's favorite beer and dropped it on top of a coaster. "Don't try lying to me. I live with you, remember? I know you're cool."

"You live with me, that's how you know I'm not cool."

Marlene had meant it to be teasing banter, but she could tell it didn't come across that way. The problem was, she really did know she wasn't cool. Not the way Abby was. Abby brought life into every room she entered and not just because she always wore something flashy and fun. Tonight was no exception. She was wearing a wig Marlene had seen on her before—bright blue with curls framing her face and a perfectly placed lock swinging in front of her matching horn-rimmed glasses. Her rings were each the twisted end of a different ornate spoon handle. Marlene's simple suit and brown loafers screamed dull.

Abby leaned over the bar, pointing at her with one of those ring-studded fingers. "We're going to have to work on that."

"On what?"

"Your confidence. And with you believing me. I never tell a lie, so if I say you're cool, you're cool."

Marlene got a little lost in the swirling depths of Abby's eyes, glittering with mischief. "Okay."

"That's a start. How was work?"

While Abby cleaned glasses and sliced limes, Marlene mumbled generalities about her day and sipped her beer. Abby had been right, Riveter's was dead. Apart from the two of them, the only other people in the bar were a couple in a booth across the room. They didn't look like they were thrilled to be there and they spent more time looking at their phones than each other. The single waitress was equally interested in her phone.

"Did you get a lot done at your studio?" Marlene asked to change the subject from her boring day.

"Sure did." Abby spun a lime on the cutting board. "I started a new canvas this morning. It needs more time to show itself to me, but that's always the fun part. Getting to know a new piece."

"I bet," Marlene said. When that sounded uninspired, she said, "I saw some of your art at Workhouse last year. At the Pride show. It was really great."

"Thanks." The way Abby's face lit up at the compliment made Marlene's stomach squirm. "I don't remember seeing you there."

The blood froze in Marlene's veins. Why had she brought up the Workhouse show? That's where she'd met Dawn and she did not want to think about Dawn ever again.

"I, um, left pretty early."

To Marlene's horror, Abby's face split into a wide grin and she leaned over the bar again, bringing the scent of that intoxicating perfume closer. "You mean you got laid that night."

"Oh God." Marlene couldn't stop the words from falling out of her mouth or stop the fire that erupted on her cheeks and neck. She dropped her face to the bar, trying to hide, but Abby wasn't easy to fool.

"I'm sorry." Abby patted her arm. "I didn't mean to embarrass you."

"I'm not embarrassed. Okay, maybe a little."

"You shouldn't be. There's nothing wrong with getting lucky." Abby stroked her fingertips across Marlene's sleeve. "Plus it's really cute when you blush."

Before Marlene could think of a response or get her face under control, the door opened and a new customer came in. Any hope Marlene had to recover was dashed when she heard the new customer's voice.

"Hey, sexy lady," Penelope said as she settled in on the other side of the bar. "What you got for me tonight?"

"For you? Anything." Abby spread her arms wide on the bar, her back to Marlene and her large breasts on full display for Pen. "What're you in the mood for?"

Pen's eyes flicked down to Abby's low collar and the ample cleavage it revealed and a smile crawled onto her face. Marlene was very familiar with that look on Pen's face. Intimately familiar. Her body reacted in ways she was not comfortable with.

Marlene tried to focus on the sultry music pumping from the speakers over the dance floor, but it wasn't quite loud enough to cover Pen replying, "I have a couple things in mind."

They went on like that for a long time, Abby making suggestive remarks, Pen replying in kind. While Abby shook a martini, Pen glanced in Marlene's direction, but Marlene hurriedly looked away. She hadn't spoken to Pen since they spent the night together. Since she'd run out in the morning and confessed to Ellie that she had slept with a woman for the first time. She'd wanted to talk to Pen. More than once. Before Dawn when she was trying out her new life.

Enjoying sex for the first time was confusing enough. Trying to learn a whole new way to be herself was something else altogether. Ellie had helped with the clothes. She had taken Marlene shopping to try to re-create the rush of excitement Marlene had felt in Pen's coat. The trip had been more successful than Marlene could ever have imagined and Ellie did her the added favor of showing her the wonders of men's pants. The pockets were huge. More than that, they felt good on her. She looked at herself in the changing room mirror at Macy's and burst into tears. Ellie had been startled and so uncomfortable, but Marlene had loved the feeling.

She still hadn't told Ellie about the lessons with Abby. When Marlene had first asked for help with dressing like a lesbian, Ellie had spit platitudes about how there wasn't one single way to dress because there wasn't one single way to be gay. That might've been true, but if there were a thousand ways to be a lesbian, how could Marlene figure out the one that fit her? She had figured it out, no thanks to either Pen or Ellie. At least she thought she had. Until Dawn dropped her bombshells. Marlene wondered if she was hiding the lessons with Abby because it felt like she failed to learn the lessons from Ellie.

Her train of thought was broken by a peel of laughter from Abby. She was leaning even closer to Pen than she had leaned to Marlene. Her breasts were practically in Pen's lap. And she was doing that thing feminine women did where they bat their eyelashes. If she'd been doing that to Marlene, she'd be in a puddle on the floor. Pen was not in a puddle, but that was probably because that sort of thing happened to her all the time.

At some point during the laughing and flirting, it occurred to Marlene that Pen and Abby might actually do something. Pen might have a girlfriend now, but no one flirted that hard without meaning it. When Pen asked for another martini before she'd even finished the first one, Abby leaned over and whispered something in Pen's ear. Whatever she said, it made Pen's eyebrows dance.

Oh God, they're going to have sex.

Once the thought appeared in Marlene's mind, she couldn't get it out. Her brain was practically screaming it at her. Her cheeks heated up again but this time she didn't hide her face. She couldn't look away. She continued to watch the build up to what would be an amazing night for both Pen and Abby.

Somewhere in the cacophony of her mind, a new thought surfaced. Abby lived down the hall from Marlene. If she brought Pen home for sex, Marlene would certainly hear it. Pen wasn't quiet and Marlene had no doubt Abby would be very vocal. The thought of hearing Abby in the throws of passion with someone else made Marlene sick with jealousy.

"Ellie was right. This was a terrible idea," she mumbled to herself.

"What was a terrible idea?" Abby had appeared in front of her, a fresh beer in one hand and a look of confusion on her face. Marlene had been so caught up in the nightmare of Abby bringing Pen back to their shared home, she hadn't noticed Abby approach. In fact, now that Marlene looked, she saw Pen's girlfriend at her side. Kieran was drinking the second martini and Pen had transferred all the innuendo and piercing stares to her as though Abby had never existed.

Marlene looked back to Abby and struggled to answer the question. "Um, drinking. On a Wednesday. Work tomorrow."

"I doubt a second beer will kill you," Abby said.

To her surprise, Marlene found the bottle in her hand empty. To her greater surprise, she found Abby still smiling and bubbly as ever. Wasn't she upset that Pen had ditched her so cavalierly? Apparently, the situation didn't bother her because Abby was her normal, happy self through Marlene's second beer and Pen leaving with Kieran not long after.

CHAPTER TWELVE

Abby nestled further into the sofa cushions, pulling her legs closer to her chest. She reveled in the comfort of the cushions hugging her. This was, by far, the best sofa she'd ever had. Marlene certainly had better taste than Josie, and it looked like Abby was lucky enough to benefit. It certainly made their lesbian movie marathon more comfortable.

In fact, lots of things were more comfortable with Marlene these days. When she first moved in, Abby had worried it would be awkward to live with someone who was essentially a stranger. A quiet, shy stranger at that. But they fell into a routine relatively quickly and really got along, despite their personality differences. Of course, it didn't hurt that Marlene was alluring in that sweet, handsome way Abby enjoyed so much.

Sneaking a glance across the sofa, Abby studied her roommate. She was stretched along the length of the chaise section of the sofa, bare feet peeking out from fluffy blue sweatpants. Her legs were too short to cover much ground, and, while relaxed, she wasn't slouching. Marlene was clearly at rest, her eyes fixed on the screen and a throw pillow in her lap, but she wasn't exactly relaxed. She held too much tension in her thin shoulders to ever truly relax, but the usual crinkles of worry or focus were gone from her eyes. Part of her wondered if Marlene's tension was Abby-related or just her natural state, but she had no way to really know.

A burst of sound drew Abby's attention to the screen as the camera panned out and the credits rolled. Marlene watched the entire list of names with quiet determination, then raised the remote and muted the TV.

"What did you think?" Abby asked.

"Is it just me or was that, um, weird?" Marlene asked.

Laughter burst out of Abby. "It's not just you. *Bound* takes campy to a whole other level. Like a cringey level."

"Okay, I'm so glad you said it." Marlene turned to her. "What was with her voice? And the scene with the briefs?"

"That's just Jennifer Tilly's voice I'm afraid. As for the briefs, I have no answers, only questions."

Marlene shrugged and ran a hand through her hair. "I guess."

"Apart from being weird, what did you think? Did you like it?"

"Yeah I think so. It was campy, but there was something great about it, too." Marlene's eyebrows scrunched together as she spoke and she stared off toward the darkened kitchen, her eyes unfocused. "I liked seeing Corky. She carried herself like a butch woman. I don't know if I've seen that before."

"You probably haven't. There aren't a lot of authentic depictions of butch women in movies."

"I've seen a lot of movies with lesbian side characters, but nothing like this, where we were the center of the story."

Warmth spread through Abby. This was exactly what she wanted for Marlene. To have that moment she'd had years ago when she first found queer movies. "It's pretty cool, right? Seeing someone like you get a happily ever after."

"Other than the fact that I could never be with a woman with that voice? Yeah. It was pretty great."

"I'll be honest, there aren't a ton of a movies with queer women. It's getting better, but when I first started watching, *Bound* was one of the few. Definitely one of the better produced and one of the happiest, too."

Marlene lifted an eyebrow. "Happy? They ended up together, but they were both tortured and beat up. They had to do and see a bunch of terrible stuff."

"But they were alive."

"Is that a high bar?"

"Very." Abby sat back on the sofa and clicked back to the title screen showing Gina Gershon and Jennifer Tilly in leather jackets.

"There you have it. *Bound*. It's a classic, but flawed. Sadly, that's why the film section of this course will be so short."

"All lesbian films are flawed?"

"Isn't everything in life flawed?" Abby clicked through the film library until she reached their next film. "*Better Than Chocolate*. It's from the same era, so there is tragic nineties hair galore, but slightly less violence."

One of Marlene's eyebrows shot up as she examined the menu page. "It's a bit risqué to have naked women on the cover though, isn't it? Is this going to be like *Cruel Intentions* where it's just lesbians for titillation?"

Abby laughed. "Definitely not. You won't find exploitation here. It's only authentic queerness in my class."

"If you say so. Not that I mind naked women, of course."

"For the record, there can be sex and nudity and all the yummy stuff without the exploitation. Lesbians can appreciate a nice-looking naked woman, too."

"We sure can." Marlene's cheeks blazed red and she stammered, "I mean, respectfully appreciate."

"Of course. But there is problematic treatment of trans characters and whole bucketful of homophobia in this one. Like lots more than we saw in *Bound*. There has to be a bad guy, of course."

Marlene groaned and dropped back onto the sofa. She was just pretending to pout, but it was the most relaxed she'd looked all day. "I might need a snack before we move on. Does this Lesbian 101 class include lunch breaks?"

"It's your class, it can include anything you want. Let me whip up some lunch for us."

Before Abby could stand up, Marlene sat straight and held out her hand. "No, don't. Let me order something. You're already teaching me, you don't have to cook for me, too."

The chivalry was pretty adorable, and Abby wanted to be lazy today, so she relented. Still, it wasn't fair to take too much advantage. "I just made us a Saturday afternoon movie lineup. It wasn't exactly difficult labor."

"Well, you still deserve a free meal for your efforts."

While Marlene ordered them delivery sandwiches, Abby clicked into her email. She wasn't expecting anything earth-shattering in there. Most of her friends were text-based communicators and her mom wasn't allowed access to a computer in the nursing home. Most of the contents of her inbox were ads and junk mail from stores she hadn't shopped at for ages. Still, she liked sorting through them in case something interesting showed up.

Marlene stretched her neck and tossed her phone onto the cushion between them. "Food will be here in thirty minutes." She sounded tired, but not in a coming-apart-at-the-seems way. More in a lazy-Saturday-afternoon-on-the-sofa-in-sweats way.

They sat together in comfortable silence for a while, a light breeze tossing the leaves outside around and making the sunlight dance on the polished hardwood floor. Eventually, Abby found an email that piqued her interest and she clicked on it. "Have you ever done one of those meal kit delivery things?"

"The ones where they send prepared meals that you just heat up in the microwave?"

"No, the ones with portioned ingredients so you cook the meals yourself but don't end up with an extra five pounds of kale rotting in the fridge."

Marlene chuckled quietly and shook her head. "Nope. I lived alone until last year. It didn't make sense to get something like that when it's just me."

Abby set aside her tablet in favor of conversation. "You've never lived with anyone until last year? Really?"

Marlene shrugged. "Really."

"And the person who lived with you before me was your ex, right? Dawn?"

Marlene stiffened visibly, but nodded and turned toward Abby. "Yeah. She moved in pretty quick after we started dating."

"What about before her?" Marlene didn't run away or look too uncomfortable, but Abby still asked, "Is this okay to talk about? We can change the subject if you'd rather."

"It's fine. I never got to the moving in stage with any of the men I dated. Nothing ever got serious with them. Most of my relationships with men just—I don't know. Petered out?"

"It didn't feel right with them?"

"Definitely not. They were nice guys, I guess. It wasn't them, it was me. I used to say that, but now I know it's really true."

Marlene was surprisingly comfortable discussing her past. She even made eye contact with Abby a few times, which wasn't something she did often, even during easy conversations. Abby decided either Marlene needed to talk about this stuff or she wanted to connect with her new roommate. Either way, Abby was keen to know more about her.

"Do you think you'd ever date men again?" Abby asked. "Have you figured out how you identify?"

"I'm a lesbian." Marlene said it with such conviction, it made Abby want to wrap her in a hug. She remembered all too well the power in finding the label she identified with when she was first coming out. "Don't get me wrong. I considered bisexuality. Since I'd dated men and some of them I really cared about."

"But it didn't fit?"

"No." Marlene blushed as she said, "It wasn't the same at all. The way I feel with a woman is nothing like I felt with men. And I'm not just talking about sex. It's the way I feel more like myself when I'm with a woman. It just feels right in a way it never did with men."

"That's great. It's hard sometimes to figure yourself out. Sounds like you know yourself pretty well."

"I ought to after thirty-eight years in here," Marlene said, waving her hand around to indicate her body.

"It takes some people much longer than that. And some folks never find out."

"How about you?" Marlene asked.

"Oh, I am intimately familiar with this." Abby mimicked Marlene's gesture to indicate her own, much curvier body. "But it's fun to keep researching."

Marlene looked away and hugged her throw pillow hard. "I, um, meant how do you identify? Do you date men?"

Abby stretched out her legs, twisting her ankles around to stretch muscles sore from a busy Friday night of bartending. "No men for me either. I'm a gold star."

"A gold star?"

"It means I'm a lesbian who has never had sex with a man." Abby watched Marlene's shoulders bunch up. "Which I now realize makes it seem like I'm saying I'm a better lesbian for never having sex with men. I'm sorry, that's not how I meant it at all."

"It's okay," Marlene said. "I wasn't offended. I just hadn't heard the term before."

"This lesson was free then. I still think I'll stop saying that. I don't think there's anything special about me not being with men before women. I was pretty young when I realized it was gross when men hit on me. It wasn't a long walk from there to lesbian."

"How young?"

"I came out in high school." Abby leaned back and smiled at the memories of her oversexed, overconfident teenage self. "And I was so loud about it. Asked out my friend Sherry right in the middle of the lunch room with half the school watching."

"Did she say yes?"

"God no. Sherry wasn't the loud type. Not like me. Maybe if I'd asked her in private she would've given it a shot, but she also wasn't gay, so I had two strikes against me."

Marlene had released the pillow and leaned into the conversation. She looked like she wanted to take notes. "What about the rest of the school? Did they give you a hard time?"

"Not really. I was the first girl in my school to develop, as my grandmother put it. The guys were too busy staring at my tits to call me names. And the girls already were calling me names, so it didn't matter."

Abby's smile faltered as she remembered the thrill of finally getting attention. The slight shift when she realized it wasn't quite what she expected. She'd told her mother what her grandmother had said about her new breasts. The way men would like her now. How she should appreciate it because they would only be interested for so long. Then her mother had sucked out all the sourness with her rage. Abby had never seen her grandmother angry until she watched from the parked car as Abby's mother had screamed in her face. That was the day Abby had found the power of her curves. Had taken her own power back from the wolf-whistlers and the boys who tried to grab her in gym class.

Marlene was kind enough not to let the silence linger. "But you dated girls in high school? That's cool. I wish I'd known then. Would've saved me a lot of time."

"I'm sure some of those relationships with men were meaningful." When Marlene didn't agree, Abby asked, "Weren't they?"

"My college boyfriend was an asshole, but the rest weren't too bad."

"Weren't too good, either?"

"It wasn't their fault," Marlene said again.

"Women aren't that much better," Abby said, hoping to take the strain from Marlene's mahogany eyes. "I've dated some real jerks, too. Loserdom knows no gender."

Marlene smiled and her shoulders did relax. She still seemed tired, though, so Abby decided they'd done enough sharing for the day.

"I'm going to sign us up for a meal kit delivery service. Any allergies?" Abby asked.

"No allergies. Let me get you my credit card, I'll pay."

Abby tapped the email link. "Nope. We'll split it."

Marlene opened her mouth, clearly intent to argue. Abby kept her eyes on her, making the challenge clear. She could tell Marlene wanted to insist, maybe even point out how much more money she made than Abby, but she wisely reconsidered. Their lunch arrived and Marlene hurried downstairs to collect it.

While filling out the form and picking their first meals, Abby tried to decide if she found Marlene's offer to pay charming or annoying. On the one hand, she undoubtedly did make more than Abby and the offer to pay could be seen as chivalrous. On the other hand, Abby hated it when people waved their wealth around. She never would have suggested an expense she wasn't prepared to share equally.

As they debated over the merits of pork eggroll bowls versus Mediterranean pasta with halibut, Abby decided that Marlene was being charming and decided she liked Marlene for it.

CHAPTER THIRTEEN

No matter how hard Marlene tried, she couldn't seem to focus on her work. Brad had given her the task of reviewing the entire area's cash-on-hand averages. It was an important task that kept all of them safer, but even the stark reminder that bank robberies were on the rise in the area couldn't grab her attention.

The problem was Brad, of course. Marlene had been on edge ever since Lucy's retirement, but Brad's last visit and his not-so-subtle hints about her fashion choices had sent her into a spiral. She'd been dwelling on it since, always terrified that he'd show up again, uninvited and unannounced. How many hints would he make before he started handing out punishments? Worse, the uncertainty was starting to affect her performance. She found herself less likely to engage with the older clients, worried they might trust her less because she wore a men's suit. Even if she'd known those customers for years, she found reasons to avoid them.

Outside her office, Ellie stood and held out a hand to her client. Marlene watched the interaction more as an excuse to stop her own work than any real interest in Ellie's. The client looked to be in her seventies or eighties and held Ellie's hands in both hers. She even patted Ellie's hand in that grandmotherly way older ladies tended to do. Ellie's smile was warm and welcoming, exactly as it always was. When it came to women, Ellie's appeal crossed generations.

Once the client had shuffled out of the branch, Ellie pushed through Marlene's office door and dropped into her guest chair.

"You have that smug 'I made a sale' look," Marlene said.

Ellie waved her hand dismissively. "Just a CD. It wasn't much, but I think the commission will make my goal for the month. That's a week earlier than last month."

"I told you to stop gloating."

"I'm not capable. Arrogance is my oxygen."

"You're my best friend, Ellie," Marlene said. "I know that better than anyone else."

Ellie leaned back in her chair and crossed one ankle over her knee. If Marlene had been in a better mood, she would've found some banter to take Ellie down a peg. As it was, she needed the normality of Ellie's obnoxiousness to keep her sane.

"Hey did you miss a haircut?" Ellie asked.

Marlene ran a self-conscious hand through her hair. It was getting longer and starting to tickle her ears and the back of her neck. She had, in fact, canceled her last haircut. After Brad's comments, she was afraid to keep it so short. She'd scoured the internet for a style that would be short enough to feel good while also being feminine enough to appease Brad. All she'd found was short bobs and pixie cuts that were nowhere near her new style. The idea of going back to something that didn't fit her made her sick to her stomach, but then so did the idea of getting fired. She couldn't make a decision so she decided to not do anything at all.

Before she'd come out, Marlene hadn't cared much about her hair. She'd grown it out to just beyond her shoulders and thrown it up in a ponytail every day. For special occasions, she tried to turn her thin, stick-straight hair into something pretty and had always failed. Nothing felt right and she didn't like thinking about it too much.

Then she'd gone to bed with Penelope and everything had changed. Well, the going to bed with Pen hadn't done it. Having sex with her while wearing that suit jacket had changed things pretty significantly, though. She recognized that disinterest in her hair as displeasure. She started consuming her news exclusively from Rachel Maddow and decided that's how she wanted to look. The first time she cut her hair, she was terrified, but she'd researched queer stylists in the DC area and found one who was as kind as she was enthusiastic.

She'd cried when she saw herself in the mirror after that first cut and she hadn't missed an appointment since.

Until two weeks ago when she panicked.

"I was busy that day. I'll get it cut soon," Marlene said.

She squirmed in her chair and her silk blouse clung uncomfortably to her skin. That was another thing she was trying out. She figured if she paired a woman's blouse with her men's suit, it might go over better. When she'd bought a new wardrobe, she'd kept all her old women's suits and slacks. Part of the decision was concern that she'd change her mind on this new style, part was a reluctance to throw away thousands of dollars-worth of clothes just because they didn't feel right anymore. Now she was putting them to use.

Apparently, that change hadn't escaped Ellie's notice, either. She sneered and asked, "What's with the pink blouse? Is that your cleavage showing? Why do you look weird today?"

"I don't know what you're talking about." Marlene avoided eye contact. "And stop looking at my boobs. It's not professional."

Ellie screwed up her face. "I'm not looking like that. Gross."

"Wow, you really are making me feel great today."

"I'm not being an ass. You just don't look comfortable."

"Maybe that's 'cause my best friend said I look awful."

"Not awful, just..." Ellie curled her lip and said, "Girly."

Marlene rolled her eyes, but knew there wasn't any conviction behind it. She did look girly and she hated it, but she didn't have a choice. She shook her mouse to wake up her computer. "I have work to do and there's a customer waiting."

Ellie's head whipped around just in time to see David, the other account representative, greet the newcomer. Ellie was incredibly competitive with David and she swore at seeing him beat her to a sale. She hurried to the door.

"Want to grab a beer at Riveter's tonight?" After a beat, Ellie said, "If you go home and change first."

Marlene turned away from her work long enough to flip her middle finger at Ellie. "No thanks. Abby's off tonight and we're hanging out."

"You've been doing that a lot recently." Ellie's eyebrows waggled suggestively. "You two have been getting close."

"No, we haven't."

"This is the second time you've turned down hanging out with me."

Marlene still hadn't told Ellie about the lesbian lessons. She wasn't sure whether Ellie would mock her or be pissed she hadn't been asked. Either way, Marlene didn't want to deal with her friend's feelings on the matter, so she deflected. "You turn down hanging out with me all the time."

"Yeah, but that's normal for me. It isn't for you."

"Maybe your company isn't as unforgettable as you think it is." Marlene went back to her reports. "Besides, we signed up for a meal kit service and our first order is being delivered today."

"Let me get this straight." Ellie released the door handle to turn her disbelieving gaze on Marlene. "You're trying to deny that you're getting close with your roommate by admitting you're skipping a chance to flirt with women in order to go home and cook with said hot roommate?"

"Yeah."

"Seriously?"

Marlene abandoned her spreadsheets again. "I'm not going to flirt with anyone at Riveter's anyway."

"Right, because the woman you want to flirt with will be in your house."

"No. I don't flirt with women at Riveter's. I just sit there and watch you flirt with women," Marlene said.

To Marlene's surprise, Ellie blushed and sputtered. "I'm not going to flirt with anyone. I don't know anyone there. Why would I flirt?"

Marlene scrunched her eyebrows together and adjusted her shoulders against the uncomfortable shirt. "Since when do you need to know someone to flirt with them?"

"I don't."

Marlene blinked and asked, "Then why won't you flirt with them?"

"I just don't want to."

"Neither do I."

"Okay then. We won't go." Ellie blushed even harder and scurried out of the office.

Marlene would've chased after her to figure out what that weirdness was all about, but her cell phone buzzed with a new message. It was a message from Abby that their meal kit had arrived, followed by a string of celebration and food related Emojis.

Abby's excitement was so infectious, it even transferred through text. Marlene didn't realize she was grinning like a fool until Ellie wrapped on her office window and made a faux swooning face. Marlene used her middle finger to great effect for a second time and then forced herself to truly look at her computer screen for the first time in ages. Still, the goofy grin didn't leave her lips.

Austin yanked the door open before Abby even had time to let her hand fall. Instead of the excitement she usually showed when Abby stopped by, there was barely contained panic in her eyes.

"Whoa. Everything okay?" Abby asked.

Over Austin's shoulder, Abby could see the motley crew that made up their D&D group milling around and chatting. The weight of their presence was clear in Austin's strained features.

"Everything's great."

No sooner was the lie out of Austin's mouth than she was hustling back to the tiny kitchen at the back of her apartment. Abby set her lute in a corner and added her strawberry, honey, and goat cheese crostini to the crowded snack table. Austin hurried back out of the kitchen, carrying a box of flavored sparkling waters to the entertainment center she'd set up as a makeshift bar.

"You look amazing." Austin tossed the words at Abby as she dashed back into the kitchen.

Abby chuckled at her friend's frantic pace. She was never like this when they were working at Riveter's. It was usually impossible to shatter her calm. But having a dozen elves, mages, and bards crammed into her one-bedroom apartment was apparently enough to kick her into gear.

"She's right you know." Beth, their dungeon master and usual host of the festivities, arrived beside Abby. "You do look fabulous tonight. New wig?"

Abby gave a little curtsy and pretended to fluff her hair. "Not a new wig, just a new style to an old one."

"Well, it's fabulous. I'm so excited you got settled so you can blow us all away with Elanderose's high fashion."

"I'm happy, too. I hated showing up here half-dressed."

"You could never be half-dressed, even if you don't have your full wardrobe at your disposal," Beth said.

Austin rushed through the room again, tossing a sweaty smile Beth's way as she rearranged chairs around the coffee table. It would be a squeeze to get them all around the table, but they were a pretty laidback group. They could make it work.

Jacki, the only single-class warrior in their group, joined them. She had to hop forward to avoid Austin streaking through the room, and that brought her closer to Abby. Closer than was really necessary, but Jacki always did love being as close to Abby as she could get without angering her girlfriend.

"Poor Austin is going to run herself ragged. Why aren't we at your house tonight, Beth?" Jacki asked.

Beth rolled her eyes. "My husband started another one of his projects last weekend. Ripping out the wainscoting in the dining room."

"He hasn't finished replacing it?" Abby asked.

"He hasn't finished removing it. He got distracted Sunday afternoon and now we have lumber and nails all over the first floor. I told him not to do it, but you know how men are."

"No, I don't," Jacki and Abby said in unison.

"Aren't you lucky," Beth deadpanned.

The three of them shared a laugh and Abby felt lighter than she had in months. It hadn't occurred to her how unhappy she'd been. Not just when she'd been unsettled after Josie, but when she'd been with Josie, too. They'd been so poorly suited and it hadn't occurred to her at the time. In fact, she rarely talked to Josie about D&D, despite how much she loved it. Part of her had known Josie wasn't thrilled at the idea of Abby flaunting Elanderose in public.

She allowed herself a moment to wonder how Marlene would feel about it. The lesbian lessons were silly, but it was bringing them closer and Abby really liked that. Marlene seemed to enjoy spending time with her and getting to know her. And she'd certainly been interested in Abby's look the first time she'd seen Elanderose. Maybe Abby should tell Marlene more about her D&D group. Maybe she'd want to come.

The very idea of straitlaced Marlene at D&D night made Abby giggle, and Jacki, ever attentive, picked up on it.

"It's good to see you your old self again. You've got your outfits and props," Jacki said.

Beth said, "And you're happy again. That's nice to see."

Abby leaned close to Beth and raised a flirtatious eyebrow. "Wasn't I happy before? You could've made me happier, you know."

"Don't try your flirty thing with me." Beth laughed. "You know it won't work."

"What flirty thing? Do I have a flirty thing?"

"You're kidding right?" Austin asked as she passed by. "You flirt with everyone."

"I do not," Abby said.

Jacki leaned in closer. "You could flirt with me more often."

"No, I can't. Your girlfriend would destroy me, both in the game and in real life." Abby said. "Besides, I don't flirt. I'm just happy. Life's good right now."

Beth said, "That's wonderful. You deserve it. But I knew that already because you didn't try that hard with the flirting. You must be dating someone new. You always look your best when you have a new lady and you don't try nearly as hard with the flirting. Who is she?"

"She doesn't exist. I'm single."

Jacki said, "No way. I heard you moved in with someone new. A cute little baby gay."

"Excuse me?" Abby heard the edge in her own voice, but she couldn't help it. Her jaw tightened and blood rushed to her face, leaving her cheeks tingling.

Jacki continued on, oblivious to Abby's rising anger. "A late bloomer or something like that, right?"

"Marlene is not a late bloomer and she's not a baby." Abby's ears were starting to ring and the plastic cup in her hand crinkled as she gripped it harder. "It took her longer than some of us to come out and that's okay."

Jacki raised her hands in surrender. "I didn't mean anything by it."

"Yeah, well that's a jerky thing to say about someone. She's going through a lot right now and she doesn't need people making fun of her."

Jacki lowered her voice and her hands. "I'm really sorry. I didn't mean to make fun. Honestly."

One or two of the conversations around them faltered and Abby realized she'd raised her voice, something she rarely did. Austin was staring at her through the pass-through, but Abby couldn't tell if she was concerned about Abby or nervous that the party mood was souring. Abby took a long breath and let it out. She was overreacting. She knew it. She just couldn't shake the sad puppy dog look in Marlene's eyes every time her ex came up. That woman had done a number on her and she didn't deserve it. Maybe Marlene had a point with these lesbian lessons after all. Sometimes queer women could be cliquish and judgmental. It would be easy to feel like an outsider in a group like this.

"It's okay," Abby said, though she wasn't entirely sure it was. "But we're not dating. We're just roommates."

The tension broke and everyone went back to their conversations or, in Austin's case, their frantic cleaning of a messy kitchen.

Beth completed the cure in her joking way. "I read a romance novel like that once."

"How did it end?" Jacki asked.

A smile spread slowly across Beth's face. "In the same bed."

Jacki laughed and Abby found herself laughing along. It was all so ridiculous. And she knew one thing for sure, she and Marlene weren't going to end up like Beth's romance novel.

Abby said, "Sounds yummy, but that's not going to happen with us."

Beth said, "Why not?"

"Well, Marlene is super hot and really sweet."

"I'm not hearing a problem," Beth said.

"I've got a roommate just like that." Jacki turned and shot her girlfriend, dressed in form fitting wizard's robes, a meaningful wink.

"She's just like my ex." Abby sighed wistfully. "More worried about her job than her own happiness and I'm not letting myself get caught up in that again."

CHAPTER FOURTEEN

Y ou don't have to worry, Mrs. Pendergast. I can take care of
this for you."

"Are you sure?" Mrs. Pendergast held her old-fashioned valise-
style purse in her lap, the stiff handles clutched in her hands. The
leather handles squeaked from the force of her grip. "I know it isn't
your job."

"It's not only my job, it's my pleasure," Marlene said. She tried
to project kindness with her smile, but Mrs. Pendergast seemed just as
frightened of her smile as someone else would be of a scowl.

"Well, if you insist." Mrs. Pendergast's words were hesitant and
stilted, but her relief was palpable.

"I do insist." Marlene collected the neatly written deposit slip
and checks. "You just wait here and I'll be right back. Make yourself
comfortable."

"Oh, yes. I will."

As Marlene headed to the teller line, she thought back to the
first time Mrs. Pendergast had come into her branch. She'd arrived in
the lobby, the same old but well-preserved handbag clutched tight to
her chest, and looked around with watery, nervous eyes. It had taken
some persuading for Marlene to convince her to step into her office.

That had been two years ago, the day after Mr. Pendergast had
suffered a heart attack and passed away. Mrs. Pendergast needed to
pay the funeral home for the upcoming service, but she didn't know
how to write a check. Or how much money she had in her various
accounts.

"Reginald took care of all that," she'd said in explanation. "He gave me cash for the groceries once a week and handled everything else."

The difficulty came in the fact that Mrs. Pendergast did not have any identification apart from a long since expired passport that listed her simply as Mrs. Reginald Pendergast. She did not have a single document containing her first name apart from her marriage certificate. She'd never had a driver's license or a credit card. She'd never worked outside the home. Her only identity was as Reginald's wife and now Reginald was dead and she was an eighty-two-year-old woman who hadn't signed her first name on a document since 1956.

Marlene had spent the last two years handling nearly every aspect of Mrs. Pendergast's finances. Marlene had set up her social security and annuity deposits. She'd arranged her automatic bill pay and ordered her checks. Marlene was well-aware that Mrs. Pendergast had gone from being dependent on Reginald to being dependent on her banker, but Marlene didn't care. She was a sweet woman with no one else in the world and Marlene would gladly spend an hour a week making sure she had money in the bank and a friendly face to count on.

Marlene rounded the corner and saw Ellie leaning on the teller line's high granite counter. Her eyes sparkled with amusement and her posture projected comfort. As Marlene approached, Felice said something that made Ellie laugh. She leaned farther into the counter and crossed one foot over the other, the leather sole of her two-toned Oxfords clicking on the marble floor. Marlene tried to adjust the high waist of her women's slacks. The tiny zipper dug into her abdomen and the flap of the fake pocket chafed her thigh. She felt like an idiot in this outfit, one she hadn't worn since before coming out.

"Hey, boss," Ellie said.

Before Marlene could scold her, Felice raised an eyebrow. "Didn't she tell you to stop calling her that?"

"Yeah, but she says stuff like that all the time," Ellie said.

"Then why don't you do it?" Felice took Mrs. Pendergast's deposit and ran it while keeping a disapproving eye on Ellie.

Ellie shrugged and grabbed one of the cheap, flavorless lollipops from the basket on the counter. Marlene was busy deciding whether or not she should weigh in on the argument when she noticed Felice's eyes go wide. She was staring over Marlene's shoulder and there was only one person who could rattle Felice.

Marlene closed her eyes, then took a deep breath. She noticed with a sort of detached resignation that her shoulders were up around her ears and her stomach had twisted itself into one big, painful knot. Releasing the breath, she tucked her hair behind her ear and plastered on her widest smile as she spun. Brad was dressed in one of his endless collection of generic navy suits and wide-collared white shirts. His usual look of distaste was also fully in evidence.

"Great to see you again, Brad." Marlene had finally learned not to hold out her hand. He would never shake it. "You remember the team."

Marlene indicated Felice and Rachel, the other teller working, as well as Ellie. Brad didn't even bother looking at them. He wasn't really looking at Marlene either. He had a habit of looking just over her left shoulder. The lack of eye contact made her skittish.

"Hey, Brad." Ellie grinned around her lollipop, her lips faintly blue and the stick jutting out at a sharp angle. "Nice of you to spend so much time here at the Main Street Branch. We always love seeing you."

Brad's eyes darted over to Ellie, taking her in from the tip of her lollipop's stick to the toes of her men's shoes and back again. Ellie had never been the type to wither under that sort of inspection. She shoved her hands deep into her pockets and rocked forward on her toes, her grin spreading the longer he glared at her.

After a long, tense moment, Brad's eyes snapped back to the spot over Marlene's shoulder. "Are you free for a chat?"

The abrupt request threw Marlene for a moment, and she nearly tripped over her shoes to lead him back to her office. Felice called her back, handing over the receipt and what was surely intended to be a supportive half-smile. It looked more like a grimace. Brad walked two steps ahead of Marlene on the way back to her office. It wasn't until she saw the pale pink of Mrs. Pendergast's shawl that she remembered she had a client.

Marlene rushed ahead to get to the office door first. "I'm just finishing up with a regular client. Wait here and I'll just be a moment."

Brad did not wait outside her office. He nearly clipped her heels following her into the little glass cube and positioned himself behind her chair like a suspicious bodyguard or a disapproving father. Neither of those attitudes were likely to set Mrs. Pendergast at ease. Marlene could hear the tiniest startled gasp from her client as her boss settled in behind her.

Mrs. Pendergast accepted Marlene's introduction, but it did nothing to set either of them at ease. In fact, Marlene found herself more stifled than she could ever remember in a conversation with a client. She tried to make up for her distraction by asking Mrs. Pendergast a few questions about her neighbors and friends, but it was clear no one in the room was interested in or comfortable with the conversation. Fortunately, Mrs. Pendergast didn't stay long. Marlene walked her out of the office, but not to the branch door as she usually did.

Using the excuse of ensuring Mrs. Pendergast made it down the stairs safely, Marlene took a moment to gather herself before going back to face Brad. It didn't do any good. She was so nervous, she made Mrs. Pendergast look relaxed. Fortunately, she had decided to wear one of her old outfits today. Brad seemed to approve of the silk blouse and high-waisted women's pants more than the men's suits. He hadn't given her the sort of disappointed inspection he'd given Ellie, at least. Still, she missed the confidence she felt when she wore the clothes she liked. Her men's suits felt like armor. This frilly blouse felt like wearing a paper dress in a hurricane.

When she arrived back at her office, Brad was sitting in her chair, intent on his phone. She hovered by the door a moment, then settled awkwardly into one of the client chairs. Brad made her sweat for two minutes while he finished typing an email, then dropped his phone on the desk and leveled his gaze at her. Marlene crossed her ankle over her knee, then thought better of it and awkwardly turned the movement into crossing one knee over the other. It wasn't a graceful movement, but Brad didn't comment. He just stared at her left earlobe.

"Why didn't you talk to your client about a mortgage product?"

Marlene's brain felt like it was caught in quicksand. She stammered her answer as words slowly made their way from her brain to her mouth. "You mean Mrs. Pendergast? Her home's paid for."

"An equity product then. There's always room for improvements on real estate."

"She's eighty-two." When he didn't respond, she said, "She's on a fixed income. She doesn't have room in her budget for an equity line payment."

"Was that deposit you made for a new account?"

"No, it was a dividend check from her electricity co-op."

Brad smiled without any hint of joy. "If she has money to invest in stocks, she has money to invest with us."

Marlene's heart was beating so fast she was having a hard time catching her breath. What was he talking about? He didn't know anything about Mrs. Pendergast or her financial situation. At the same time, maybe he had a point. She had been awkward with her client and she probably could have done better.

"You're right," Marlene said. "I haven't talked with her about her full financial profile in a while. Next time she comes in, I'll make sure to ask more probing questions."

Brad smirked and leaned forward, propping his elbows on her desk and crinkling the papers there. "Every time you let a client walk out the door without offering them a new account or service, you run the risk of there not being a next time."

Marlene opened her mouth to protest when a burst of laughter cut through the moment. Twisting in her chair, Marlene saw Ellie arrive at her desk, a pretty woman in tow. Ellie was laying the charm on thick and, as usual, her voice rose with each laugh and bit of witty banter.

"Close the door," Brad said through clenched teeth.

Marlene hopped up to obey, but the closed door did little to muffle Ellie's enthusiastic conversation. As she settled back into the client chair, Brad didn't look at Marlene. He kept his disapproving glare fixed on Ellie.

"You're going to need to do something about her," he said.

"Who? Ellie?"

He nodded, his knuckles white he was gripping his own hands so hard. "I can tell you're friends, so I know that will be hard for you, but I need you to be a leader here, Marlene. In fact, the friendship itself is problematic."

Marlene's face started to tingle as the blood rushed out of it. "How is our friendship problematic? I'm friendly with all the branch staff. That's why we're such an effective team."

Brad ignored the explanation, continuing as if she hadn't spoken. "We've talked before about the importance of traditional values. FTL clients expect our bankers to look a certain way." He finally met her eyes, his lip curving. "Ellie is not the type of person they expect."

"Ellie is a great banker and her clients love her."

Brad gave the young woman seated at Ellie's desk a significant look. "I'm sure some of them do. That's also a problem."

Marlene's mouth went dry and her heart was still hammering in her chest. Was Brad implying what she thought he was implying? Was he saying that he had a problem with Ellie because she was a lesbian? What would he say if he found out she was a lesbian, too? How could this possibly be happening? It felt like a threat from the 1950s, not something a manager would say these days. But then she had seen enough homophobia even in her short time being out to believe it. Was her job at risk here?

Brad stood abruptly, buttoning his jacket. "I encourage you to put some distance there."

Marlene had intended to say something. She couldn't form the words. She couldn't even stand or say good-bye as he marched past her, yanking the door open with what seemed unnecessary force. The door closed with a thud, sending a burst of air at her back and ruffling the too-long hair at the nape of her neck. She sat and stared at her empty desk chair. The spot he'd sat when he threatened her friend's career. Threatened her career.

Marlene wasn't sure how long she sat there, but the door opening again broke her out of her stupor. Ellie leaned her head in and asked, "Hey, you okay?"

Marlene whipped around, worried that Brad would see them talking. When she didn't see him, she drooped back into the chair, her shoulders finally relaxing. "Yeah. I'm fine." Ellie opened her mouth to say something, but Marlene sat up and said, "You know what? No. I'm not fine. I could use a drink."

"Thought so. Meet me at Riveter's at five thirty."

"Make it five fifteen," Marlene said.

Chapter Fifteen

Marlene slid onto the barstool and immediately felt more herself. The clothes helped. She'd gone home and ripped her way out of the silk blouse and women's dress slacks so quickly she nearly lost a button. Putting on the loose jeans and baby blue button-up felt like taking a deep breath.

Unfortunately, while Marlene had found her comfort, Ellie seemed to have lost all hers. She was perched on the very edge of her barstool and she was bouncing her right knee so frantically that the keys in her pocket were jingling. The ringing added a discordant note to Riveter's usual trancey music.

"Okay, you have to tell me what's going on." Marlene put her hand on Ellie's knee to stop the twitch. "You're acting weird."

Ellie didn't argue. Instead, she sagged on her stool. "Sorry, I just had a shitty day."

Marlene bit back her sigh. The last thing she wanted to do was talk about work, but the least she could do for her best friend was help her work through whatever this was. "Want to tell me about it?"

"You're my boss, I can't complain about my job to you."

"I'm also your best friend, so spill."

Ellie shrugged, then drained her beer. "You know that business loan I was working on?"

"The one for the bakery around the corner?"

Ellie nodded and said in a rush, "Yeah. That one. Well, it turns out things are more complicated than I originally thought and it'll probably fall through and I feel like shit because I all but promised the client it would work out and I don't know how to tell her it won't."

"Are you sure it's dead? What's the problem?"

"She has way more debt than she originally quoted and the building appraisal came in low."

"Have you talked to the underwriter? Who is it?"

Ellie groaned as she explained everything she'd done to push the deal through. She went over every little detail with the sort of professional enthusiasm Marlene had never felt for the work. As she drank her beer and listened, Marlene realized that Ellie would make a great manager one day. She had an eye for detail and a passion for service like Marlene, but she also had a genuine love for the process. The more she talked, the more she relaxed and the more Marlene tensed up.

In an effort to stop her spiral, Marlene searched for something else to focus on as Ellie continued to talk through her problem. As usual, her eyes were drawn to Abby. She had taken to wearing her natural hair more these days. Well, natural was a stretch given the bright, cherry-red color, but it wasn't a wig and it suited Abby's steel gray eyes and pale skin. Marlene had never been a hopeless teenager, but she could relate to the crush.

Peeling her eyes away from Abby, Marlene put a hand on Ellie's shoulder and gave her a light squeeze. "I'm sure we can work something out. I'll call Brad in the morning about a manager's override."

"You think he'll go for it?"

"Won't hurt to ask."

Ellie scoffed and waved at Abby. "You sure about that?"

Abby returned Ellie's wave as she mixed a drink. Marlene forced herself not to watch. "Not at all."

Ellie growled and ran her hands through her hair. "You know what I need?"

Marlene rolled her eyes at the smile growing on Ellie's face. "To dance out your feelings?"

Ellie hopped off her stool. "You know me so well."

Marlene watched as Ellie bolted to the dance floor and started grinding on the first girl she made eye contact with.

"I would ask what's up with her, but she's always like that," Abby said from the other side of the bar.

Marlene laughed and grabbed a coaster from the stack Abby put between them. "Yeah. She hit puberty and stuck there. Never matured past sixteen or so."

Abby stood a coaster up on edge and spun it. Marlene already had hers spinning, and she slapped it down expertly a split second before Abby got hers.

"You're getting good at this," Abby said.

"I have a good teacher."

"Speaking of which." Abby reached beneath the bar and pulled out a battered paperback. "Your next lesson. I grabbed it from my studio today."

Marlene's nerves spiked and she compulsively looked around, worried someone else would overhear. The stools on either side were empty, and no one nearby was paying any attention. She forced herself to take a deep breath as she took the book. The cover was a simple black-and-white photograph showing a pensive woman chewing on her fingernails.

"*The Price of Salt?*" As she handled the book, Marlene noted the creases and the droop of pages and cover. This book had been read many times.

"It's a classic. One of the first novels with lesbians who didn't end up dead, alone, or married to men."

"There are books about lesbians?"

"Lots. And the best part? Some of them have happy endings."

Marlene fanned through the pages, the smell of paper briefly filling her nostrils. "I like happy endings."

"I noticed. We're gonna take a break from movies for a while. Too many of them are depressing."

"I appreciate it."

"Well, we might make an exception for the movie version of this one." Abby gave her a wink. "Cate Blanchett's in it."

"I like Cate Blanchett even more than I like happy endings."

Abby's laugh made Marlene's heart stutter. "Same here."

Setting the book down carefully, Marlene looked up to find Abby smiling at her. It wasn't the suggestive, flirty smile she used with everyone else, and she liked the relaxed, friendly smile even more. "Seriously. I may not have mentioned it, but it means a lot that you're teaching me."

"I always keep my promises. Besides, it's actually fun. Delving into queer culture. I haven't thought about it for a while," Abby said.

Marlene's heart was thudding again, but this was nothing like the fearful racing heart she'd felt at work. This was the pleasant reminder that Ellie was right, Marlene still had a crush on Abby. She'd hoped familiarity would temper it, but it hadn't. If anything, the more she got to know Abby, the more she liked her for herself, not just because she was outrageously sexy.

Ellie burst into the comfortable silence like a sweaty, panting wrecking ball. All her earlier hesitation had vanished behind a wide smile and sparkling eyes. "Hey, Abby."

"Hey, Ellie. Having fun out there?"

"For sure. Can I get another beer?"

"Nope. You'll have to ask someone else. I'm officially off the clock." Abby took the book from the bar and dropped it into her purse behind the bar.

Ellie's eyes widened, giving the distinct impression she'd never been turned down by a woman for anything in her life. She glanced over at Austin, pulling beers from two taps at once while taking orders from customers three deep on her side of the bar. Then she looked the other way at the only other bartender who was setting up a ridiculously long row of shot glasses in front of a giggly bunch of twenty-somethings. She looked back at Abby and pouted her bottom lip out. For a moment, Marlene didn't think she'd get her way, but this was Ellie and apparently not even Abby could resist her charms.

With a sigh and an exaggerated roll of her eyes, Abby reached into the cooler and grabbed a bottle. She barely had the top twisted off before Ellie gave her an air kiss and took her beer back onto the dance floor.

As Abby added the drink to Ellie's tab, Marlene played with another coaster. If only she could figure out how to do that. How to brew that mix of sex appeal and confidence that could win over a woman like Abby. That could keep a woman like Dawn.

Just as she was sliding into another bout of self-pity, Abby dragged her out of it with a question. "Why aren't you out there on the dance floor?"

Marlene's voice squeaked when she asked, "Me?"

"Of course you. Don't you dance?"

Not in a long time. Even in her head it sounded too sad to say aloud. She liked to dance, even though she wasn't great at it. She usually danced with Ellie when she was in need and she'd spent most of her relationship with Dawn on that dimly lit floor. But dancing required rhythm, which was too closely related to sex for her to be confident in now, and joy, which was a long way off.

Instead of that explanation, Marlene gave an excuse that felt easier. "I don't have anyone to dance with."

Abby tossed her apron on the bar. "You do now."

"Oh no. I wasn't asking for you to dance with me."

"Doesn't matter. I'm offering." Abby turned toward the corner and the exit from the bar, but stopped and turned back to Marlene, a look of concern washing over her features. "Unless you aren't interested. I'm sorry. I didn't mean to push."

Great. Now there was guilt to add to Marlene's insecurity and sadness. Abby had looked so happy at the prospect of dancing. Now she looked as nervous as Marlene felt. If Marlene chickened out, Abby wouldn't go alone. She would sit at the bar or go home alone, deflated and disappointed. Marlene would do just about anything to stop that from happening. Even dance badly in front of the woman who consumed her thoughts day and night.

"I'm interested," Marlene said. Then again, with more confidence and a forced smile. "I'm very interested."

It was worth it to see Abby's face light up. She hopped excitedly and hurried off to the flip-up section of the bar so she could join the crowd. Marlene slid off her stool, landing on feet slightly numb with trepidation. She didn't even have time to give herself a pep talk before Abby took her by the hand and led her onto the dance floor.

Crossing onto the dance floor was like stepping into another room. The lights dimmed, the temperature rose, and the energy went through the roof. Riveter's kept their dance floor bathed in a subdued purple light to match the crushed purple velvet of the booths. The upside was that Marlene knew the panic in her eyes and the nervous sweat on her forehead were less visible here. She could pretend she was mostly invisible. She could pretend she was someone else. That had gotten her into trouble the night she met Pen. She'd allowed herself to be someone else that night. Someone who danced with women. Someone who pressed close to them when the beat slowed. Someone who let them kiss her and then kissed them back.

Tonight, she let herself be someone else, too. She let herself be a woman who hadn't had her heart broken. She let herself be a lesbian who knew what the hell she was doing. She let herself be someone who Abby wanted to dance with not out of pity, but out of interest. Maybe even out of lust.

She settled into her new skin just as Abby turned to her and started to dance. It was an incredibly sexy dance. Her arms lifted and her hips spun to the beat. Marlene told her body to mimic her dance because she wasn't capable of creating her own movement. Not when Abby was moving like that.

Ellie found them quickly. More quickly than Marlene would have liked. She settled in next to Abby, in the spot Marlene was desperate to fill had she been more confident. For a few songs, Ellie and Abby seemed to compete for who would be more ridiculous in their dancing. Marlene stayed in their orbit and laughed along with them, but they focused more on each other than on her. That suited Marlene just fine, since it took some of the pressure off. Then the song changed and so did Abby and Ellie.

Abby leaned over close to Ellie and whispered something in her ear. Ellie laughed, but then she moved closer to Abby. They danced closer and closer to each other, Abby trailing a hand down Ellie's arm once and constantly making little comments Marlene couldn't hear but guessed were just as flirty as her demeanor. As the song continued, Marlene found it less and less comfortable inside the new skin she'd put on for the dance floor. She spent more time in her head worrying than in her body dancing. Once or twice other dancers bumped into her and she realized she'd been standing still. Was it possible Ellie's mystery girl crush was on Abby? It made sense. Not even her best friend would see Marlene as a true threat for the affections of a woman like Abby. The thought had her looking for an exit.

Marlene felt a touch on her hand and turned, expecting to have to apologize to another dancer she'd blocked. Instead, she found Abby, her eyes glimmering pale lavender, her smile ecstatic.

Abby leaned in close and shouted over the music, "I thought I'd lost you there for a minute. You okay?"

Marlene realized dancers had separated her from her friends. Ellie was barely visible through the crowd now, her attention entirely on a new partner with blond pigtails and a diamond eyebrow ring sparkling in the low light. But Abby hadn't let her get too far away. Abby had come after her. She didn't want to dance with Ellie. She wanted to dance with Marlene. The thought simultaneously terrified and electrified her.

Marlene said, "Yeah, I'm good."

Marlene fell into the rhythm again, Abby dancing closer this time. After another song she realized she was more than good. She was great. She might even characterize herself as happy.

CHAPTER SIXTEEN

Abby wandered around Merrifield Garden Center, flitting from one plant to another like the pollinators she hoped to bring to her balcony in the spring. Austin occasionally passed by in her search for interesting green additions to her tiny apartment. She was far more productive than Abby, filling her side of their shared cart to overflowing. Meanwhile, Abby's side was bare as she still searched for the first item on her list.

Abby was determined to find milkweed, but she kept getting distracted. Sometimes she was distracted by Austin's silly jokes. Sometimes by another shopper wandering through the sunny greenhouse. Sometimes by thoughts of Marlene and the way they'd danced together after her shift the night before.

Mostly it was thoughts of Marlene.

"Spit it out," Austin said.

Abby looked up to see Austin brandishing a snake plant at her like an accusatory finger. The rounded stalks were somewhat intimidating, but not nearly so much as Austin's fixed stare.

"You usually take a long time to shop." Austin nestled the snake plant in beside her variegated pothos in the center of the cart. "But today you're even worse than usual."

Abby couldn't argue with Austin's point. It had been her idea to shop for plants together and Austin had only agreed because she liked hanging out with Abby. That and Austin loved potted plants and the brightness they brought to any living space. Still, this outing was supposed to be about them spending time together without the pressures of work and here Abby was, ignoring her friend and incapable of finding even a single plant on her list.

"I can't find milkweed," Abby said. "Their website said they had it."

"You're kidding, right?"

"What do you mean?"

Austin pointed at the low bench in front of them. It was covered in small plastic pots, overflowing with the classic thin leaves and tall stalks she'd been looking for. Abby knew that, come June, those stalks would be bursting with spiky orange flowers and then the endangered monarch butterflies would come.

"Okay, so maybe I'm a little distracted," Abby said.

She collected the heartiest looking of the bunch, and then another just for good measure. One could never have too many butterfly visitors.

"I don't suppose your distraction has anything to do with your dance partner from last night?"

Abby avoided Austin's eye as she marked milkweed off her list. "Have you seen blue aster? That's next on my list."

"Maybe." Austin crossed her arms and said, "But I won't tell you where until you answer my question."

"I can find it on my own you know."

"Of course you can. I'll just wait here for the next hour while you search for it."

Abby laughed and rolled her eyes. "Okay, it's possible that I've been thinking about last night a little."

Austin's smile grew and she pointed across the greenhouse. As they walked together toward the display, Austin asked, "Is she a good dancer?"

"She's an excellent dancer, as I'm sure you saw."

"Mostly I saw her tripping over herself whenever she looked at you."

Abby had seen it, too. The glazed look Marlene got when she moved close. Her hesitance and her shyness. Abby usually liked confident, bold women, but Marlene's vulnerability was even more alluring. She showed incredible trust in Abby to be vulnerable around her, and Abby wanted someone who trusted her. After all, trust was sexy as hell.

"It was cute, right?" Abby asked.

"If you say so."

Austin picked up one of the blue asters, making a face. They weren't in season yet, so the face wasn't entirely unwarranted, but Abby had no problem putting in the time to nurture a flower until it was ready to bloom. She took the plant from Austin's hands and set it next to the milkweed.

As they swung around a young family on the way to the citrus section, Austin said sarcastically, "So you're falling for the banker. Didn't see that one coming."

"I'm not falling for her. I just like her. I didn't think I would, but she's not nearly as stuffy as I thought. She likes to cook and she takes an interest in my paintings. More than Josie ever did. And she's thoughtful."

An image of Marlene, staring intently at the screen while they watched a movie popped into her mind. The way she turned that gaze on Abby while they talked about their dating history. Her eyes had been so intense. Searching without invading.

"Almost too thoughtful." Abby laughed as she sorted through painted ceramic pots. "I've never met anyone who's treated me so well without also treating me like I'm helpless. And she's completely immune to my flirting. I don't know why I love that, but I do."

"From what I've seen, she's not as immune to your flirting as you think she is," Austin said. She snatched the plain blue pot from Abby's hand and replaced it with a similar one with polka dots. "Just be careful, okay?"

"Aren't I always?"

"Not when it comes to your heart. You fall fast and hard and I don't want to see you hurt again."

Abby said, "Thanks, but I think I'm safe this time."

"That's what you say every time."

"This time it's true."

Austin laughed. "You say that every time, too."

They stared at each other for a long moment. Austin's eyes held all the gentle concern of a friend, and Abby was momentarily overcome. How could she be so lucky to have Austin in her life? She set the pot down and wrapped her arms around Austin's neck, resting her cheek on her friend's shoulder.

"I love you, ya know that?" Abby asked, her voice muffled by Austin's shirt.

"Right back at ya, babe."

Abby gave her a big squeeze, then let go before the tears welling in her eyes had a chance to fall. Austin's eyes looked a little misty, but in true masc lesbian fashion, she tried to shake off the emotion by shoving her hands in her pockets and squinting off into the distance. Abby collected herself first, dabbing a finger at her bottom eyelid to stop a tear from ruining her makeup. Austin cleared her throat and they went back to their plant shopping.

Abby was able to focus better now. Everything felt better when she had a good chat with her bestie. She couldn't quite tell if Austin approved, but it didn't matter. She just needed to say out loud that she liked her roommate more than she'd expected. That would probably be enough to keep her from thinking about her too much.

Even though she was chivalrous and sweet and everything Abby liked in a girlfriend, she was never destined to be the one for Abby. She was still the same old career obsessed, strait-laced woman who would tire of a girlfriend like Abby. It was much better that they remained friendly roommates and nothing more. She could like Marlene and maybe even fall for her, but she would be content with the fluttering feelings of attraction and nothing more.

Still, as they wandered through the sun-warmed greenhouse, Abby's mind was firmly fixed on Marlene on the dance floor. The way she was hesitant and sweet. The way she hadn't quite had the nerve to dance until Abby pushed her. Not pushed. Encouraged? Supported? Whatever she had done, it had given Marlene the strength to relax and be herself. If only she could do that more. Abby liked Marlene relaxed. She liked Marlene when she was herself. When Marlene was like that, Abby was completely entranced by her. She knew she shouldn't be, so she tried to keep her emotions in check, but Abby had never been good at checking her emotions. She was a woman who lived her life out loud. Abby collected plants and let herself imagine a world where Marlene was brave enough to let herself live out loud, too.

❖

Ellie didn't knock before entering Marlene's office. She just pushed through the door and flopped down in the client chair.

"Your roommate is a hell of a dancer," Ellie said. "You looked like you were having fun out there with her."

Marlene had been waiting for this for a week. Ellie was never one to let something like that go without a long round of teasing. She'd spent a lot of time thinking about dancing with Abby. She'd actually just spent a lot of time thinking about Abby. It was time Marlene was honest with herself, even if she knew there was no chance in hell Abby felt the same way.

"I was having fun. Not just dancing. I have a lot of fun with her all the time." Marlene pushed the words out in a rush, but they felt good to say. "Remember how I told you I was having trouble sleeping?"

"Yeah."

"I'm still having trouble sleeping." Ellie's eyes were fixed on her. It wasn't the teasing look she usually wore when they were talking about Abby. It was quiet. Understanding. Marlene said, "She's all I can think about. She's so hot and funny and smart. Maybe you were right. Maybe it was dangerous to have her move in."

"It's about time you figured it out," Ellie said.

"I know." Marlene ran a hand through her hair and stared through the window. "I just thought we could be friends."

"You don't need more friends. You got me."

The mock indignation on Ellie's features made Marlene laugh and that helped relax her. At least for the split second she stopped thinking about Abby.

"The more time I spend with her, the more time I want to spend with her," Marlene said.

Ellie sat forward, resting her elbows on her knees, her reasoned, calm demeanor was so out of place it was almost unsettling. "Have you thought of telling her how you feel?"

"God no." The thought sent an ice-cold spike of dread through Marlene's limbs. "She doesn't feel the same way."

"How do you know?"

Marlene swallowed her pride and returned her stare to the window so she didn't have to see Ellie's pity or skepticism. "I know.

She doesn't flirt with me the way she flirts with you and Austin and—other people."

Marlene couldn't bring herself to name Penelope. Not when she was so sure Abby was interested in her. Not when she knew she couldn't compete with Pen's prowess in the bedroom.

"Abby doesn't flirt with me," Ellie said. She actually looked like she believed it.

"No? What did she say to you on the dance floor the other night?"

"Did she say something to me? I don't remember that."

"You don't remember the way she leaned in close to you, rubbed her hand down your arm, and whispered in your ear? 'Cause the way you smiled, I'm pretty sure whatever she said was memorable."

Ellie shrugged. "Apparently not. I don't think she did any of that though. If she did, it wasn't flirting. It was trying to talk to me over the music."

"Sure. Whatever you say."

"Seriously. She wasn't flirting with me. And she doesn't flirt with everyone else, either."

Marlene said, "She flirts with every butch woman who walks into Riveter's. That's her type."

"You're that type," Ellie said.

"Yeah, well, apparently not enough cause she doesn't flirt with me."

"Or maybe she doesn't do what you think of as flirting because she really likes you."

Marlene hadn't thought of that, but she made sure not to let the thought penetrate. She couldn't get her hopes up only to be humiliated when nothing came of it. "It's nice that you think so, but you're wrong."

"I get that you're trying to protect yourself," Ellie said.

"That's not what I'm doing."

"Yes, it is, and you should stop. Tell her how you feel so you can get some sleep."

Marlene picked up her long-neglected coffee cup. "Telling Abby I have feelings for her won't help me get more sleep."

"Exactly. Because instead of lying awake thinking about her down the hall, she'll be in your bed with you, and neither of you will be sleeping."

Marlene had the cup almost to her lips when Ellie's words smashed into her brain with the force of a high-speed train. Mental images she'd been shunning for weeks sprang into her mind's eye and left her breathless. Her hand shook and coffee sloshed over the lip of her cup soaking through her shirt and splattering her pants.

"Oh crackers." Marlene sprang to her feet, lukewarm coffee dripping onto her office floor.

"Crackers?" Ellie's face twisted in between confusion and laughter.

Marlene traded her empty mug for a fistful of tissues. They didn't do much to dry the coffee, but the damage had been done anyway. "Abby doesn't curse."

Ellie said. "Now you're picking up her habits. You're such a lesbian."

Marlene was going to ask what she meant by that, but realized she knew. Abby had explained the lesbian couple habit of "twinning" during an early lesson. That queer women often started to dress alike after being together a long time. That was the same lesson when she learned about toaster ovens, the butch/femme dynamic, and Subarus. Her hand froze in the middle of dabbing at her shirt. Had the lessons really worked? Did she know how to be a lesbian now?

Shaking off the thought in favor of the problem at hand, Marlene examined her outfit. "Do you think I can save it?"

"Not a chance." Ellie had taken her phone out of her pocket and was tapping around in it.

Ellie was right, of course. She'd chosen a plum-colored top and gray slacks today. The blouse might not show the stain too badly, but the pants were a disaster. In fact, they might be permanently ruined.

"No big loss," Ellie said. "I hate that shirt. Why are you showing off your cleavage like a femme? Go home and put on a suit. You look weird."

"I can't. I have a managers meeting this afternoon," Marlene said distractedly.

"What does that have to do with your outfit?"

Marlene hadn't told Ellie about Brad's comments, either about her appearance or her friendship with Ellie. She might be willing to dress more feminine, but she wasn't going to ruin her friendship with her best friend. Not for a new manager who would probably be gone in a couple years.

"I have to go home and change." Marlene grabbed her keys from her top drawer and hurried to the door, avoiding Ellie's eye. "Can you cover the branch while I'm gone?"

"Obviously," Ellie said, not looking up from her phone.

Marlene made it home just after noon. She had a half hour to change and make it across town to the managers meeting. She was so absorbed with concerns over traffic, she didn't notice that her bedroom lights were on until she was standing at the foot of her bed, staring at both glowing bedside lamps.

"Hey, roomie. What're you doing home so early?"

Marlene's body was numb as she turned to the door of her ensuite bathroom. She moved on instinct, turning to the sound of Abby's voice the way a flower turns its face toward the sun. All the feeling rushed back into her limbs at the sight of Abby, standing in front of the sink, her cherry-auburn hair limp with moisture, the towel wrapped around her, showing off more of her body than Marlene should be seeing.

As her eyes traveled over Abby's creamy calves and small round toes, heat built in patches across Marlene's skin. She became hyperaware of the cotton blouse brushing against her abdomen. Of the slight breeze from the air vent fanning against her overheated cheek.

Abby was standing in her bathroom, wearing a towel. A fine mist of steam still covered the mirror. Had Marlene arrived five minutes earlier, Abby would have still been in the tub. Naked under soapy water. Or perhaps she would have been standing as the water drained away beneath her, rivulets of water tracing down her neck to the valley between her breasts.

Marlene's keys dropped from her fingers, smacking hard against her ankle before flopping quietly to the carpeted floor. She realized her mouth was hanging open and snapped it shut, averting her eyes from her towel-clad roommate.

"Seems like you have a case of the dropsies today," Abby said, a twinkle of laughter in her voice.

"Huh?"

Abby waved a finger in her direction. "Did your coffee cup share the same fate as your keys? I'm guessing those slacks didn't come with that stain."

"Oh. Yeah. I spilled my coffee." Marlene bent to pick up her keys, giving both her eyes a place to land and her hands something to do. "I came home to change."

"Sounds like a good plan. Sorry to be in your space."

"It's fine." Then because she didn't want to make this weird, she said, "I'm glad the tub is getting some use."

Perhaps it was a miscalculation, because rather than going back to her room to get dressed, Abby used the comment to start chatting as if she wasn't almost naked in Marlene's bedroom. "You really ought to take a bath in that thing. It's amazing."

Marlene forced herself to calm down. This was a normal thing. A conversation with her roommate. It didn't matter that she was in a towel. In fact, it was amazing they hadn't seen each other in states of undress like this before.

"I'm not a bath person." Abby's eyebrows shot up, so Marlene explained, "I get in the tub and think about all the things I should be doing and it stresses me out."

Each word made her body cool another degree until Marlene thought there was a chance she'd survive this encounter after all. Then Abby's voice became a teasing purr and she said, "Maybe you need someone in there with you to help you relax."

The air solidified in her throat and Marlene made a sound somewhere between a choked laugh and a whimper. Marlene's mind instantly created a very vivid, very explicit image to connect with Abby's suggestion.

Before Marlene could formulate a coherent reply or even a coherent thought, Abby said, "I'm sorry. I made you uncomfortable. I shouldn't joke like that."

The regret in Abby's voice gave Marlene the strength to meet her eye. Her expression was impossible to read. She wasn't smiling that usual teasing smile, but there wasn't regret or sadness in her eyes either. If Marlene had to guess, she'd call it interest. Or a challenge?

Before she could talk herself out of it, Marlene asked, "What would you do if I called your bluff one of these days?"

To her surprise, Abby blushed as hard if not harder than Marlene usually did. Then she took her lower lip between her teeth and looked Marlene over from messy hair to polished flats. "It wasn't a bluff. If you'd called it, I would be running fresh water in there right now."

Marlene reached out and grabbed the corner of her dresser as her vision swam. Blood roared in her ears and she couldn't take her eyes off that corner of Abby's lip, trapped between her teeth. Her lips were always a glistening, blazing red. The color always made Marlene think of cherries. Would they taste like cherries? What would they feel like against Marlene's lips? Against her neck? Marlene's breath came in a shallow gasp and she gripped the dresser to stop herself from taking that one step forward to close the gap between them. She would find out what those lips tasted like and she would set the fuse on the explosion that would destroy her life. It would probably be worth it.

"I'm sorry." Abby's words drifted slowly into her lust-soaked brain. "I really have made you uncomfortable now."

"I'm not." Marlene stuttered to a stop and tried again. "Would you really?" She caught herself again and straightened her spine, throwing more confidence into her voice. "I'm not uncomfortable."

Abby had never teased her like this. Had never flirted with Marlene the way she flirted with the others. But with everyone else, Abby had laughed it off. Had taken a step back. This time she took a step forward. She fixed her eyes on Marlene's lips. "Yes. I can tell how comfortable you are."

They were so close, Marlene could smell the lingering fruity scent of Abby's shampoo. She could feel the moisture on her skin. The heat and the freshness. All she had to do was lean in. Their lips were so close. Marlene could kiss her now, right here on the threshold between her bedroom and her bathroom. She could finally discover the flavor of those lips she dreamt of every night. Feel the silk of Abby's skin and the ecstasy of her touch.

But then what? Marlene had stood here before. On the brink. And she'd been standing almost in this exact spot when Dawn had told her she wasn't worth it. That she was too much work. That she was unlovable. The words had broken her, but she had survived.

Marlene wouldn't survive hearing those words in Abby's voice. They would come with regret and the kindness, but they would come nonetheless. They would crush Marlene with their weight. They would destroy her completely. She was already so helpless and they'd never even kissed. How could she survive being dumped by a goddess like Abby when she'd known the bliss of intimacy with her? She couldn't. She wouldn't.

Marlene took a step back on wobbly knees, but found they held. "I should get changed."

Abby made a little sound like a sigh and the intensity left her eyes. She was back to the sweet, funny roommate in a heartbeat. "I should, too."

Abby took a long side step to get around Marlene, one hand holding her towel in place. Marlene counted her own breaths as Abby padded across the floor. As Marlene was starting her fifth breath, Abby stopped in the door. Marlene couldn't help herself, she turned to look.

"For the record," Abby said. "Yes. I really, really would."

She put a hard, suggestive emphasis on the second repetition of really. Then she pulled the bedroom door shut behind her and Marlene was alone in her bedroom, the faint scent of shampoo in her nose and the even fainter hint of steam clinging to her skin. She had to sit on the edge of the bed for five minutes before she could gather the strength to walk to her closet.

CHAPTER SEVENTEEN

When Abby arrived home after a long day at her studio and an even longer evening helping Austin rearrange her living room, she expected the house to be dark and silent. Well, not dark. Marlene always left the lights on for her, even when she was working at Riveter's and wouldn't be home until so late it was actually early. None of her exes had never done that.

As Abby climbed the stairs, she flipped off the lights behind her, each switch reminding her how thoughtful Marlene could be. It wasn't just the lights. Abby hadn't had to pour herself a cup of coffee in weeks. She hadn't unloaded the dishwasher in ages either, and Marlene washed her towels any time she did a load of linens. She didn't even ask, she just did it.

Abby was well-aware that she was heading into dangerous territory here. Marlene was thoughtful, sure, but in every other substantive way she was just like Josie. Just like Daniella and Christine, too. She was just as uptight and career driven. Just as methodical and logical. The same personality type of all the exes who had broken Abby's heart. The personality type that loved the idea of adventure, but thrived on the mundane.

Everything about Marlene fit the mold. Even the lesbian lessons. They were Marlene's attempt to fit her sexual awakening into a box she understood. An attempt to logic her way out of the intensity of her feelings. Abby would never fit into one of those boxes Marlene needed to survive. Any relationship between them wouldn't last.

The knowledge dragged at Abby's steps, but, if she was honest with herself, it wasn't enough. She chastised herself even as she smiled. She didn't fit into those neat boxes. She wasn't ordered and logical. Which was why she would still try with Marlene. She was going to fall hard for this sweet, sexy woman and she would get her heart broken again. But it wouldn't stop her. She couldn't help herself. When something felt right, she just went for it. One of the many ways her relationships were doomed from the start.

When she climbed the last stair into the living room, she was surprised to find it occupied. Marlene was snuggled into her corner of the couch, her eyes zipping across the page of a crisp new paperback. She was so absorbed in the book, she didn't notice Abby arrive. She remained hyper focused on the story, her legs tucked up close to her chest and the pages turned toward the warm glow of the lamp on the side table.

Abby watched her for a moment. Her body was just as tense as always, curled as it was into a tight ball. For the first time, however, Abby recognized the tension as intensity. She was lost in the fictional world on the page. Completely transfixed. There was a passion in that to which Abby could relate. A single-mindedness at odds with the logical, mundane existence she'd just been contemplating. Josie had never read like that. Or watched a movie the way Marlene did either. Was it because she was studying, or was it because she loved the fantasy?

Marlene finally looked up, her eyes taking a long time to focus on Abby's face. When they finally did, she scrambled to sit up straighter and dropped her book. Abby's heart did a little fluttering dance at the dusting of pink on Marlene's cheeks. Oh yeah. She was in trouble. But she couldn't bring herself to care.

"Sorry to startle you," Abby said.

Marlene grabbed the book off the floor and shoved it onto the side table. "No problem."

"That doesn't look like my copy of *The Price of Salt*." Abby dropped onto her side of the couch and kicked off her shoes. "Did you give up on it?"

"No. I finished it last week. It was really good."

"I'm glad you liked it. You should've told me you were done. We could've talked about it. Lesson is not complete until I read your book report."

Marlene's eyes went wide for a moment, but then she narrowed them in suspicion. "You're teasing me, aren't you?"

Abby laughed and feigned innocence. "Me? Never."

She was expecting a comeback of some kind. Maybe a dry joke or a sarcastic remark. Instead, Marlene just watched her, a slight curve to her pale lips as she stared across the couch. Abby's smile faltered for a heartbeat under Marlene's inspection. If she didn't know better, she'd think there was a challenge in those eyes. Maybe even a hint of desire. She'd thought Marlene would be a tough nut to crack. That she'd have to be the one to make the first move if anything were to happen between them. Maybe Marlene had a few surprises in her after all.

No sooner had she thought it, than Marlene gave herself a little shake and broke eye contact. "I should be getting to bed, I guess. My eyes are tired."

"Oh don't go yet. It's early." Abby hadn't meant to say it. Prudence would tell her to let Marlene go, but she didn't want to be prudent. She wanted to spend more time with Marlene.

"Do you really want to talk about the book, because I might be too tired for literary analysis."

Abby said, "No, we'll save that for our regular Monday night lessons. How about a movie? We moved on, but there are a lot more good ones you haven't seen."

"Actually..." Marlene's words trailed off as Abby snagged the remote and pulled up her movie library. Abby's jaw dropped. The last time they'd watched a movie together there had been a handful of titles in Marlene's library, most of them purchased by Abby as part of their two-week lesbian movie binge. Now there were dozens, stretching several pages, and all the covers were very familiar to Abby.

"You've been doing research on your own, I see," Abby said. "Did you think you'd get extra credit?"

"You said we couldn't go through everything together."

"Yeah, but this is, like, every lesbian movie ever made."

As Abby searched through the titles, Marlene burrowed further into her corner of the couch, her shy demeanor reasserting itself.

"Remember how you worked doubles both days last weekend?" When Abby nodded, Marlene said, "I didn't really have anything to do, so I did a Google search for lesbian movies. I haven't watched all of them yet."

Abby raised an eyebrow at Marlene. "You watched everything that came up in a Google search for lesbian movie? That does sound like a fun weekend."

When Abby waggled her eyebrows suggestively, Marlene blushed hard. With that reaction, it was pretty clear she had actually put "lesbian movie" into Google.

"It was a dangerous search, I'll admit," Marlene said. "But I found my way out of the porn eventually."

"Not all the way out. I see you have *Below Her Mouth* on here." When Marlene blushed even harder, Abby smiled. "I love making you do that."

"I'm glad you're enjoying this," Marlene said, rubbing at her cheek.

"I am." Abby stopped teasing and surprised even herself with her earnestness. "It's fun living with you."

"Yeah right. I bet it's super fun for you, teaching a baby gay the ropes."

"Hey, stop doing that." Abby set the remote on the coffee table and scooted across the couch. She put her hand on Marlene's knee, hoping it wouldn't be too much. "Don't call yourself that. It's a mean thing that your ex said and it isn't true. You're a better person than she will ever be and you shouldn't let her make you feel like this."

Marlene stared at her hand for a moment. Abby couldn't tell if Marlene liked it being there, but she didn't back away or ask Abby to stop touching her. In fact, she seemed to relax a little. Eventually she managed to transfer her gaze from Abby's hand to her eyes.

"You really think so?" Marlene asked in a quiet voice.

"Of course. She was a jerk. You deserve better."

"I meant you really think it's fun living with me?"

The desperate hopefulness in Marlene's voice made Abby's heart break. It made her want to find Dawn and give her a paper cut between her fingers. Even more than that, it made her want to pull Marlene into a hug. She was absolutely certain Marlene wasn't ready for that, though, so she settled for giving Marlene's knee a light squeeze.

"Of course I mean that, too," Abby said. "You're a really great roommate."

Marlene's lips battled to form a smile, but she eventually managed it. "Thanks."

"How about *Crush*?" Abby asked.

Marlene's smile was far stronger this time. "I love that one."

Marlene woke with a crick in her neck and her right shoulder aching. That wasn't surprising because she woke up with her cheek pressed into the arm of her couch. The weak morning sunlight peeking through the blinds inches from her face made her squint as she blinked herself awake. She was covered in the blanket that was usually draped across the cushions behind her. She didn't remember crawling beneath it, but then she didn't remember falling asleep on the couch.

It took her sluggish brain several long seconds to recap the previous night. She remembered Abby coming home and discovering her stash of lesbian movies. They'd made it through *Crush* and most of *Carol* before her memories got fuzzy. The things that stood out were Abby crying openly when things got mushy on screen and laughing at all the jokes, no matter how silly.

Nothing made Marlene feel so much like a robot studying human life as watching Abby laugh. She was so good at it. So open. She threw her head back and guffawed in a way Marlene could never remember laughing in her life. How did she do that? Let herself go so easily. Marlene knew she looked ridiculous when she laughed. When she was a kid, her dad would give her this look when she laughed too loud. He would shush her in movie theaters. When she was a teenager, Marlene's puberty-inspired embarrassment was all the inspiration she needed to tame her reactions.

Clearly, Abby had not tempered herself like that. Or maybe she had and she worked out of it. She obviously was comfortable with herself. Marlene was hoping these lesbian lessons would give her the same confidence. She always thrived when she felt prepared in school and work life, surely she could do the same with her personal life. Except she still wasn't laughing like that. She wasn't as nervous as she had been before, but that was just because Abby made everything easy. She was comfortable around Abby. Except when she let herself look at Abby's lips. Or think about her touch.

Abby had put a hand on her knee last night. Had let her hand linger on her thigh. Just the thought of that touch was enough to wake up the rest of Marlene's body. How could a simple, friendly touch be so powerful? And it had been friendly, she was sure of it. As much as she wanted to read something into it, Abby hadn't meant to do anything more than show her support.

A sound from the kitchen dragged Marlene out of the bittersweet thoughts of Abby's hand on her thigh. She rolled over, not quite ready to sit up. The kitchen light was on and she could hear the purr of the coffee maker. The opposite side of the couch was empty, but the couch's other blanket lay rumpled across the cushions. Had Abby slept on the couch, too?

Marlene shot up too fast, making her sore neck throb. She didn't feel the pain because her head was too busy spinning with the tantalizing realization that she had slept mere inches from Abby. If Marlene had rolled over in the night, might they have touched? The couch was deep enough that they could have curled up in each other's arms. Shared a blanket. Pressed their bodies close together.

"Morning, sleepyhead." Abby emerged from the kitchen, a steaming mug of coffee in her hand. "Hope you didn't have any early plans. I couldn't bring myself to wake you up. You looked so comfortable."

Marlene took the coffee cup and cradled it between her hands. The warmth spread through her fingertips, and she took a sip to avoid answering. Abby was dressed in her paint splattered overalls, her hair damp and pulled back into a high ponytail. If they had slept together on the couch, Marlene had dozed right through her getting up to shower, dress, and make breakfast. She hadn't slept that deeply in ages.

"Thanks, but I don't have any plans for today. I'll probably just hang around the house," Marlene said.

Abby snatched up the blanket and folded it. "I'm heading to my studio to paint for a while. You're more than welcome to come if you want."

"You'd let me watch you work?"

"Sure. Why not?"

Marlene shrugged. "I thought it might be too personal to share."

Abby tucked the blanket back into place and smoothed out the wrinkles. "You should know by now that I don't think anything is too personal to share. Besides, it can get lonely in the studio all by myself. You'd be keeping me company."

"That sounds nice," Marlene said. "If you're sure."

Marlene had never dressed so fast in her life. She was determined not to hold Abby up, but Abby just chuckled and shook her head when Marlene appeared back in the living room, less tousled but struggling to catch her breath. They drove separately at Marlene's request. She wanted to be sure she could leave after she looked around so Abby could focus on her work. Any convenience on the back end was probably negated by the annoyance of having Marlene tailgate her all the way across town so she didn't get lost.

Abby's studio was one of many housed inside a converted motel way out past Leesburg. Traffic in the DC suburbs was intense no matter the day or time, but they were working against the flow this crisp Saturday morning. Even without traffic, the drive was long and tedious. As she pulled into a parking spot next to Abby, she did the mental calculation of how long the drive from here to Riveter's would be. She cringed at the very thought.

"Why don't you get a studio closer to home?" Marlene asked. Once the words were out of her mouth, she realized it was the first time she'd spoken of her condo as Abby's home. The thought brought an unexpected warmth to her chest and pulled at the corners of her mouth.

Abby unlocked the door, giving it a lift and shove with her shoulder. It still groaned and squealed as it opened. "Gosh, I'd love to one day, but everything closer to the city is way outside my price range."

Marlene stepped inside the room and knew at once this place was Abby's. Everything from the beaded curtain in the hallway leading to the tiny bathroom to the worn but enticing couch against one wall screamed her flashy but comforting personality. The concrete floor and industrial sink were dotted with splashes of paint, but the rest of the room was neat as a pin. From the racks of canvases to the shelves of supplies, everything had its place. Even the small stack of cardboard boxes in the corner looked like they were exactly where Abby wanted them.

"It's not much." Abby's voice was uncharacteristically quiet. "But it's enough for me."

"It's amazing," Marlene said. "I can see why you love coming here."

She turned to look at Abby and was immediately glad she did. Abby's face had been hesitant, almost questioning, but Marlene's words brought the light back into her eyes. Almost as though Marlene's approval meant something to her, though she couldn't imagine why that would matter to Abby. She couldn't help but stare. Abby's eyes always had the ability to draw her in, but there was something else in them this morning. Something joyous and terrifying all at once. If Marlene believed in magic, she'd believe there was some in this room. At least for Abby there was. Marlene stared into those sparkling eyes and, to her utter shock, Abby stared back into hers. Normally, Marlene would look away. Break the connection before she got lost in it. But she couldn't. Not here in this magical place with Abby. She wanted to feel the pull of another person. To get sucked into someone else's orbit.

That was the best part of her discovery she was attracted to women. To find out she too could experience those intense feelings other people talked about. Attraction and desire. She'd never felt that before. She'd never been so drawn to someone she couldn't stand to be without them. She felt that now and it was like being reborn. Of course, there was the flip side of that intense emotion. The pain when it shattered was just as life changing. She'd never hurt so bad as she had when Dawn left. She'd put herself away and decided not to pursue her attraction to Abby because she didn't want to feel that pain again. But what if she was brave just this once? What if she let Abby pull her in? Loving Dawn had felt like running when she'd only ever walked. Instinct told her this would be different. Loving Abby would be more like flying.

The thought of loving Abby broke the spell. It was way too early and way too scary to think about love. In fact, she shouldn't be thinking about her attraction at all. Abby was her roommate and her teacher and it should stay that way. It was so much safer that way.

Marlene pulled her eyes away from Abby and they landed on the painting above the couch. It was a dizzying mix of colors from deep, royal blue to the most delicate lavender. The colors swirled and touched, mixing and separating in a chaotic, hypnotic sweep. Marlene couldn't take her eyes off it, but the movement made her almost queasy. She took a few slow breaths and focused on one corner, where a thick stripe of blue curled in on itself. The paint was so thick that shadows dotted the crevasses. The final curve of blue was like the inside of a bowl and Marlene ached to reach out and trace the scoop with her fingertip.

Abby's voice floated into her thoughts. "Do you like it?"

Marlene's queasiness had left as she focused on one point. Now she took in the whole canvas again and saw the beauty in the madness. There were more deep brushstrokes like the one in the corner. There were also shiny flat patches and paint caked so thick it was like mounds of clay.

"It's incredible." Marlene took a step closer to the couch and the canvas took up most of her field of vision. "How do you get the brushstrokes like that?"

Abby's hand settled on her shoulder, gentle pressure encouraging her to turn and sit. Marlene moved because she would do anything Abby asked her to do with a touch like that. Once she was settled on the couch, she realized she was facing a half-finished canvas propped on an easel in front of her. Abby was already heading to the shelf full of tubes of paint and brushes.

"I'll show you."

CHAPTER EIGHTEEN

The moment Abby finished cashing out, she slumped against the bar. She knew there were folks waiting for drinks, but she also knew someone else could darn well help them. She had been taking more day shifts recently, which usually meant a drop in tips. Today, however, Riveter's had been busier than she'd ever seen it for lunch and the crowd never thinned out. Today felt less like a sleepy day rotation and more like a Friday during Pride Month and she was more than ready to head home to put her feet up.

"Hey there, hot stuff," Austin said from over her shoulder. "You feeling okay?"

"I'm not sure. Why don't you feel me and let me know?"

Austin laughed at the teasing flirtation and threw an arm over Abby's shoulders. "If only you meant it. You look exhausted."

"I feel exhausted." Abby pushed herself off the bar while Austin took off her coat and hung it in the back. "Today was rough."

"Well, hopefully the trend continues. I need some work done on my hunk of junk car and I could tell by the way my mechanic's eyes lit up that it'll be an expensive job."

Abby was only partially listening. Her phone chimed an incoming text message from Marlene, and the sight of her name on the display set off a flurry of tingling in Abby's chest. She wasn't even pretending she didn't have a crush anymore. Last weekend when Marlene had visited her studio, there had been a moment she thought Marlene might kiss her. They'd stood there, staring into each other's eyes, and it was even more intense than when they'd spent the night dancing here at Riveter's. Marlene hadn't made a move, but it was clear they were both feeling more than a roommate vibe. Sooner or later, Abby would get to find out if Marlene was as sweet a lover as she was a roommate.

"Earth to Abby." Austin waved a hand in front of her face. "You still with me?"

"Sorry," Abby said. "Just lost in thought."

Austin pointed to Marlene's name on the screen. "Yeah, and I'm pretty sure I know what thoughts those are. Enjoying time with your roommate?"

Abby chose to ignore the sarcastic emphasis Austin had put on the word roommate. "Yes, actually. It's really fun living with her."

"Fun?" Austin's skepticism laced every word. "Living with a banker is fun?"

"She's not just a banker. She's also an art lover and an avid reader." Abby didn't mention that some of that reading had been assigned. "And she's also a very conscientious roommate and a sweet butch."

"Sounds like you're talking about a girlfriend, not a roommate."

"Turns out I wouldn't be opposed to the idea, even though she is a banker. But she hasn't made a move."

Austin deadpanned, "I'm shocked."

"What does that mean?"

Austin tucked a towel into her waistband. "It means she's so skittish I'm surprised she doesn't sleep under the couch. You know you're going to have to make the first move, right?"

Abby sighed as her phone dinged again. "Yeah, probably."

"Is that a problem? You've made the first move before."

"But I'm worried about moving too fast and screwing things up."

"Because she's skittish."

"Because she's recovering from a broken heart."

Austin rolled her eyes. She'd never been the type to form lasting relationships, so she had very little patience with vulnerability. Of course, she was fifteen years younger than Abby, so she had plenty of time to learn what it was like.

Abby finally checked Marlene's message and her smile must've given her away. Austin asked, "What's your skittish roommate have to say?"

Abby swatted at Austin's arm. "She's checking on me. I'm usually home by now so she's making sure everything's okay at work."

Austin made a sound like a cat throwing up a hairball. "She's worse than Josie. Who checks in on their roommate?"

"A sweet, caring person." Abby checked her watch. "Besides, we were supposed to cook dinner together and I'm sure she's starving."

While Austin made a face, Abby shot off a quick reply that she was headed home now after a long day. Marlene instantly replied that she would start cooking dinner so it should be ready when Abby got home.

"Oh thank God," Abby said.

Austin looked over her shoulder to read the exchange. Then scoffed and walked away.

If that's okay with you, Marlene texted.

Abby texted back, *It sounds perfect and very thoughtful. Thank you.*

Abby watched as the three dots popped up on her screen. After a moment, they disappeared. After another moment, they came back. This dance happened another two times before the screen went blank for a long time. Finally, Marlene texted back a thumbs up emoji. Abby laughed, picturing Marlene at home, composing several responses and deleting them all. Maybe she was skittish, but it was adorable as all heck.

"Hey, smiley." Austin poked her shoulder. "Weren't you headed home?"

Abby gave her a quick hug before grabbing her coat and fighting through the thick crowds to get out of the bar. The drive home was uneventful, but the longer she spent behind the wheel, the more the exhaustion of the day settled into her. By the time she reached her front door, it was a struggle to put one foot in front of the other.

She noticed the music while she dragged herself up the stairs. Last week's lesson had been on lesbian musicians, one of Abby's specialties since Riveter's played exclusively queer women. The smoky, sultry voice was the sort that was very popular in lesbian music, but Abby knew instantly who it was.

When she'd told Marlene about Chris Pureka, Marlene had been skeptical. To be fair, Abby might have oversold the singer, but she'd been completely honest and accurate when she described Pureka's voice as "a lesbian orgasm set to acoustic guitar." Marlene had listened as intensely as she did everything else, and apparently she'd at least been impressed with the song "Burning Bridges" as it was currently blasting from their speakers.

The music was loud enough to cover her arrival as she stepped into the kitchen. Marlene was at the sink, her thin frame moving in time with the beat. The part that stopped Abby in her tracks, however, was the realization that Marlene was singing along. Chris had a lower register, and it was certainly within Marlene's range. In fact, Marlene could give Chris a run for their money. Abby's heart skipped and skittered in her chest, listening to Marlene sing.

She had the same smoke in her voice, but there was a freshness to Marlene's tone that was distinctly different. A lightness that was so unlike the tightly wound woman who made the sound. It made Abby wonder if there was a relaxed soul underneath Marlene's tense exterior just waiting to be found. Waiting to be cherished. Waiting to feel safe. A burst of desire shot through Abby. Not sexual desire, though that was simmering beneath the surface every time Marlene swayed her hips. This desire was to be the person who helped Marlene come out of her shell. The one who earned her trust. The craving to be that person for Marlene was almost too much to bear.

Marlene slapped down on the faucet, cutting off the stream of water. She spun on her heel, belting the chorus, and stopped dead when she saw Abby. Marlene's cheeks blazed so red they were almost purple and she stammered to silence. Abby picked up the chorus where she left off, finishing the last two lines. The song finished and Marlene made a lunge for the wireless speakers, clearly intent on turning the music off. Abby intercepted her, twining her fingers between Marlene's and pulling her back into the middle of the kitchen as the next song started.

"Oh no you don't," Abby said as Marlene tried to return to the sink. "Dance with me."

For a moment, Marlene stood frozen and Abby feared she'd pushed too hard. But the next song that came on was an upbeat dance remix of a classic Tracy Chapman song, and Marlene relented. Abby couldn't get her to sing again, but they danced to three more songs before the oven timer announced dinner was ready.

❖

Brad had been bent over the desk, going through paperwork for more than twenty minutes without looking at or speaking to Marlene. As usual, he was in her chair, leaving her to sit across the desk like a visitor in her own office. It didn't help that she knew it was a power play, it made her feel small every time. He was a full foot taller than her and the chair she was sitting in hung lower than her office chair, so he towered over her. As always when he was here, she felt like a third grader waiting to be scolded by the principal.

"I notice you've been making an effort to dress more appropriately at work," Brad said without looking up.

He spoke with a distinct air of disapproval. As though she were doing what he asked, but it wasn't quite enough. That she wasn't quite enough. She couldn't think of a response, so she remained quiet. Maybe he would elaborate. Praise her or give more details on how she could earn praise. He didn't say anything. He flipped the page and scratched out a few notes with a fountain pen. It was like he'd said the words and immediately forgotten she was in the room.

After another three minutes of silence, the door opened and David walked in. Marlene turned to him, expecting that he'd come to her with a question or concern. She was his boss, after all, and he was the newest account representative at the branch. He had a lot of questions, most of them proving he hadn't listened particularly well during his month of training.

To Marlene's surprise, Brad set down his pen and stood, shaking David's hand. "David. Good to see you. Settling in?"

"Yes, sir."

Brad made a gesture toward the paperwork on the desk. "I can tell. Your numbers are impressive. If I didn't know better, I'd think you'd been selling mortgages all your life."

They laughed together in that chummy, manly way that grated on Marlene's nerves. Not to mention, the paperwork Brad was reviewing was for cash orders over the last few months and had nothing to do with David's sales performance. She assumed her professional smile, the one that telegraphed interest but never quite met her eyes, and waited to field David's question. At least it would be a chance for her to show Brad how well-versed she was in company policy and how she handled staff.

She waited in vain. After showering David with compliments about how he was quickly becoming indispensable, Brad asked about his wife and how she was settling into their new house. As they chatted, Marlene realized Brad knew more about David's personal life than she did. She also realized that Brad had never once asked her about herself. He didn't know anything about her romantic life or whether she owned a home or if she had any hobbies. As Brad and David continued to chat like old friends, Marlene felt more and more isolated.

Just when the frustration became too much to bear, Ellie pushed through the door. Marlene waited to see if Brad would turn his attention and personal questions to Ellie, but he ignored her as though she were a piece of furniture. Even when David looked over and nodded, Brad did not so much as glance in Ellie's direction.

"Hey, boss," Ellie said, giving the men a wide berth. "My customer has a question about cashing savings bonds as executor of an estate."

Ellie's question was somewhat complex and they went back and forth for several minutes, checking documentation and procedures. All the while, Brad and David discussed their golf games. At some point, Marlene thought they made plans to play a round that weekend, but she'd been on hold with the Treasury Department at the time, so she couldn't be sure.

More than once, Marlene tried to draw Ellie's attention to the men. She wanted to share an eye roll or some acknowledgement that they were being ignored. Ellie, as usual, was oblivious. As a manager, Marlene appreciated that her employee was single-minded about helping her client. As a friend, it annoyed her immensely. Sharing a moment with Ellie would have at least validated Marlene's growing frustration. Instead, her question answered, Ellie collected her paperwork and returned to her desk.

Without anything else to do, Marlene returned to the tiny, uncomfortable client chair and waited for Brad and David to finish their conversation. But Brad had unbuttoned his jacket and was standing at ease, hands in his pockets. It was a posture that spoke to complete comfort and showed he wasn't ready to end his conversation.

The longer the men chatted, the more Marlene's frustration turned to fear. Clearly, Brad wasn't as standoffish with everyone as he was with Marlene. In the real world, that wouldn't bother her at all. She didn't like Brad and she didn't want to connect with him on a personal level. But in the professional world, she was all too aware that an engaged superior was the best chance for career advancement. After all, she'd had that with Lucy and she had no doubt that connection had helped grease the wheels with her promotions. It was bad enough that she didn't have a connection with her boss, but then there was the fact that her employee did have a connection with him. If Brad liked David and didn't like her, there was every chance that a promotion or two for him could put her job at real risk. How soon before Brad moved her out of one of the bank's best branches and put David in this office? Or worse yet, what if Brad fired her in favor of him?

The office door opened again, making Marlene jump. This time it was Felice, her head teller, standing in the doorway. Felice gave her a smile and a friendly greeting before turning her attention to David.

"Mrs. Templeton is on the line for you, David. She has a question about that account you opened for her last week," Felice said.

David excused himself, shaking Brad's hand. His eyes settled on Marlene for a half-second, but that was the only acknowledgement he gave that he had spent the last twenty minutes in her office without ever stating his purpose for being there.

"Felice, your customer survey scores are excellent this month. Well done," Brad said after David left.

Felice had been backing out of the room, but she stopped to thank him for the compliment. He asked a couple of questions about how things were going on the teller line and if she needed anything from him. The conversation wasn't personal, but it was still friendlier than any conversation he'd had with Marlene.

The wheels in Marlene's head went back into motion. So Brad didn't have an issue with all women. Movement caught Marlene's eye and she turned to see Ellie shaking hands with her client. Felice looked over, too, but not Brad. It was like he had decided Ellie didn't exist. Just like he'd decided Marlene didn't exist. The dots weren't hard to connect. Brad was fine with women, just not queers.

Marlene shook the thought from her head. Brad was gruff and old-fashioned, but it was a bridge too far to assume he was homophobic. After all, he hadn't had personal conversations with her. He didn't know she was gay. Unless he assumed her dress and hairstyles were enough of a tell. But Marlene had changed her clothes. The wildly uncomfortable woman's suit and silk blouse she wore today were testament to that. And she was growing her hair. It must be something else that was holding her back.

The thought occupied her all day and into her drive home. The days were getting longer as winter came to a close, but the sun was setting as she neared home. It wasn't quite dark enough to trigger the streetlights to come on and most folks didn't have lights on in their homes. Apart from the occasional headlights flashing in her eyes, the twilight was darker than usual. The lighting fit her mood a little too well. All day she had felt defeated. All day she'd tried to engage with Brad and he had ignored her. It was starting to feel inevitable that her career would take a serious hit from this management change. As much as she hated her job, she had worked hard for this success.

As she pulled to a stop at the red light for her turn onto Legato Road, she turned to look at her condo. She'd intended to give herself the usual pep talk about parking in her driveway, but she noticed the lights were on in a couple of windows of her building. Was one of them her condo? Was Abby up there, on the balcony? She'd tried more than once to go out there over the last couple of weeks, but it still wasn't quite warm enough to sit outside and read.

Today was warmer than it had been all year, though. Maybe Marlene could convince Abby to grab a blanket and a cup of tea and they could sit on the balcony and watch the sun set. Or just chat. Abby had mentioned being close to finished with her latest painting. Maybe she had a picture? She'd love to sit and listen to Abby talk about her day, as long as she didn't have to talk about hers. Anything to make her feel like an interesting human. Someone worth spending time with.

She was wondering whether she should start boiling water for tea as she turned onto her street. Abby liked the decaf Earl Grey she'd ordered online. Surely she'd be interested in a pre-dinner cup. She waved to Mr. Phan as she passed, and he actually waved back. He didn't smile, but then she had never seen him smile at anyone other than his dog. Her blouse caught on her watch as she turned the wheel and she decided she would take this awful suit off before she started water for tea. It wasn't until she threw her car into park that she realized she had just parked perfectly in her driveway. She wasn't too close to the air handler or the post for the balcony. She hadn't had to readjust, either.

Marlene had just hopped out of the car when she received a text message from Abby.

I'm determined to sit on the balcony tonight. Want to join?

Chapter Nineteen

A bby hopped out of bed with her regular vigor even though she could tell by the streetlights glowing against the curtains that it was earlier than usual. She'd never been the type of person to linger in bed, trying to go back to sleep when she was already awake. She'd gone to bed early the night before. Well, early for her. She was still stuck in the day shift rotation at the bar, but there were perks. Like hugging a steaming mug of tea between her hands so she could watch the sunset on her new balcony for the first time.

She'd been surprised that Marlene had joined her and even more surprised to learn that Marlene was going to suggest it herself. Marlene hadn't struck her as the type to brave the cold to appreciate a sunset, but then her roommate seemed full of surprises these days. She was an incredible listener. She hadn't said much while they'd shared the sunset, just fixed her eyes on the horizon and asked about Abby's work in progress. Abby could chatter on about her work indefinitely, so she was careful to keep tight hold of her tongue so as not to dominate the conversation. But Marlene had rebuffed all Abby's attempts to ask about her day and had instead asked a few more leading questions. Most surprising of all was how she actually seemed to listen to the answers.

As Abby showered, she thought over the conversation. As wonderful as it had been to talk about her work, it hadn't taken long to discover that Marlene wasn't happy at her own job. She avoided the topic most days, but last night had been more than usual. Abby also couldn't help but notice that the way she dressed for work didn't match the way Marlene dressed at home or at Riveter's. Abby could tell it was a costume and she made a mental note to talk about code switching in their next lesbian lesson. Whether it was a conscious choice or not, she was worried Marlene was doing herself emotional harm by changing how she presented at work. It might be better for her career to dress more feminine, but it wasn't doing anything good for her mental health.

Abby was absorbed with the ways she needed to be gentle in that conversation while she got dressed and didn't notice the smell of coffee until she arrived in the kitchen. She was already headed for the coffee pot when she noticed the steaming mug sitting in front of her empty barstool.

"Good morning." Marlene looked up from her phone with a sheepish smile. "I heard you getting ready so I made you a cup."

"Thank you. That's sweet."

Marlene's smile grew wider at Abby's words, but she quickly went back to her phone. While she scrolled through the news, Abby tested her coffee. It was at the perfect temperature since it had been sitting out waiting for her and she took an experimental sip. She moaned as the creamy bitterness coated her tongue.

It was absolutely perfect. She had backed off on the creamer recently, leaving a subtle difference in the comparative shades of their two cups. Marlene must've been paying attention on the rare occasions when Abby made her own cup and adjusted. Funny how Josie had never managed to do that. Not that she ever made Abby's coffee for her. She could barely be trusted to keep the pot warm when she left for the day.

Abby's mug froze halfway to her lips. Now wasn't that interesting. Instead of comparing Marlene to Austin or any of her other friends or former roommates, here she was comparing Marlene to her ex. Abby chuckled to herself as she finally took her sip. She knew exactly why she was comparing Marlene to her ex.

"What?" Marlene asked.

Abby decided it was safer to play dumb. "Hmm?"

"You did your mischievous laugh."

"I have a mischievous laugh? How is it different from my regular laugh?" Abby asked.

Marlene's eyebrows scrunched together as she pondered the question. "Your funny laugh is—I don't know how to describe it. Unguarded?"

"How so?"

Marlene set her phone down and shifted to face Abby. "You throw your head back and laugh with your mouth wide open."

Abby scowled. "I laugh with my mouth wide open? That doesn't sound attractive at all."

"Oh gosh, no." Marlene looked horrified and she leaned in. "It is. Confidence is sexy."

The words made Abby's skin tingle. She leaned in, too, bringing them dangerously close to each other. Abby was enveloped by the musky, vanilla scent of Marlene's perfume. "Did you just call me sexy?"

She expected Marlene to lean away. She always shied away from banter like this. But Marlene didn't run away. She stayed right where she was, though a dusting of pink colored her cheeks. "I think I called you attractive."

Abby's smile grew so wide it made her cheeks ache. "I'll take that."

The need to lean closer, to see how far she could take this moment, was so strong it made Abby's vision quiver. She forced herself not to move. To test how comfortable Marlene was with this moment. She listened to the breath whistle across Marlene's slightly parted lips. Her eyes were drawn to those lips. The thin line of them. The hint of a bow on her top lip and the hint of a pout of the bottom. They were pale pink like cotton candy and Abby was desperate to taste them. To discover what kind of kisser Marlene would prove to be.

She would be hesitant at first, of course, but that would make the kiss all the sweeter. As Marlene said, confidence was sexy, and Abby knew the first brush of their lips would impart confidence to Marlene. Then she would lean in and Abby would get her first real taste. Then who knew where Marlene would take them. Abby hoped she would be eager. That she would slide her hand into Abby's hair to hold her close.

Abby stole a glance up at Marlene's eyes to distract herself from the pleasant fantasy. Marlene's eyes, too, were fixed on the lips inches from her own. There was a hunger in her stare. A need that Abby ached to satisfy. Maybe it was time for her to make a move. Marlene certainly seemed eager enough. But the thought of moving too fast and losing her chance held her in place. As she agonized over the decision, Abby pulled her bottom lip between her teeth. She was close enough that she could hear Marlene's hitched breath.

For a heartbeat, Abby believed Marlene would pluck up the courage to make a move, but she didn't. A second passed. Then another. Marlene's phone rattled on the counter, an obnoxious electronic beep bursting from it. The sound made Marlene jump and she leaned back, her eyes finally jerking away from Abby's lips.

Abby sighed as Marlene checked her message. She sipped her coffee and made her decision. Marlene wouldn't make the move, so Abby would just have to do it herself.

"It's Ellie." Marlene scrambled to her feet, grabbing her briefcase. "I have to get to work. Have a great day."

Abby let Marlene get to the door before she said, "Hey, I'm working day shift again today. We should get off work at the same time. Want to meet me somewhere for dinner out?"

Marlene smiled but panted like she was short of breath. "Sure. Yeah. I'd like that."

"Excellent. I know just the place. I'll make a reservation and text you the details."

"Do I get to know where?"

Abby said, "Not until you get there. It's a surprise."

"Sounds fun." Marlene's expression was slightly pained, belying the comment. "See you tonight."

Marlene hurried out of the room and Abby sat down, smiling as she lifted her mug to her lips. Marlene clearly had no idea what she intended, but that was fine. This was going to be even more fun than she thought.

Her morning banter with Abby sustained Marlene through a tedious day. She didn't even notice how uncomfortable her outfit was or how long her hair was getting. She didn't get mad when

David messed up yet another credit card application, requiring an embarrassing call to the customer for more information. She didn't even worry that Brad might walk in any second to make her feel small and worthless.

She got all the way to the end of her day before her happy bubble burst. It happened while she was locking up the front door with Ellie at five o'clock.

"Want to get a beer with me?" Ellie asked.

"Not tonight, sorry." Marlene checked the parking lot for lingering cars and then pulled down the shade. "I'm going out to dinner with Abby."

"Nice. Way to go, pal."

Ellie held up her hand for a high five, but Marlene just stared at it. "What do you mean?"

"You finally asked her out. It's about time."

Marlene's brain felt like it was pressed against a bug zapper. "I didn't ask her out."

"It's cool she made the first move. What matters is you're going on a date," Ellie said.

"Date? No. What? It's not a date." Marlene pressed her body against the door, the shade rattling against the glass. "We've just been cooped up too long. Because of winter."

"Breathe, pal. You're hyperventilating."

"No, I'm not." She was, though, so she forced herself to take two long breaths. "We're just letting someone else cook for us."

Ellie spoke gently. "Whoa, relax. Tell me what happened."

"Nothing happened." Marlene's chest was feeling tight. Was this a date? She didn't want to go on a date. Well, that wasn't true. She couldn't stop picturing Abby's lips this morning. They were so round and luscious. Marlene had never kissed a woman who wore lipstick before and she was desperate to know what it felt like. What it tasted like. Then Abby had bitten her bottom lip and Marlene had thought she'd explode right there in the kitchen. "She just asked if I wanted to meet her for dinner. Our schedules lined up."

Ellie laid a hand on her shoulder and the pressure felt good. Comforting. "It's a date, Marlene."

"It is?"

"Yeah, and that's a good thing." Ellie's eyes were shining like she might cry, but Ellie didn't cry. She didn't do any emotions other than sarcastic and horny. "Look, I've never seen you this happy. Like ever. And you know what? You deserve happiness."

Ellie's words echoed in her mind while she drove to the restaurant. She didn't know if she believed them exactly, but she wanted to. She was pretty sure she'd been happy with Dawn. After all, she had to have been happy for it to hurt so bad when it ended, right? That had been the reason she decided to take a break from dating. But if she was happier than Ellie had ever seen her when she wasn't even dating Abby, how good would it get after tonight? How good would it get when they finally kissed? Or when they slept together?

Marlene jerked the car back into her own lane just in time to avoid colliding with the Jersey wall. The car behind her blared its horn and she waved apologetically in the rearview mirror. She definitely needed to avoid this train of thought while driving. Instead, she forced herself to focus on the road and just let whatever happened tonight happen. It would take all of her will power not to either get her hopes up or get so nervous she turned around and went home, but she remembered how good things felt when she spent time with Abby. She would focus on that rather than thinking about Abby's lips and hopefully she would make it to the restaurant alive.

Abby paced outside Mon Ami Gabi and tried not to be nervous. She wasn't having much luck. She wasn't the type to get nervous on a first date, but then she also wasn't the type to trick someone into a first date. She'd been wrestling with the guilt of that from the moment she'd told Austin about her plan.

"So you asked her on a date, but you didn't tell her it was a date?" Austin's scowl had been enough to make Abby take a step back. "That's manipulative, Abby. You know how nervous she is."

"That's why I took the pressure off by not telling her."

"You also took away her chance to say no. What if she isn't ready?"

Abby was sure Marlene was ready, but Austin had helped her see that it wasn't her place to make that decision. She hadn't wanted to explain to Marlene over text message or a phone call, so she forced herself to wait until Marlene arrived to explain. The delay was killing her. Now she had a bad case of first date nerves and an even worse case of liar's guilt. The combination was not fun.

Added to all that, Abby hadn't had a chance to go home and change before their reservation, so she was still wearing her work clothes. She gave her shirt a sniff and wrinkled her nose. Nothing like tricking someone into a first date and then showing up smelling like booze and dishwater. She grabbed her bottle of perfume from her purse and gave herself a healthy spritz. It didn't cover up everything, but it would make for better groveling if she didn't stink.

Marlene walked around the corner from the parking garage and smiled when she spotted Abby. Her genuine, wide smile made Abby's heart flutter. There was nothing like the butterflies of a new crush. She lived for this feeling. For the potential of love.

"Hi," Abby said.

Marlene looked like she was struggling to smile but not too big. She tucked a lock of hair behind her ear and looked away, only to look back a moment later. "Shall we head inside?"

Abby looked through the window at the white tablecloths and the wine glasses. The waiters in crisp white shirts and black ties. Mon Ami Gabi was one of her favorite romantic spots. The food was French, but approachable. The staff was always attentive, but not too attentive. The whole atmosphere screamed date.

Abby sighed and took Marlene's hand, leading her away from the door. Once they were tucked away from prying eyes and ears, Abby looked up. Marlene's eyes were inquisitive with a sliver of confusion. Or was that hope?

"I really like you," Abby said. The words were harder to say than she thought they'd be.

"I like you, too."

Abby decided to take a crumb of hope from that and hurried on. "I want this to be a date. I should have made that clear this morning."

Marlene's whole body stiffened, but when she didn't run away, Abby decided to be hopeful. When she didn't actually respond, Abby felt herself deflate. She shouldn't have gotten her hopes up. She shouldn't have done all this. Marlene would never trust her now.

"Just because I want this to be a date, doesn't mean it has to be." Abby forced the rest of the words out and she forced herself to mean them, despite her disappointment. "If you don't want that, we can just be friends. I just need to know so we're on the same page."

It wasn't as hard as she'd thought it would be to put on a smile. Abby was used to smiling. Even when things didn't go her way. Even when they hurt. What surprised her was the tentative, shy way that Marlene smiled back at her.

"I want this to be a date, too."

Her hope returned so quickly it made Abby lightheaded. "Really?"

Lines of concentration appeared on Marlene's forehead, and she said in a rush, "Yeah, really."

Marlene's obvious hesitation did nothing to temper Abby's excitement, but she forced herself to take a deep breath and not go too wild tonight. She knew Marlene needed gentle treatment, and Abby was prepared to let her set the pace. She could do this. Marlene wanted to do this, and that was enough.

"Great." Abby couldn't stop staring at Marlene's lips, especially when they turned up in a full smile. "Let's get this date started."

CHAPTER TWENTY

Abby was having an amazing day. She had finished her rotation on day shift at Riveter's and would head back to the night shift that she loved next week. She'd spent the morning at her studio, finishing her latest piece. It was one of her favorites, the colors sang and the brushstrokes had all the centrifugal movement she loved. She had spent the rest of her afternoon on the balcony with a trashy romance novel and a cup of herbal tea. It had been a perfect day.

Of course, she couldn't deny that today was so good because last night had been darn near perfect. With all her worries about Marlene not wanting their dinner to be a date, she had expected at least a little tension. There was a bit early on, but it melted away quickly. Before the waiter even came to take their drink order, Marlene was smiling and asking about her day. They didn't have all the usual first date getting-to-know-you chitchat to lead the conversation, but it didn't matter. Their undeniable chemistry made it all feel so natural. Marlene had even walked her to her car after, though she didn't lean in for a good-bye kiss. That would come. And Abby knew the wait would be worth it.

With her spirits so high, Abby decided to get fully dolled up. After all, she hadn't had the opportunity to go full pinup girl in a long time and she missed it. The dress choice was easy. She plucked her favorite dress from the hanger and felt sexier just looking at it. The puff sleeves and sweetheart neckline showed off acres of creamy skin from her neck down to a peek of cleavage. The gathered circle skirt flared from her ample hips and the bright floral print dazzled. She topped it off with a tiny red belt high on her waist and a pair of red polka dot platform heels.

Abby whistled while she painted her face. She had done cat eye makeup nearly every day since her early teens, but today she outdid even herself. Some pearl powder and a cherry lip later, she felt like she could take on the world. She gave herself a little wink in the bathroom mirror and went back to her bedroom to finish the look.

Selecting a wig made her giddy. She loved her new hair color, it looked like cherry cola in the sun and fit her better than the old pink, but she happily gathered it up to tuck away tonight. She chose a relatively simple wig, platinum blond with victory rolls in the classic Betty Grable style. The weight of a wig always made her chin shoot into the air. It was a little boost of confidence she hadn't realized she was missing.

Abby was just skipping down to the living room when she heard the front door open. She hadn't realized it was so late, but the only thing that made her feel better than wearing her favorite dress and wig was knowing Marlene was home. She considered striking a sexy pose but didn't want Marlene to think she was aiming at seduction. It was important for her to signal in every way that she was comfortable taking things slow. Instead, she went into the kitchen to get Marlene a beer.

Abby was twisting the top off the beer when Marlene stepped into the kitchen. It was all worth it to see Marlene's eyes go wide and her jaw drop open. Abby felt sexy and confident just being in these clothes, but it certainly didn't hurt when she got reactions like that.

"Welcome home," Abby said in her best sultry voice.

When she saw Marlene's throat bob from a hard swallow, Abby held out the bottle. Marlene missed the first time she reached for it. That probably had a lot to do with the fact that her eyes were glued to Abby. Specifically, Abby's thighs beneath the wide skirt.

"Thanks," Marlene stammered. "Where are you headed off to?"

"I'm not going anywhere."

"Really? I just thought you were headed out because you're dressed so nice."

The comment was innocuous enough, but given Abby's experience with Josie, it felt more like a rebuke. She turned away, but not fast enough to hide the frown the creased her cheeks. One deep breath brought her back to herself and she was smiling again when she said, "Nope. These are just the clothes I like to wear. They make me feel pretty and that makes me feel good."

"You are pretty." Marlene stammered the words and continued in a rush, "Not just pretty. Gorgeous. You look amazing."

Well, she couldn't deny how good that made her feel. And Marlene's awkwardness was so adorable, Abby couldn't help but forgive her. After all, she didn't know she'd pushed a button. She stepped around the counter and Marlene moved toward her. She reached out a hand like she might touch Abby, but then seemed to change her mind. She set the hand on the counter and leaned against it, trying desperately to look like that's what she intended all along.

Abby was such a sucker for this. The awkwardness early in a relationship. The hesitation and the pining. The women she dated never seemed to be as confident as she was, and Abby thrived in these moments when she could guide a partner out of their uncertainty. The road would be longer with Marlene, she was sure, but gosh would it be a fun trip.

Abby stroked gentle fingers along Marlene's hand. She stopped at the feel of cold metal beneath her fingers and wiggled Marlene's thumb ring.

"Thank you," Abby said. "That's very sweet of you to say."

Her touch and her words had all the desired effects. Marlene's cheeks dusted with color and her eyes went straight to Abby's lips. They were standing close enough that Abby could see the rapid rise and fall of Marlene's chest and feel the warmth of her body.

"I should, um, get into the clothes I like to wear, too," Marlene said. "I'll just go upstairs and change."

Without another word, Marlene turned and hurried out of the kitchen. Abby shrugged to the empty room and went to the fridge to start making dinner, not exactly deflated, but not feeling quite as happy as she'd been ten minutes before.

❖

Marlene knew she'd messed up with her comment about Abby's clothes before dinner, but she didn't know what she'd said wrong. Abby wasn't exactly angry, but there was a heaviness to their conversation while they cooked and ate. Marlene was desperate to fix it, and she got her chance while they were washing dishes.

"You got home early today," Abby said. "How'd you manage that?"

"It was a slow day, and it was Ellie's turn to close. She always forces me to leave early if she can."

"She's a good friend." Abby looked over her shoulder, squinting through the balcony doors. "Want to sit on the balcony? The sun's setting and it's so pretty."

That's when Marlene had the best idea ever. "Or we could go for a walk. There's a park on the other side of the neighborhood with a pond. We could watch the sunset over the water."

Abby's enthusiastic reaction was all the confirmation Marlene needed that she'd made the right call. That sparkle in her eyes that had dimmed when Marlene made her comment was back with force.

While they walked, Marlene asked about Abby's day. She talked about finishing her latest piece with such unbridled joy it made Marlene's heart ache. When had she ever talked about something with that much excitement? When had she ever felt that much excitement? Not for a long time, if ever.

"The best news, though," Abby said. "Is that I've sold a bunch of paintings online. Did I tell you I started an Etsy store?"

"No, you didn't, but that's a great idea."

"I wasn't sure it would do well. All my paintings are unique, and prints do better online."

"Plus they're tactile." When Abby gave her a confused look, panic flared in Marlene's chest. Not again. She said the wrong thing again. "Not that you touch them. It's just…I don't know what I mean."

"No, please, tell me. It's okay."

Marlene took a deep breath and pulled up the image of Abby's work in her mind. "You use a lot of paint."

Abby chuckled. "You're telling me. You should see my bills from Art Supply Warehouse."

"It's a good thing." Marlene fought the impulse to run away. She could explain this. She could make Abby see the compliment in her words. "There's a depth to your work. They feel three-dimensional. The real magic is getting in close and seeing the brush strokes."

It took a moment for Marlene to realize Abby had stopped walking. She turned, expecting to see confusion or anger in Abby's expression. Instead, Abby was smiling. Smiling and her eyes were shining in the fading light.

"You get it."

Marlene's instinct to run was somehow stronger now that Abby was looking at her like this. "Doesn't everyone?"

Abby laughed her happy laugh. The one that was unrestrained and wide open. Marlene knew from the tone of it Abby wasn't laughing at her, but laughing at everyone else. The realization made her heart thud hard in her chest.

"You'd be surprised how few people understand me," Abby said.

Marlene shrugged and fell back into step beside Abby, but her chest was fit to burst with pride. This amazing, confident, beautiful, sexy, talented woman appreciated Marlene seeing her. Marlene making her feel good. It felt like a moment out of someone else's life.

After a few moments of silence, the practical part of Marlene's brain kicked back into gear. "If you've sold that many paintings, you must have a lot of shipping to do. I can't imagine they'll fit into your Mini. You can borrow my SUV. Or I can drive you."

Abby's hand slipped into hers and gave her a squeeze. The swell of emotion in her chest tripled at the touch.

"That's a sweet offer," Abby said. "And I'll definitely take you up on it."

Marlene expected Abby to drop her hand, but she didn't. She held it the whole time they walked and it only took a few minutes for Marlene to remember to twine her fingers in with Abby's. She occasionally glanced over at Abby as they walked, but her face was fixed on the glowing horizon. The sun was behind the trees until they crested the hill at the center of the little park. Then it burst onto them, showering Abby's upturned face in golden light. She looked like a bronze statue, high on a pedestal and far out of Marlene's reach. Then she turned her face to smile at Marlene and she looked human again. Attainable for the first time since Marlene had met her.

"How about you?" Abby asked. "How's work?"

All the pride and happiness that had filled her since they started this walk dropped out of Marlene and left her dizzy and weak. She tried to cover the moment by pointing out a bench and leading Abby over to it, but the distraction didn't work. Once they were settled, Abby leveled those kind, inquisitive eyes on her. She held Marlene's hand in both her own and said, "I'm here to listen. You can tell me."

Marlene did the last thing she expected. She told Abby about work. About Lucy's retirement and Brad's arrival. The way he didn't seem to like her. The way he was harder on her than Lucy had been. She left out her fears that he didn't like her because she was a lesbian, but she had a feeling Abby had picked up on that.

"My sales numbers are fine, but they're starting to dip," Marlene said. "I'm worried about my job for the first time since I started at the bank."

"Is this dip in your number a normal market thing?"

If she'd been talking to anyone else, she would've said yes. She'd probably even lie to Ellie about it because it was easier than admitting the truth. But Abby would see through her. She wanted Abby to see through her.

Marlene took a deep breath and said, "No. It's me. My conversations with clients aren't as deep as they used to be. I'm missing the easy stuff."

Abby ran her thumb along Marlene's palm and the pressure was so soothing Marlene closed her eyes to focus on the sensation.

Abby said gently, "Do you think maybe it's because you don't feel right? You don't feel like yourself at work, so you're not making those connections anymore?"

Marlene shrugged but couldn't open her eyes. She wanted to feel Abby's comfort, but she couldn't stand to see her pity. "That might have something to do with it."

"Then I would encourage you to be yourself. You're an amazing person, Marlene. When you let people see that, they connect with you. That's what's gotten you this far and you'll continue to be successful if you keep doing that."

Marlene worked hard to keep the words far away from her heart. They were too much. The idea that someone as incredible as Abby thought she was an amazing person was enough to make her head spin. So instead of thinking about it too much, she opened her eyes and turned to the sun setting over the pond in front of them. She focused on the salmon and pink of the sky, cut through with the last golden rays of the sun. The colors distracted her. They were easy. Naming the shades rather than thinking about her feelings and her fears.

Abby seemed to sense her need to shut down. She continued to hold Marlene's hand, but she turned her attention back to the sky. Pulling Marlene's hand into her lap, she leaned back against the bench as the light faded.

Soon, the pressure in Marlene's chest eased and she thought about what Abby said. She was right, of course. Marlene wasn't comfortable and her clients could sense it. The feeling in her office had shifted since Brad took over the area. Since Marlene changed to suit him. Her professional success came from her confidence that she had her clients' best interests at heart. With Brad breathing down her neck about everything, her thoughts were scattered and she lost her confidence. That wasn't right for her, and it wasn't right for her clients.

By the time the sun dipped beneath the horizon, Marlene felt calmer than she had in ages. She knew what she had to do. She had to be herself. A month ago, she didn't know who that was. It wasn't just Brad. Dawn had taken that from her, too. But when she was with Abby, everything was different. If she could catch the eye of a bombshell like Abby, she could do anything. And more than just catch her eye. Abby thought she was an amazing person.

A streetlight hummed into life a few yards away. The light glowed blue-white and cool like moonlight mixing with the dying sunlight. Abby's face glowed in the strange new light. Her eyes shone ghostly gray. She had never looked so beautiful as she did in this moment. Like a fairytale princess come to life on a park bench in the suburbs. And she was looking at Marlene. Smiling at Marlene. Holding Marlene's hand and sharing this delicate moment with her.

Before she could lose her nerve, Marlene reached out. She ran her fingertips along Abby's jaw. It was smooth and soft, the curve full of the same magnetic energy of the brushstrokes on canvas. Abby held still, waiting. Wanting. Marlene could feel how much she wanted this moment, and it gave her courage.

She curled her fingers around Abby's cheek, cupping her face like the delicate, precious thing it was. She leaned in slowly. She breathed deep, taking in the mingled scents that were Abby. Powder and sweet, floral perfume. Then her eyes fluttered shut.

Abby's lips were exactly as luscious as they looked. Kissing them was like falling into clouds. Like running through heavy snow. Like the first bite of cheesecake. Her kiss was overwhelming and gentle, just like the woman herself. Marlene held her close, trapped in the wonder of this perfect kiss.

When Abby's lips parted, Marlene couldn't help herself. She deepened the kiss with a groan of pure delight. She finally discovered what lipstick tasted like. Slightly waxy with a hint of something like dark chocolate. In an instant, the taste of lipstick on a beautiful woman's lips became one of her favorite flavors. The taste of Abby's lips was nothing compared to the fine wine of her tongue. The longer the kiss lasted, the more Marlene knew she would never kiss anyone like this again.

Nothing else could ever feel this right.

CHAPTER TWENTY-ONE

Marlene's eyes sprang open at four o'clock and she sighed with a sense of inevitability. She had learned not to try going back to sleep. She wouldn't be able to. The bouts of insomnia that had cropped up occasionally in her life had become more frequent after Dawn left. Abby moving in marked a change from frequent to daily. If she'd thought the shift from roommate to girlfriend would help her lust-soaked mind settle, she was mistaken.

Throwing aside the covers, Marlene contemplated her day. It would have been a long, difficult one even if she'd gotten a full night's sleep. The end of the month coinciding with the end of the quarter meant constant pressure to close out loans and drum up one last credit card sale. She didn't want to start her day by rolling around under the covers, searching for another few minutes of sleep. Better to get up and get started.

The light over the oven threw a warm, orange glow over the countertops. Marlene left it at that while she boiled water and prepared a pot of herbal tea. It was a blend Abby had found at a tea shop and was supposed to help calm nerves. Marlene wasn't sure how effective it was, but it tasted good and they both liked it. She decided to make a whole pot instead of a single cup. Abby was closing at Riveter's tonight, so she'd be home in another half hour or so.

Marlene took her steaming mug onto the balcony off the kitchen. Before Abby moved in, she hadn't spent much time out here. She hadn't done much before Abby moved in, actually. She worked and she watched TV and she went to Riveter's. Now she read more and listened to music. She enjoyed sunsets and spent time outside. It was remarkable how much better everything felt. Like she'd shut herself away and was only now spreading her wings.

Since her eyes had already adjusted to the dark, Marlene left the balcony light off, too. The sun wasn't close to rising yet, but Legato was a busy road dotted with streetlights. Setting her mug down on the railing, Marlene looked out into her half-lit neighborhood.

She could see into some of the other condos. Most were dark at this hour, but a few windows glowed with lights. Had those folks left a light burning for roommates or loved ones who got home late, or did they just prefer a nightlight? Marlene didn't know much about her neighbors, so she wasn't sure whose houses were dark and whose were lit. For the first time since moving in, she wondered about their lives.

There was the young couple with the toddler and the Mercedes who seemed to be perpetually laughing. What was going on in their lives that made them so happy? Or Mr. Phan. Was it Mrs. Fluffy barking all day long on Saturday and Sunday, or some other dog Marlene had never met? Mr. Phan was quiet, but Mrs. Fluffy struck Marlene as the kind of dog who always demanded attention. And did that mystery dog bark all day during the week? Would Marlene be able to hear it if she were home?

Abby would know. Not only was she here during the day, she was the sort of neighbor who would strike up a conversation with them. She would know why the young couple was so happy. She would know what these peoples' lives were really like. What happened on their balconies when Marlene wasn't home to watch. Not only because she was here, but because she cared. She cared about people. Showed an interest in their lives. She let people in.

"Couldn't sleep again, huh?"

Abby's voice from the balcony door soothed the worries from Marlene's mind. It didn't matter why the dog barked or why the young couple had never introduced themselves to her. Abby was here.

"I slept," Marlene said. "For a few hours."

Abby joined her at the railing and ran a thumb across Marlene's cheek. "Not enough. You'll be exhausted at work today."

Marlene leaned into Abby's touch. Her skin was warm and soft and smelled like soap. "It's Friday and I don't work tomorrow. I can survive one day without sleep."

Marlene didn't want to think about her day. She wanted to think about Abby touching her and the sunrise an hour or two off. Leaning in, she interrupted Abby's next words with a kiss. Abby didn't seem too upset at the interruption. She cupped Marlene's face in her palm and brought that enticing flavor of lipstick.

"Did you make enough tea for two?" Abby asked after breaking the kiss.

"Of course. Here, take mine, I haven't had any yet."

Before Abby could object, Marlene pressed the mug into her hands and hurried back inside. She wasn't even over the threshold when she started chiding herself. She had to stop doing this. Every time they kissed, Marlene found an excuse to run away. There was always something to fetch or a question to ask or something that would break the intimacy. She wasn't doing it consciously, but she always found herself disengaging.

Her nerves were completely unfounded, she told herself as she snagged another mug from the cabinet. Hadn't Abby made it clear she wanted Marlene? Hadn't she proven in everything she'd said and done that this was what she wanted? Sure, she'd never initiated a kiss, but it was clear she wanted to. She was obviously holding back to make Marlene more comfortable and all that did was make Marlene feel like more of a heel. A woman who needed to be treated with kid gloves. Well, she would prove she wasn't fragile. She would march back out there with her tea and she would show Abby just how comfortable she was kissing and maybe even touching.

When she went back out onto the balcony, Marlene found Abby leaning on the railing, looking out over the neighborhood just like Marlene had done. Abby raised the mug to her lips and blew steam from the surface, sending it roiling into the semi-darkness. She was so beautiful, so effortlessly stunning, that Marlene stood and watched her for a moment.

"Are you going to come join me or just stare at my butt?" Abby smiled over her shoulder.

Marlene's stomach twisted with worry. "Oh no, I wasn't looking at your butt."

"No? Too bad. I have a nice butt. Don't you think?"

"Yes, you do. Of course, you do. I just don't want you to think I was objectifying you." When Marlene tripped over her explanation, Abby laughed. "You really like teasing me, don't you?"

"Yeah, I really do." Abby turned a smile on her that made Marlene's knees go wobbly. "But I also really want you to stare at my butt sometimes."

Marlene's mouth went dangerously dry and she knew she wasn't up to the task of drinking her tea right now. Her throat would close up around the hot beverage and she'd choke. She set her mug down on the little table between the wicker chairs and squeezed her palms together.

"What if I told you I already do that?" Marlene leaned against the railing, trying to channel a suave, devil-may-care attitude. "I stare at your butt and your lips and your…um."

She couldn't pick a word that would sound both sexy and respectful, but since her eyes were glued to Abby's cleavage, the message was pretty clear. Abby's laughter made that much clear.

Abby set her tea down next to Marlene's and squared her shoulders, presenting an even better view. "If you told me that I would be very pleased."

Her smile certainly looked pleased. Maybe even a little hungry. It wasn't only her smile. Her eyes sparkled in the low light, her pupils so wide the thin ring of pale gray was barely distinguishable. Marlene could almost feel the way those eyes raked over her body. The very tip of Abby's tongue peeked out to caress her upper lip. There was something in her posture—in the set of her shoulders and the straining of her fingertips against the railing—that spoke clearly of her desire to devour.

Marlene recognized the hunger because she felt it herself. She was drawn to Abby. To her body and her energy. Being around her was like an itch that only intensified when she scratched. Each sight of Abby led to a need to kiss her. Kissing her was becoming a need to touch. She knew what would happen if she touched Abby, and, though the thought of sex with Abby frightened her, it also overwhelmed her with need.

Marlene hadn't realized she'd been leaning toward those enticing lips until they touched her own. She melted into them. Devoured them. Exploded into them. She knew she was kissing too rough when her teeth scraped against Abby's, but she couldn't pull back. In fact, she pushed farther forward, with lips and tongue and body.

And oh, that body. The way it fit against her own like they were a matched pair. The way Abby's curves melted her sharp angles. Marlene rested her hand on Abby's hip, holding her close as they kissed. Abby's hands went around her neck, the weight of her arms there surprisingly sensual.

All the worries and fears that kept Marlene awake too late and woke her up too early evaporated in the heat of Abby's kiss. In the feel of her skin under Marlene's fingers. A moment of panic enveloped her as she realized she'd slipped her hand under Abby's shirt. She nearly pulled away, but then Abby pressed into Marlene's palm. She knew encouragement when she felt it and Marlene wanted to be encouraged. If she could touch Abby like this—sensually if not intimately—it would sate her hunger for a while. Or so she thought.

The longer their lips and tongues caressed, the higher her hand crept up Abby's side. Marlene waited for Abby to pull back. To make a joke. That's far enough, tiger. Don't get ahead of yourself. Something to cool down the moment. But Abby didn't pull back. She didn't make a joke. She let Marlene touch her and the more Marlene touched Abby, the more she wanted to touch Abby.

Her hand slid up the gentle swells of Abby's side, soaking in the feel of her skin like sun-warmed silk. She slipped her other hand onto Abby's hip and then around to the small of her back. Abby gasped as their bodies pulled even closer, until they were pressed together from knees to necks.

Marlene didn't lose her nerve until her fingertips brushed against stiff lace. Abby's bra. Containing the enticing flesh of Abby's breasts. Abby didn't pull away, so she let her fingers linger against the lace. If she let them linger there long enough, she might pluck up the courage to move her hand farther up. To cup Abby's breast or wrap her fingers around her hard nipple. She might even be bold enough to slip her thigh between Abby's leg. To press against her heat and see if Abby would rock against her. If they would fall into a rhythm that might take them off this dark balcony and into one of their bedrooms. The thought caught her body on fire and she broke the kiss, finally out of oxygen.

"Wow." Abby's throaty voice was pitched low and breathless. "I should ask you to look at my butt more often."

"That was okay?" Marlene's heart thudded so hard against her ribs she worried Abby wouldn't be able to hear her words. "Not too fast?"

Abby gently scraped a long fingernail across Marlene's jaw. It sent shockwaves through her nerves. "Trust me. You cannot possibly go too fast for me," Abby said.

Marlene's breathless laugh sounded more like a cough, even to her. "I'll keep that in mind."

"You will after this morning." Abby picked up her mug and headed into the house. "Good night."

WHEN IT FEELS RIGHT

CHAPTER TWENTY-TWO

Next week we should try the deli that just opened on the corner of Fifth." Ellie held open the door and Marlene gratefully stepped into the branch. "I hear they make their own chips."

The wind had been brisk outside, and Marlene ran her fingers through her hair to settle it back in place. "Why would I want homemade chips when I can have the fries at Havabite?"

"Have you ever tried homemade chips?"

"No. I like fries."

Ellie gestured for Marlene to proceed her up the stairs. "You could try something new, you know? It's worked out for you recently."

Marlene tripped on the stair and shot Ellie a sharp look. "Not here."

Ellie said, "Come on, boss. Everyone here knows you prefer the fairer sex. I'm not spilling any secrets."

"It's not a secret," Marlene said as she pushed open her office door. "I just don't like to talk about my personal life at work."

"That's a very good policy. Though you don't seem to be following it," Brad said from inside Marlene's office.

Marlene's heart sank. Ellie's eyes went wide, then she turned and strolled back to her desk. Marlene would have given all the money in her 401(k) and the deed to her condo to be able to follow. She tried to compose herself as she turned to face her boss, sitting in her chair, his hands steepled in front of him.

Marlene hurried in, leaving the door propped open behind her. "Brad. Sorry to keep you waiting." When he didn't respond or move, she said, "I would've cut my lunch short if I'd known you were here."

Brad glanced at his watch, then pressed his fingertips back together. "I'm surprised you had time to take a full lunch. I can't remember the last time I had the luxury of a full half hour away from my work."

Even through the chill of embarrassment, Marlene forced herself to think about what Abby told her the other night. She should be confident. Be herself. She was good at this job and that was because of her commitment to her clients. "The restaurant is an old client of the branch. A couple of us go once a week to check in on them. See if they need anything. It makes them feel special that we're as loyal to them as they are to us."

Brad gave her one of his usual smiles. Every time he did this, he looked like he was smelling something unpleasant. He said, "I'm sure you've made the point. No need to waste more time with them."

"I don't think showing a customer we appreciate them is a waste of time."

The moment the words were out of her mouth, Marlene regretted them. Brad slowly dropped his hands to the arms of her chair, pushing himself to his feet while never taking his eyes off her. He looked remarkably like her father in that moment. Like Brad, she'd never seen her father in anything but an expertly tailored suit and a look of disappointment.

"Not to worry." Brad put his hands on his hips and pushed his shoulders forward. He towered over her and Marlene was acutely aware of their height difference. "You'll get used to how things work around here soon enough."

Something in Marlene snapped and she said, "I've been a branch manager for several years now."

His pretense at kindness vanished along with his forced smile. "Not for me, you haven't. My managers don't confuse work time with personal time."

It took every ounce of Marlene's strength to continue standing tall as he rounded the desk and marched out of her office. She counted to ten after he left, giving him time to get down the stairs, before she released the breath she'd been holding. Regret flooded into her. What had she done? Why had she antagonized him like that? There was a difference between confidence and insubordination and Marlene was pretty sure she'd crossed that line. And for what? Her weekly falafel lunch with Ellie?

"What a fucking asshole." Ellie burst into the office.

"Watch your language." Marlene hadn't meant to snap at her friend, but she was way too on edge to deal with Ellie's emotions right now.

"He deserves it. You've been here ten times as long as he has."

"And he's my boss."

"So what? You're allowed to run your branch the way you see fit."

Ellie's voice was giving Marlene a headache. Or maybe that was the rising panic. She should have been working, not wasting precious work time hanging out with Ellie. Whatever excuse they gave, those lunches were about hanging out, not buttering up a client. Why had that seemed like a good idea before? Brad was right, Fairfax Title and Loan owned her time from eight to five, Monday through Friday. Until six on the days she closed. Hanging out with her best friend was not part of the equation. Why had she ever thought it was?

"He's right."

Ellie gaped at her. "What? How can you say that?"

"I'm being lazy. I should be working during lunch. I've certainly got enough desk work to do."

"There's a reason we clock out for lunch," Ellie said.

"I'm on salary."

"Even more reason to protect your breaks."

Marlene dropped into her chair. "I don't get breaks, Ellie. That's the point."

Ellie actually stepped back at that. "No. Don't let him do this to you."

"We both need to get back to work."

"Marlene."

Marlene held up her hand to silence Ellie. If she had to hear one more word, she would scream or cry or both and she couldn't do either at work. She had invested too much time in this career to lose it over something so ridiculous as a lunch break. It was all she had.

"We have to get back to work," Marlene said.

Ellie was pissed, that was obvious, but Marlene didn't have time for her emotions. Once Ellie had stormed back to her desk, Marlene took a few deep breaths to calm herself. She nearly choked on the incredibly strong, astringent smell of Brad's cologne. It was all over her chair, completely filling the air around her.

Marlene's phone buzzed with an incoming message and she glanced at the screen. It was a text from Abby and she read it in hopes it would make her feel better.

Hey you! Want to take a long lunch tomorrow? I was thinking a romantic picnic in the park.

Marlene laughed bitterly. Of all the times to receive a text like that, now was the worst possible one. She could imagine how well that would go over with Brad. Or Ellie. She wasn't in the right headspace to politely decline at the moment, so she tossed her phone into her desk drawer and turned back to the piles of work on her desk.

By the time Marlene got home after work, she had almost managed to put the worst of her day behind her. Ellie had left without a good-bye, which annoyed her, but she'd come around. She always did. Still, Marlene's shoulders were tight and her head ached as she climbed the stairs to her condo.

All of that melted away when she stepped onto the landing to see the dining room table set, a steaming plate of fish and sauteed vegetables waiting. It wasn't the barramundi that eased away the stress of the day, though. It was Abby, standing next to the table in a tight mod dress and platform go-go boots, smiling like she'd just won the lottery.

No one had ever looked at Marlene the way Abby did. The abrupt shift in mood made her eyes well with tears, but she held them in. It was way too early in their relationship for Marlene to turn into a blubbering mess.

"Hey, cutie," Abby said.

Abby walked over and kissed her on the cheek. Marlene leaned into the contact but appreciated that Abby hadn't tried to kiss her on the lips. Their previous kisses had been amazing, but Marlene wasn't sure she could repeat the performance in her current, turbulent mood.

"You made dinner already?"

Abby took the briefcase out of her hand and carried it over to her office. "Yeah. I have D&D tonight, so I have to leave soon. I'm so glad we get dinner together before I go, though."

"I'm really happy about that, too. It was a rough day at work."

Abby returned from her office and took Marlene's hand. "I figured it was a bad day when you didn't answer my text."

Marlene cringed. She'd forgotten about the text until she was leaving work, but then it took her the entire drive home to figure out a way to decline without hurting Abby's feelings.

"Sorry about that. It sounds like a great idea, but maybe for the weekend?" She took a breath and tried to make the words not sound rehearsed. "I doubt I can get that much time away during the work week and I wouldn't want to rush."

Abby ran a thumb along Marlene's jaw line, making her skin tingle. "I'm up for it whenever you are."

"Great. Thanks."

Abby's smile showed no sign of disappointment. No worries about how they could make this work. None of the turmoil Marlene felt every moment of every day. She started to turn back to the table, but Marlene caught her arm. She spent two seconds looking into Abby's questioning eyes before pulling her into a heated kiss. Marlene slid her hand up along the back of Abby's neck, holding her close while she explored her mouth. She poured everything she had into that kiss. Every moment of doubt was a challenge that she could conquer with this kiss. Every terrible day would burn away in the passion she poured into Abby. Abby could take it. Abby would want a woman with this level of intensity. She knew she was right by the delight in Abby's eyes when she broke the kiss.

"Just let me change real quick, then we can have dinner," Marlene said.

Abby just nodded, her eyes still shining from the kiss. But Marlene wasn't as fast as she had intended. She stripped naked in her closet and stared at her pathetic excuse for a wardrobe wondering how she ever thought she could be a good partner to a woman as exciting and outgoing as Abby.

Walking into Riveter's felt so different these days, Marlene had a hard time believing it was the same bar. First of all, everyone who worked there seemed to know who she was. Before she started dating Abby, Austin would give her a disinterested smile and move on. Now she waved and called Marlene by name. There were three or four other bartenders, a pair of bouncers, and several bar backs who did the same, if somewhat less enthusiastically than Austin.

Then there was the way Abby greeted her. Even tonight, when the bar was busy and every table was full, Abby still made time to throw Marlene a wink. She finished pouring a row of shots for the boisterous group taking up half the bar, and then came over to Marlene's normal spot. She grabbed Marlene's favorite beer on the way over to the obvious annoyance of the handful of thirsty patrons waiting for her attention.

"Hey, hot stuff." Abby leaned over the bar and gave Marlene a quick kiss. "Missed you."

The kiss shocked Marlene far more than the friendly welcome from strangers. She loved kissing Abby, and she didn't mind public displays of affection. In fact, she and Dawn had done more than their fair share of kissing in this very bar and this one with Abby was chaste in comparison. But this was Abby's workplace. Marlene would never consider kissing anyone at the bank.

Still, there was something to be said for Abby's varied ideas about professionalism. The women waiting for drinks now looked less annoyed at Abby and more annoyed at Marlene. Were they jealous? Marlene couldn't remember a time in her life when women had been jealous of her. Not like this. Most of those women were much more attractive than Marlene. Abby could have any one of them from the looks of it, and they were all disappointed she wasn't kissing them. How had she missed the fact that half the women in this bar were here to drool over her girlfriend?

Abby's worried voice pulled her attention away from the jealous women. "Was that okay?"

Was it? Marlene wasn't sure. Part of her stomach still coiled in embarrassment, telling her the kiss wasn't appropriate while Abby was on the clock. Part of her stomach coiled with a far warmer, more pleasant sensation that started with the enticing press of Abby's lips and was sharpened by the jealousy of strangers.

"It was fine." Marlene tried to shake off the last of her worries. "More than fine. Good. Do it again?"

Abby's lips curled up at the request and she leaned forward. This kiss was far more intense, though Marlene still couldn't bring herself to part her lips. Just when Marlene was forgetting about the rest of the world, Abby broke the kiss.

"Do I get one of those?" Pen said, leaning on the bar beside Marlene.

Marlene's throat tightened, making it hard to breathe. Of all the people to show up right now, why did it have to be Pen? No matter what those strangers across the bar thought, Marlene wasn't the smooth one here. She wasn't the one with all the right moves. That was Pen. Now all of them would see they had no reason to be jealous of Marlene, even with a knockout like Abby as her girlfriend.

Abby laughed and slid down the bar, leaning an elbow on the worn wood so she and Pen were inches apart. "You get anything you want from behind this bar."

The words sliced across Marlene's mind, making her thoughts sluggish. Had Abby really just said that? Was she really flirting with someone else right here in front of her girlfriend?

"Let's start with two martinis." Pen caught her bottom lip in her teeth as her eyes raked up and down over Abby's body. An image flashed in Marlene's mind's eye. Pen looking at her like that, her hands following her eyes, while her naked body hovered over Marlene's. "I'll come back for the rest later."

Abby snatched a green bottle off the shelf behind her but kept her eyes on Pen. "Don't tease me. You know my heart can't take it."

Pen said, "Like I'd ever disappoint you."

Abby's laughter and the rattle of ice cubes against the metal shaker couldn't compete with the ringing in Marlene's ears. There was no mistaking that look between Pen and Abby. They couldn't take their eyes off each other. It was like Abby had forgotten anyone else existed. Forgotten Marlene existed.

Marlene didn't hear the rest of the banter between them, she was too busy fighting off nausea. All that registered was the happy tinkle of Abby's voice. Marlene didn't even take a breath until Pen collected her two martinis and took them back to her table.

"Let me go help Austin for a second," Abby said, finally acknowledging Marlene again. "I'll be right back."

She didn't wait for a response, just hurried back to the patrons she'd ignored earlier. How different Marlene felt looking over at the group now. They didn't seem all that angry that Abby had helped two people who'd been waiting less time than them. One of the group—a twenty-something whose pale green shirt was buttoned all the way to the top button—even winked at Abby when she placed her order. Abby didn't wink back, but she did bat her eyelashes enough that the kid kept chatting her up. She even stuck around and chatted after collecting her beer.

Not every interaction Abby had was like that, but most of them were. The more masculine presenting the customer, the more Abby flirted. After a few minutes, Marlene couldn't watch anymore. What had she expected? She knew Abby. Knew how exciting and gorgeous she was. Of course everyone wanted her. Of course she could find a dozen more compelling women. Marlene just hadn't expected to watch it happen.

Marlene reached over to snatch up a stack of coasters from behind the bar, then stood one on its edge. She flicked one side, sending it spinning like a coin. She remembered the night all those weeks ago when Abby had shown her the game. She'd said it would keep her from getting glue under her fingernails. Marlene scoffed and slapped the coaster down. The woman sitting on the nearest barstool jumped and looked over.

"Sorry," Marlene said. "Nervous habit."

The woman shrugged and turned away. Of course she did. Nothing interesting to see here. Just a boring, middle-aged lesbian whose girlfriend was right over there, flirting with the world. She flicked another coaster, shaking her head. This time she slapped the coaster a little harder than before.

"You're getting good at that," Abby said from the other side of the bar. There was a sparkle in her eye, but Marlene knew it was from the flirting with other people. Not from her.

"Yeah."

Abby tilted her head to the side. "You okay?"

Marlene slapped another coaster down. She hadn't hit it correctly and it bent. "Fine."

"Bad day at work?"

Marlene couldn't remember. All she could remember was the way she insinuated she'd be meeting up with Pen later. "Not really."

"Did you get into a fight with Ellie?"

Marlene shrugged. They weren't as close as they had been, but Marlene knew it was her fault. She'd been spending all her time with Abby. When she reached for another coaster, Abby laid her hand on top of Marlene's to stop her. Marlene did her best not to melt under that touch, but she'd always been powerless with Abby.

Abby said, "Hey, talk to me. What's going on?"

Marlene's shoulders slumped. She knew she was being a brat, but she couldn't help asking, "You sure you wouldn't rather talk to Penelope?"

"Of course not. What do you mean?"

Marlene looked up. Big mistake. Abby's gray eyes looked almost blue tonight with the low light and her robin's egg blue wig. They also looked open and caring and not at all like a woman who was looking for other options. She looked at Marlene like she was the only person in the world.

Marlene swallowed her embarrassment and said, "You were flirting with her."

"Flirting? With Pen?" Abby laughed as though it was the most ridiculous thought in the world. "No, I wasn't."

The dismissive tone made Marlene's hackles raise. "Yeah, you were. You always flirt with her."

"We're friends."

Marlene leaned forward, lowering her voice so no one else could hear. "You said she was welcome to anything behind the bar."

"I meant drinks."

"You didn't mean drinks and she knew you didn't. The way she looked you up and down? That wasn't about a martini."

"Pen's a flirt, you know that." Abby waved her hand and grabbed Marlene another beer from the cooler. "She doesn't mean anything by it."

Marlene didn't point out that Pen had flirted with her once and she had certainly meant a lot by it. Instead, she said, "Okay, but what about the others?"

"What others?"

"You were flirting with everyone who ordered a drink from you. That kid in the fully buttoned shirt?"

"Bartenders flirt, babe." She ran her fingernail along Marlene's jaw. "It's just part of the job. You know I only mean it with you."

Did she know that? Marlene wasn't so sure. For one thing, she hadn't started flirting with Marlene until recently, and now the times she did felt so empty. Marlene tried to shake the feeling off. The pet name and the touch along her jaw went a long way to breaking down her resolve. After all, she hadn't touched anyone else. Not even Pen.

"Sorry to interrupt." Austin put a hand on Abby's shoulder. "What's a pink lady? Is it one of your drinks with the egg whites?"

"Sure is. Who wants it?"

Austin pointed out an older couple across the bar. The shorter one with silver hair waved and Abby waved back. Turning to Marlene, she said, "Duty calls."

Once Abby left, Austin turned to her. Something in her questioning look made Marlene wonder how much of their conversation Austin had overheard. She asked, "Everything okay?"

Austin was Abby's friend, not hers, so no way she was telling the truth. Instead, she pretended to think Austin was asking if she needed another drink. She raised her full bottle and said, "I'm good."

Whether Austin believed her or not, she accepted the answer. With another friendly wave, Austin went back to work, leaving Marlene alone with her beer and her doubts.

Chapter Twenty-three

C ongratulations, you graduated."
Abby held out the mug she'd just bought at a novelty shop in Dupont Circle. It featured two pairs of entwined scissors on a pride flag background.

Marlene grabbed the remote and paused her movie. "Uh, what?"

"You're officially a lesbian. I have nothing left to teach you."

"But we haven't had a lesson in over a week."

Abby dropped onto the couch, sitting closer than usual now they were a couple. "That's because you know everything there is to know about queer culture."

"I don't think that's true."

"Oh yeah? What's the mug mean?"

Marlene smiled. "It's about scissoring. Which most lesbians don't really do but straight men seem to think we all do."

Abby asked, "Can you cite an example of this coming up in queer entertainment?"

"*Booksmart.*"

"See? You know it all. You could teach this class next semester."

Marlene looked at the mug, rubbing her thumb across the painted ceramic. "You're just quitting because we're dating, aren't you?"

"Absolutely." Abby laughed and leaned back on the couch. She had hoped Marlene would take this well, and it looked like humor was the right angle. "It's weird for me to teach my girlfriend how to be a lesbian."

Marlene's eyebrows shot up to her hairline. "I'm your girlfriend?"

"Is that okay?"

"It's very okay."

Marlene sounded relieved, which melted another little piece of Abby's heart. One day she would convince this woman how special she was.

"You're probably right," Marlene said. "I don't approve of student/teacher relationships, even without the age gap."

Abby laughed and pulled her knees up to her chest. "You're adorable, you know that?"

Marlene's blush was worth every moment of uncertainty. Abby glanced at the TV and recognized the character's fur-lined leather jacket.

"*Saving Face* again?" Abby asked.

"Sorry. I really like it." Marlene reached for the remote. "We can watch something else."

Abby laid her hand on Marlene's. "No way. It's one of my favorites, too."

Marlene scooted over to the far edge of the chaise section of the oversized couch. "We could share if you want. There's plenty of room."

Abby most definitely did want and she wasted no time snuggling close. Marlene pulled a blanket over them before starting the movie. It was remarkably domestic and Abby couldn't help notice how quickly they'd fallen into a comfortable romantic relationship. Abby was the sort to fall hard and fast. Apparently, Marlene was, too.

Abby curled closer, drawn to the warmth of Marlene's body against hers. Marlene's hand slid onto Abby's thigh, just above her knee. The movement was slow, almost hesitant, but the burning heat of her palm hypnotized Abby.

"Is this okay?" Marlene asked, her voice low.

"It's great."

Abby slid her hand up and down Marlene's forearm, the fine hairs on her skin baby soft and inviting. The butterflies in Abby's stomach fluttered harder, but she forced herself to keep her focus on the screen. She was so close to getting lost in this moment, but she didn't want to. Marlene was special. So very like all her other girlfriends but also decidedly different. Abby had to be sure that, if they decided to get hot and heavy on the couch, it wasn't too much, too soon.

Then the universe decided to truly test Abby. Marlene was drawing light circles on her thigh, her fingers traveling higher and higher with each pass, when the characters on screen started to have sex. They both knew it was coming a moment before the scene shifted.

Abby swallowed hard when the montage began. It took all her will power to keep her hand still on Marlene's arm. The screen flashed with nipples and mouths and smooth, naked skin. Music thrummed low and sensuous. Abby became very aware of how her breast pressed against Marlene's side. Then she became aware of how Marlene's breathing had slowed. She could feel the rattle of her long, deep breaths.

Abby pried her eyes off the screen to look over at Marlene. She was transfixed by the intimacy on the screen, her lips barely parted. Abby moved her slow stroking from Marlene's forearm down to her wrist. Marlene's eyes flicked off the screen. They landed on Abby's lips and held.

Abby leaned close to Marlene's ear and whispered, "You must like this scene."

Marlene's hand was higher on Abby's thigh than before. In fact, it was moving to territory that might be considered scandalous.

"You're breathing is ragged." Abby drew out the last word, adding the hint of a groan.

She leaned back, hoping to see a blush on Marlene's round cheek. Instead, she found a sparkle in her eye. If she didn't know Marlene better, she might've called it mischievous. Abby leaned in, too, closing for the kiss she craved. But Marlene didn't capture her lips. Instead, she brushed her cheek along Abby's until her lips landed on Abby's throat just beneath her ear. At the same moment, she slid her free hand into Abby's hair.

The combination of the kiss on her neck and the hand in her hair had Abby desperate. She tilted her head back, allowing Marlene access to any part of her she wanted. Marlene left a trail of kisses down the column of her throat and back up, nipping at the hinge of her jaw. Abby's eyes fluttered shut when Marlene grazed her teeth along Abby's earlobe. Her breath hitched and she shifted from gently stroking Marlene's arm to grabbing fistfuls of T-shirt over Marlene's abdomen.

"Now whose breathing is ragged?" Marlene whispered into her ear.

Abby panted, "You have that effect on me."

"Do I?"

Marlene hadn't said it in a cocky way, which Abby might've expected given the way she was currently melting under her touch. It wasn't even flirty. It was a little unsure and a little proud, but definitely not cocky.

"You know you do."

Now Marlene kissed her. And not the polite but confident first kiss. This kiss was hungry. It was the kiss of a woman who was full of need and desire and Abby kissed her back in kind. She'd been fighting so long to keep herself in check and now Marlene told her with lips and touch that she didn't have to hold back anymore. That she was ready and willing. And it wasn't just her kiss. Marlene's hands were both at work now, sliding beneath her shirt and caressing every inch of her.

Marlene had magical hands, setting off sparks of delight across her skin. Sending her mind spinning and her heart pounding. Abby pulled her close, her hands slipping under Marlene's shirt and tugging at the band of her sports bra.

"Is this okay?" Abby asked, barely managing the breath to speak.

"God yes. Please touch me."

Marlene didn't have to ask twice. When Abby cupped her breast, Marlene's nipple was rock hard against her palm. They were perfect breasts. Small and firm with sensitive nipples. Abby wanted nothing more than to taste her skin, but there were acres of fabric between them. She was just considering how to get their shirts off when Marlene's hand pressed against the lace of her bra. Abby gasped so loud she even startled herself.

"Oh shit. I'm sorry." Marlene scuttled back toward the center of the couch.

Abby could see panic in Marlene's eyes and said, "Baby, that was a good noise."

"Oh, okay. Sorry." Marlene shook her head and wouldn't meet Abby's eye. "I'm not good at this part. Honestly? I'm not good at any of the parts, but I'm especially not good at this part."

Abby could see her starting to spiral and her heart ached. She took Marlene's hand in hers and brought it to her lips, kissing along the knuckles. "Sweetheart, it's okay."

"No. It's not. We were having a moment and then I screwed it up. I'm sorry."

Marlene tried to pull her hand away, but Abby wouldn't let her melt down like this. She reached out and took Marlene's face in both her hands. She turned her face until their eyes met and, when they did, the panic in Marlene's eyes dissipated a degree. She took a long breath and her shoulders relaxed. Abby leaned forward a little, gauging Marlene's reaction. When she didn't bolt, Abby leaned in and pressed a soft kiss against her forehead. She felt Marlene's sighed breath against her neck. She pressed a kiss against her cheek, then her nose, then her other cheek, and, finally, gently as she could, against her bottom lip.

"There's nothing to be sorry about," Abby whispered. "I want everything you have to give and I won't ask for more. Whatever you want to happen tonight will happen, and nothing that you don't want to happen will. Okay? You're safe with me."

"I know."

"Do you want to sit back and watch the movie?"

Marlene pulled back and looked into Abby's eyes. "No. I want to kiss you again. Can I?"

Abby nodded, expecting a shy, hesitant kiss. And the first one was. Marlene deepened the second kiss, though. She pressed forward with her tongue on the third and she slipped her hand underneath Abby's shirt again on the fourth. Abby tried to go slow. She didn't press and she didn't have expectations, but her body thrilled at each touch. Marlene fell back into their shared intimacy as though there had been no pause.

When Marlene pulled her shirt off and started a line of kisses down her chest, Abby couldn't hold back her moan. This time it didn't scare Marlene off. When Marlene slipped the bra strap off her shoulder and took Abby's nipple into her mouth, her gasp turned into a desperate whimper. Marlene actually chuckled around her mouthful.

When Marlene would have transferred her attentions from one breast to the other, Abby pressed her back against the couch. She reached for the hem of Marlene's shirt, but hesitated. She stopped and looked into Marlene's eyes. They were hazy with lust and unfocused, but Abby made sure she was listening. If they didn't talk about this now, it would hover over the rest of the night and possibly the rest of their relationship.

Abby said, "If you aren't ready, we don't have to do anything. We can have some pants-on fun here and leave it at that. But if you're worried that you're not good at sex…"

"I'm not," Marlene whispered.

Abby slid one, square cut fingernail across Marlene's jaw. "Baby, why don't you let me be the judge of that?"

Marlene was clearly torn. Her hands hadn't left Abby's skin and they were creeping back toward her naked breasts. "I don't want to disappoint you."

"You never could, darling. You can trust me, okay?"

Marlene looked straight into Abby's eyes and nodded.

Abby pressed her palm into Marlene's thigh, running her hands up toward her straining hips. "So do you want me to keep going?"

Marlene's nod was far more enthusiastic this time, her tongue skating across her lips.

"I love body language as much as the next girl," Abby said with her most seductive grin. "But consent is sort of my kink. I need you to say it. Do you want to have sex with me?"

"God yes."

The way Marlene's voice crackled when she said the words made Abby's stomach swoop with excitement. She didn't have long to enjoy the sensation because Marlene lunged forward and enveloped her in another kiss that made her mind go blank. She didn't just focus on Abby's breasts, but found and exploited all the sensitive spots on her neck and chest that made Abby's skin tingle and burn.

Pressing Marlene back against the couch, Abby took some time to indulge herself in exploring Marlene's sensitive spots. She ran her tongue slowly across the soft plane of Marlene's abdomen, relishing in the muscles flexing beneath her. When she kissed up Marlene's side, Marlene spread her arms across the back of the couch, gripping the cushions with white-knuckled fists. Abby climbed off the couch and settled on the floor between Marlene's legs. Then she took one pink-brown nipple into her mouth and Marlene unleashed a whimper that sizzled through every nerve ending and landed with a shock in her core. With some experimentation, she discovered that Marlene enjoyed a light scrape of teeth across her nipple. That made her whole body quake and her breathing hitch in delicious ways.

Abby couldn't wait another second. She hooked her fingers beneath the waistband of Marlene's sweatpants and pulled them down slowly. She'd been right about Marlene's eagerness. The moment she felt the first tug, Marlene lifted her hips so Abby could slip her pants off.

"Keep talking to me, okay?" Abby said, her eyes on Marlene's. "If something is too much or not enough, let me know. I have to learn your body, too."

Marlene nodded before dropping her head onto the back of the couch. Abby took a moment to appreciate the scene before her. Marlene's body was thin to the point of willowy, and all her muscles were pulled into tension. Her chest heaved, sending her small breasts rocking up and down. Kneeling between her legs, Abby could appreciate every pale line of skin, every freckle, every fine hair that made up Marlene's body. Abby slid her hands up the insides of Marlene's thighs and watched her struggle to remain still. To let Abby lead and allow herself to follow. It wasn't vulnerability exactly, but it was conscious trust.

Abby followed the path of her hand with her lips, slowly trailing kisses up Marlene's thighs. Marlene quivered with each touch. Her skin was so soft. It looked like raw marble under a full moon. Abby opened her mouth for the next kiss, her tongue darting out to taste. Marlene's skin carried the faintest hint of salt, and Abby's mouth watered as her scent filled her nostrils.

When Abby reached the apex of her thighs, hunger nearly overwhelmed her. Before she could lean in, Marlene said, "Wait."

Abby rocked back on her heels immediately. "Okay. Too fast?"

"No. It's good. It's very good."

Marlene grabbed the throw pillow from beside her and held it out. Abby took it, looking at it with more than a little confusion. Marlene blushed and said, "For your knees."

A laugh bubbled out so unexpectedly it made Abby light-headed. She shoved the pillow under her knees, then pulled Marlene down into a heated kiss.

"You're so flipping sweet, you know that?"

Then she pushed Marlene back against the couch and spread her wide open. Abby loved going down on women. She loved the taste and the feel and the utter bliss of bringing another woman pleasure with her mouth. Marlene tasted like salted watermelon and Abby drank her in. She forced herself not to be too eager, to listen for any instructions Marlene might give. The only instruction Marlene gave was a string of nearly incoherent words in which the words "Abby" and "yes" featured prominently. Abby lost herself in the taste and smell and heat of this woman. When Marlene's words stopped, Abby wrapped her arms around her thighs, holding her in place for the explosion to come.

Marlene came with a roar of pleasure, her body shaking. She curled forward then arched back and Abby barely managed to keep hold. Marlene stammered apologies as Abby pressed her back into the couch, her mouth easing Marlene through her peak. At some point she broke off enough to ask permission to go inside, permission Marlene eagerly gave, and then she went to work again with fingers and tongue. Marlene's second release was even louder than the first, but she managed to stay seated on the couch through it.

As her cries died away, Marlene collapsed back into the cushions. Abby's heart hammered in her chest, watching Marlene so utterly at rest. She panted and her face was pointed at the ceiling, but her arms lay limp at her sides and her knees slumped against the couch. Better even than bringing her pleasure, Abby reveled in bringing Marlene peace.

For Marlene, coming down off the high of her orgasms was almost as blissful as having them. She had been so terrified of this moment. Of whether she could move past her fears and let herself feel good. She hadn't even been able to masturbate since Dawn left. Every time she was turned on enough to try, she remembered how Dawn had used her that last night before tossing her away and shame overwhelmed her. She'd been so worried that would happen with Abby. That she would get close to the point of ecstasy and then fall into that pit of fear.

She should've known better. She should've known Abby would protect her. Would care for her and guide her through it. God, how had she gotten so lucky? How had Abby chosen her? She didn't deserve this kind of gentleness, but she knew how incredible a gift it was and she wasn't going to let it go.

Abby slid out of her, sending one last, powerful aftershock through Marlene's limbs. A soft, almost imperceptible kiss on her thigh made Marlene open her eyes. Abby was smiling up at her. The warmth in her eyes made Marlene's heart sing, but the eroticism of her kneeling there, between her legs, made other emotions rocket through her.

She needed Abby.

Needed to hold her and touch her and make her feel all the things she was feeling now. Her body had craved release, but it was desperate to give in kind.

Marlene slid forward, then pulled Abby into a wet, needy kiss. She could taste herself on Abby's tongue, and the desperation inside her magnified beyond reason. She hadn't intended to coax Abby to lie down on the rug or to lower herself between her legs. She hadn't intended to press their bodies together until Abby arched and moaned. But she did those things and Abby followed her lead, ceding control of their lovemaking to Marlene eagerly.

The only time she took a break from showering kisses across every inch of Abby's skin was when she reached back for the pillow. When she slipped it beneath Abby's head, she was rewarded by another hungry kiss. She had to file that information away for later. Dawn never cared about her romantic gestures, but Abby certainly did.

And just like that, her confidence broke. Thinking of Dawn in this moment was a terrible mistake. The pit of fear opened beneath her feet and she was tumbling away from the confidence Abby's touch had given her. Marlene screwed her eyes shut against the doubt and kissed Abby harder. Abby's arms snaked around her and pulled her down until their bodies were pressed so hard together there was no room for Marlene's fear. She forced herself to focus into this moment. She wanted this. She wanted Abby.

Marlene's fingertips brushed against Abby's erect nipple and their kiss faltered with her gasp of pleasure. Confidence returned in a trickle, but she could make it a river. She could stay present. Marlene lost herself in Abby's mouth and body. She moved from one breast to the other until Abby's body quivered beneath her. When she sensed the pleading edge to Abby's movements, Marlene slid her hand lower.

Abby moaned as Marlene's fingertips brushed the curls between her legs. Doubt gripped her again and Marlene couldn't stop her hand from trembling. She tried to cover it, but Abby knew she'd faltered. The longer it took to compose herself, the more doubt crept in. What if she couldn't do this? What if she couldn't make Abby feel all the things she'd felt? How could she deal with Abby's disappointment?

She was spiraling and she knew it, but she didn't know how to get back into the moment. Then Abby's hand was on top of hers. Her thumb rubbed along Marlene's wrist and the trembling stopped. Abby's fingers twined with hers and then their hands were moving again, sliding through the slick curls and further.

"Is this okay?" Abby whispered.

Marlene sighed as heat pooled beneath her fingertips. "Yes. Is it okay for you?"

Abby's head titled back, creasing the pillow. "I love having your hands on me. You're amazing with your hands."

Marlene's heart thudded in her chest. Was that true? Abby had clearly enjoyed the way Marlene had touched her breasts. But this was different, wasn't it?

Marlene's fingers slid across Abby's clit and they both groaned. Abby was so wet. So ready. And Marlene had done that. She wanted Marlene, the evidence of that was coating both their hands. Marlene rolled her fingers and Abby followed along with her hand. She wasn't touching herself. She was touching Marlene touching her. After a few slow strokes, Marlene realized Abby wasn't even leading the way. Marlene was the one choosing where to touch and how hard. Which meant all those delicious noises Abby was making were from her hands.

Abby opened her eyes and stared into Marlene's. There was a haze across the shining steel of her irises. All desire and lust and, Marlene was certain, trust. Marlene nodded and Abby's hand fell away from hers. She curled it up above her head and let her eyelids roll shut.

Marlene explored her clit the way she'd explored the rest of her body, testing different strokes and pressures. Finding all the ways she could make Abby gasp. The more she touched, the more she wanted to touch. The more she wanted to discover exactly what Abby liked. Within moments, her body was arching and tensing. Then Abby was screaming Marlene's name. All her fears and doubts were completely banished by her name on Abby's lips.

Propping herself up on her palm for a better angle, she slid two fingers inside as her first orgasm melted away. She kept her thumb on Abby's clit, stroking as best she could from both directions.

"Oh God." Abby groaned. "Don't you dare stop."

Then Marlene was chuckling, low and throaty, and teasing Abby. Who was this person that was suddenly so confident in bed? Marlene didn't have a chance to wonder because Abby was clenching around her and screaming again, a bead of sweat trickling down her forehead to soak into her hairline.

She coaxed one more weak cry of pleasure from Abby before collapsing, exhausted onto the rug beside her. Abby curled toward her, throwing her leg over Marlene. Marlene held her close, basking in the afterglow, as their skin cooled in the chill air and their breathing slowed. She trailed her fingertips across Abby's thigh, reveling in the weight of it on top of her. In the crackle of electricity between them.

"Are you cold?" Marlene asked. "Should I get a blanket?"

Abby pulled her closer and mumbled against her shoulder, "Don't you dare get up."

"Good." Marlene pushed a strand of hair off Abby's temple. "I don't want to stop looking at you."

Abby's breathing was slow as she offered a sleepy version of her usual blinding smile. "You're amazing."

The words had barely passed Abby's lips when her eyes closed. Marlene beamed as she watched the slow rise and fall of her back as she painted lazy circles on Abby's skin. Those words of affirmation echoed in Marlene's ears until she fell asleep herself, a smile fixed on her lips.

CHAPTER TWENTY-FOUR

Abby pushed open the door to her studio and pulled in a lungful of air. The mingled scents of stretched cotton and acrylic paint filled her nostrils and lifted her heart. Of course, her heart was about as light as it could possibly be already. Waking up next to Marlene, their naked bodies pressed tight together as they shared a single throw pillow, was about as blissful as anything Abby could imagine. Okay, the stiff muscles and aching shoulder from sleeping on the living room floor dampened the perfection a little. But only a very little.

She wanted nothing more than to stay there, wrapped in Marlene's arms. Then spend a leisurely morning in Marlene's massive tub, soaking away all the pleasant aches from their night together. Unfortunately, she had promised to meet Penelope at her studio before work and she couldn't get out of it. She'd hoped to steal one more kiss from Marlene before she left, but she'd been sleeping too peacefully. All she could do was leave a note explaining where she'd gone along with a promise to make it up to her when she got home from work.

Abby was puttering around her studio, happily replaying memories from her magic night with Marlene, when Pen knocked on the open door.

"Thanks for meeting me so early." Pen greeted her with a one-armed hug.

"No problem. What're you looking for anyway? You weren't clear when we talked."

"That's cause Kieran was in the bathroom and I didn't want her overhearing. It's a surprise for her birthday."

"Aw. That's sweet. Your first birthday together as a married couple."

Pen cringed. "Never say the M word around me. That is never going to happen."

Abby patted her cheek and gave her a wink. "I hate to break it to you, but you are already there. Everything except the paperwork."

Pen rolled her eyes and turned her back, heading for the wall where Abby's best work hung. "I want something dramatic for her. Something one of a kind."

"You know me, one of a kind and full of drama."

"That's what I love about you."

Abby said, "I'll sell a piece to you, but only on one condition."

"What condition? I gave up my hall pass, so if you wanted to break in that couch I have to regretfully decline."

Abby stepped in front of Pen and crossed her arms, killing the flirtatious banter. She hadn't meant to be so aggressive, but remembering the pain in Marlene's voice last night made anger flash white-hot in her chest. She shoved her finger in Pen's face. "Tell me you're not the one who made my girlfriend think she's bad in bed."

Pen held up her hands and took a step back. "What? Marlene's not bad in bed."

"Obviously she isn't. Did you tell her she was?"

"Of course not. Even if she had been, I'd never say that to anyone, especially their first time with a woman. What kind of asshole would do that?"

Abby hadn't really believed Pen was the culprit, but it was nice to hear her say it. She shook the anger off and stuck her chin in the air. "Dawn, I'm guessing. Sorry to accuse you. I know you aren't cruel."

"It's fine. If you want someone to kick Dawn's ass, I know a few people who could do the job. Now that most of my clients are Georgetown rich I hear some wild stuff."

"That's not really my style, but I appreciate the offer."

Abby turned her attention to the artwork, but Pen didn't let her off that easy. She strode up beside and leaned close. "So you know Marlene isn't bad in bed, huh?"

Abby searched for a funny quip or a sarcastic comment, but she was too blissfully happy to joke about her night with Marlene.

"Holy shit, are you blushing?" Pen asked. "I didn't know you were capable of blushing."

She laughed and swatted at Pen's shoulder. "Of course I'm capable." She waved a hand at the piles of pale blue curls on her head. "Underneath the makeup and wigs, I'm just a gushing girly girl."

"You don't have to look under the makeup and wigs to tell." Pen smiled at her with the most genuine expression Abby had ever seen on her face. "I'm really happy for you, Abby. You deserve it. And Marlene's great."

Abby's heart did a little skip. She was happy for herself. All her heartbreaks felt like a lifetime ago. All her loneliness and nights of doubt had fled in the night while she slept in Marlene's arms.

"You have no idea."

Pen said, "Nope, but I look forward to you telling me all about it. When's the wedding?"

Abby swatted her shoulder again, but this time with even less conviction. "Oh shut up and look at my paintings, would you?"

They talked about the ones on the main wall first. Abby pointed out the ones that had sold already and made a mental note to schedule a trip to FedEx with Marlene. Pen asked a few questions and commented on one canvas or another, but nothing there caught her eye. Abby had a pretty good sense which would be the one, but she wanted to make Pen work for it. She had precious little time talking to her friends about art, she wanted to take advantage. Not to mention it didn't hurt to give her Realtor friend the full tour since she had rich clients with deep pockets now. Maybe one of them was looking for a housewarming gift?

Most of her attention, however, was on Marlene. Abby assumed she'd woken up by now. Hopefully, she wouldn't be too disappointed to find herself alone. She had D&D tonight, but maybe she could skip one week? They might even make it up to one of their bedrooms tonight.

Because she was preoccupied with thoughts of Marlene, she missed the moment that Pen tumbled to the concrete floor. The sound startled her so much she screamed. Turning to see Pen face down on the floor, struggling to right herself terrified her.

"Are you okay?" Abby asked as she squatted at Pen's side. "What happened?"

Pen's face was oddly passive. She wasn't even grimacing in pain. "I'm fine. Help me to the couch, would you?"

"Are you sure you should move? Did you hit your head?"

"Not my head, just my ass. Help me to the couch."

Abby tried to be gentle, but she was so shaken up, she couldn't really remember the procedure. Pen didn't really seem to need her help. In fact, she spent most of the time giving Abby detailed instructions on how to move her, almost like she had been through this before. The only difficulty came in getting her down on the couch since Pen couldn't put weight on her foot and Abby didn't know how to move her. They managed it eventually, but Pen was left groaning in pain by the end.

"I'm so sorry." Abby knelt in front of Pen, working at the tight laces on her Oxfords. "What happened?"

"Twisted my ankle. Not your fault," Pen said through gritted teeth. "I have bad joints."

She hadn't initially reacted like she was in pain, but she certainly was now. Probably because of the clumsy transfer to the couch. If only Abby's couch wasn't so low, it would've been easier.

Pen said sheepishly, "I might have to beg a ride home from you. Not sure I can drive with this ankle."

"Of course. Anything you need. Just let me get this shoe off."

Abby tried to be delicate, but Pen's ankle was already looking painfully swollen. She had to scoot close to Pen and hold her foot in top of her folded knees. As she slid the shoe off, Pen's head fell back on the couch with a groan of relief.

"What the hell?"

Marlene's voice cut through Abby's concern. She was bent low over Pen's leg, so it was awkward to turn and look over her shoulder. By the time she did, Marlene was already whipping back out the open door. A bouquet of red roses dropped to the floor and bounced, spraying bruised petals onto the paint speckled floor.

Marlene could barely see the pavement beneath her feet and she couldn't remember where she'd parked her car. The spots in front of

Abby's studio were taken when she arrived, so she had to park farther away. Her head whipped around, desperately seeking her car, but she could barely see the parking lot in front of her.

All she could see was Abby.

Abby on her knees, her head barely visible between Pen's legs. Pen with her arms stretched across the back of the couch. Her head thrown back and her eyes closed. And that moan. The whole scene was exactly like the one from this time last night. Only Abby had been kneeling between Pen's legs instead of hers.

Marlene squeezed her eyes shut to block out the images. Tears stung her eyes. She should have known she would never be enough for Abby. She wasn't a good girlfriend and she wasn't a good lover. Why else would Abby sneak out of the house so early to find the release she'd needed?

Marlene's eyes finally landed on her SUV and she took off toward it. Her head spun as she struggled to take in air. Her lungs wouldn't inflate. Her mind wouldn't stop showing her images of Abby. Panic ripped through her, and she squeezed her hands into fists. A sharp pain bit into one palm as she squeezed too hard on her keys. She gasped and opened her hand, her keys tumbling out and rolling underneath her car.

"Fuck." Marlene dropped to her knees, rocks cutting into her skin through her thin slacks. "Shit. Fuck. Shit."

Marlene had to reach to the full stretch of her arm to grab the keys. Her fingers were shaking so hard she could barely keep a grip on them, but she managed to drag them out and get back to her feet just as she heard running footsteps behind her.

"Marlene." Abby skidded to a halt beside her. "Hey, where are you going?"

She didn't want to turn—she didn't know if she could handle seeing Abby right now—but she had no choice. It was Abby. It wasn't like she had the choice to walk away now. In truth, she'd never had a choice. She'd always been under Abby's spell. She turned and saw confusion on Abby's face and that confusion made her furious and despondent all at once.

The tears came no matter how hard she fought them. She was such an idiot. One stupid decision after another led her here to this moment. She should never have asked Abby to move in. Ellie had been right. She'd had a crush and she pretended not to for what? To get lessons on being a lesbian? A fat lot of good that had done her. Now she had the education to realize she was living one of those classic lesbian story arcs. Destined to be crushed by love and die alone and sad.

"Are you okay?" Abby asked.

"Am I okay? What the fuck kind of question is that to ask me right now? How the fuck am I supposed to be okay?"

Abby took a step back, her eyes widening in shock. It wasn't until she registered the echo of her voice off the building that Marlene realized she'd shouted.

"Okay," Abby said in a low, calm voice. "Why don't you take a deep breath and tell me what's going on?"

"I don't think I'm the one who owes you an explanation. I'm pretty sure I don't owe you a goddamn thing."

"That's not how this is going to be." Abby's voice was calm. Painfully calm. Heartbreakingly calm. "That's not how I'm going to be treated."

Marlene ignored the voice in the back of her head that told her to stand down. She'd stood down her whole life. She never spoke her mind. Today, she would speak her mind. "I'm not thrilled with how I'm being treated in this relationship, either."

"Tell me what you mean by that."

Marlene snapped. The voice in the back of her head cut off abruptly and her vision narrowed to a fine point. "If I need to lay out for you why what you were doing with Penelope is wrong, you clearly don't see this relationship the same way I do." Abby started to speak, but Marlene couldn't hear her words. All she could hear was herself saying, "I should've known. I've seen you flirt. Hell, I've seen you flirt with her more than once."

Now she was getting the reaction she expected from Abby. Her cheeks were flaming red and her eyes were the cold steel-gray of a slashing knife. "That's my personality. I'm a flirt. I've told you that before. Heck, it's practically a job requirement of a bartender to flirt. It doesn't mean anything."

"What you were doing in there with Pen just now means something." Marlene couldn't do it anymore. She couldn't look at

Abby. She turned back to her car and tried to open the door, but Abby's hand slammed into the glass next to her face, making her jump.

"Nope. You don't just get to say something weird and vague like that and just drive off," Abby said.

Marlene whirled around to face her, her heart ramming against her ribs so fast she was surprised she hadn't passed out. "Weird and vague? It's weird and vague to be pissed to find you cheating on me? I just saw you literally kneeling between her legs. I'm supposed to just be okay with that? I told you I don't like it when you flirt with her and you brush me off. Now I find you fucking her and you think you can just brush that off, too?"

If she'd expected an indignant reply or an attempted denial, she was destined to be disappointed. Abby blinked rapidly for a few moments, then took several steps back, her eyes narrowing and her jaw set.

Abby's voice was cold as frozen stone when she said, "Obviously you don't think very highly of me."

"It's pretty clear you've been keeping your options open from the start," Marlene said, throwing her arm out to indicate the still open door of Abby's studio. "Did you ever really think of this as a relationship?"

"Whatever it was, I think it's best we end it now," Abby said in that same cold monotone. Without another word, Abby turned and walked back to her studio, for all the world like she was the wronged party.

CHAPTER TWENTY-FIVE

Marlene adjusted her position in her chair, trying to project confidence by throwing her shoulders back and pushing her chin into the air like her father had taught her. It didn't work. She didn't want to have this conversation. She knew she had to, but she also knew it would not go well.

Throwing her shoulders back also didn't help her confidence because the position pushed the big, floppy bow on her new blouse so high it tickled at the edge of her vision, distracting her. Not to mention the padded bra was pushing her breasts up almost to her chin. She'd bought both on an impromptu shopping trip after work the night before. She'd told herself it was necessary because she needed clothes for work that would fit into Brad's specific style requirements, but it was a lie. She had clothes. She just didn't want to see Abby.

Everything was wrong. Marlene knew that much, but she was no longer sure what. The image of Abby kneeling between Pen's legs was still fresh as ever, sending icicles of shame and anger through her, as they had when she marched blindly to her car yesterday morning. But then there was the look in Abby's eyes when she had walked away.

Abby had walked away.

That was the scary thing that made no sense. She had looked like she was hurt and confused. How did that make sense? She had been cheating. Marlene had caught her having sex with another woman, but she was the one who looked hurt. Despite the evidence she'd seen with her own eyes, doubt kept creeping into Marlene when she thought of the look on Abby's face.

The longer that doubt gnawed at her, the more it cooled her anger and the more it made her wonder. Sure, Abby was a flirt, but Marlene would never in a million years think the woman who had been so gentle and patient and thoughtful a lover would be a cheater. It just didn't make sense.

Marlene shook herself and the shame came flooding back in. "Of course it makes sense. It's Pen."

No. It wasn't just Pen. It was Marlene. The part she wouldn't say out loud, even sitting here alone in her office, was that it made sense not because who Abby had cheated with, but who she'd been dating in the first place. If there's one thing Marlene knew from her relationship with Dawn, it was that she couldn't satisfy a woman in bed. She couldn't satisfy Dawn enough to keep her around. She couldn't satisfy Abby enough to keep her faithful.

So she had avoided Abby the previous night. It had been Abby's D&D night, so she'd known that, had she come home at all, it would be late. There was a chance she'd just stay at her studio, but all her stuff was at the condo. If she spent one more night in the condo, Marlene wanted to be in bed long before she came home, but she'd been lying awake. Part of her hoped Abby would come bursting into her room, crying or raging—Marlene would accept either—and demand they talk. Part of her knew there wasn't a chance in the world. Most of her wondered if Abby really had gone to D&D. But if she'd gone to Pen's house instead, she hadn't spent the night.

They were both up late. Marlene stared at the ceiling until early into the morning, listening to the sounds of suitcases being packed and carried downstairs. At some point she had dozed off, but it wasn't restful sleep. Once she'd dressed for work, she went out on the balcony to scour the parking lot. Abby's Mini was in the driveway, but Marlene could see it was stuffed to the brim with Abby's possessions. Marlene took a cold satisfaction in knowing this would be the last time she saw the car there. Her dangerous, ridiculous experiment had blown up in her face, just as Ellie had predicted.

Marlene forced herself to stop thinking about Abby and snatched up her office phone. "Ellie, can you come in here please?"

Ellie didn't bother to answer. Marlene could see her put the phone down and hop out of her chair. A slice of frustration cut through her. Was there anyone in her life that treated Marlene with respect? How hard would it have been to act professionally?

"I'm glad you're ready to talk," Ellie said as she dropped into the visitor chair. "You've been walking around all day like someone ran over your cat."

"Close the door, please."

Ellie shrugged and hopped back out of the chair. Marlene studied Ellie's appearance while she yanked the door shut. Ellie was wearing a new suit, too, but hers was from the men's department, tailored to hug her thin frame and looking incredibly comfortable. Marlene shifted her shoulders again and the bow rubbed against her chin.

"Spit it out. Did you and Abby have a fight?"

"This is not about personal matters," Marlene said. The chill in her voice went well past professional and nearly tipped over into rude, but she wasn't in the mood to deal with Ellie's antics. "We're at work and we're going to talk about work."

"Okay. Fine. Sheesh."

Marlene cleared her throat and waited for Ellie to look at her. That was a tactical error. This was going to be so much harder now that she had to look into her friend's eyes.

"While the bank's dress code technically lets us dress however we want." Marlene kept her voice as even as possible. "FTL expects more feminine attire from our female employees."

While the silence stretched, Marlene thought of Ellie sitting in that chair the day after her birthday last year. When Marlene told her about Pen. About her life changing. Ellie had congratulated her. Had listened to her and comforted her.

Ellie said, "You've got to be fucking kidding me."

"Please use appropriate language."

Ellie had taken Marlene to get her first suit. To buy men's pants and have them tailored to fit her diminutive frame. When Marlene had been afraid she'd get in trouble for shopping in the wrong section, Ellie had accompanied her. Had been a good friend.

"Fuck my fucking language. How could you say that to me?"

"We have a code of conduct," Marlene said.

"Which doesn't say I have to dress like a fucking Barbie." Ellie's face was twisted with anger and hurt. Marlene could barely hear her for the ringing in her ears. "Are you telling me I can't dress how I feel comfortable?"

"It's about maintaining a professional atmosphere."

"Bullshit. It's about Brad's bullshit misogyny, isn't it?" Marlene didn't answer, but Ellie clearly knew she didn't have to. "Look, you might be willing to change for him, but I'm not."

"What's the big deal with dressing in more feminine clothing while you're at work?" The words stung Marlene's tongue, but she ignored it. She had a job to do.

Ellie pushed herself out of her chair and leaned over the desk. In all their years as friends, Marlene had never seen her look so vulnerable and so furious. It suddenly occurred to her that this might be the end of their friendship.

"I spent years pretending to be someone else, Marlene. For my mother and my stepfather. For my friends who would hate me if they knew I was gay. For the world. I won't do it again. Not even for you."

Ellie pushed off the desk and marched to the door. Marlene watched her go, but didn't know what to say. Why was Ellie being like this? It wasn't so hard. It was just a few hours a day. If Marlene could do it, why couldn't she?

"I know who I am and I like who I am," Ellie said. "I thought you'd finally figured out who you are, too. I really hope this isn't it."

Then Ellie was gone. She hadn't turned to look at Marlene as she'd spoken. She didn't turn to look at her when she got back to her desk and sat down. She just went back to work like nothing had happened. Marlene watched her for a long time. She wasn't sure what she was hoping for. Just like she hadn't been sure what she'd been hoping for with Abby last night.

Having that conversation was necessary. Brad had all but ordered her to do it. It was the right thing for the branch and she was the one who had to make these tough decisions and have these tough conversations. That's what a manager had to do. Brad had actually said those words. Still, it didn't make it any easier. It didn't make the sick, bitter taste of betrayal leave her mouth or curb the loneliness soaking into her skin.

Eventually, Marlene peeled her eyes off Ellie's back and rigidly set shoulders. She pushed her chin higher into the air, failing again to find the confidence her father insisted the gesture would bring. The bow was choking her and the bra was too tight. She couldn't take a full breath. She told herself the same words she'd told Ellie. Only a few hours and then she could go home and change.

Only problem was, without Abby there to cook with and share the couch with, it wouldn't feel the same.

Abby was feeling a distinct sense of déjà vu as she hauled boxes and suitcases into her studio. She hadn't even gotten the last ones out and here she was, bringing everything back. The couch looked just as uninviting as it had the last time she'd slept here, but what could she do? She wasn't going back to the condo, that was for darn sure.

The tears started when she tried to get the last suitcase out of the Mini's tiny back seat. She wasn't crying about Marlene, she told herself as she wiped aggressively at her streaming nose, she was frustrated with the bag. The way it went right in last night when she loaded it into the car but couldn't seem to fit through the same door now. How had the dimensions of this stupid suitcase changed so drastically overnight? She yanked at the handle and a corner stuck on the roof. She pushed on the top and the wheels snagged around the seat belt. The harder she tried to mold it to the opening, the less it worked.

Abby marched back into her studio, leaving the car door open and the suitcase sticking out of it. She couldn't deal with this now. Not when she was so mad and sad and tired. That was the worst of it. How tired she was. Exhausted to her bones with yet another heartbreak. She dropped onto the couch and threw her arms over her eyes.

Why did this keep happening to her? And why did it have to happen with Marlene of all people? It was silly, she knew, to mourn this relationship so hard when it had only existed a matter of days. Josie leaving had hurt, but nothing like this. And she knew why. The further she got from her last relationship, the more she saw all the ways it didn't work. All the things she ignored. All the one-sided happiness. Part of her knew it would never last with Josie, no matter how much she wanted it to.

But she hadn't forced any of that with Marlene. She hadn't squeezed into a box so she could pretend at happiness and Marlene hadn't either, she was sure of it. Marlene had been insecure and wary, but she had been herself with Abby. If there was one thing Abby was sure of, it was that their relationship had felt right for both of them. So why had it all blown up in her face?

Because Marlene had never known her at all. She had created an image of Abby in her head and that image was nothing like the real thing. How could Marlene think so little of her? Think that she would ever cheat? Think that she was keeping her options open? The cruelty of her words—of her thoughts—were worse by far than the other breakups. Not even Josie would accuse her of cheating. So what had given Marlene the idea that she could do that?

Whatever the cause, Abby didn't have time to agonize over this now. She needed to get to work, and that meant she needed to get that darn suitcase out of her car. Marching to the bathroom, Abby carefully slid a finger under each eye, wiping away the damage done by crying without further smudging her eye makeup. If she couldn't feel good, she could at least look good. That done, she went back to her car. She surveyed the scene and made a decision. She would get this suitcase out right now and she wouldn't accept failure as an option.

Brute force and determination did the trick. She took hold of the handle with one hand, pressed down on the top with the other, and held the seat belt of the way with her foot. One almighty yank and the suitcase popped free as though it had never been stuck. Inside was her favorite bell skirt and red button-up top. It would be harder to get ready in the rudimentary studio bathroom, but she would show up to work tonight like nothing was wrong. She always did.

Austin waited until after the moderately busy bar had all been plied with beverages before she stepped up close to Abby's ear and asked, "What happened?"

She hadn't told Austin about the breakup, but it didn't surprise her in the least that she'd figured it out. Austin was intuitive and Abby didn't have a poker face. "It's over."

Austin reached for a hug but Abby stepped away. She couldn't do this. Not here. Not now. She'd start crying and she didn't want that. She needed this place to feel good.

When she saw the hurt on Austin's face, she regretted the instinct to pull away. "I'm sorry. I just can't talk about this here."

"I understand. Why don't you come over to my place and we can talk about it?"

"Sure. It'll be a few days, though. I've got to get my stuff out."

"Do you need help?"

"No. I'll do it while she's at work. I've already paid this month's rent. I can leave most everything there while I find a place to land."

Austin offered her couch again and Abby refused for the same reasons as last time. She needed a real bed and her own space. She would be pickier this time. She wouldn't put herself in the same position again. She had an idea of where to stay while she found her own place, but she didn't want to hurt Austin's feelings by telling her.

An hour later, Abby was too busy to obsess over either Austin or Marlene. The usual evening crowd was a drink or two in, and the noise level in the room was high enough to drown out conscious thought. She was so busy, in fact, that when her cell phone buzzed in her pocket, she was forced to ignore it for several long minutes. She spent those minutes telling herself it wasn't Marlene, and she was right. When she finally had a chance to glance at the screen, it was Pen, asking when they could arrange delivery of the painting she'd bought.

Abby texted back, *I can deliver it tonight after work if you want*

After a moment of hesitation, she added, *Did you and Kieran finish renovating that guest room? I could use a place to crash for a few days.*

Chapter Twenty-six

As if the horrible bow from the previous day's blouse hadn't been enough, Marlene's latest outfit had a high standing collar with a tie at the neck that poofed into a flower shape. It didn't just occasionally hit her chin, it constantly rubbed on her cheek and made her feel like she was being devoured by a hydrangea. Whatever had possessed her to buy the damn thing, she had no idea. She couldn't wait to get home and rip it off. She might even throw it onto the ground and stomp on it.

Lost in thought over her terrible outfit, she didn't see the person approaching her office until the door swung open. Marlene jumped out of her chair, anticipating attack. David looked as panicked as she was.

"I was just checking in. You remember the managers meeting, right? At headquarters in thirty minutes?" David asked.

Her panic at the unexpected intrusion flipped to panic of missing a meeting. That was all she needed. Brad would fire her on the spot. She grabbed her briefcase and was set to sprint out when she remembered how chummy David and Brad were. If he saw her lose it, she'd be in real trouble.

Forcing herself to move slowly and speak calmly, she said, "Thank you, David. I was just heading out."

Once she was down the stairs to the main lobby, she picked up her pace. As soon as she turned the corner outside the front door, she sprinted as fast as her short heels would allow. Her attempts to stay upright distracted her sufficiently to be startled by another unanticipated visitor.

Penelope climbed out of her car next to Marlene's, leaning heavily on a cane, her face twisted into a mask of fury. She threw her finger out, pointing at Marlene, and opened her mouth to speak. Then her eyes slipped off Marlene's face and landed on the monstrosity on her neck.

Whatever Pen had been intending to shout, Marlene was pretty sure it wasn't the words that made their way out. "What in the Stepford Wife hell are you wearing?"

Marlene's defensive stance faltered, and she reached for the fabric flower, trying to block it from view. "What are you doing here, Penelope?"

Pen's eyes snapped back up to meet hers and she said in a low voice edged with barely repressed rage, "I'm here to tell you that you're an idiot. And not just for that stupid blouse you're wearing."

It took Marlene until that moment to realize she hadn't been directing any of her anger at Pen. She'd saved it all for Abby since Abby had been the one she'd been in a relationship with. Seeing Pen here, standing in her bank parking lot, looking her in the eye, after what she'd done, fury like nothing she'd ever felt flared white-hot in Marlene.

"How dare you show up where I work. This is beyond inappropriate," Marlene said in a low whisper.

"You know what's inappropriate?" Pen asked in a voice far too loud for public. "The way you acted toward Abby."

"Not here." Marlene looked around the empty parking lot.

"Then tell me where we can talk because I'm not leaving until I rip you a new asshole."

Fear of embarrassment quickly overcame her anger and Marlene unlocked her SUV. "Get inside and keep your voice down."

Marlene checked all around, making sure no one saw them getting into her car together, while Pen clambered into the passenger seat. Once she had the door firmly shut, Marlene said, "You have five minutes. I have a meeting."

"I don't care about your meeting. Why would you say those things to Abby?" Pen asked.

Marlene's control broke and she threw her arms in the air. "Oh, I don't know. Maybe it has something to do with how she left my bed and hopped right into yours without taking a breath?"

Lines of indignation and confusion etched Pen's face. "What in the hell are you talking about?"

That was not how Marlene thought she'd react. Not by a long shot. Pen had never been coy about her conquests before. She was respectful of her bedfellows, Marlene included, but she didn't hide or deny anything they'd done together. Why would she do that with Abby? All the confusion she'd felt after Abby's hurt reaction flared again.

"She was kneeling between your legs, her head bent over your lap. You were moaning. It doesn't take a genius to figure it out," Marlene said.

"No one would ever accuse you of being a genius." Pen glared at her and Marlene had never seen such a look of disgust on her face. "We were not having sex."

Now she was just being insulting. Marlene had no interest in being made a fool of by Abby and she certainly wasn't interested in it from Pen. "Sure, and I bet next you'll tell me you haven't been flirting with Abby either?"

"Of course I have. I flirt with everyone and so does she. It doesn't mean anything."

"It means something to me." Marlene hadn't meant to shout, and her eyes darted around the parking lot again. She needed to get control of herself. She couldn't have anyone at work see or hear any of this, but she was so mad and confused. Pen was sitting here, acting like cheating didn't matter. Like she hadn't ruined everything. Pen could have anyone she wanted. Hell, she'd already had just about everyone and she could have them all again. All Marlene had was Abby. At least she used to have Abby. Couldn't she just have one thing? One person to make her feel for one heartbeat the way Pen must feel all the time. Unstoppable. Invincible. Happy.

Pen spoke with remarkable calm given the way Marlene had shouted. "Your insecurities are not my problem and it's a damn shame they're Abby's."

Pen just didn't get it. Someone like her never would. It wasn't insecurity. It was the way everyone else walked through the world like they belonged. Like they had it all figured out and so the world gave them what they wanted. Marlene never got what she wanted. Even when she did, she never got to keep it.

"I shouldn't have to explain, but I will anyway." Pen shifted her weight and showed off her cane. She winced at even that brief movement and went back to her previous posture quickly. "I twisted my ankle at her studio and Abby was helping me take my shoe off. My foot was swelling and it hurt."

Marlene didn't accept the answer right away, but she allowed that it could account for the position where she'd found them. Pen's moan had been different from the ones she remembered from their night together. Was it because it was a sigh of relief? Honestly, Marlene didn't know her well enough to decide.

"How could she possibly have been doing that anyway? My pants were on," Pen said.

"I didn't look closely enough to notice," Marlene snapped back.

"But you still accused Abby of cheating?"

Marlene dropped her head into her hands. She peeled apart the memory in her head. Had Pen been wearing her pants? She hadn't noticed. "I jumped to conclusions, okay. Your reputation proceeds you, especially with me."

"What about Abby's reputation? Why don't you trust your girlfriend?" Pen asked.

"It's not about trusting Abby." Why had she been so sure Abby was cheating on her? What had she done? "What could Abby possibly see in me?" Marlene's chest was too tight to take full breaths. Her words were weak and quiet without enough air behind them. "I don't know anything. What can I offer Abby when there are more experienced women out there? Women like you. Women who are good at being girlfriends. Women who are good at sex."

"You know it isn't a turn on to be so damn insecure. In fact, it's a total turnoff."

"That's easy for you to say. You're amazing in bed," Marlene said in a strangled whisper.

"Yeah. That's true. I am." Pen's smirk was disgusting, but her voice was kind. "But you are, too, and even if you weren't, that's no reason to treat Abby like garbage."

Marlene couldn't stop blinking as Pen's words penetrated her mind. She thought of the ways Pen had moved beneath her when they'd gone to bed together. The way Abby had moved. But Pen was just trying to make her feel better, right? Not that she'd done that at all today, but her words didn't make sense.

"You don't think I'm bad in bed?"

"I didn't say that. I said you were amazing in bed. Much better than not bad," Pen said.

"That's not true."

"Of all the people you know, who do you think would be best qualified to determine if someone is good in bed?"

"You."

"Exactly."

"I know I'm not good, though."

"Tell me why," Pen said.

Marlene didn't want to. She didn't want to talk about it. She didn't even want to think about it. But she did all the time. It was why she had been so nervous with Abby. It was why she couldn't even touch herself.

"Before Abby, I dated a woman named Dawn."

Pen said, "Yeah. I know Dawn."

Of course she did. Marlene didn't want to know how well, so she didn't ask. "She broke up with me. Right before Abby moved in."

"Okay."

Marlene swallowed hard. She closed her eyes so she didn't have to see Pen's face when she admitted the thoughts she'd never been able to put into words. "We had sex the night before. I don't—um—I don't know when she decided to leave, but she rented a truck and she got her brother to take the day off work."

"So she'd planned it. She knew she was leaving before she had sex with you."

Marlene nodded, begging Pen to understand so she wouldn't have to say the words.

"Breakup sex is pretty shitty if you ask me, but that actually means she enjoyed having sex with you. She wanted it one last time."

"You don't get it." Marlene spoke the next words to her steering wheel. She wasn't sure she wanted Pen to hear the words anyway. "She was giving me a chance to save the relationship. If I'd been better—if I'd filled her needs—she would've called it off. She would've stayed."

Pen was quiet for a long time. Eventually, Marlene mustered the strength to look over. Pen's eyes were kind, all hint of her anger completely gone. "Is that what you really want? For Dawn to have stayed?"

Marlene shook her head. "No, but I can't help wondering if I could have made her stay."

"Did she tell you that was the point of the sex, or did you just spin this whole narrative in your head?"

"It's not a narrative."

"So she didn't say it. You just assumed it?"

"She said something." Marlene swallowed hard against the thickness in her throat. "She said butches don't bottom."

Pen's laughter was so unexpected Marlene jumped. "First of all, that's utter bullshit. Anyone can bottom. Butches can do whatever the hell they want, just like femmes or anyone else."

"You don't get it."

"Hey, Marlene." Pen waited for Marlene to look at her before she asked, "When we had sex, where was I when I came?"

The thought of their night together didn't send a thrill through her the way it used to, especially given her current mood, but she still remembered every moment vividly. Looking down at Pen's face, frozen in a moment of pure ecstasy, had been incredible. And she had been looking down. Pen, for all her confidence and butchness, had wanted Marlene to top her.

"I'm pretty sure you're like me," Pen said, saving Marlene from answering the question. "At least you were a switch like me that night."

This had not been covered in her lesbian lessons, but Marlene could figure out from context clues what Pen was talking about. Maybe later she would take time to figure that part out for herself, but right now she only had the energy to allow that maybe Dawn had been wrong.

"Look." Pen sat back, cradling her cane between both hands and looking for all the world like some suave billionaire. "You're being an idiot, we've established that."

"Hey."

Pen ignored her and continued. "I understand. I was an idiot for so long it might as well have been a career. I kept myself unhappy for years because I didn't think I deserved love."

"But your girlfriend?"

"Yeah, she forced me to stop being an idiot." Pen's lips curled in a wistful smile. "If a woman like her thinks I'm enough, than I must be."

Images of Abby ran through Marlene's head. The way she always made Marlene accept her successes. The way she wouldn't let her get down on herself. The way she made Marlene feel like the coolest person in a room, even when she wasn't.

Pen yanked the handle to open her door. "If a woman like Abby thinks you're enough, you damn sure are enough. I wasted a decade when I could have had the woman of my dreams. Don't be as big an idiot as I am. You can fix this."

Five o'clock hadn't rolled around yet, so Abby didn't have a lot to do. There were a few early arrivals at Riveter's—there always were—but mostly she was just standing around, polishing glasses and waiting for the night to start. Normally, this was a fun part of the evening. The music coming through the speakers was still low and the lights were still high. The atmosphere was charged, like the air before a thunderstorm. Waiting on the edge of excitement. The tension wasn't exciting to Abby today. Nothing was as exciting as usual to Abby these days.

Austin strolled up to her. "How're you doing?"

"I'm fine."

"You don't really look fine."

"I don't really feel fine, but I'm getting there," Abby said.

"I'm really sorry things worked out this way. I really thought Marlene was better than the others."

Abby put the glass down but didn't pick up another. She couldn't think of a compelling reason to do much of anything. "I'm starting to wonder if anyone is better than the others."

"Don't do that," Austin said. She looked so defeated, just as defeated as Abby felt. "Don't let her change you. My Abby wouldn't give up on love because of one jerk."

She was right, of course. Abby wasn't the type to let a breakup crush her. Make her sad, sure. Make her question the whole idea of happiness? Never. The truth was, Abby had thought Marlene was different, too.

The door crashed open, drawing Abby's attention. Austin stiffened beside her, prepared as always to be half bartender, half bouncer. When she saw it was Marlene rushing toward her, Abby's lungs froze. It was such a cruel irony, the way her body reacted to the sight of Marlene with regret now when so recently she had taken Abby's breath away in a much more pleasant way. Less than a week had passed, but already she had adapted to her new reality.

"You've got a lot of nerve coming here," Austin said with a growl.

Marlene's eyes darted up to Austin's face, but only for a second. They returned to Abby and stuck. She still had beautiful eyes. Brown like rich hardwood and set into her round, soft face that made her look like a shy teenager. But she wasn't shy and she wasn't so young. There were lines around her eyes Abby hadn't seen before. Maybe they were strain and maybe they were pain.

It wasn't just her face that had changed. She was wearing the most ridiculous outfit Abby had ever seen on her. A floral shirt with an oversized fabric flower on the neck and pants cut to accentuate her hips. Marlene looked like she'd been dressed by someone who had never met her but had a vague sense of what a professional woman was supposed to wear. Her hair was too long. Everything about her appearance was wrong.

"It's okay." Abby turned to see Austin's incredulity. "Can you give us a minute?"

Abby walked to the corner of the bar. It was as far as they could get from the patrons nursing their drinks and Austin's scowl.

"Thanks for giving me a chance to talk. I know I don't deserve it," Marlene said.

Abby crossed her arms and forced herself to look into Marlene's eyes. "This isn't about what you deserve. It's about what I deserve. I want an explanation. How could you think so little of me?"

Marlene said, "You're right. You do deserve an explanation. I'm the jerk here. You didn't do anything wrong."

Abby forgave her the interruption, since she was obviously eager to explain. At least she recognized that she had screwed up. That was an important step. She decided to wait and see what her other steps were like.

Abby said, "Then what exactly happened?"

"I misunderstood what I saw." Marlene fumbled through the explanation, her words tripping over one another. "I rushed to judgment. I just talked to Pen. She explained that I didn't see what I thought I saw. I'm so sorry. I saw you kneeling there in front of Pen the way you had with me the night before and I just lost my mind. I wish I could take it all back."

Marlene stopped speaking, going silent with that hopeful smile that used to melt Abby's heart. It did not melt her heart today. In fact, it stoked her already raging anger. She was so furious she had trouble forming her thoughts. Her ears rang and her teeth locked together, grinding against each other until her jaw ached. She was silent so long she had the opportunity to watch the smile melt off Marlene's face.

"Let me get this straight." Abby's voice trembled with forced calm. "It took Pen to convince you? You could believe her but not me?"

"Not exactly." Marlene's stammering was worse now. Her eyes darted around the room, never looking in one direction for too long. "We hadn't discussed monogamy or anything like that. It wasn't about cheating. It was just about being with someone else. Someone like Pen. And so soon after we had been together."

"Stop." Abby had barely said the word when Marlene's mouth shut with an audible click. The silence felt good. Not having to hear Marlene's voice felt good. Abby had been angry before in her life, but she could not remember feeling anything like this. This hurricane of anger, sadness, and deep, penetrating exhaustion. "You don't know me at all."

"It's not you." Marlene was practically hopping on her toes, eager to make everything so much worse. "It's me. Don't you see? I could never understand what you saw in me in the first place. I thought you were just—I don't know—being nice?"

Abby's thinly controlled calm cracked. "Being nice?"

"That came out wrong."

"No, Marlene. I think it came out just exactly how you intended it." Abby's fury had taken over her conscious mind. "You thought that I gave you a pity fuck and then had to go see Pen after to get myself taken care of."

Abby hadn't cursed in years, and the foreign word felt good on her lips. Felt powerful. She had never been the sort to revel in another's pain, but the way Marlene flinched at her anger felt powerful, too.

"You think what? I faked it with you? Never wanted you? I don't know how you think apologies go, Marlene, but this isn't it."

"Abby, please."

"No. Go, Marlene. Just go."

Tears rimmed Marlene's eyes. Soon they would cascade down her round cheeks. It didn't feel good to see that, but they were an end. At least Abby had her answers, even though she felt foolish for wanting them.

Marlene said, "Please give me another chance."

It was tempting. Despite it all, Abby still knew she had the capacity to love Marlene. To maybe even be happy with Marlene. All she had to do was say yes.

"I can't do that." Abby took a deep breath and the air spread her lungs to the point of pain. "I love myself too much. You should try it sometime. You'll never find love with someone else when you hate yourself so much."

"I do love myself. I can love myself."

"You don't and you know why? You've been hiding behind your job and your image for so long you don't even know how to have your own life. You let everyone change you. You bend over backward to be professional and successful. You think it makes you an adult, but all it really does is keep you alone." Abby indicated the ridiculous blouse and tiny heels with a sneer. "You don't love yourself. That's why you've put this costume back on."

Marlene took a step back. Her lips trembled and then the tears broke through the barrier and poured down her face. The tears were Abby's final straw.

"And you don't get to do that. You don't get to cry. You don't get to act hurt here. Not after what you did. Not after what you thought."

Marlene's head dropped and Abby's heart thudded hard against her ribs. Why did she have to do that now? Why did she have to be so sweet and injured?

The gesture thawed her enough to say, "I'm going to say this because there's part of me that will always care about you. Stop letting that job do this to you. Stop letting Brad do this to you. Stop letting him change you. You're worth standing up for."

Abby couldn't stand there anymore. She couldn't wait for Marlene to respond or watch her go. It was too much. All of this was too much. She turned around to find Austin nearby, holding out a clean bar towel. That was when she felt the tears on her own face. They were mostly tears of anger, but they were mingled with tears of sadness and so many tears of regret. She took the towel but waved Austin off. Her feet carried her away from the bar and the staring patrons toward the stockroom. Once she got there, she collapsed onto the stool in the corner and covered her face with the towel. She sobbed for so long her throat hurt and her arms ached from holding up the towel.

Chapter Twenty-seven

Marlene's mind was empty and her heart was numb as she drove home from Riveter's. She probably should have gone back to the bank, but she couldn't stand to walk past all those staring eyes. She couldn't stand that Ellie wouldn't stare. Ellie hadn't looked at her or spoken to her since their argument. That was to be expected, but it was still too much for Marlene to bear.

She'd thought it would be worth it to miss the managers meeting when she drove to Riveter's. That she'd be able to explain or take the hit for it if only she had Abby back. Now she had nothing and nothing she could do would change that. So instead she drove home so early there wasn't any traffic. She couldn't remember ever driving home this early. At least not since she was promoted to branch manager. Other folks had an early day once a week if they worked Saturday. Marlene never took hers. There was always something to do. A client to call. A loan to close. Some reason to keep her at the job Abby thought she hid behind.

Abby.

Her name was like a drumbeat in Marlene's mind as she drove. Her voice was like a knife. How had things gone so wrong? After Pen's visit, she thought everything would be okay. God, could that really have just been this afternoon? Today felt like it had lasted a lifetime. Maybe it was the roller coaster of emotion. Her day had started empty and alone. Then Pen's talk had given her hope. After her visit to the bar, Marlene wasn't sure she'd ever feel hope again.

She knew she wouldn't feel happiness again. She would never have with anyone else what she'd had with Abby and now it was clear she would never have Abby. She didn't deserve Abby. Not after the way she acted.

That thought filled the emptiness of her mind as she attempted to park in her driveway. It was a complete disaster. She had to pull out and start over twice. She eventually managed to get the SUV parked, but she wasn't sure she'd ever be able to get it out again. Her final parking space was so close to the balcony column that she had to climb over the console and get out through the passenger door.

She didn't notice Mr. Phan and Mrs. Fluffy watching her until she was out of the car. Mr. Phan's look of disapproval was expected. Mrs. Fluffy stared at Marlene and then squatted to pee on the sidewalk, maintaining eye contact the whole time. Marlene couldn't help taking the act as a sign of aggression.

Marlene could barely muster the energy to open her front door. The rest of her strength was used up by climbing the stairs to her bedroom. Staring at the double doors, she thought of Abby's first day in the condo. She unlatched the slide lock on the second door and threw them open together, but she didn't feel grand walking across the threshold. She felt like a child pretending to be a princess while home alone after school.

Taking a moment to relock the second door, Marlene's thoughts stuck with Abby and the day she moved in. That had been three months ago, almost to the day. It was a new record for Marlene. Building and ruining a friendship in less than a quarter. Building and ruining a relationship in less than a week actually wasn't a record for her. She was the queen of fucking up when people cared about her. Probably because Abby was right. She had never learned to love herself. She certainly didn't love herself now. After all, she was to blame for the cold, empty condo around her and the cold, empty life she lived inside it.

Because she couldn't help punishing herself, Marlene walked down the carpeted hall to the door of Abby's bedroom. She couldn't really call it Abby's bedroom anymore though, could she? The bed was stripped down to the bare mattress and the closet was empty. A few boxes stood in the corner, neatly packed and ready to be collected.

The last remnants of their time together. Marlene wondered if she'd even had time to fully unpack.

The guest bathroom was equally bare. The counter was gleaming and the fake lemon scent of glass cleaner still hung in the air. Even in her leaving, Abby had been considerate. Far more so than Marlene had ever been.

Even as she chastised herself, Marlene heard Abby's voice in her head, telling her this was why she was alone. She was so quick to berate herself. So eager to tear herself down. Why was that? The world was doing a fair job on its own, why was Marlene so eager to join in the pile-on? She caught a glimpse of herself in the freshly cleaned mirror. The ridiculous blouse and the pleated slacks. The way her hair hung limply just above her shoulders. Marlene slapped at the light switch, plunging the room into darkness. The light spilling in from the hallway showed her outline but not her features.

In this light, she looked how she felt. Like an empty shell, waiting to be filled up by someone else. That's what she'd always been. A vessel for everyone else's expectations. First her father and his insistence on her professional success. Then one boyfriend after another, looking for arm candy or comfort or God knew what. Even Lucy had molded her into what she wanted. The daughter she'd never had. A protégé. Then Lucy had moved on and left her to Brad. And here she was, letting Brad change her into what he wanted. A woman who hated herself and bent to his vision. A woman in her place.

The only thing Marlene had ever done for herself was love women. Pen had opened Marlene's eyes to a chance at happiness. At pleasure. At a life lived outside the costume of femininity she'd tried to wear for so long. Then Dawn had shown her that women could be just as cruel and careless as men. But Abby. Abby had let her be herself. Abby had taught her without molding her. Had supported her and loved her. She hadn't said the words—neither of them had—but Abby had shown Marlene more love in a week-long relationship than anyone else Marlene had ever been with.

Marlene's head swam and her heart ached. She couldn't think anymore. She couldn't regret. She went back to her bedroom and briefly considered crawling into bed and letting this terrible day end before most people even ended their workday. The bed looked too big and too cold, though. She wandered into her bathroom, drawn by the massive tub in the corner. Abby had used the tub more than once. Marlene never had. Yet another luxury item she collected but didn't care about.

It took her a lot of trial-and-error fiddling with the dual knobs to find the right water temperature. Once the tub was noticeably filling, she stripped naked, tossing her work clothes into a heap in the corner. She doubted she could ever wear the outfit again.

Watching the water level rise with an apathy bordering on catatonia, Marlene waited, shivering slightly. Once the tub was full, she turned off the taps, only then realizing she should have used bubble bath or bath salts. The water looked so sad, just clear, steaming water rather than the scented, bubbly oasis she saw in movies. It didn't matter, though, she'd never bought bubble bath in her life and she wasn't even sure what bath salts were other than a cheap street drug on the news.

She carefully climbed the two stairs built into the tub enclosure and then over the rim. She yelped in pain, the water far hotter than she had anticipated, but she was already halfway in the tub and couldn't decide whether to yank her foot back out or put the other one in. She spent a long few moments, gritting her teeth through the discomfort, one leg in, the rest of her awkwardly perched on the rim. Eventually, she adjusted to the heat and decided she might as well climb the rest of the way in.

Each time a new body part met the water, Marlene hissed and waited to adjust. The tub was divided into two sections, one larger and wider, one smaller and tucked into the corner in a roughly heart-shaped design. She didn't know which side she should use, but the smaller side seemed logical. If she thought she'd be more stable in the smaller end, she was mistaken. When she sat down, her butt slid along the slippery bottom, dunking her head below the scalding water. She came up sputtering and choking, but managed to wedge herself against one side so she didn't slide down again.

She was not comfortable. She had to keep her legs locked and fully stretched out to stay still. The water was still too hot and her shoulders were cold where they stuck out. One elbow was stuck between her side and the tub wall and the pressure of the hot water around her neck was not unlike a pair of hands around her throat.

Obviously, she was doing this wrong. Abby had loved this tub. Said she'd never felt so relaxed as when she soaked in here. Other people raved about bubble baths on the weekend and dozing off in the comfort of their tubs. Marlene was so utterly bad at life, she couldn't even take a bath right.

The tears she'd been holding back since Abby told her to stop crying came then. They burst out of her in a sob she knew the neighbors would be able to hear. She didn't care. In fact, she sobbed again, louder this time to try pushing the shame out. She forgot to be quiet and she forgot to be small and she cried like she never had in her life. She cried for the loneliness she'd never be able to shake and she cried for hurting Ellie. She cried for herself wearing clothing that made her feel horrible and she cried for the fear of losing her job. But more than anything, she cried for Abby. For the need to have Abby in her life. For the love she felt way too soon and way too strong. For losing a woman who looked at her like Abby looked at her. Who touched her how Abby had, body and soul. She cried and she did not feel better.

Eventually, she ran out of tears. She splashed water on her face and found it wasn't too hot anymore. In fact, it was deliciously warm. She wasn't uncomfortable, either. Her shoulders had slipped underwater, and the warmth had eased some of her tension. She wasn't holding herself in place. Her body had found an equilibrium between floating and lying in the tub. Marlene wiggled her toes, letting the warm water slide between them.

When the water got cold, Marlene drained the tub and climbed out. Wrapping herself in a towel, she caught sight of her reflection in the mirror. Her eyes were puffy and red-rimmed, but her skin looked smooth and lightly pink. She wiped steam off the mirror so she could see to comb her hair.

Marlene knew her hair had gotten long, but she hadn't stopped to think about how long. As she combed out tangles, she thought back to when she'd last had hair this long. It was before she came out. Before she'd accepted how much she hated the feel of cold, wet strands of hair sticking to her back and shoulders the way they were now. She stood there and stared into the mirror, seeing the woman she had been before she'd come out. Before she did anything for herself.

She hadn't meant to throw the comb down so hard, but the sound of the plastic cracking against the tile by her foot was wonderfully satisfying. She grabbed her cell phone from the bedroom but returned to look at herself in the mirror while it rang. Her stylist picked up on the fourth ring, her voice thin and strained.

"Hey, Raven," Marlene said. "If I paid you triple, would you be able to cut my hair right now? I know the workday's over and you want to get home to your family, but it's an emergency. I'll pay whatever you ask."

CHAPTER TWENTY-EIGHT

How are you?" Austin asked as she let Abby into her apartment.

Abby sighed. "I don't really know how to answer that question."

Austin pulled her into a long hug and Abby held on tight. Austin gave the best hugs. Her height and her powerful arms mixed with her warmth were like a weighted blanket, driving the sadness out of Abby's bones. Well, most of it. It would take more than one hug to erase the disaster of this week.

Once Abby was settled on the couch, her legs tucked beneath her and a bottle of her favorite kombucha in hand, she felt almost ready to take on the tale of her breakup. She didn't want to rehash it all, but she was prepared to throw all that anger and indignation Austin's way. There was no one better to vent to than her best friend.

"I didn't hear much of what you two said the other night, but I think I got some of the story." Austin said. "Was it the flirting thing?"

Abby choked on her sip of pineapple-peach deliciousness. "What is that supposed to mean? What flirting thing?"

"You flirting with everyone. Is that why Marlene broke it off?" Austin asked.

"I don't flirt with everyone."

"Abby." Austin said her name with a disbelieving air. "Of course, you do."

"I'm nice to everyone. That's not flirting."

"Call it what you want, it clearly bothered Marlene."

"How do you know that? Did she say something to you? Why didn't you tell me?"

"You need me to tell you that your girlfriend didn't like you flirting with other people?" Austin asked.

"I'm a bartender. It's part of the job," Abby said.

"Well then, you do that part of the job really well." Austin's eyebrows crinkled together. "Wait, you really don't know how much that bothered her?"

Abby wasn't about to admit that it had come up during the breakup. Austin didn't need to know that. "What did she say to you?"

"She didn't say anything. I just saw her in Riveter's like a week and a half ago? You were flirting with Pen and Marlene looked like she was going to cry right there at the bar. I thought you talked about it?"

"We did talk. I told her it wasn't like that," Abby said.

"That doesn't sound like an apology," Austin said.

How dare Austin act like this was her fault? "Because I didn't have anything to apologize for." Abby's voice grated at her throat. "Why are you attacking me like this? Aren't you supposed to be my friend?"

"I am your friend."

"Then stop blaming me for my broken heart." Abby's voice rang off the windowpane. She took a slow breath to calm down, but it didn't do much.

Austin leapt out of her chair and dropped on the couch next to her. "I'm sorry. I wasn't trying to blame you. Even if that was the reason, it doesn't make you the bad guy."

"Because I'm not the bad guy here," Abby said. But was she? Marlene had mentioned the flirting, but it wasn't like that was the issue. The issue was Marlene thought Abby was the type of woman to cheat. To sleep around. That wasn't her fault. That was all Marlene.

Austin pulled her into a hug, but Abby couldn't bring herself to hug back. She was too emotionally bruised. Too raw. She let Austin hug her and then offered a weak thank you before Austin went back to her side of the couch. Still, she couldn't get the accusation out of her mind, no matter how ridiculous it was.

"That was a really shitty way to start this conversation," Austin said. "I'm sorry, Abby. I don't know what came over me."

"Do you think I would sleep around?"

"What? No. Never."

"But I flirt with everyone, so it would be reasonable to think I would act on the flirting." Abby hated saying the words, but maybe they were true. If Austin's first thought was the breakup was about the flirting, and Austin knew her better than anyone else, maybe it was the issue. Why would Marlene think that of her unless Abby had given her reason to be suspicious?

"No, of course not. I know you better than that," Austin said.

"But Marlene doesn't."

"That's her fault. She didn't take the time to get to know you," Austin said with surprising heat.

"We've only really known each other for three months. You've known me for years and you still thought the flirting was the problem," Abby said. Austin blushed and looked away. "She assumed I was keeping my options open. That I hadn't fully committed to her."

"But that's not what you were doing," Austin said.

"Maybe I was?"

Abby closed her eyes and tried desperately to see herself from someone else's perspective. Was it really so outrageous for Marlene to think she would cheat? She did flirt. She always had. Ever since she was a teenager. She'd always been heavier than her friends and that meant her body developed first. It had been fun to use the extra attention to her advantage. She'd gotten very good at flirting and teasing with her body, but it had always been about feeling powerful in her own skin. Marlene couldn't know that, of course. All she saw was her girlfriend openly flirting with other women.

"Wait. Are you saying you were trying to sleep with Pen?" Austin asked.

"No way. I have no interest in Pen." Abby set her drink down. It was starting to sweat and she didn't like the clammy feeling on her palms. Or maybe her palms were clammy because she was embarrassed. "But I've used my tits and sexy banter to get my way my whole life."

"That doesn't mean you're doing anything wrong. All of us know you don't mean it."

"Marlene didn't."

"Marlene was waiting for a reason to prove she wasn't good enough for you. I barely know her and I can tell her self-esteem is in the toilet," Austin said.

"And me flirting around her sure didn't help that." Abby dropped her head in her hands. Maybe she should have had this conversation with Austin the other night. If she had realized how unkind she'd been to Marlene, maybe she wouldn't have blown up like she did.

"Her insecurities are not your fault."

"Everyone keeps saying that," Abby said into her hands. "But if my actions made her feel bad about herself, aren't I partially to blame? I flirt to manipulate people and it works. Even if it's just to make me feel good, it's still a manipulation."

"It's harmless."

"It's anything but." Abby could see it all so clearly now. How had she missed this for so many years? How had her friends let her get away with this? "It's not fair to the people in my life. It keeps all my relationships shallow."

"I don't think our relationship is shallow."

Austin looked so hurt, a pang of regret shot through Abby. She probably should be having this conversation with someone else, but it was too late now. All she could do was start repairing the damage she had done.

"It's not shallow, Austin. You're one of the most important people in my life. But don't you see? When I joke and flirt with you, I'm usually deflecting. Protecting the parts of me I don't want you to see or ask about."

"We all do that."

"But I do it better, darling." Abby caught herself lowering her voice to a coy drawl. "Sorry. See? I do it all the time and I don't even think about it."

"As far as bad habits go, you could do a lot worse."

"Yeah, but it is a bad habit. I could use my flirting powers to make a partner feel special. By focusing all my attention on her. That would've meant the world to Marlene."

"Maybe so," Austin said.

There was a bittersweet note to Austin's response, but it wasn't half as bitter as Abby's. "But it's too late now."

Austin was quiet for a long time. Abby didn't look at her. She looked at her hands and thought about the last three months. How wonderful it had been to get to know Marlene. To grow close and fall for her. It had been the first relationship in a long time that had formed organically. No dating app or setup from a friend. Just her making a new friend who turned out to be more than that. Maybe it was that organic growth that had made the relationship feel so special so fast. Maybe it had been Marlene herself.

Flirting felt good. It made her feel powerful and sexy and special. But Marlene made her feel powerful and sexy and special, but also seen and heard in ways that other girlfriends hadn't. She felt cared for, and that was so much more powerful than flirting ever made her feel.

"I'm sorry it didn't work out," Austin said.

"Yeah. Me too."

❖

"We need to talk."

Marlene could see Ellie preparing for a fight by the way her shoulders stiffened and her knees bent ever so slightly. She turned from the copier, a glower in place and her jaw set. The moment she saw Marlene, though, her body relaxed. Maybe a little too much since she dropped the pages she'd been holding.

It felt good to see Ellie relax around her. It had been too long since her friend looked at her like this. Like she expected to be happy after their conversation. She decided to lean into the feeling. Or more accurately, lean into Ellie. She reached out and wrapped her arms around Ellie's shoulders, pulling her into a hug.

"I'm really sorry for everything I said and did. I was a jerk. I hope you can forgive me some day," Marlene said.

Ellie didn't return the hug, but at least she didn't push Marlene away. Normally she wouldn't have hugged someone without their permission, but she was starting to learn that it was okay to make a big gesture and show people how she felt.

"You're wearing a tie," Ellie said.

Marlene had played this moment over in her head a million times. Sometimes Ellie forgave her. Sometimes Ellie told Marlene never to talk to her again. None of the possible outcomes Marlene imagined included a random comment about her attire. Marlene pulled back from the hug to find Ellie staring at her, her mouth slightly open as she scanned Marlene from head to toe.

"It's my favorite tie." Marlene smoothed the royal blue silk along her chest. "You gave it to me as a coming out present. It's the first tie I ever owned."

"It matches your hair."

Marlene laughed and rubbed the short hairs at the back of her neck. She loved the new cut. It was even shorter than she'd worn it after coming out. It faded down the sides of her head until it was so tight against her scalp she could barely see it. The crown pulled into a pompadour, though she wasn't great at styling it yet so there was a single, stubborn curl over her forehead. She supposed it was all the more striking because of the vivid blue hair color.

"Do you like it?"

A slow smile crept across Ellie's face. "You look like such a dyke right now."

Marlene's heart raced with a surge of adrenaline. It was a feeling she used to hate, but it was growing on her. "That's what I was going for."

Marlene smoothed her tie again, this time buttoning her pinstriped suit jacket, too. It hugged her shoulders and her chest. She'd had the suit tailored back when she'd bought it months ago, and she was happy to find that it still felt perfect even after weeks hidden in the back of her closet.

Ellie's face fell. "So are you done with the bows and the heels and all that shit?"

"Completely done."

Marlene had tossed all those clothes, both the new ones and the ones she'd hung onto after coming out, into a massive garbage bag and donated them to a charity store.

"That's good. I've missed my friend," Ellie said.

"I've missed me, too."

"How long will it last this time?"

Marlene deserved that, she knew it. She'd be doing a lot of groveling today and she'd prepared for it. Before she could assure Ellie, however, she heard a familiar voice behind her.

"What the hell is going on here?" Brad asked, his voice vibrating with rage.

Marlene turned to look at him and was thrilled to see his face purpling with anger. This interaction was going exactly how she'd imagined it would.

Marlene kept her voice professional and calm. "Ellie, could you excuse us, please?"

Before Ellie could make it back to her desk, Brad stepped in front of her, blocking her path. "Marlene was supposed to have a discussion with you about your clothing and manner." The last word came with a curled lip and disgusted once over. "Obviously that didn't happen."

"Actually, it did," Ellie said. "And I told her what I'll tell you. I am not violating the bank's dress code and I won't be changing either my clothing or my manner for you."

"I think I know the dress code of my own institution."

"Obviously not." Ellie always loved a good fight, and Marlene could see how eager she was for this one. "I made absolutely certain before I took this job that there would be space here for my queerness."

Marlene watched with interest as Brad shuddered at the word. Not too very long ago, she would have been mortified to see such obvious contempt from a superior. But she'd finally lost interest in what people like Brad thought of her.

"This is a workplace. There's no place for anyone's lifestyle here," Brad said.

"It's not a lifestyle. Being a lesbian is who I am," Ellie said.

"Whatever you want to call it, it doesn't belong in the workplace."

"Well, you can't fire me for being a lesbian."

Now that she allowed herself more perspective, Marlene could see that Brad usually had tight control over his emotions. She could also see that his control was slipping. He usually chose his words carefully, preferring to let the listener infer what he wanted rather than issue a direct command. Apparently, he'd had enough of that. He glanced around the lobby, noting the empty desks, before he let his sneer really show.

"No, but I can fire you for insubordination." Brad's smirk was infuriating and Marlene's contempt for the man grew by the second. "A woman wearing pants, let alone a men's suit, is not appropriate for a bank."

Marlene's blood pounded through her veins, making it hard to hear anything else. Here it was. He was finally doing it. Finally punishing the two of them for the crimes of being women and being queer. She'd been so worried about this moment. Had been avoiding it ever since Lucy retired. But now that it was here, she wasn't scared. She was excited. A little voice in the back of her head reminded her that she was brave. That she was worth fighting for. That voice sounded a lot like Abby, and it gave her strength.

Marlene took a step forward, positioning herself between Ellie and Brad. She allowed herself a smile. "I won't let you talk to my employee that way, Brad."

"I see today is a day for insubordination all around." He transferred his glare to Marlene. "I've had it with the two of you. You've been spoken to, but you refuse to listen. There's little enough room for women in a bank. Unless, of course, they're behind the teller line wearing a smile. You're fired. Both of you. Get out of my bank."

Marlene heard the click of heels over the pounding of blood in her ears. It sounded like victory. Brad stepped back, taking in the woman standing in Marlene's office door. He stood up straighter and forced a smile, but there was sweat on his brow and his face was still red.

"You didn't say you were meeting with a client, Marlene." He straightened his tie, adjusting the too-large knot under his chin. "You shouldn't have kept a client waiting."

"I'm not a client," the woman said. "And this conversation has been very illuminating."

Ellie was looking back and forth between Marlene, Brad, and the newcomer with open-mouthed confusion. Marlene felt an overwhelming desire to laugh so hard she cried.

"Brad, allow me to introduce Daniela Miller from Human Resources." Marlene held up the paper in her hands. With everything that had happened in the last few minutes, she'd forgotten the reason for her trip to the copier. "She asked to meet with me when she received my letter of resignation."

Ellie finally found her voice. "You're quitting? Why?"

Daniela took a step forward, positioning herself at Marlene's shoulder. "She alleged discriminatory treatment from her direct supervisor. I asked for an interview to determine the validity of the claim, but it seems I don't need to burden Ms. Diggs with documenting your conduct. Do I, Mr. Carter?"

"There's a perfectly reasonable explanation for this," Brad said.

"Why don't you tell me what it is?" Daniela indicated the door of Marlene's office. Once Brad had gone inside, she asked Marlene, "Ms. Diggs, would you mind if I borrow your office for the rest of the day?"

"It's not my office anymore," Marlene said.

"I'd like the opportunity to change your decision. I think you'll find your working conditions will be very different after today."

"It wasn't just Brad's behavior." Marlene thought of all the ways she'd twisted herself into knots for this bank over a decade long career. "I don't think banking is for me."

"Your record speaks differently. I'd still like the opportunity to try."

"We'll see," Marlene said.

She could tell by the twinkle in Daniela's eye as she closed the office door that this was a woman who loved the chase. Maybe she could find a way to keep Marlene at FTL, but it would take a lot.

"You're seriously still quitting?" Ellie put a hand on Marlene's shoulder, drawing her attention away from the closed door.

"Yeah. I am."

"But you're the best."

"I hate this job, Ellie." Marlene gave her friend a sad smile. "Seeing you every day is the only good part of this job. The work makes me an anxious ball of stress."

"Why didn't you say anything?"

"I didn't know how bad this place was for me. I've been doing a lot of thinking and I just want to do something that makes me happy," Marlene said.

"What do you have in mind?"

"I don't know. I'll figure it out eventually."

"Wait. You quit your job without a backup? You?"

The way Ellie said that, with disbelief bordering on panic, really did make Marlene laugh. "Yeah. Me. I'm going to take some time off and figure out what I want."

"I have a feeling you know one thing you want."

"Yeah."

"How are you going to get Abby back?"

"I'm hoping showing up looking like myself is a good start. What do you think?"

Ellie pulled her into a bone-crushing hug. "I think it's a great start."

CHAPTER TWENTY-NINE

Thursday night was one of Abby's favorite nights to close, and tonight had been a lot of fun. The crowd had been lively, and the regulars had adapted pretty well to her new no flirting policy. In fact, most of them had seemed to enjoy the more authentic interactions. Even better than the energy of the crowd was the way they left promptly at the two a.m. closing time.

She and Austin had spent the next hour cleaning and restocking, chatting and laughing like old times. If she didn't let herself stop and think about the way she still missed Marlene or the way Pen and Kieran's guest bedroom had the cold, sterile feel of a hotel room, she would say that she was starting to feel almost like her old self.

Almost.

"Want to grab some fries and milkshakes over at the diner?" Austin asked.

Abby pushed through Riveter's back door and stepped out into the chill damp of early morning. It felt like rain soon and Abby pulled her jacket close around her.

"Not tonight. Pen's a light sleeper and I don't want to come in too late."

"Your loss. Peach milkshake season just started."

Austin stepped down onto the cracked cobblestones of the alley, shrugging into her coat. She waited for Abby to set the alarm and lock the door, but she was clearly itching to go. She was three steps ahead of Abby as they crossed into the dirt parking lot behind the bar.

"What the hell?" Austin said.

Abby had been digging in her purse for her keys, so she hadn't noticed Austin stop in her tracks. "What?"

Instead of answering, Austin pointed to a pair of cars in the middle of the lot. Abby squinted to see through the hazy glow of the streetlight. She saw the shimmer of her Mini and the hulking shadow of a much larger vehicle beside it, but that was about it. She took another step forward and a chunk of the shadow peeled away from the rest.

"Is she for real?" Austin asked.

"Is who for real?" Abby was starting to get nervous. She wasn't afraid of the dark and DC wasn't nearly as dangerous as everyone seemed to think, but she didn't love the idea of shadows moving in the dark. Instead of fighting to understand, she did the logical thing and walked right toward her car. She only got a few steps before she stopped again. With the street light farther behind her, she could make out the figure now.

It was Marlene. But it didn't look like the Marlene she'd seen last. This Marlene wasn't hunch-shouldered and hang-jawed. This Marlene was striding forward, her chest out and her chin up. She wasn't wearing some ridiculous women's power suit, she was wearing dark jeans and a tweed sport coat over a *Star Wars* graphic T-shirt. And her hair. It was cut short on the sides and styled up on top. She stopped a few feet away from Abby, the streetlight glowing off cobalt blue hair.

Perhaps for the first time in her life, Abby had no idea what to say. Her hands felt tingly and too big and she didn't know what to do with them. She could feel heat on her face and an even more persistent heat in her lower belly. When she first met Marlene, Abby had thought she was cute. As they got to know each other, she found her intriguing and charming. Now she was the sexiest thing Abby had ever seen on two legs.

Marlene seemed just as unsure what to do or say as Abby. For a long time, they just stared at each other. If Abby was honest, she couldn't think of much else she'd rather be doing than staring at this butched-out version of Marlene, standing there looking confident if a little nervous.

Austin cleared her throat, breaking the silence. "I'll leave you two alone to talk."

Marlene finally broke their eye contact and Abby swayed on her feet. She had been so absorbed in those beautiful brown eyes, it was like they were holding her up. She didn't hear the exact words Marlene said to Austin, but there was a thank you in there and a handshake passed between them. Abby struggled to compose herself in the lull. She didn't think she'd ever see Marlene again, much less see her like this.

"Is it okay that I'm here?" Marlene asked. "I didn't want to disturb you at work and I don't know where you're staying."

Abby couldn't help herself. "I'm staying with Penelope."

Marlene didn't flinch. She gave a small smile and said, "She's a good friend. I'm glad you have her in your life."

Somehow, this perfectly appropriate answer stoked Abby's anger. What right did Marlene have to come here, looking this hot and saying the right thing? "What? You're not going to accuse me of staying with her to make you jealous?"

"That's not the sort of thing you would do." Marlene looked at the toes of her boots. "I deserve that though."

Now that made her feel like a jerk. How was this going so badly for Abby? She sighed and shook off her anger. It wasn't like her to be catty. Besides, hadn't she just decided she had contributed to Marlene's feelings? She ought to be more understanding.

Abby sighed and said, "Shouldn't you be in bed at this hour? You have work tomorrow."

"I don't actually." Marlene's smile showed a relief Abby had rarely seen there, and never when she spoke about work. "I quit."

Abby was so shocked by this answer, she took a step back. "You what?"

"I quit. Turned in my resignation. They're trying to talk me into coming back, but they don't have anything to offer that I want."

The more Abby looked at her, the more transformed Marlene appeared. It wasn't just the clothes or the hair. It was the way she held her body. The way her shoulders sat relaxed but not slumped. The way her chest rose and fell more fully, as though she was taking free, unlabored breaths. This version of Marlene—this confident, comfortable woman—was exponentially more enticing than the Marlene who had come home exhausted every day. Or even the

Marlene who had watched movies or cooked dinner with her. This was the Marlene that Abby had been sure was there, but had never shown herself until now.

Abby's heart swelled to see Marlene this happy, but she doubted the change was permanent. Everyone felt good when they had a day off from work.

"If you're not going back to the bank, what do you have lined up?" Abby asked.

"Nothing."

"Nothing?"

"Well, I have a lot more lesbian movies to watch. And I have a dozen books to read. I'll start there," Marlene said.

"I meant for work. You're starting a new job soon, right?"

"Eventually, yeah. But I'm taking some time off. I have to figure out where I can work with this hair."

Abby laughed as Marlene ran a hand through her new, shorter cut. "I was going to ask about that."

"Do you like it?" There was a note in Marlene's voice—a quiet, pleading hope that Abby would approve.

"It looks great. Why blue?" Abby asked.

Marlene took a step closer, catching Abby's eyes with hers. It was too dark to make out the shade of brown, but Abby had plenty of memories of those eyes. They'd always had the power to capture her—hold her spellbound.

"It's the same color yours was the night I first saw you."

Abby's mouth went dry and her tongue felt too big for her mouth. All she could manage was a mumbled, "Oh."

Marlene reached out to take Abby's hand in hers. Her fingers were trembling, but her shoulders were firm and she never released Abby's eyes.

"I went home with Penelope that night," Marlene said in a whisper.

Abby slipped her fingers between Marlene's. They were warm from her pocket and her palm was soft. "I remember."

"For months, I've been sad looking back on that. Not because it happened, but because it didn't happen with you," Marlene said.

Abby tried to swallow, but her mouth was still too dry. The air in the parking lot felt heavier than it had a moment ago. Marlene was leaning closer. Not close enough for a kiss, but close enough to bring the electricity of her presence into Abby's orbit.

"I wanted to go home with you that night," Marlene said.

"You did?"

"Yeah."

Marlene felt so warm and so solid. Abby slipped her other hand on top of their joined ones. The back of Marlene's hand was just as soft as the palm, but stronger where knuckles and tendons gave her solidity.

"I'm not sad about that night anymore. I had to figure out a lot of things about myself before I was good enough to go home with you," Marlene said.

The words were like a bucket of water poured over Abby's head. She fell out of the trance Marlene's eyes had dragged her into and her jaw tightened painfully. "You see, this is the whole problem. You were always good enough. There was nothing wrong with you then and there is nothing wrong with you now."

Marlene pulled Abby back in with a gentle yank on their entwined hands. Abby was so surprised by the gesture—so out of character for the hesitant woman she had fallen for—that she stumbled forward. Marlene slid an arm around her waist, supporting her and drawing her close.

"I know that now. I didn't then." Marlene brushed her thumb along Abby's spine as she spoke, sending little bolts of electricity through Abby's limbs. "The only person I really had to convince was me."

"Exactly." Abby could barely force her lips to form the words. She was far more interested in pressing her lips against Marlene's. In remembering her taste. In letting herself fall all over again. No matter how much she told herself they had more to say to each other, she couldn't stop staring at Marlene's lips.

"I've done that now, and it's because of you. Because you gave me the space and the support to be myself. Because you love yourself and your gift is that you show other people how to do that, too."

Abby's heart was beating so fast, she felt lightheaded. Was this really happening? Was Marlene really here, holding her and saying all the right things? Had she really quit her job and colored her hair and found herself?

"I used to live in a black and white world, Abby. Either or. Be normal. Girls in pink dresses and boys in blue suits." Marlene brought Abby's hand to her lips and pressed a kiss on her knuckle. "You showed me a world full of color. It's hard to be a girl who likes blue suits, but you made me brave enough to be me. You brought color into my world."

Abby's brain was so busy buzzing with all Marlene's words that she wasn't sure it was a conscious decision to lean forward. It wasn't until her lips brushed against Marlene's that she realized what she was doing. She had fully intended to stop herself. To step back and finish the conversation. They couldn't make a fresh start without talking. But then Marlene tilted her head and pressed forward into the kiss and all thoughts of ending it vanished from Abby's mind.

Marlene had always been a good kisser, but confidence made her an amazing kisser. Her lips parted, deepening the kiss, and Abby was swept away. The first touch of their tongues was blissful. Marlene was gentle and strong. Her desire was evident in the passion of her touch with lips and tongue, but she wasn't insistent. She led and Abby was more than happy to follow.

Marlene broke the kiss. "I'm sorry. I didn't mean to do that."

Abby was slow to recover. Her eyelids felt glued together. Her body was on fire. Her heart so full. She recovered enough to realize Marlene was trying to step back, to separate their bodies as well as their lips. Abby was having none of that. She squeezed down on Marlene's fingers to prevent their escape and reached out for Marlene's other arm, wrapping it back around her side.

"I should be the one to apologize. I kissed you, but we have more to say," Abby said.

There was a sparkle in Marlene's eye that told Abby she was well-aware that she had been forgiven already, but, to her credit, she didn't take advantage. That's one of the many things Abby loved about Marlene. Even when she hadn't believed it, she had been brave.

"You're right," Marlene said. "I have more to say."

"I do, too, but you go first."

A hint of fear flashed in Marlene's eyes, but she overcame it quickly. She tightened her arm around Abby's waist, once again making it hard for Abby to focus on her words.

"I want to be that kind of partner for you, too. I want to be supportive and loving in a way I couldn't be until I loved myself. Will you give me another chance? A chance to love you right this time? Because I do. I love you, Abby."

Marlene may have wanted to say more. In fact, Abby was pretty sure her lips were still moving when Abby pulled her into another kiss. This time, she wasn't interested in following Marlene's lead. She wasn't interested in a reconnection. She was interested in making Marlene's toes curl. In showing Marlene how much those words had meant. Her kiss was a promise of more to come once they were in a place with a bed.

Abby ended the kiss by sucking Marlene's bottom lip into her mouth with a scrape of teeth. Marlene's eyes were clouded with the same lust that was coursing like fire through Abby's veins, but she had her own apology to make before they acted on it.

"To be clear, I love you, too." Abby's words made Marlene's lips twitch up in a punch-drunk sort of smile. "And I'm sorry, too."

"You don't have anything to be sorry for."

"Yes, I do." Abby took a deep breath and placed her palm on Marlene's chest. "I flirt with everyone and it isn't fair to you."

"I trust you."

"Thank you, but that doesn't mean it's okay. I flirt because I like attention and, honestly, it gets me what I want. That's not fair to the people I flirt with anymore than it's fair to a partner who would of course worry about my intentions. It's also not fair to me, because it keeps me from having honest interactions with people."

Abby slid her fingers up Marlene's shoulders and into the short hair at the back of her neck. She liked the way it tickled her fingertips and she liked even more the way Marlene shuddered at the contact.

"I'm going to work on it, but maybe you can help me if I backslide?" Abby batted her eyelashes at Marlene and noted the way her breath hitched. "We could work out some sort of punishment and reward situation."

Marlene's jaw fell open. "As long as you keep flirting like that with me."

"Always."

Marlene's goofy grin was so endearing, Abby had to place a kiss on the corner of her mouth. Then on the other corner. She slid her hand higher into Marlene's hair, up where the strands got longer, glowing bright blue in the moonlight.

"I really do like this color on you. What are you going to do when it washes out?"

"My stylist says it'll fade over the next six weeks. I'll pick a new color before then." She leaned down to put an open-mouthed kiss on Abby's neck. "You make me want to try every color of the rainbow."

The kiss awakened a new series of desires in Abby. It wasn't until her eyes were rolling shut that Marlene's words sunk in.

"Wait. You didn't use temporary color?"

"Nope." She slid her lips distractingly along Abby's neck. "I don't want to be temporary. I don't want to wear a costume anymore. I want to be brave."

"You'll have to be brave to be with me." Abby gasped as Marlene's lips wrapped around her earlobe. Her hands were also making an interesting journey along Abby's side. She made an experimental fist, holding on gently but firmly to Marlene's hair. It was just the right length for a fistful. That would come in handy later. "Oh yeah. I really like the way this hair feels."

"So do I," Marlene said. "It feels like me."

Abby tamped down her hormones, focusing on the words. Marlene had been here before. Or at least close to here. It hadn't worked out then, but Abby knew in her marrow that things were different now. Marlene was different now. Everything felt so new and fragile.

"How do you know this is the right thing to do?" Abby asked.

Marlene shrugged and her cheeks glowed with her smile. "When it feels right, you just know."

EPILOGUE

I s this seat taken?"
When Pen spoke from over her shoulder, Marlene had been splitting her focus between the beer bottle, sweating on a coaster in front of her, and Abby, mixing what looked like a very complicated drink across the bar.

Pen didn't wait for her to answer, but dropped onto the next stool. She dropped her phone on the bar and ran a hand through her hair. A few gray hairs flashed in the low light, but Pen was the kind of woman who made salt-and-pepper hair look sexy.

"What a day." As Pen spoke, she waved to Abby, who spread a wide smile between them. "At least the work week is half over."

"Um, it's Thursday night."

"When you're a Realtor, the weekends are the busiest workdays."

Abby presented the complicated drink to the rail-thin blonde and waggled an empty martini glass in their direction. Pen gave her a thumbs up, then made a heart shape with her two thumbs and pointer fingers. Marlene again lost herself in watching Abby make a drink.

Even though it was a simple martini this time, Abby's movements were no less impressive. Her hands flew across bottles, snatching them up, pouring, and setting them back in place in a single movement. She had a grace that was unparalleled, and it wasn't just mixing drinks. Marlene watched her paint occasionally and saw the same economy of movement. The same intense focus. It was confidence that made her fingers so nimble. A deep belief that she could perform the action flawlessly, and so she did. Of course, there was one place where Marlene appreciated Abby's confident dexterity more than any other.

Pen cleared her throat, reminding Marlene that she'd been silent for too long. She shook off the pleasant thoughts that had been coursing through her mind to look over at Pen. There was a knowing half-smile on Pen's face that told Marlene she knew exactly what kind of thoughts had preoccupied her.

"Fortunately," Marlene said, belatedly joining the conversation. "I don't have any experience with busy workweeks at the moment."

"I was going to ask how the job search is going," Pen said.

"I'm keeping my options open."

In truth, Marlene hadn't started her job search in earnest. She would have to soon, of course. Her savings were substantial—having no life for over a decade had done wonders for her nest egg—but they wouldn't last forever. The problem was, she couldn't decide what to do with her life.

Pen asked, "The bank didn't beg you to come back?"

"They did, but their offer wasn't good enough."

After FTL fired Brad, they offered his position to Marlene. She couldn't think of anything she wanted to do less, so they instead offered her old branch back, with a significant raise. She did think about that one for a little while. She missed seeing Ellie every day. She even missed some of her clients. She liked helping people like old Mrs. Pendergast who was lost when it came to her finances. But helping those people and seeing Ellie every day didn't make up for the stress, the unrealistic quarterly goals, and the entire banking culture that had become all about selling rather than serving. She turned the position down. She didn't know what she wanted to do for work yet, but she knew it wasn't that.

"Good for you," Pen said. "Hold out for something that feeds your soul."

The comment surprised her coming from Pen. She'd always struck Marlene as the type who worked herself to exhaustion in search of the almighty dollar.

"Really?" Marlene asked. "Does selling houses feed your soul?"

Pen laughed and scrunched her eyebrows together. "Yeah. It does actually. Why? You think a job can't be fulfilling unless it's curing cancer or ending world hunger?"

"I guess it can. I just haven't ever found one that did."

"Which is why it isn't time for you to go back to work yet."

"Yeah, I guess you're right," Marlene said.

"I'm always right. Didn't you know that about me?"

Pen threw her arm around Marlene's shoulders, pulling her into a side hug. Marlene immediately tensed up. She and Pen had formed a tentative friendship in the month since Pen had shown up in her office to tell her off, but this was still the first time they'd touched since their one-night stand.

Once she got over the initial shock of first contact, Marlene had to admit the hug was nice. It didn't feel anything like the way they'd touched that night, of course. If she had to characterize the hug, she'd call it brotherly. Something akin to camaraderie but reserved for two women both occupying the masculine end of the lesbian spectrum. Looking at it that way, Marlene's chest swelled with pride. This side hug probably meant nothing to Pen, but to her it meant she was being accepted as a butch woman. That her lesbian lessons had been a success.

"Hey, you two," Abby said.

Abby set the martini in front of Pen. It was murkier than most the ones Abby made and had far too many olives. Her hands now empty, Abby shifted over to stand in front of Marlene and set her elbows on the bar. It was a calculated move, one that pressed her breasts together and up high enough for more than the usual amount of cleavage to show. Marlene's eyes latched onto the spot and a stirring started low in her belly.

"Mmm, delicious," Pen said after sipping her drink. "You know just how to treat a girl, Abby."

Abby's eyes remained fixed of Marlene as she said, "You have no idea."

"Here I thought I always came first with you."

"If you were with me, you would always come first."

"If you were with me, we'd always come together," Pen said.

"Now that's really how you treat a girl."

"That's why I always come out on top."

"I prefer a switch," Abby said.

"I'd be anything for you."

Marlene listened to the rapid-fire banter with a growing amusement. Abby and Pen had kept up this dynamic for so long, they were like expert tennis players, volleying and returning with expert precision. Abby's ability to carry a pun too far was only surpassed by Pen's. Marlene was tempted to let them keep going until they ran out of road, but she knew that might take hours.

She and Abby had talked often about the flirting thing, and had made a deal. If Abby slipped and flirted with strangers or friends, she had to make it up to Marlene in the bedroom. It wasn't about punishment or even reassurance, it was just a fun way to keep from falling back into old habits. The deal seemed to work well for both of them, since they had a hard time keeping their hands off each other most nights.

Marlene cleared her throat and raised an eyebrow at Abby. The most rewarding thing was the way Abby's cheeks dusted pink.

"Shoot." Abby gave Marlene an apologetic smile. "Sorry. I forgot."

"Oh hell. Did I do something wrong?" Pen asked.

"No, it wasn't you." Abby straightened, adjusting her shirt back into a more professional position. "I'm just backsliding."

"It's okay." Marlene smiled. "You're cute when you get caught."

"You know we don't mean anything by it, right?" Pen looked genuinely worried as she set her drink down.

"Of course." Marlene waved her finger between herself and Abby. "It's just a thing we have. We're all good."

"Once I pay up." Abby had a sparkle in her eye as she turned back to Marlene. "I have to close out a tab, then I'm going to run to the stockroom for a little while. Austin can cover for a bit."

Marlene's jaw nearly hit the bar. Was Abby suggesting what she thought she was? They'd done a fair amount of making out in quiet corners of Riveter's, but a quickie in the stockroom was a different story all together. Just the thought of it made Marlene's fingers tingle in anticipation.

"I didn't mean to get you in trouble," Pen said.

"It's okay." Abby gave Marlene a wink. "It's good trouble."

Now it wasn't just Marlene's fingers that were tingling, it was her face and her lips and most of her body. Abby was definitely suggesting what Marlene thought she was and she was more than happy to see where this went.

Once Abby had floated off to the register, Pen leaned close. "I don't know what just happened, but I guess you're welcome."

Sliding off her stool, Marlene slapped Pen on the back in one of those brotherly gestures. "I owe you one."

She was halfway across the room when her mind caught up with her. If she had known a year ago that Pen would be her friend and Abby would be her girlfriend, she wouldn't have believed it. Nothing this perfect had been on her horizon then. The direction her life had gone since Pen had told her she walked gay, since she'd slipped Pen's coat on and seen her reflection in the window, since Abby had shown her she was special, and since she had decided she should love herself, was like something out of a dream. She owed Pen more than a slap on the back.

When she got back to her empty barstool, Pen was absorbed in her phone. She looked up when Marlene said her name.

"What's up?" Pen asked. "I thought you had somewhere better to be right now."

Marlene looked over just in time to see Abby slip through the door behind the bar. "Trust me, I'll make it quick."

Pen's leer was just like the one she'd had that night she'd changed Marlene's life forever. It was reassuring to Marlene that Pen could change so much, but also be completely the same. It gave her hope.

"I wanted to say thank you."

"You already thanked me."

"I don't mean for tonight." Marlene took a deep breath and looked around. The table where she'd sat with her friends for Ellie's birthday was hidden behind a wall of people, but she knew exactly where it was. "I meant for picking me up that night. For telling me I was gay."

"I just told you that you walk gay," Pen said.

"Yeah, but you also told me I was gay. That I was wearing a costume. You put the pieces together for me. You helped me find myself."

Pen laughed low and shook her head. "I'd love to say I was being altruistic that night, but you know that's not true. I was just trying to get laid."

Marlene thought back to the calculating way Pen had pissed her off. Then how she'd followed Marlene outside and casually offered her coat. She'd known what she was doing. Maybe she had just been trying to get laid, but, if so, she went about it in a rather unorthodox way. Something in the sparkle of Pen's eye that night told Marlene she might've had more than one goal.

"I don't care what your motives were. You helped me and that means a lot," Marlene said.

"It feels good, doesn't it? To figure yourself out."

"Yeah. It feels really good."

"Don't stop doing that. Though I don't suggest using the same method when you figure out the job thing," Pen said.

Marlene wanted to be annoyed, but how could she be? "You're obnoxious, you know that?"

Pen stood up and put a hand on each of Marlene's shoulders. "And you walk very, very gay, you know that?"

"Yeah. I do know that."

Before she could talk herself out of it, Marlene pulled Pen into a tight hug. It was probably too tight a hug, but Marlene didn't care. Her life was more than she could have ever hoped for and it was at least partially because of Pen. Of course, the woman who was responsible for the biggest change in Marlene was waiting for her back in the stockroom, so Marlene didn't linger.

She pulled out of the hug, slapped Pen on the shoulder again, and marched off toward the stockroom, walking in as gay a manner as she could muster.

About the Author

Tagan Shepard (she/her) is the author of seven books of sapphic fiction, including the 2019 Goldie Winner *Bird on a Wire*. When not writing about extraordinary women loving other extraordinary women, she can be found playing video games, reading, or sitting in DC Metro traffic. She lives in Virginia with her wife and two ridiculous cats.

Books Available from Bold Strokes Books

Curse of the Gorgon by Tanai Walker. Cass will do anything to ensure Elle's safety, but is she willing to embrace the curse of the Gorgon? (978-1-63679-395-5)

Dance with Me by Georgia Beers. Scottie Templeton mixes it up on and off the dance floor with sexy salsa instructor Marisa Reyes. But can Scottie get past Marisa's connection to her ex? (978-1-63679-359-7)

Gin and Bear It by Joy Argento. Opposites really can attract, and as Kelly and Logan work together to create a loving home for rescue cat Bear, they just might find one for themselves as well. (978-1-63679-351-1)

Harvest Dreams by Jacqueline Fein-Zachary. Planting the vineyard of their dreams, Kate Bauer and Sydney Barrett must resist their attraction while battling nature and their families, who oppose both the venture and their relationship. (978-1-63679-380-1)

Outside the Lines by Melissa Sky. If you had the chance to live forever, would you take it? Amara Rodriguez did and it sets her on a journey to find her missing mother and unravel the mystery of her own heart. (978-1-63679-403-7)

The No Kiss Contract by Nan Campbell. Workaholic Davy believes she can get the top spot at her firm if the senior partners think she's settling down and about to start a family, but she needs the delightful yet dubious Anna's help by pretending to be her fiancée. (978-1-63679-372-6)

The Value of Sylver and Gold by Michelle Larkin. When word gets out that former Boston homicide detective Reid Sylver can talk to the dead, the FBI solicits her help on a serial murder case, prompting Reid to assemble forces once again with Detective London Gold. (978-1-63679-093-0)

When It Feels Right by Tagan Shepard. Freshly out of the closet Marlene hasn't been lucky in love, but when it comes to her quirky new roommate Abby, everything just feels right. (978-1-63679-367-2)

Lucky in Lace by Melissa Brayden. Straitlaced stationery store owner Juliette Jennings's predictable life unravels when a sexy lingerie shop and its alluring owner move in next door. (978-1-63679-434-1)

Made for Her by Carsen Taite. Neal Walsh is a newly made member of the Mancuso crime family, but will her undeniable attraction to Anastasia Petrov, the wife of her boss's sworn enemy, be the ultimate test of her loyalty? (978-1-63679-265-1)

Off the Menu by Alaina Erdell. Reality TV sensation *Restaurant Redo* and its gorgeous host Erin Rasmussen will arrive to film in chef Taylor Mobley's kitchen. As the cameras roll, will they make the jump from enemies to lovers? (978-1-63679-295-8)

Pack of Her Own by Elena Abbott. When things heat up in a small town, steamy secrets are revealed between Alpha werewolf Wren Carne and her human mate, Natalie Donovan. (978-1-63679-370-2)

Return to McCall by Patricia Evans. Lily isn't looking for romance— not until she meets Alex, the gorgeous Cuban dance instructor at La Haven, a newly opened lesbian retreat. (978-1-63679-386-3)

So It Went Like This by C. Spencer. A candid and deeply personal exploration of fate, chosen family, and the vulnerability intrinsic in life's uncertainties. (978-1-63555-971-2)

Stolen Kiss by Spencer Greene. Anna and Louise share a stolen kiss, only to discover that Louise is dating Anna's brother. Surely, one kiss can't change everything...Can it? (978-1-63679-364-1)

The Fall Line by Kelly Wacker. When Jordan Burroughs arrives in the Deep South to paint a local endangered aquatic flower, she doesn't expect to become friends with a mischievous gin-drinking ghost who complicates her budding romance and leads her to an awful discovery and danger. (978-1-63679-205-7)

To Meet Again by Kadyan. When the stark reality of WW II separates cabaret singer Evelyn and Australian doctor Joan in Singapore, they must overcome all odds to find one another again. (978-1-63679-398-6)

Before She Was Mine by Emma L McGeown. When Dani and Lucy are thrust together to sort out their children's playground squabble, sparks fly leaving both of them willing to risk it all for each other. 978-1-63679-315-3)

Chasing Cypress by Ana Hartnett Reichardt. Maggie Hyde wants to find a partner to settle down with and help her run the family farm, but instead she ends up chasing Cypress. Olivia Cypress. 978-1-63679-323-8)

Dark Truths by Sandra Barret. When Jade's ex-girlfriend and vampire maker barges back into her life, can Jade satisfy her ex's demands, keep Beth safe, and keep everyone's secrets...secret? 978-1-63679-369-6)

Desires Unleashed by Renee Roman. Kell Murphy and Taylor Simpson didn't go looking for love, but as they explore their desires unleashed, their hearts lead them on an unexpected journey. 978-1-63679-327-6)

Maybe, Probably by Amanda Radley. Set against the backdrop of a viral pandemic, Gina and Eleanor are about to discover that loving another person is complicated when you're desperately searching for yourself. 978-1-63679-284-2)

The One by C.A. Popovich. Jody Acosta doesn't know what makes her more furious, that the wealthy Bergeron family refuses to be held accountable for her father's wrongful death, or that she can't ignore her knee-weakening attraction to Nicole Bergeron. 978-1-63679-318-4)

The Speed of Slow Changes by Sander Santiago. As Al and Lucas navigate the ups and downs of their polyamorous relationship, only one thing is certain: romance has never been so crowded. 978-1-63679-329-0)

Tides of Love by Kimberly Cooper Griffin. Falling in love is the last thing on either of their minds, but when Mikayla and Gem meet, sparks of possibility begin to shine, revealing a future neither expected. 978-1-63679-319-1)

Catch by Kris Bryant. Convincing the wife of the star quarterback to walk away from her family was never in offensive coordinator Sutton McCoy's game plan. But standing on the sidelines when a second chance at true love comes her way proves all but impossible. (978-1-63679-276-7)

Hearts in the Wind by MJ Williamz. Beth and Evelyn seem destined to remain mortal enemies but are about to discover that in matters of the heart, sometimes you must cast your fortunes to the wind. (978-1-63679-288-0)

Hero Complex by Jesse J. Thoma. Bronte, Athena, and their unlikely friends must work together to defeat Bronte's arch nemesis. The fate of love, humanity, and the world might depend on it. No pressure. (978-1-63679-280-4)

Hotel Fantasy by Piper Jordan. Molly Taylor has a fantasy in mind that only Lexi can fulfill. However, convincing her to participate could prove challenging. (978-1-63679-207-1)

Last New Beginning by Krystina Rivers. Can commercial broker Skye Kohl and contractor Bailey Kaczmarek overcome their pride and work together while the tension between them boils over into a love that could soothe both of their hearts? (978-1-63679-261-3)

Love and Lattes by Karis Walsh. Cat café owner Bonnie and wedding planner Taryn join forces to get rescue cats into forever homes—discovering their own forever along the way. (978-1-63679-290-3)

Repatriate by Jaime Maddox. Ally Hamilton's new job as a home health aide takes an unexpected twist when she discovers a fortune in stolen artwork and must repatriate the masterpieces and avoid the wrath of the violent man who stole them. (978-1-63679-303-0)

The Hues of Me and You by Morgan Lee Miller. Arlette Adair and Brooke Dawson almost fell in love in college. Years later, they unexpectedly run into each other and come face-to-face with their unresolved past. (978-1-63679-229-3)

A Haven for the Wanderer by Jenny Frame. When Griffin Harris comes to Rosebrook village, the love she finds with Bronte de Lacey creates a safe haven and she finally finds her place in the world. But will she run again when their love is tested? (978-1-63679-291-0)

A Spark in the Air by Dena Blake. Internet executive Crystal Tucker is sure Wi-Fi could really help small-town residents, even if it means putting an internet café out of business, but her instant attraction to the owner's daughter, Janie Elliott, makes moving ahead with her plans complicated. (978-1-63679-293-4)

Between Takes by CJ Birch. Simone Lavoie is convinced her new job as an intimacy coordinator will give her a fresh perspective. Instead, problems on set and her growing attraction to actress Evelyn Harper only add to her worries. (978-1-63679-309-2)

Camp Lost and Found by Georgia Beers. Nobody knows better than Cassidy and Frankie that life doesn't always give you what you want. But sometimes, if you're lucky, life gives you exactly what you need. (978-1-63679-263-7)

Felix Navidad by 'Nathan Burgoine. After the wedding of a good friend, instead of Felix's Hawaii Christmas treat to himself, ice rain strands him in Ontario with fellow wedding-guest—and handsome ex of said friend—Kevin in a small cabin for the holiday Felix definitely didn't plan on. (978-1-63679-411-2)

Fire, Water, and Rock by Alaina Erdell. As Jess and Clare reveal more about themselves, and their hot summer fling tips over into true love, they must confront their pasts before they can contemplate a future together. (978-1-63679-274-3)

Lines of Love by Brey Willows. When even the Muse of Love doesn't believe in forever, we're all in trouble. (978-1-63555-458-8)

Manny Porter and The Yuletide Murder by D.C. Robeline. Manny only has the holiday season to discover who killed prominent research scientist Phillip Nikolaidis before the judicial system condemns an innocent man to lethal injection. (978-1-63679-313-9)

Only This Summer by Radclyffe. A fling with Lily promises to be exactly what Chase is looking for—short-term, hot as a forest fire, and one Chase can extinguish whenever she wants. After all, it's only one summer. (978-1-63679-390-0)

Picture-Perfect Christmas by Charlotte Greene. Two former rivals compete to capture the essence of their small mountain town at Christmas, all the while fighting old and new feelings. (978-1-63679-311-5)

Playing Love's Refrain by Lesley Davis. Drew Dawes had shied away from the world of music until Wren Banderas gave her a reason to play their love's refrain. (978-1-63679-286-6)

Profile by Jackie D. The scales of justice are weighted against FBI agents Cassidy Wolf and Alex Derby. Loyalty and love may be the only advantage they have. (978-1-63679-282-8)